24/2/22

The Promise

The Promise

LESLEY PEARSE

MICHAEL JOSEPH
an imprint of
PENGUIN BOOKS

MICHAEL JOSEPH

Published by the Penguin Group

Penguin Books Ltd, 80 Strand, London WC2R ORL, England

Penguin Group (USA) Inc., 375 Hudson Street, New York, New York 10014, USA

Penguin Group (Canada), 90 Eglinton Avenue East, Suite 700, Toronto, Ontario, Canada M4P 2Y3
(a division of Pearson Penguin Canada Inc.)

Penguin Ireland, 25 St Stephen's Green, Dublin 2, Ireland (a division of Penguin Books Ltd)

Penguin Group (Australia), 250 Camberwell Road, Camberwell, Victoria 3124, Australia
(a division of Pearson Australia Group Pty Ltd)

Penguin Books India Pvt Ltd, 11 Community Centre, Panchsheel Park, New Delhi – 110 017, India

Penguin Group (NZ), 67 Apollo Drive, Rosedale, Auckland 0632, New Zealand
(a division of Pearson New Zealand Ltd)

Penguin Books (South Africa) (Pty) Ltd, 24 Sturdee Avenue, Rosebank, Johannesburg 2196, South Africa

Penguin Books Ltd, Registered Offices: 80 Strand, London WC2R ORL, England

www.penguin.com

First published 2012
1

Copyright © Lesley Pearse, 2012

The moral right of the author has been asserted

Set in 13.5/16pt Garamond MT Std
Typeset by Jouve (UK), Milton Keynes
Printed in Great Britain by Clays Ltd, St Ives plc

A CIP catalogue record for this book is available from the British Library

ISBN: 978–0–718–15704–3

www.greenpenguin.co.uk

To Maureen with love
Because you're worth it.

Chapter One
July 1914

Sheltering from the heavy rain in a doorway, he looked across the street to the little bow-windowed milliner's.

Just the name 'Belle' in gold italic writing above the window made his heart race a little faster. He could see two ladies silhouetted inside, and the way they moved suggested they were excited by the pretty hats on display. He had achieved his objective, to discover if Belle had realized her dream, but now he was here, so close to her, he wanted much more.

A plump, rosy-faced matron joined him in the doorway to shelter from the rain. She was struggling with an umbrella which had blown inside out. 'If it don't stop raining soon we'll all get webbed feet!' she remarked jovially as she tried to right her umbrella. 'I don't know what possessed me to come out in it.'

'I was thinking the same myself,' he replied, and took the umbrella from her to straighten out the spokes. 'There you are,' he added as he handed it back to her. 'But I expect it will do the same again in the next gust of wind.'

She looked at him curiously. 'You're French, aren't you? But you speak good English.'

He smiled. He liked the way English women of her age didn't hold back from asking complete strangers questions. French women were much more reticent.

'Yes, I am French, but I learned English when I lived here for a couple of years.'

'Are you back here on holiday?' she asked.

'Yes, visiting old friends,' he said, for that was partially true. 'I was told Blackheath was a very pretty place, but I didn't pick a good day to visit it.'

She laughed and agreed no one would want to walk on the heath in such heavy rain.

'You must live in the south of France,' she said, looking at his tanned face appraisingly. 'My brother holidayed in Nice and came back as brown as a conker.'

He had no idea what a conker was, but he was glad the woman seemed prepared to chat, hoping he might learn something about Belle from her.

'I live near Marseille. And that shop over there reminds me of French milliners,' he said, pointing to the hat shop.

She looked over to it and smiled. 'Well, they say she learned her trade in Paris, and all the ladies in the village love her hats,' she said with real warmth in her voice. 'I'd have popped in there myself today if the weather wasn't so bad, she's always got time for everyone, such a lovely young woman.'

'So she has good business then?'

'Yes indeed, she gets ladies coming from all over to buy from her, I'm told. But I must make my way home now or there won't be any dinner tonight.'

'It was a pleasure talking to you,' he said, and helped her put her umbrella up again.

'You should go over there and buy your wife a hat,' the woman said as she began to walk away. 'You won't find a better shop, not even up in Regent Street.'

After the woman had gone he continued to look across the street to the shop, hoping for a glimpse of Belle. He had no wife to buy a pretty hat for, and he hardly needed an excuse to drop into an old friend's shop. But was it wise to stir up the past?

He turned to look at his reflection in the shop window beside him. Old friends back in France claimed he'd changed

2

in the two years since he last saw Belle, but he couldn't see any difference himself. He was still as lean and fit: hard work on his small farm kept him that way and his shoulders were even broader and more muscular. But perhaps his friends meant that the old scar on his cheek had faded and contentment had softened his angular features to make him look less dangerous.

Ten years ago, in his mid-twenties, when he'd needed to be able to strike fear into people, he'd taken some pride in hearing that his blue eyes were icy and there was menace even in his voice. But while he knew he was still capable of violence if it was needed, he had retired from that world.

If the older woman's praise for Belle was representative of how everyone in this genteel village felt about her, the more scandalous parts of her past couldn't have followed her here. That was good. He of all people knew how past mistakes, wrong turns and shameful episodes were often very hard to live down.

Now, as his mission had been accomplished, he knew the wisest thing would be to go back to the station and catch a train into London.

The tinkling of a door bell alerted him that someone was leaving Belle's shop. It was both the ladies, who he guessed were mother and daughter, for one looked to be in her forties, the other no more than eighteen or so. The younger one ran to a waiting automobile with two pink- and black-striped hat boxes in her hands, while the older woman looked back into the shop as if saying goodbye. Then suddenly he could see Belle in the doorway, as slender and as lovely as he remembered, wearing a very demure, high-necked pale green dress, her dark shiny hair piled up on her head with just a few curls escaping around her face.

All at once he didn't want to be wise; he had to speak to her. The rumblings of war which had started a year or two ago had become increasingly louder in the last year, and since the assassination of Archduke Franz Ferdinand of Austria back at the end of June, war was now inevitable. Germany would undoubtedly invade France and as he would have to fight for his country, he might not live to see Belle ever again.

As the two women drove off, Belle closed the shop door. Unable to resist the impulse now she was alone, he darted across the street through the rain, pausing for just a second or two to watch her through the glass in the door. She had her back to him as she arranged some hats on little stands. There was a row of tiny pearl buttons down the back of her dress, and he felt a pang of jealousy that he would never be able to undo them for her. She bent forward to pick up a hat box from the floor and he had a glimpse of shapely calves above pretty lacy ankle boots. He had seen her naked at the time he rescued her in Paris, and felt nothing then but concern for her, yet now the sight of just a few inches of leg was arousing.

She turned as the door bell tinkled and on seeing him her hands flew up to her mouth and her eyes opened wide with shocked surprise. 'Etienne Carrera!' she exclaimed. 'What on earth are you doing here?'

Her voice, the deep blue of her eyes and even the way she said his name made him feel weak with longing. 'I'm flattered that you remember me,' he said, removing his hat with a flourish. 'And you are looking even more lovely. Success and married life suit you.'

He took a couple of steps nearer her, intending to kiss her cheek, but she blushed and backed away as if nervous. 'How did you know I was married and here in Blackheath?' she asked.

4

'I called in at the Ram's Head in Seven Dials. The landlord there told me you'd married Jimmy and moved to Black-heath. I couldn't leave England without seeing you, so I caught the train out here in the hope of finding you.'

'After all you did for me I should have written to you when I got married,' she said, looking both anxious and flustered by his sudden appearance. 'But . . .' she faltered.

'I understand,' he said lightly. 'Old friends who have been through so much together do not need to explain. I always knew from the way Jimmy never gave up in his quest to find you after your abduction that he must love you very deeply. So I am just happy that things worked out for you both. I heard that he and his uncle have a public house here.'

Belle nodded. 'It's the Railway, just down the hill. I'm sure you remember me telling you about Mog, my mother's housekeeper. Well, she married Garth, Jimmy's uncle, two years ago in September, then Jimmy and I got married soon afterwards.'

'And you got your hat shop at last!' Etienne glanced appre-ciatively at the pale pink and cream decor. 'It's lovely, as feminine and chic as you are. A woman out on the street told me you couldn't get better hats even in Regent Street.'

She smiled then and seemed to relax a little. 'Why don't you take off that wet raincoat and I'll make us both a cup of tea?'

'Are you still on your farm?' she called as she went into a little room at the back of the shop.

Etienne hung his coat on a hook by the door, and brushed his damp fair hair back with his hands. 'I am indeed, but I also do a little translating, which is the reason I came to Eng-land to meet with a company I have done work for in the past,' he called back.

'So your life is about more than chickens and lemon trees

now?' she said as she came back into the shop. 'Please tell me you *have* kept to the straight and narrow?'

Etienne put his hand on his heart. 'I promise you I am a pillar of polite society,' he said, his voice grave but his blue eyes twinkling. 'I haven't escorted any more young girls to America, and neither have I rescued any from the clutches of madmen.'

He had never forgiven himself for not making a stand when the gangsters he had worked for back then blackmailed him into delivering Belle to a brothel in New Orleans. He might have partially redeemed himself two years later when he rescued her in Paris, but in his eyes that didn't wipe the slate clean.

'I really don't believe you could ever be a pillar of society,' Belle giggled.

'Do you doubt my word?' he said with pretended pique. 'Shame on you, Belle, for having such little faith! Have I ever lied to you?'

'You once told me you'd kill me if I tried to escape,' she retorted. 'And you later admitted that wasn't true.'

'That's the trouble with women,' he smiled. 'They always remember the little, inconsequential things.' He reached out and touched a pink feathered hat on a stand, marvelling that her determination and talent had paid off. 'It's your turn to tell the truth now. Is your marriage all you hoped for?'

'Much more,' she said, just a little too quickly. 'We are very happy. Jimmy is just the very best of husbands.'

'Then I am happy for you,' he said and gave a little bow.

Belle giggled again. 'And you? Do you have a lady in your life?' she asked.

'No one special enough to settle down with,' he said.

She raised her eyebrows questioningly.

6

He smiled. 'Don't look like that, not everyone wants marriage and stability. Especially now with war coming.'

'Surely it will be averted?' she said hopefully.

'No, Belle. There is no chance of that. It is only weeks away.'

'That's all men talk about these days,' she sighed. 'I get so weary of it. But look, why don't you come home with me now and meet Jimmy, Garth and Mog? They'll be so excited to meet you after all this time.'

'I don't think that would be appropriate,' Etienne said.

Belle pouted. 'Why ever not? You saved my life in Paris, and they'll be very disappointed and puzzled that you called here but wouldn't come and meet them.'

He looked at her thoughtfully for a moment. 'When you moved here you also left the past behind.'

Belle opened her mouth to protest but shut it again, realizing he was quite right. From the day she married Jimmy she had firmly closed the door on her time in America and Paris. Etienne may have opened it again by coming to see her, and she was glad he had, but Jimmy might not see it that way.

'What about Noah?' she asked. 'Will you see him? You became such good friends when you were searching for me, and I'm sure you'll remember Lisette who took care of me in the convent before you took me to America. Noah fell in love with her, and they are married now with a baby on the way. They have a lovely home in St John's Wood.'

'I have kept in touch with Noah,' Etienne said. 'Not perhaps as well as I should have, but then he's a journalist and writing comes much easier to him than it does to me. But he is such a well-known columnist now that I can even read his work in France. In fact I'm having lunch with him tomorrow, near his office. We will always be friends, but I won't call at his home. We both feel Lisette needs no reminders of the past, especially now with a baby coming.'

Belle gave a rueful smile, understanding exactly what he meant. Lisette had also been forced into prostitution when she was a young girl, which was why she had been so kind to Belle. 'Respectability comes at a high price. I like Noah and Lisette very much, but although we keep in touch, and visit each other now and then, we are always careful to avoid talking about how and why we met. I know that is the right thing to do now both Lisette and I are married, but it does prevent us from being really close friends.'

'Does the past affect your relationship with Jimmy?' Etienne asked, his eyes boring into her, daring her to lie to him.

'Sometimes it does,' she admitted. 'It's like having a splinter in your finger which you can't get out, yet you can't help but prod it.'

Etienne nodded. He thought her description very apt. 'For me too. But in time a splinter works its way out and the hole it left will become filled with new memories.'

Belle laughed suddenly. 'Why are we being so gloomy? For all of us – you, me, Jimmy, Mog, and Lisette too – despite all the troubles we had, good came out of it. So why are humans so perverse that they choose to dwell on the bad times?'

'Is it the bad times we dwell on, or the beautiful moments that lifted us up during the bad times?' he asked, raising one eyebrow quizzically.

Belle blushed, and he knew she remembered only too well the moments they'd shared.

Despite being taken against her will to America, Belle cared for him when he was seasick on the voyage. Long before they reached New Orleans they had become very close, and on the night of her sixteenth birthday she had offered herself to him. He didn't know how he restrained himself that night; he wanted her despite his wife and two young sons at home. The memory of her firm young body in his arms, the sweetness of her kisses, had inflamed him so often over the years. Yet he was very glad he hadn't succumbed to her charms that night – he carried enough guilt about her without that too.

'Whenever I read anything about New York I think of you showing me all the sights,' she said. 'I have to take care I never mention that I've been there, or I might have to explain when and who I was with. I never asked you if you enjoyed those two days too. Did you?'

'It was the most fun I'd had in a long time,' he admitted. 'You were so wide-eyed, so eager to see everything. I felt so bad when we had to continue the journey to New Orleans, knowing I'd got to leave you there.'

'It wasn't so bad at Martha's,' she said, putting one hand on his arm as if to reassure him. 'I never blamed you, I always understood that you had to do it. And anyway, when two years later in Paris you came bursting through the door to save me from Pascal, you more than made up for everything.'

She involuntarily shuddered as she always did when she remembered the horror Pascal put her through. That madman had imprisoned her at the top of his house, and if Etienne hadn't managed to find her she had no doubt Pascal would've killed her.

And Etienne hadn't only rescued her, he'd healed her by sitting beside her bed at the hospital, letting her cry, talking to her and giving her hope for the future. She remembered too the day Noah told her that Etienne's wife and two sons had died in a fire at their home. To her shame her first reaction had been that Etienne was now free, not horror that his loved ones should die in such a barbarous way.

Etienne noticed her shudder, and aware that his unexpected visit and their shared past were troubling her, he felt
he must bring them both back to the present.

'I'm going to enlist in the army when I get back to France,'
he said.

'Oh no, surely not,' she gasped.

Etienne chuckled. 'That's always the female reaction, but
it's my duty, Belle. And once again my past will catch up with
me because I evaded the compulsory national service as a lad
by coming to England.'

'Will they punish you for that?' she asked.

He grinned. 'I'm hoping they'll just be glad to put a gun in
my hands,' he said. 'I won't be welcoming all the drill and
having to take orders, and I'm not naive enough to think it's
the path to glory, but I love France, and I'll be damned if I'll
stand by and see it fall into the hands of Germans.'

She looked at him speculatively. 'You are resourceful and
brave, Etienne, you'll make a good soldier. But I'd much
rather you were safe on your farm growing lemons and feeding chickens.'

He shrugged. 'In this life we can't always choose the safe
and pleasant road. I have a violent past, I know the worst
man can do to man. I thought I'd never have to put that to
use ever again, but it seems that is exactly what my country
needs me for now.'

'You are a good and honourable man,' she sighed. 'Please
keep safe. But if you're sure you really don't wish to come
and meet Jimmy, I ought to close the shop and go home. We
always like to have a meal together before he opens the bar
for the evening.'

'Yes, of course, I mustn't delay you,' he said, but made no
move to pick up his hat and coat. He wanted to tell her that
he had always loved her, he wanted to take her in his arms

and kiss her. But he knew it was too late. He had had his chance back in Paris and he hadn't taken it. Now she belonged to another man.

'You'd better leave first. I don't want anyone remarking that I was seen walking down the street with a stranger,' she said bluntly.

At that Etienne put on his coat. 'I found what I was looking for,' he said quietly. 'That you are happy and secure. Stay happy, love Jimmy with all your heart, and I hope one day I will hear through Noah that you have a whole brood of children.'

He took her hand and kissed it, then turned quickly and walked out.

'Au revoir,' Belle murmured as the door closed behind him, tears prickling her eyes for there was so much more she would have liked to say to him. So much more she wanted to know about his life.

At sixteen she had thought she loved him. It still made her blush to remember how she'd stripped off her clothes and got into his bunk and invited him to share it with her. He had been such a gentleman; he'd held her and kissed her, but took it no further.

As an adult looking back on the horrors she'd experienced before meeting Etienne, being snatched from the street by her home, then taken to Paris to be sold to a brothel and raped by five men, she supposed that she might have felt she loved anyone who was kind to her after such an ordeal.

Yet it couldn't have been just because Etienne was kind to her, or that he was strong, sensitive and affectionate, because those girlish dreams about him had stayed with her throughout her time in New Orleans and the voyage back to France.

When he reappeared to save her life, her innocence was

long gone and she knew more about men than any woman should. But he must have felt something for her too: why else would he come rushing to Paris two years later when it was reported to him that she'd disappeared?

Throughout her convalescence after the rescue, she waited and hoped for an admission of love. She sensed he did love her from the way he looked at her, and the tenderness he showed her. Yet he didn't take her in his arms and admit he wanted her, not even when they parted at the Gare du Nord and she was crying and making her own feelings very clear.

She'd done her very best to erase their parting from her mind, and the yearning she felt for him for so long after, even when she was safely home with Mog, and Jimmy was talking of marriage. So why did he have to come here today to drive that particular splinter back into her heart?

She had told him the truth. She and Jimmy were very happy. He was her best friend, lover, brother and husband all rolled into one. They had the same goals, they laughed at the same things, he was everything any girl could want or need. He had healed the horrors of the past; in his arms she had encountered exquisite tenderness, and deep satisfaction too, for he was a caring and sensitive lover.

Jimmy was her world; she loved the life she had with him. Yet all the same she wished she could have told Etienne how wonderful it was to see him again; that he'd been in her thoughts so often over the last two years and that she owed him so much.

But a married woman could not say such things, and neither could she encourage him to stay in her shop any longer. Blackheath was a village, people were small-minded and nosy, and there would be plenty of them glad to gossip about seeing a handsome man talking to her in her shop.

She began to tidy up, dusting off the counter and picking up some stray tissue paper from the floor.

Yet she couldn't help but ask herself why, if everything was so good for her, she felt there was something missing in her life. Why did she read about suffragettes in the newspaper and feel envy that they had the guts to stand up for rights for women in the face of hostility? Why did she feel a little stifled by respectability? But above all, why was it that Etienne's voice, his looks and the touch of his lips on her hand, still had the power to make her shiver?

She shook herself, opened the drawer where she kept the day's takings and emptied them into a cloth bag which she pushed into her reticule. She secured her straw hat to her hair with a long hat pin, flung her cloak over her shoulders and took her umbrella from the stand by the door.

She paused at the door before turning off the lights, and reminded herself of the day she opened her shop. It had been a cold November day, just two months after Mog and Garth's wedding, and she and Jimmy were due to be married just before Christmas. Everything had been new and shiny that day. Jimmy had indulged her by buying the small but expensive French chandeliers and the glass-topped counter. Mog had found the two button-backed Regency chairs and had them re-upholstered in pink velvet, and Garth's present to her was paying the two decorators who had done such a fine job of turning the dingy little shop into a pink and cream feminine heaven.

She sold twenty-two hats that first day, and dozens of other women who came in to look had been back since to buy. In the eighteen months since then there had been fewer than seven days in total when she hadn't sold one hat, and those were all in bad weather. The average week's sales worked out at fifteen hats, and though it meant she had to work very hard to keep up with the demand, and use an out-worker to help her, she was making a very good profit. During the summer she'd bought in plain straw boaters and trimmed them herself, and that had proved very profitable. Her shop was a resounding success.

'As is everything in your life,' she reminded herself as she turned out the lights.

Etienne went straight to the station, but having found he'd just missed a train and had twenty-five minutes to wait for the next one, he stood by the window by the ticket office and looked at the Railway public house across the street.

He had never quite understood English bars, the rigid opening hours, men standing at the bar drinking huge quantities of beer, then staggering home at closing time as if they could only face their wives and children when drunk. French bars were far more civilized. They were never seen as a kind of temple to get drunk in, for they were open all day and a man wasn't considered odd if he drank coffee or a soft drink as he read the newspaper.

The Railway at least looked inviting, with its fresh paint and sparkling windows. He could imagine that on a cold winter's night it was a warm, friendly haven for men to gather in.

As he looked at it, a big man with red hair and a beard came out of the front door. He was wearing a leather apron over his clothes, and Etienne guessed that this was Garth Franklin, Jimmy's uncle. Stopping to look up at water spurting out of a broken gutter and running down the front of the building, he called to someone inside.

A younger man joined him, and Etienne knew immediately that this was Jimmy. He was bigger than he'd imagined, as tall as his uncle and with the same broad shoulders, but he was clean-shaven and his red hair was neat and slightly darker than Garth's, perhaps because he'd oiled it down. The pair, who looked like father and son, stood there looking up, discussing the broken gutter, seemingly oblivious to the rain.

Jimmy suddenly turned, his face breaking into a joyful smile, and Etienne saw it was because he'd seen Belle coming towards them.

She was struggling to hold the umbrella over her and holding her cloak around her shoulders, but she ran the last few yards towards the men. As she reached them, her umbrella was tilted back and Etienne noted that her smile was as bright as her husband's.

Jimmy took the umbrella from her with one hand, while with the other he caressed her wet cheek, and kissed her forehead. Just those small, tender gestures told Etienne how much the man loved her.

He had to turn away. He knew he should feel at peace to be sure Belle was truly loved and protected, but instead he felt only bitter pangs of jealousy.

Chapter Two

Belle looked up from sketching, frowning with irritation at the din coming from downstairs in the bar. She expected such noise on Saturday nights, especially near closing time, but not at eight o'clock on a Tuesday.

Mog's homemaking skills had come into their own since they all moved to Blackheath. The living room was large, with two sash windows looking on to the street. During the afternoon and evening it was bathed in sunshine, and Mog's choice of decor, pale green wallpaper with a small leaf motif, moss-green velvet curtains and a sumptuous Turkish carpet she had bought at an auction, was very attractive yet homely.

The previous owners of the pub had left the huge couch behind, probably because it had seen better days, but Belle and Mog had made a loose chintz cover for it and matching ones for the two armchairs they'd brought from Seven Dials. Garth was always teasing Mog about aspiring to be 'gentry', and said that she'd be insisting on getting a maid before long. But both he and Belle knew that she would never trust any-one else to clean her home; she loved it too much to have any outsider poking around in it.

Normally the living room was a serene retreat from the hurly-burly of a busy pub. Belle loved her evenings sitting at the table by the window working on her hat designs, but real-izing that with all the noise tonight she wasn't going to be able to concentrate, and overcome by curiosity, she decided she would go down and see what was going on.

As Garth didn't approve of women behind the bar during

the evenings, she could only peep round the door. Yet even with a limited view she could see it was filled to capacity with young men, all clamouring to be served. But the most surprising thing was that they came from all walks of life. Some were City gent types with bowler hats, dark suits and starched white shirts, others were manual workers in flat caps and grubby overalls, but almost every other occupation and style of dress between these two extremes were accounted for too. Jimmy and Garth were struggling to keep up with the supply of beer.

'What on earth's going on?' she asked Mog, who was washing glasses in the kitchen. 'There must be at least eighty men in there. What made them all come in tonight?'

'They've all been enlisting in the army,' Mog said, and shook her head as if she was bewildered by such madness.

On 4 August, two weeks earlier, Germany had invaded Belgium and therefore England had declared war on Germany. Since then no one had talked about anything else. The newspapers were full of it, men stood on street corners discussing the likely outcome, even the women who came in to Belle's shop talked about it, some afraid that their husbands or sweethearts would join up, others claiming it was every able-bodied man's duty to go and fight.

Belle knew, as everyone did, that the British army was small, but it was also often said that its soldiers were better trained than any other European army. She hadn't expected that ordinary men like these would start clamouring to join up.

'What, all of them?' Belle exclaimed as she peeped round the door to the bar again. 'They aren't even men, they're mostly boys!'

Now she knew what had caused their excitement, their flushed cheeks and sparkling eyes made her feel chilled. She had recognized a few of them as sons, brothers or husbands of women she knew, and wondered what their reaction would be to their menfolk enlisting.

'There was a soldier playing a bugle outside the church hall apparently,' Mog said, as if that was an excuse for them to be so impulsive. 'Garth went by there this afternoon and saw them flocking in to sign up. He came back with a similar light in his eyes, but mercifully they're refusing anyone over forty.'

Belle felt a pang of fear run through her. 'Jimmy wouldn't want to join up too, would he?'

'Not if he's got any sense,' Mog said, grimacing as if the thought appalled her. 'But men are funny creatures – who knows what goes on inside their heads? Most of them just want a bit of adventure, so let's hope it's true that it'll all be over by Christmas.'

Garth opened the bar door and called to Mog to hurry up with the glasses and asked her to come and serve too. Belle thought he must be hard-pressed to lose his prejudice against women behind his bar as she went upstairs again. But once back in the living room she found herself worrying about Jimmy.

Up until now his view had been that soldiering was for professionals, not a bunch of hot-headed amateurs. Yet whatever he said, Belle suspected that pressure from other men and a surge of patriotism might very well change his mind. Mog was probably right in saying that most recruits just wanted an adventure, but some of their number would be killed or wounded, and Jimmy could well be among them.

Just the possibility of losing Jimmy made her eyes fill with tears. She couldn't, and didn't want to, think about life without him. She wiped away a stray tear, not understanding why in the past few weeks she'd become so emotional about everything. Only the previous day she'd burst into tears on opening a box of trimmings from her supplier and finding he'd sent four rolls of red ribbon instead of one each of red, pink, blue and yellow.

But then ever since the day in June when Etienne turned up at the shop, she'd not been herself. The weather had turned very warm just after his visit, bringing in a sudden demand for straw boaters. She'd had some put by, already trimmed, so there was no real need for panic, but she did panic, rushing down to her supplier in Lewisham and buying up almost his entire stock. Yet instead of buckling down and getting the hats trimmed up, she found herself idly staring out of the shop window. She'd nodded off several times during the day, then at night couldn't go to sleep. She could be hungry all day, yet when Mog dished up the evening meal, often her appetite had gone. Her ability to concentrate appeared to have left her too; she couldn't seem to stick at anything for more than half an hour.

At first she thought it was just because Etienne had stirred up old memories; she certainly had been guilty of frequent daydreams. But now she wondered if it was just the war, as it was hard to look ahead when you couldn't foresee what the future might bring. Yet could impending war and uncertainty really account for her feeling over-emotional, woolly-headed and weary? She hadn't confided in Mog or Jimmy because there was nothing tangible to describe, and anyway she was afraid to say anything to either of them in case she let slip about Etienne calling on her.

She felt bad about that. What could be more natural than sharing the delight in seeing an old friend again? But of course the truth was that she was afraid she would say something that would make Jimmy realize her feelings for Etienne had been more than just friendship.

It was as plain as the nose on her face that she couldn't have a better husband than Jimmy. She didn't think that many one-time whores could claim they'd never had their past thrown back in their face in a moment of anger or jealousy.

But Jimmy had never done that. He was kind, steady, sensitive to her needs, and would do absolutely anything for her. Yet even more unusual, and something she truly valued, was that she had the kind of freedom in her marriage that was almost unheard of. He never interfered with her business, he was proud that she was doing so well, and if she should fail, she knew he'd be supportive. And he worshipped her.

Common sense told her that even if Etienne had told her he loved her when they were in Paris, and she'd married him instead of Jimmy, it would never have become the kind of serene relationship she had now. Noah had been right when he pointed out on the journey back to England that Etienne was dangerous. He didn't mean that Etienne would ever physically hurt her, more that he was a deep, complicated man with a complex and dark past.

But he was gone for good now. By now he might even be fighting the Germans. She just hoped he would stay safe.

'Penny for them!'

Belle spun round in her seat at Mog's remark. She'd been so deep in her guilty thoughts that she hadn't heard her come into the room.

Marriage had done wonders for Mog. All through Belle's childhood in Seven Dials, she had been a kindly and loving mouse. She'd scuttled about her work, cooking, cleaning and mending, always in dark, shapeless clothes, her hair scraped back tightly from her face. She had seemed much older than Annie, Belle's true mother, even though they were the same age.

Now her clothes were fashionable, fitted well and showed off her small but shapely body. She might have a few strands of grey among the brown now, but she wore her hair in a chignon, with a few loose curls around a face that glowed from fresh air and happiness. She might be thirty-eight, but today, in a pink- and black-striped dress with pin tucks on the bodice, she looked ten years younger.

Mog had made her dress herself, but she was such a skilful seamstress that it could have come from the very expensive gown shop further up Tranquil Vale. She told anyone who asked that she'd been a housekeeper before she married Garth, and they assumed by her demeanour that she'd worked for gentry.

No one would ever guess she had spent her entire adult life until now as a maid in a brothel, and carried inside her head more knowledge about that profession than the whole female population of Blackheath.

'You were miles away,' she said to Belle, smiling fondly. 'Care to tell me about it?'

Mog had been like a mother to Belle for her entire life, and she was the one Belle could normally confide in about anything. But she couldn't admit anything about Etienne, Mog would be horrified that any man other than Jimmy ever crossed her mind.

'My thoughts aren't worth anything,' Belle sighed. 'It's just the war, the madness down in the bar. It's unsettling.'

Mog looked down at the hat Belle was drawing, frowning because she saw it was almost funereal, not Belle's usual frothy style. 'You've been looking a bit peaky for a couple of weeks now,' she said. 'You couldn't be up the duff, could you?'

Belle's mouth dropped open in shock, partly at Mog using the kind of slang she used back in Seven Dials, but even more because it had never occurred to her to consider she might be having a baby.

'No, of course not,' she said. 'Well, I don't think so. I can't be! Can I?'

Mog chuckled. 'Well, if I didn't know you better I'd have thought you didn't know how babies are made,' she said.

Belle blushed and giggled. Since Mog married Garth she never said anything about Belle's time as a whore, and even when she spoke about the days when she was the maid and Belle's nursemaid in her mother's brothel, she somehow avoided all reference to what went on elsewhere in the house. So the oblique reference to it now was surprising.

'I hadn't considered that possibility,' Belle replied.

'Well, consider it now,' Mog said tartly. 'I noticed you turned green last night when I was preparing that ox tongue. You couldn't get out the kitchen fast enough.'

'It was just that it smelled funny.'

'Maybe so, but it's never bothered you before. When was your last monthly?'

Belle tried to think. She could remember one back in May when there was a brief heatwave, but that was all. She told Mog this. 'That isn't to say I haven't had another one, I just can't remember,' she added.

'If that was the last one you'd be three months gone now,' Mog said, looking at Belle speculatively. 'Have you had any other symptoms?'

'Well, I've felt a bit odd,' Belle admitted. 'But not sick or anything.'

'Don't look so worried,' Mog said lightly. 'If you are having a baby it's a gift from heaven, and it's something to rejoice about. I keep hoping I might be lucky, but maybe I'm too old.'

That brought Belle up sharply. It had never occurred to her Mog might want a baby. Yet by the wistful look in her eyes, that was exactly what she had hoped for when she married Garth.

'You aren't too old,' Belle said quickly. 'Women have babies right up till they are in their mid-forties. But I'm not sure that this is the right time for either of us, not with the war on.'

'Well, I know I'm not having one,' Mog sighed. 'But maybe you are, and war or no war, we're all going to love an addition to the family. Just think how excited Jimmy will be!'

'Don't say anything,' Belle warned her. 'I don't believe I'm that way.'

Mog just looked at Belle with the same smug expression she always had when she thought she knew better. 'I wouldn't dream of telling Jimmy anything we discussed in private, but I'd better go back down there now and wash some more glasses.'

After Mog had gone, Belle put her hand on her stomach. It was as flat as it always had been, but it was rather nice to imagine there might be a tiny baby growing inside her. Back in New Orleans, and Paris too, it had been something to fear, and she'd used all the preventive measures she'd known to make sure it never happened.

She also was familiar with most of the first symptoms of pregnancy, as the other girls in New Orleans were always talking about them. Sudden aversions to certain smells were common, as were tender breasts and being sick in the mornings. But her breasts weren't tender and neither had she felt sick.

Having a baby once you were happily married was the natural order of things. But for some reason Belle hadn't expected it to happen to her.

She picked up her pencil and began drawing again, but her heart wasn't really in it, and when she heard Garth ring the bell down in the bar for last orders, she was glad that the evening was almost over.

It took a long time for Garth and Jimmy to usher everyone out of the bar. Belle looked out of the living-room window and watched as groups of men lurched across the road in twos and threes, with rubbery legs, arms around one another's shoulders. She saw one fall flat on his face. She had no idea whether they would be off tomorrow to the training camp in France, or if it took longer to arrange, but it was frightening to think that within a few weeks they could have guns in their hands. They were shop assistants, clerks, bricklayers and gardeners; the nearest most had come to a gun was on a rifle range at a fair. Her stomach tightened in fear for them, and she had a premonition that some wouldn't make it to their next birthday.

She shook herself out of such maudlin thoughts and went downstairs to help, as there would be a great deal of clearing up after such a busy night.

Half an hour later, the bar and tables were wiped down, stools and chairs stacked on them, and most of the glasses were washed and dried. Mog looked exhausted. Garth was out in the back yard hosing it down, muttering to himself about the pools of vomit and the filthy state of the lavatory.

'We've taken more than a whole week's takings tonight,' Jimmy said as he took a tray of clean glasses and replaced them on the shelves under the bar. 'But I hope to hell we don't get another night like this one.'

'You won't join up too, will you?' Belle asked him anxiously.

He laughed, stopping what he was doing to pat her cheek. 'What, and leave you, the prettiest lady in London? Of course I won't, at least not unless they make it compulsory. And that's unlikely, because who would run everything in England if everyone under forty was sent to France?'

'The old codgers like me,' Garth called out from the yard. 'And if I have to clean up a mess like this again I'll lie about my age and volunteer.'

Jimmy fell asleep that night almost as soon as he got into bed, but as always he had one arm around Belle, curled into her back. She lay there in the darkness listening to his gentle breathing, and moved his hand down on to her belly. She had got over the shock of Mog's suggestion now, and here, tucked so cosily into bed, the thought of her and Jimmy having a baby was a good one. She could imagine Mog and Garth cooing over him or her, always ready to lend a hand, as loving as grandparents. Jimmy would make a superb father too; he was loving, patient and so big-hearted.

But would she make a good mother? She knew nothing about babies, having no younger brothers or sisters, and brought up as she was, she'd never even held one in her arms. The closest she'd ever got to a baby was seeing women in Seven Dials with one tucked into a shawl in their arms. Here in Blackheath many of the mothers had nursemaids who walked their charges in a perambulator on the heath.

Would she be able to keep her shop going? While she certainly didn't like the thought of giving it up, she wasn't going to do what her own mother had done and hand over the baby to Mog.

Thinking of Annie, Belle wondered how she'd react to becoming a grandmother. Would she be indifferent? Or see it as a chance to make amends?

Belle had hoped when Annie helped her to get the shop they might become closer, but that hadn't come about. If

Belle didn't go and see her once a month, there would be no contact at all.

Annie was still running the boarding house in King's Cross that she'd acquired when the old place in Jake's Court had been burned down, and doing very well for herself. No one would ever guess by her elegant clothes and genteel manner that she'd once owned a brothel. Belle suspected that she kept having a daughter a secret too, so she wasn't likely to be enthusiastic about a grandchild.

Belle ran her hand over her stomach and silently vowed she was going to give her child all the love and affection she'd never received from her mother.

Chapter Three

Belle fanned herself with a newspaper. It was so hot in the shop that she felt she might just melt. Not for the first time in the past few days of stifling heat, she wondered who it was that decided women had to wear so many clothes.

She was wearing a camisole, chemise, drawers and stockings, over those a petticoat with yards of material, and then a fitted dress with long sleeves and a high neck. They were all damp with perspiration and her feet hurt because they were swollen with the heat, but she supposed she was luckier than most women who felt obliged to suffer a boned corset too.

It was four in the afternoon and she hadn't had a single customer since ten that morning. Earlier there had been plenty of people walking by on their way up to the heath. Most of the ladies had been carrying parasols, and if only she'd thought to stock a few she might have made some sales today.

But it was very quiet now for a Friday, a lull perhaps because the fair was opening on the heath tonight. Last year she'd been really excited by it; Jimmy had taken her there on the Saturday night and they'd had a wonderful time on the swingboats, the carousel and the helter-skelter, and gone home with a coconut and a goldfish he'd won. But she had no enthusiasm this year. It might be the last weekend of August, and to everyone perhaps the finale of summer, but the grass on the heath was brown and dusty through lack of rain. It would be even more crowded this year because everyone was out to enjoy themselves while they could, putting the war to the back of their minds.

Since the busy night when so many young men had enlisted, there was less talk about it, but plenty of grousing about rich people who were stockpiling foodstuffs. In some cases they'd cleaned shops out, and the word was that it was bound to make food prices soar. But Belle had sold more hats, as many sweethearts were rushing to get married.

She wished she and Jimmy could go to the seaside tomorrow; it would be heaven to feel a sea breeze and escape the stink of drains, which kept making her feel sick. But with the fair on, she knew he couldn't leave Garth and Mog to run the pub alone.

She moved over to the open door of the shop, desperate for some cooler air, and stood leaning against the doorpost, idly wondering if she should tell Jimmy about the baby tonight. Just two days ago she'd finally gone to see Dr Towle in Lee Park, and he had confirmed she was indeed about three and a half months pregnant. Almost as soon as Mog had suggested she might be, the symptoms arrived. First, she was becoming ever more sensitive to smells and she'd gone off drinking tea. But now her breasts were tender and fuller, and the waistband on her petticoat was tighter.

Only Mog knew so far, and she seemed to think it wasn't quite proper to tell Jimmy and Garth yet. Belle thought that was the silliest thing she'd ever heard, as what could be more natural than to inform her husband he was going to have a son or daughter? But she had noticed that women around here didn't talk about pregnancy, and because she was afraid of making a social gaffe, she was keeping it to herself for now.

A young couple were coming up the street. The girl, who was probably younger than Belle, was small and slender, wearing a pale pink ruffled dress and a straw boater. She was holding the arm of a man a few years older than her; he had the look of a bank clerk with his formal dark suit and stiff collar. The girl was gazing up at him as he spoke, hanging on his every word. As she appeared far too young to be married, it was unusual that there was no one else with them to act as a chaperone. Belle privately thought it preposterous that a young couple couldn't take a walk together without tongues wagging, but that was how it was around here.

When she and Mog had first come to live in Blackheath, they had to bow to all these peculiar and restricting niceties, just so they would fit into the community and attract no gossip. Belle played along with it, but inwardly felt a little superior because she knew so much more about men and life in general than any of the simpering women she made hats for.

Yet now she was going to be a mother she felt a little saddened and worried by her worldliness. How would she be able to bring a daughter up to be chaste, to teach her that she must obey her husband and all the many rules of etiquette so she would fit in with polite society, when Belle herself had flaunted them all?

She watched the young couple until they turned the corner up by the heath, then looked down to her left, toying with the idea of closing up as the street was now deserted. There was a heat haze on the road further down, which looked like a pool of water. She wondered if that was what a mirage was, for she'd heard that people in deserts often saw water ahead when it wasn't really there.

All at once a strident yell and the sound of rumbling carriage wheels broke Belle out of her reverie.

Looking back to her right, she saw a small carriage drawn by two brown horses was being reined in by the driver, and at the horses' feet a woman was lying crumpled on the ground. The driver must have been going at quite a speed, and it looked as if she had walked out right into his path.

As Belle darted to help, the driver climbed down from the carriage.

'She stepped out without looking. I could have driven right over her,' he gasped, his face ashen with fright.

'You did well to stop,' Belle said as she knelt down by the woman.

Her hat had fallen off and her fair hair was hiding her face. Belle smoothed her hair back cautiously, half expecting that she would have a grievous injury if one of the horses' hooves had struck her a glancing blow. But there was no blood, just a graze on her forehead which appeared to be from hitting the ground. Whether she had tripped and then been knocked unconscious by the fall, or had fainted, Belle didn't know as she hadn't seen it happen. The woman was young, perhaps in her early twenties, and very well dressed in a pale blue gown.

'Can you hear me?' Belle asked, running her eyes over the woman's body, looking for anything that might suggest further injuries.

The woman's eyelids fluttered and then opened. 'What happened?' she asked, her voice faint and indistinct.

'I think you must have fainted, but you were lucky you weren't mown down by the carriage,' Belle said. 'Can you move your arms and legs?'

The woman looked at Belle vacantly, clearly in shock.

Belle turned her head to look at the driver, a small, plump man wearing green livery. He was wringing his hands and appeared equally shocked. 'Did you actually hit her?' she asked.

'I don't know,' he replied. 'She just walked off the pavement and as I yelled at her she dropped like a stone. I pulled so hard on the reins it was a wonder the horses didn't rear up. She might have been struck by a hoof, but I was that close to her I couldn't see past the horses. But it weren't my fault.'

'No, of course not,' Belle said, and pulled the woman's dress down to cover her legs. 'There isn't any blood, and she seems stunned rather than injured. I think she fainted.'

A few people had gathered now, and though Belle knew you weren't supposed to move someone with an injury, she couldn't leave the woman in the road. She saw a big, dark-haired man among the bystanders, and beckoned to him. 'Could you help me get her into my hat shop?' she asked. 'I could call a doctor from there.'

'I'm all right,' the woman said in a quavering voice. 'If you'd just help me up.'

The big man came forward, leaned over and lifted the woman as if she weighed nothing. Belle picked up the blue hat lying in the road and indicated where her shop was.

'You look shaken up too,' she said to the carriage driver. 'Would you like to come in as well and I'll make you a cup of tea?'

'That's kind of you, miss,' he said. 'But I've got to pick up the mistress.'

Belle had learned in her time in Blackheath that servants were often very nervous of displeasing their employers. 'Well, if you are sure you are all right,' she said. 'I expect the young lady will be fine, I'll take care of her.'

The big man was just putting the woman down on a chair as Belle got to the shop. She thanked him before he left, and then turned to the injured woman. 'I'm Belle Reilly,' she said. 'Can you tell me your name?'

'Miranda Forbes-Alton,' she said, lolling back in the chair. She was very pale and the graze on her forehead had a lot of grit in it.

31

For some reason the name Forbes-Alton rang a bell, but Belle couldn't think why that was. 'Right, Miss Forbes-Alton,' she said firmly. 'I'm going to shut the shop door and bathe your forehead.'

Instinct told her that as the woman was badly shocked it might make her sick, and she wouldn't want an audience to it. So as she shut the door, she pulled down the blind.

First she got the woman a drink of water, and waited for a moment to check she wasn't going to be sick, before fetching a bowl of water and a clean cloth to bathe her forehead.

'I was terribly hot coming up the hill,' Miss Forbes-Alton said as Belle began to clean her wound gently. 'I was thinking I must get some water, but I don't remember anything after that. Why was I in the road?'

'I think you fainted,' Belle said. 'Have you ever done that before?'

'Not since I was at school,' she said, wincing as Belle got out a piece of grit. 'I did it several times when we had to go to communion before we had breakfast. Did that carriage hit me?'

'I don't think so,' Belle said. 'Do your arms or legs hurt?'

Miss Forbes-Alton ran one hand down her legs through her dress. 'No, it's just my head.'

'You were lucky the driver managed to stop in time. He said you walked out and dropped down right in front of him. If those horses had hit you it might have been very serious.'

Once the wound was clean, Belle went into the back room and put the kettle on to make some tea. As she waited for it to boil she looked round the door and studied the woman a little more closely. Although she was stunned and shaky, it was obvious from her voice, demeanour and clothes that she came from the upper classes. Her dainty cream shoes alone would have cost more than the most expensive hat in Belle's shop, and her blue dress was real silk.

'I have always admired your shop,' Miss Forbes-Alton called out, surprising Belle as her voice had become much stronger. She had that clipped manner of speaking that so many of her class used. 'Someone told my mother that you were French, but you aren't, are you?'

'No, I just learned millinery in Paris,' Belle called back. 'Do you live nearby?'

'Yes, in the Paragon,' she said. 'Mama bought a hat from you when you first opened. It's her favourite, purple velvet with sprigs of violets around the brim.'

Belle suddenly knew why Forbes-Alton sounded familiar. It was the name of a very snooty woman who had demanded that the hat she'd bought should be sent to her home. It was only because it was Belle's first day that she'd agreed to it, and when she'd gone round there at the end of the day, the butler had taken the hat from her without so much as a word of thanks for her trouble.

The house had been a very grand one, but then the whole of the Paragon, a Georgian terrace of three-storey houses linked by colonnades, was grand. It was probably the best address in Blackheath.

'I remember your mother,' Belle said. 'I delivered her hat to your home in the Paragon. She'll be worried about you, miss. Should I telephone so someone can come and take you home?'

Belle had only had the telephone put on in the shop a few weeks before. She'd been told by the owner of the gown shop just a few doors down that she really should have one as rich women liked to arrange a time to come and shop for gowns and hats when they could be the only customer. Until then Belle had thought a telephone a fad that would never catch on with ordinary people. But she was anxious to attract wealthier customers, so she decided to try it. Since its installation she had received several inquiries, and it was good to be able to order materials for her hats without having to make the trip to warehouses. Now she was inclined to think that in a few years all businesses and many private homes would have one.

'Please call me Miranda. And no, I don't want you to telephone anyone. I'll be fine in a minute or two.'

Belle made the tea, putting extra sugar in Miranda's, and insisted she ate a few biscuits too. Her face was still very white, but then she'd noted that most women of her class looked pasty.

'I'm not going to let you walk home alone,' she said as she gave Miranda her tea. 'I'll come with you and I'll advise your mother to call the doctor. I know it is very hot today, but that shouldn't make you faint.'

Miranda's eyes widened with horror. 'No! I don't need an escort or a doctor,' she said, her voice rising in agitation.

Belle was immediately suspicious. Most people would be grateful for help and support if they'd had some kind of turn which could have resulted in serious injury or death. And if Miranda's mother couldn't even carry a hat box home with her, she was hardly likely to have raised a daughter who was independent.

'Could it be that you've been up to something today which you don't want your family to know about?' she asked lightly.

'You are direct to the point of rudeness,' Miranda replied, looking down her slim, aristocratic nose. 'I appreciate that you've helped me, but I don't think that gives you the right to question me.'

Belle shrugged. It seemed Miranda was as hoity-toity as her mother. She guessed that she'd been brought up to believe that people in 'trade' should kowtow to the upper classes. 'I believe that any woman should offer the hand of friendship to another if they feel they have a problem. I surmise by your prickliness that you know exactly why you fainted, and you are afraid that if I walk you home your mother will insist on you seeing a doctor.'

Belle was merely stabbing in the dark, but when she saw the look of alarm on Miranda's face she knew she'd touched a nerve.

Maybe it was just that she'd felt dizzy so often lately. There had even been a couple of times when she'd thought she was going to faint. And Miranda had no wedding ring on her finger, not even an engagement ring. Was she in that kind of trouble?

Belle was well aware that she might very well offend Miranda and that could cause a great deal of trouble for her. But it wasn't in her nature to look the other way, not when her instinct told her someone needed help, so she went over to her and knelt down by her chair. 'Are you having a baby?' she asked quietly. 'You can tell me to mind my own business if you like, but if you are, you need to confide in someone. You can trust me, I won't tell a soul.'

Miranda didn't have to reply. Tears sprang to her eyes and she covered her face with her hands, all haughtiness gone.

Belle felt a huge wave of sympathy. She was familiar enough with upper-class society to know that a baby born out of wedlock would create a terrible scandal.

'Can't you get married quickly?' she asked, putting her arms around Miranda to comfort her.

'He's already married,' Miranda sobbed. 'I didn't know that, not when it happened. But it doesn't matter now because I went to see a woman today and she dealt with it.'

Belle's stomach turned a somersault. One of the girls at Martha's in New Orleans had gone to a woman who had 'dealt' with her unwanted pregnancy. She knew what it entailed.

'You went to see someone today? Did she do it with soapy water and a douche?'

Miranda nodded. 'I thought it would come away while I was with her, but she told me to go home and it would happen in a few hours. As I was coming up the hill from the station I felt dizzy, then the next thing I knew, you were there.'

Belle sensed that Miranda was naive enough to imagine that aborting an early pregnancy was quick and painless. Clearly the abortionist hadn't enlightened her for fear of losing the fee.

'How do you feel now?' she asked, putting a hand on Miranda's stomach. She was very slender but held in by a firm corset.

'I've got a dull ache,' Miranda said.

Belle took a deep breath to steady herself.

She knew the sensible thing was to let Miranda go home as she had already planned; after all, she was nothing to her. But she doubted Miranda had any idea of how fierce the pains would be, or that she was likely to lose a lot of blood. Holed up in her bedroom, it was doubtful that she could go through that without crying out. And with a house full of servants, and a bossy mother, her secret would soon be out and she'd be ruined.

Belle couldn't bear the thought of any woman having to face such an ordeal alone.

'Haven't you got a friend you could go and stay with for the night?' she asked.

Miranda looked puzzled. 'Why would I want to do that?'

Belle sighed, wondering how anyone could be so stupid. 'Because you might need help. It's a messy business,' she said.

Miranda's pale blue eyes became wide with horror. 'Then

I couldn't go to anyone I know! They'd all be outraged. What am I going to do? You're frightening me.'

Belle held Miranda's hand and looked at her hard. She wasn't exactly pretty, her nose was too sharp, her lips too thin, but there was something very attractive about her, even with her red-rimmed eyes. Belle thought back to all the tight spots she'd been in herself. She'd found her way out of most of them without help from anyone, and become stronger for the experience. But she couldn't bring herself to let this girl lose everything by sending her home. She felt her mother was the kind who would disown her if she was shamed by her.

'You can stay here,' she said impulsively.

'Here?' Miranda looked around the shop as if bewildered at the suggestion.

'I didn't mean here in the shop,' Belle hastened to explain. 'I meant out in the back room. I can make you comfortable there. There's water and a lavatory just out the back. I'll stay and take care of you too. But you must telephone home and make some excuse.'

'You'd do that for me?' Miranda's eyes filled again. 'But you don't know me! And besides, you are married, won't your husband expect you home?'

Belle knew Jimmy would be horrified at her getting involved, but she had no intention of telling him anything, at least not until it was over. She'd speak to Mog and get her help.

'I'll be truthful. I don't want this,' Belle said simply. 'But I couldn't have it on my conscience if I sent you home and you had no one to take care of you. Your reputation would be ruined if this got out. I've met your mother, remember? I can't see her being very kind to you.'

37

'Why would you care?'

'Let's just say it's because I've had some hard times in the past. Now, who could you tell your mother you are staying with?'

'Well, I told her this morning that I was going to see a friend who lives in Belgravia. I do sometimes stay overnight there.'

'The telephone is there.' Belle pointed to it. 'Use it.'

Belle went into the back room as Miranda asked the operator to put her through. She just hoped it wasn't possible for Mrs Forbes-Alton to find out that the call had come from Blackheath and not Belgravia.

The back room was the same width as the shop, but not as long, and a door at the end opened on to the small walled yard where the lavatory was. On the left of the room there were shelves to the ceiling filled with boxes of trimmings, canvas and rolls of felt. Beneath it was her workbench with her blocks and the steamer for shaping hats. To the right behind the door into the room were the sink, gas ring and a small stove she lit in cold weather. If she moved the small table beyond that, over by the workbench, she could make a bed of sorts on the floor.

Fortunately she had a few cushions, old ones from Seven Dials which she'd brought up here with the intention of making new covers for them. There was also an old but clean dust sheet left from when the shop was decorated.

She could hear Miranda speaking on the telephone, and it sounded as if her mother wasn't at home and she was giving a message to one of the servants. It was terribly hot, so Belle opened the back door and pulled the beaded curtain across it which kept out flies, then laid the cushions down and covered them with the dust sheet.

'Mama and Papa have gone out and they won't be home

until late this evening,' Miranda said from behind her. When Belle looked round she was standing in the doorway looking down anxiously at the makeshift bed. 'That was just as well as Mama would probably have quizzed me endlessly.'

'That's good. But I will have to leave you for a little while and run home,' Belle said. She could see Miranda was becoming frightened now that she knew it wasn't going to be the way she had expected. But Belle had no choice but to leave her alone. She had to go home and give an excuse to be away for the night, and she also had to get some clean sheets, towels and other necessities.

'Don't be scared, I won't be long. Why don't you take off your dress and corset? You'll be a lot more comfortable, and I'll bring you back a nightdress of mine to wear.'

Belle went out through the back door and into the narrow alleyway, telling Miranda she would come back the same way. As she made her way home she was mentally making a list of things she would need, and what she would say to Jimmy.

Luck was with her. Mog was alone in the kitchen making a cake and she said Jimmy and Garth had gone into Lewisham together to order some new chairs for the bar.

Belle found it impossible to tell Mog lies, so she blurted out the truth about Miranda.

'I know what you're going to say,' she said as she finished. 'I should have sent her home and not got involved, but I can't, Mog.'

Mog looked stricken and didn't say anything for a moment. Belle could almost see the conflicting emotions running through her.

Finally she made a gesture with her hands, an acceptance that Belle had no real choice but to help the girl. 'I think I would've done exactly the same. But Belle, these things can go badly. I've heard of women dying from it. You promise me that if anything goes wrong, if she becomes feverish, you'll telephone the doctor?'

'Of course,' Belle replied. She had already invented a little cover story for an emergency: that the close shave with the carriage earlier in the day had made Miranda start to miscarry and she'd let her stay in the shop rather than try to get home.

It was so typical of Mog that she didn't waste any further time with a lecture, but flew upstairs and found sheets, a couple of towels, a blanket and some clean rags for the blood flow. She was down again in a trice, even before Belle had finished eating a hastily made sandwich.

Mog also had some medicine in a brown bottle. 'Give her a couple of teaspoons of this every three or four hours, it will help the pain and keep her temperature down,' she said. 'Now, I'm going to tell Jimmy you've gone over to see Lisette for the night as Noah is away and she's lonely. He'll be fine about that, with her in the family way an' all. But you'll have to straighten it out with Lisette later so she doesn't let the cat out the bag.'

Belle ran upstairs to get a few things, and when she got back she found Mog packing an overnight bag, and another smaller one with a jar of soup to heat up, some apple pie and a small bottle of brandy.

'Just some bits in case you are hungry,' she said, taking the things from Belle's arms and putting them in the bag. 'And brandy in warm milk might help to settle her afterwards.'

Belle put her arms around Mog and hugged her tightly. 'You are such a good person,' she said. 'Thank you for not being angry with me.'

Mog pulled away, but held Belle's arms and looked straight at her. 'How could I be angry with you for having a big heart?' she said. 'I'll pop up there tomorrow morning before the men are about. Just to see how she is. Keep her clean, boil some water up for washing her down below. She might be sick when it finally happens, don't be too alarmed by that. But if she loses consciousness or there is a fast flow of blood, call the doctor immediately, whatever she says.'

Belle realized then that Mog must have helped girls through this before, just another part of her past she had never revealed.

'I will,' she said, suddenly scared by what she had let herself in for.

Mog hugged her again. 'I'll be there with you in spirit, if not in the flesh. Now go, before Jimmy gets back.'

Miranda was sitting on a stool by the open back door when Belle came struggling through the yard gate with her two big bags. She was still dressed and her face looked grey with anxiety.

'It's so hot,' she whimpered. 'And my stomach aches.'

'That's a good sign,' Belle said briskly. 'It means it's starting to happen. Why didn't you take off your dress?'

'I couldn't do the buttons,' she said. 'We have a maid at home, she always does that.'

'Well, there's no maid here,' Belle said, and putting down the bags, she turned Miranda around and unfastened her dress. The corset beneath her petticoat was laced so tightly it was a miracle she could breathe. Belle quickly unlaced it for her. 'Take everything else off too,' she said, and rummaged in the overnight bag for the nightdress she'd brought for her.

Miranda turned away as she took off her chemise and camisole, and Belle winced as she saw the vivid red marks the corset had made on her naked back and waist. She slipped the clean nightdress over Miranda's head, then indicated she was to take off her drawers and stockings too.

'I'm going to heat up some water for you to wash yourself properly down there,' Belle said. 'But sit down for now while I make up the bed for you.'

It was dark by nine o'clock and much cooler. Miranda lay on the bed, now made up with clean sheets, and Belle had brought one of the shop chairs in to sit on. Miranda had eaten a little soup and bread, and seemed more relaxed, and with just the light Belle used on her workbench, the workroom looked cosy.

'Tell me about the man,' Belle said. She could see Miranda was having regular pains, but so far she said they were no worse than her monthlies. 'Is he someone your family knows?'

Miranda had already said she was one of four children: two older brothers who were both married with homes of their own, and a younger sister called Amy who was twenty and engaged to a solicitor. Miranda was twenty-three.

When Belle had asked her earlier what her father did for a living, Miranda had looked surprised. 'A living?' she'd said. 'He runs the estate in Sussex of course. Is that what you meant?'

By that Belle had to assume that Mr Forbes-Alton had inherited wealth and all he had to do was keep an eye on those who worked on his country estate and brought in the money to keep a grand London house. Miranda had said they'd only recently come back from a month in Sussex. She said she had been panicking her mother would want to stay longer, as she knew she must get the abortion done quickly.

'No, my family don't know him,' she said. 'I met him in Greenwich Park back in the spring. I'd gone for a walk on my own, and I tripped on some mud. He helped me up, and as I had hurt my ankle, he offered to walk me home. He was so charming, funny, interesting and kind. My parents have been trying to get me married off for the past few years, but the gentlemen they think are suitable are always so dull and earnest.'

'And I imagine you weren't supposed to go out walking on your own either?' Belle suggested.

Miranda half smiled. 'No, Mama would've been furious if she knew. I couldn't ask Frank to call on me either as we hadn't been introduced by friends or family. So right from the start we had to meet in secret.'

Belle guessed that Frank was a complete cad. He'd taken advantage of Miranda knowing full well that as she couldn't invite him to meet her parents, he could make up any cock-and-bull story about himself without fear of being exposed.

'What did he tell you about himself?' she asked.

'Not a great deal. What was there to tell? A gentleman with private means.' She shrugged. 'He dressed well, and he said he lived in Westminster.'

'Where did you go with him?' Belle asked.

'We went for walks mostly, usually down to Greenwich because I didn't dare let anyone in Blackheath see me with him. Sometimes we took a boat up river and we'd have lunch out. I could only see him about once a week or my absence would've been noticed.'

'I meant where did he take you to seduce you?' Belle asked.

Miranda blushed. 'To a room in Greenwich.'

Belle shook her head. 'Didn't that strike you as odd when he'd told you he lived in Westminster?'

'He said his servants might talk,' she said. 'I was so in love with him by then I would've gone anywhere with him.'

'And when did he tell you he was married?'

'When I told him I thought I might be having a baby.' Her eyes filled with tears again. 'I really believed he'd tell me not to worry and we'd get married straight away. But he wouldn't even look at me. We were in a tea shop, and he just looked out of the window and said, "Then you've got a problem," not even "we've". I started crying and I could see that irritated him. We left the tea shop and then he said I knew all along he was married.'

'How crafty to make out it was your fault!' Belle exclaimed. 'What a cad!'

Miranda sighed, and screwed up her face as she got another stronger pain. 'We always made arrangements for our next meeting. When he said he'd meet me at the usual time in the rose garden in Greenwich Park the following week I felt hopeful that would give him time to think it through and he'd find a solution. He kissed me goodbye down by the Naval College in Greenwich just as tenderly as he always had. But that was the last time I saw him.'

'And I suppose you had no way of contacting him?'

Miranda shook her head. 'I had no address, nothing but little stories about people that I suspect now probably weren't even true. I went into the tea shop we often went to in Greenwich and asked the girl behind the counter if she'd seen him, but she said, "He only ever came in here with you." What else was there to do? I'd already been round to the house where he took me a few times, he'd said a friend of his owned it. But I'm afraid when I spoke to someone there it became clear to me it was a place where rooms were rented out by the hour.'

Belle took Miranda's hand and squeezed it. She could guess that finding out she'd been used as a whore, without even being paid, was the worst humiliation.

'When tonight is over you must put all this behind you,' she said gently. 'Most of us have something in our past we are ashamed of. But all you are guilty of is being a little gullible. He is the bad person for pretending he loved you.'

44

'That's the part that hurts most,' Miranda said. 'I really loved him, I risked everything to be with him. Why would anyone do that to another person?'

'I think some people are born wicked,' Belle said. 'I'd say he was a practised philanderer, but at least he didn't try to get money out of you.'

Miranda looked shamefaced. 'I did give him fifty pounds,' she admitted. 'It was just a couple of weeks before I told him I thought I was having his baby. He'd been telling me for some little time that he knew of some land just out of London that was ripe for building on. He even showed me some sketches of small houses, just perfect for young married couples who wanted an inexpensive house in the countryside but could travel into the city for their work.'

Belle could see what was coming. 'I suppose he told you his funds were tied up and he needed cash to secure the land?'

'How did you know that?' Miranda said in surprise.

'Instinct,' Belle said. 'And you volunteered your savings?'

'He wanted a hundred, but I didn't have that much,' she said. 'He promised he would give it back just as soon as he'd sold some shares.'

Belle felt a tight ball of anger in her stomach at anyone being so low. 'I hate to say this to you, Miranda, but I think you must face the fact that getting money out of you was his intention from the moment he discovered where you lived,' she said. 'His good clothes, his manner and even where you met him, indicate that he was actively looking for someone to cheat. He's clearly a man who lives on his wits.'

'Then you don't think he was married either?'

She asked that question with such hope in her eyes that Belle almost laughed at her stupidity. The loss of her money, not turning up to meet her when he said he would, wasn't evidence to her of a scoundrel; she still chose to believe he'd let her down because he was married.

'He might be, to someone as gullible as you,' Belle replied. 'But it's more likely he's got a whole string of women around London, all doting on him, keeping him and believing they are his true love.'

Belle had heard Jimmy and Garth talking many times about such men they knew back in Seven Dials who made a living out of cheating women. Mog had always said that until women woke up, got the vote and insisted on a society which wasn't run just by men, for men, there would always be a hiding place for cads and bounders.

'How did you find out about the woman who "helped" you?' Belle asked. She couldn't imagine how any woman with a family background like Miranda's had made contact with such a person.

'From a woman in the house in Greenwich,' Miranda said. 'I started to cry when the man who ran that place was sharp with me and said he didn't know Frank. She came after me and asked if she could help. I was so upset, and she was so kind, I told her about the baby, and she gave me the address in Bermondsey.'

Belle nodded. She guessed the woman in question was a whore, and one with a heart too. Sometimes she thought that the only women with big hearts were fallen women.

'It was an awful place she sent me to,' Miranda confided. 'I've never seen anything like it. There were ragged, dirty children everywhere, broken doors and windows, it was so dirty and smelly I wanted to turn and run away. But I couldn't, I had to go through with it.'

Belle could imagine what the place was like, a rotting, overcrowded tenement like the ones around Seven Dials.

'You were very brave. But if you could go through that, you can go through anything. Now, how are you feeling?'

'I think I'm losing some blood now.' She blushed scarlet at having to reveal something so personal.

'Lie back and let me look,' Belle said. 'Don't be embarrassed. You haven't got anything I haven't, and just think of me as a nurse.'

Miranda was bleeding a little, but it was mostly the soapy water the woman had used running out of her. Belle had been told by one of the girls in New Orleans who had gone through it herself that the practice was to open the sealed end of the cervix, then pump soapy water in, which acted as an irritant and made the woman miscarry. It didn't bear dwelling on what they made the opening to the cervix with.

Belle washed Miranda and fixed a piece of clean rag beneath her. She felt it wouldn't be much longer now and gave her a dose of the medicine Mog had supplied.

It was almost one in the morning when Miranda's pains became really bad. Belle could sense the strength of them by the sweat on her brow and the way she arched her back and grimaced. But she didn't scream out, only held tightly on to Belle's hand.

By half past two Belle was exhausted herself, wondering just how much longer anyone could be in such terrible pain. 'You are being very brave,' she said as yet again she wiped Miranda's face with cold water. She was writhing with the pain now, biting her bottom lip to stop crying out.

When she began to retch Belle quickly got a bowl and held it for her but with her spare hand she pushed back the sheet to look. There was a lot of fresh blood, and as Miranda once again retched, there was a rush of what looked like pieces of liver. Knowing what that meant made Belle want to retch too.

'Is that it?' Miranda gasped out.

Belle gathered up the bloody rags, placing clean ones beneath Miranda. She didn't want to look closely, but felt she must before she put them in the bucket. But there was something pale and tadpole-shaped, and knowing that must be the baby, she couldn't stop herself from crying. It was even more distressing to think she had a baby in her own womb which would be wanted and loved, while that poor little mite had to be destroyed.

'Yes, that's it,' she managed to get out through her tears. 'Has the pain gone now?'

'Yes, I just ache,' Miranda whispered hoarsely. 'What would I have done without you?'

Belle hoped that if she lived to be a hundred she'd never have to see something as hideous as that again. Silently she cursed Frank, wished he could see what his greed and wickedness had done tonight, and that he'd suffer because of it.

She washed Miranda all over and covered her up with the sheet. 'Next time you meet a young man, you bring him to me to sound out,' she whispered, and kissed her forehead. 'Now I'll make you some hot milk with some brandy in it. Then you can go to sleep.'

Chapter Four

Just after six in the morning Mog slipped in through the back gate to the shop yard. It was a beautiful morning, with the promise of another hot day ahead. Birds were singing, and at any other time she would have been reminded how lucky she was to have got away from Seven Dials and to have a loving, hard-working husband.

But she had barely slept with anxiety about Belle. Although back in the days when she worked as the maid in Annie's brothel she had taken care of six or seven girls in exactly the same predicament as Miranda, it had never come easily to her. It was a foul, shameful business, and even worse for Belle to witness it when she was pregnant herself.

Mog wished with all her heart that there was an alternative for unmarried women who found themselves in this position. But if they didn't go along with an abortion, without support from their families or the father of the child they were likely to find themselves cast out on to the streets, the workhouse the only place that would take them in. If their baby didn't die from neglect during the birth, it was likely to be placed in an orphanage, or farmed out to someone who saw child rearing as a profitable business and showed no tender care.

But Mog's main fear today was that if anything had gone wrong last night, Belle would be in serious trouble. The law might turn a blind eye to anyone helping a prostitute through such an ordeal, but not a lady of quality.

Women did die from these barbarous abortions, if not

while it was happening, then later when infections set in. Belle might not be guilty of aiding and abetting what Miranda had done, but if the girl died, her family would need to blame someone and Belle would be their scapegoat.

All was quiet and the back door was open a little to let in air. Mog pushed it open a little further to look in. Belle was fast asleep on the floor, wearing only her chemise, her hair tousled and one slender arm tucked around her head. The blonde girl on the makeshift bed was equally peaceful. She was wearing an old cotton nightdress trimmed with lace which Mog had made for Belle. Her colour looked good, not too pale, nor flushed and feverish.

Relief flooded through Mog. There was no blood, mess or anything to suggest anything out of the ordinary had taken place in the room. She could see a covered bucket outside in the yard, and guessed that any evidence was in there.

Despite her relief that all was well, there was something about the blonde girl which made her look through the door again, and to her shock she recognized her as the daughter of Mrs Forbes-Alton. Until just a few days ago all she knew of this woman was gossip: that she was bombastic and liked to keep a finger in every pie in the village. Mog had finally met her at a meeting which had been called to start a knitting group to make useful items for soldiers at the front. Mrs Forbes-Alton had been there with her two daughters, and Mog remembered them clearly because they looked so uncomfortable when their mother began to sound off as if she was running the entire show.

Mrs Fitzpatrick, the wife of a famous concert pianist who had blue blood running through her veins, had made a tentative suggestion that maybe Mrs Jenkins, who ran the village haberdasher's, could advise women what to knit and give instruction to novices as she was something of an expert.

Mrs Jenkins agreed she'd be happy to do that, and would offer a discount on any knitting wool purchased from her.

'Oh no,' Mrs Forbes-Alton had boomed out in her plummy voice. 'We can't have anyone profiting from our venture. We should buy the wool wholesale.'

Mog had seethed along with a great many other women because Mrs Jenkins had lost her husband in the war in South Africa, and just a few weeks earlier had seen both her two sons enlist. She was big-hearted, generously knitting clothes for every new baby born in the village, and had helped countless young women make their wedding dresses. Everyone knew she would be struggling to make ends meet now her sons had gone to war. But as one woman pointed out, she'd probably knit more items than anyone else in the village.

That afternoon at the meeting, both the Forbes-Alton girls had been impeccably dressed and looked the very picture of shy docility. That made it even harder for Mog to imagine that the older and plainer one had been having a secret love affair.

After the meeting feelings were running very high about Mrs Forbes-Alton and it was said that this was how she always behaved, belittling the efforts of anyone else, but doing very little herself. They said she was boastful and mean-spirited and treated her servants appallingly. So it was somewhat ironic that Belle had rescued Miranda, and saved that ogre of a woman some richly deserved shame and humiliation.

Now Mog knew what Miranda's mother was like, she felt even more sympathetic towards the daughter. She'd probably been brought up by servants, with little interest and affection from her mother. It was no wonder she fell into the arms of the first man who said he loved her. But she'd paid a very high price for a little fleeting happiness.

Hopefully she would recover physically in a few days with rest and good hygiene, but Mog knew that the mental scar of losing a baby, whether by accident or intent, was something that took a great deal longer to heal.

Belle stirred and opened her eyes as the back door creaked. She saw Mog and smiled, putting one finger over her lips and nodding towards Miranda, then got up and came out into the yard.

She closed the door behind her and taking Mog's arm, led her over to a couple of wooden boxes where they sat down in the sunshine. 'She's going to be all right, I think,' Belle said in a low voice. 'She was very brave, didn't scream or anything, and fell asleep soon after it was over, but I couldn't go through that again.'

Mog put her arm round her and held her close. She hated that her Belle had been forced to see something so harrowing.

'It doesn't bear thinking about how it would have been for Miranda if she had gone home,' she said thoughtfully. 'I've met her mother and she's a Tartar.' She went on to tell Belle what she knew about her. 'But what are you going to do with Miranda now?'

'Let her sleep for as long as possible,' Belle said, looking back at the door. 'I won't open the shop of course, not when I'm supposed to be at Lisette's. I'll walk her home later. Fortunately the friend she's supposed to have stayed with isn't on the telephone, so her mother won't find out she wasn't there. Miranda can pretend she's just having a very heavy monthly and go back to bed.'

'You'll have to get rid of that.' Mog pointed to the bucket.

'I'm going to pour some turpentine on it and set fire to it later,' Belle said. 'I can't do it now; it would be suspicious if anyone saw smoke at this time in the morning.'

'I'll take my hat off to you, you've thought it all through,' Mog said admiringly. It never ceased to astound her how after all the humiliations and terrors Belle had been through she had retained her humanity, dignity, warmth and sense of humour.

She had loved Belle as her own from the moment she held her in her arms when she was newborn, and she would have continued to love her even if she'd lost her mind and her beauty. But to see her return to England and by her own force of will open the milliner's she'd always dreamed of and make a huge success of it, that made Mog immensely proud.

Belle half smiled. 'It's not the first time I've had to plot something, but I don't know whether I can tell Jimmy. How was he last night?'

'He was fine, but then he's always easy about everything. Not like some men that fly off the handle when their missus goes out. You got a fine one there.'

'I know,' Belle said glumly. 'That's why I'm going to feel terrible lying about going to see Lisette.'

'Then don't say anything much, just launch into telling him about your baby. He'll be so thrilled about that he won't think to ask about Lisette.'

Belle looked pensive. 'I wonder if Miranda will keep in touch with me after this.'

'Do you want her to?' Mog asked.

'Yes,' Belle nodded. 'I thought she was very snooty at first, but once that was gone I found we had a lot in common and I felt very close to her. I kept thinking that it was but for the grace of God I was never in her position. But I didn't tell her I was having a baby, it didn't seem right.'

Mog sighed. 'No, but don't dwell on that. You were there when she most needed someone. Now, if you don't need me for anything, I'd better go home. Have you got anything you want me to take to wash? Don't want Jimmy seeing you with anything suspicious.'

'There's a sheet and a towel,' Belle said and got up to get them. 'I'll be home about one.'

As Mog opened the back gate a few minutes later with the soiled linen in a bag, she turned to Belle. 'I'm so proud of you,' she said. 'Perhaps in the eyes of the law you did wrong getting involved, but to me you have been brave and kind. I hope Miranda realizes that God must have been smiling on her to send her to you.'

Just after one, Belle locked up her shop, and tucking Miranda's arm into hers they set off on the walk to the Paragon. There were a great many people flocking over to the fair, children running about excited at the music and noise coming from it. Miranda looked drained and pale, but she was in quite good spirits and not in any pain. Belle had slipped out of the shop earlier and bought some Hartmann's sanitary pads for her, and it was a relief to both women that she wasn't losing much blood any more.

'Fairs look like such good fun,' Miranda said, looking across the heath towards it. 'Mama doesn't approve of them though. Amy and I have never been allowed to go. Once, a few years ago, we planned to slip out after dinner to go there, but she caught us just as we were opening the front door. There was hell to pay; she made us stay in our rooms for a week, and said only factory girls and strumpets went to fairs.'

'That isn't true,' Belle said indignantly. 'My husband took me last year and we saw a great many of the gentry there. It's just harmless fun for everyone.'

'Mama has very fixed opinions,' Miranda sighed. 'To tell the truth I'd marry almost anyone to get away from her.'

'You don't have to marry anyone to leave home,' Belle

exclaimed in horror. 'You could get a job in an office easily enough, then find a room to rent. I know girls from your background don't normally work, but now we're at war, there are going to be far more opportunities for women. And you can bet well-bred ones like you will be chosen over ordinary ones.'

Miranda squeezed her arm. 'You are so inspiring,' she said. 'As soon as I'm over this I'm going to start looking for a job. All Mama can do is cut me off, and the way I feel now that would be heaven.'

Belle thought that Miranda wouldn't be all that happy when she found out what long hours most women worked, and how low their wages were. But she was glad she'd given her something to think about.

'Before you get carried away by the notion of freedom, you must get your story for your mother straight,' she said archly. 'You can use that graze on your forehead as an excuse for feeling a little shaken, say you fell over this morning in Belgravia and you've got a very heavy monthly. Just in case anyone spots us together, it might be a good idea to say you saw me on the train and because you felt dizzy or something I walked back with you.'

Miranda nodded agreement. 'You amaze me how you think of everything. But what if anyone saw the accident yesterday?'

Belle had given that some consideration already. 'Well, I didn't recognize any of the people who were around, and I'm sure if any of them had known you, they would've come forward. But if it should get back to your mother, just deny it was you. If she comes to me, I'll back you up and say it was a stranger.'

'I can never thank you enough,' Miranda said softly. She had been very embarrassed when she woke up this morning;

no one had ever been so kind to her before. 'May I keep in touch with you?'

'I'd be upset if you didn't,' Belle said. 'I hope we're going to become good friends.'

Then all at once she remembered that Mrs Forbes-Alton would never countenance her daughter being the friend of a shopkeeper, especially as Belle's husband was a publican. It was also likely that in a few days' time Miranda might get scared Belle would talk.

'Of course, I'm not in your social set,' Belle said lightly. 'But you can always drop into the shop for a chat. And don't for one moment imagine that I might betray you by talking about this. I promise you I will never say a word to anyone else. Mog, my aunt, knows, but we are both the same, tight-lipped and loyal.'

'I know that,' Miranda said. 'I felt it as soon as you offered your help. I understand now why my mother's friends talk about you. Despite being so young, you are a deep and fascinating woman.'

Belle laughed. 'So what do they say about me?'

'Well, your beauty has been remarked on many times, along with your wonderful, stylish hats. It went around of course, as I said yesterday, that you were French, and to most that means you are a little racy.'

Belle was amused by that. 'Do you think I am?'

Miranda looked sideways at Belle and blushed. 'Well, there is something about you . . . .You're worldly, strong and under-standing of people. I hope one day you'll tell me all about yourself. How you came to be in Paris, where you met your husband, and if you ever loved a man before him.'

'I'm sure I will,' Belle said, though she suspected if she were to tell Miranda her whole story she'd have an attack of the vapours. 'Maybe this war will also help to break down social barriers; it's likely to if women of all classes have to muck in to help the war effort. I hope so; I haven't got much time for all the present-day restrictions on women.'

'It is so good to hear you say that. Mama is forever saying, put your gloves on, you must wear a hat, put your shoulders back, a lady doesn't do this or that. That was one of the things I loved so much about being with Frank, even if he was a cad. I felt free because he flouted all the rules.'

'Well, some of those rules were made to protect us,' Belle reminded her. 'But a man doesn't have to be a cad or a scoundrel to be exciting and passionate. And now you know the worst of men, you can look for the best in future.'

Belle said goodbye to Miranda at her door, then made her way home. While she was concerned about Miranda's recovery and hoped her mother wouldn't become suspicious, she was more apprehensive about going home to Jimmy.

She had never lied to him before. She was guilty of not always telling him things, but then maybe he did that too. But she couldn't tell him what she had done last night. He would be horrified.

Jimmy was behind the bar with Garth when she came in through the side door. Because of the fair the bar was packed, and very noisy. Belle went into the kitchen and found Mog making sandwiches.

'Was everything all right?' Mog said in a low voice, even though the door through to the bar was shut.

'She's fine,' Belle reassured her. 'No fever or pain, and she felt hungry this morning and was quite perky on the way home. I'm so relieved nothing went wrong.'

'My prayers were answered.' Mog rolled her eyes

heavenwards. 'But now for more earthly things. I'll be taking these sandwiches into the bar in a minute and I'll tell Jimmy you're back. Why don't you nip up and change your clothes?'

Belle had washed and was just putting on a clean chemise when Jimmy came into the bedroom. He leaned against the doorpost, watching her with a cheeky grin on his face.

'Now, there's a lovely sight, my pretty wife with next to no clothes on. Shame it's busy in the bar today, or I'd throw you on the bed and have my wicked way with you.'

Belle laughed and went over to hug him. He looked handsome in a white shirt and emerald-green waistcoat which enhanced his tawny eyes. 'I missed you last night,' she said. 'I really wanted to tell you something.'

'I hope it wasn't that you'd thought of running off with another man, but then changed your mind,' he said, rubbing his nose against hers.

'No, because I won't be able to run for very much longer,' she said, and took his face in her two hands and kissed him.

It was Jimmy who broke away first. 'Why?' he asked, looking puzzled, then his eyes dropped down to her stomach and he put one hand there. 'Are you?'

'Yes,' she laughed. 'Yes, I'm having a baby!'

He looked at her as if stunned for a brief second, and then the widest of smiles spread almost from ear to ear. 'A baby? Are you sure? When?'

'Well, the doctor couldn't be precise, but I think I'm about three and a half months, so it will be about the end of February.'

Jimmy hugged her to him tightly. 'That's the most wonderful news I've ever had, well, except perhaps when you said you loved me for the first time,' he said softly into her hair. 'Oh Belle, could anyone else in the world be as happy as I am?'

Belle moved back to look at him and saw tears rolling down his cheeks. 'Me, I'm the happiest person, because I've got you as well as the baby.'

'We must tell Mog and Garth,' he said, his damp eyes glowing with delight. 'I know Mog is going to be thrilled, but I'm not so sure about Garth, he'll need some time to get used to the idea.'

'We'll tell them when you shut the bar for the afternoon,' Belle said. She knew Mog would never let on she knew already.

'And now I've got to go back in that bar and act like nothing momentous has happened?' Jimmy asked. 'I'd like to go in there and announce it to everyone, but that isn't really the done thing, is it?'

'No,' Belle said, smiling at his boyish enthusiasm. Pregnancy was something men didn't mention or comment on outside their own family, not even when it was completely obvious. The most they would ever say was 'She's in the family way', and only then when there was some very good reason to speak out. Yet for all that, Belle had noticed that the roughest of men were more courteous and kindly to pregnant women. 'If you do you'll just embarrass them.'

'They never mind wetting a baby's head though,' Jimmy chuckled. 'And they all pat the new father on the back like he's done the cleverest thing in the world. He'll boast about his new son, then promptly ignore him until he's old enough to be useful.'

'I know you'll never be that kind of father.' Belle patted his cheeks affectionately. 'I'm banking on you sharing everything with me, even changing napkins. So get down to the bar again and smile, but say nothing.'

'I love you, Mrs Reilly,' he said as he turned to go back to the bar.

'And I love you too, Mr Reilly,' she called after him.

As Belle got dressed she thought on Jimmy's last remark about men boasting about their new son, and then ignoring him until he was old enough to be useful. He had often spoken disapprovingly of men who came into the bar every night, without a thought for their wives and children at home.

They had both seen women on a Friday night waiting outside the pub door with a baby in their arms, here and in Seven Dials, trying to catch their husbands and get their wages from them before they spent it all. Many saw nothing wrong in beating their wives, treating them like mere chattels.

Jimmy's father had deserted his mother while he was still a baby and he knew how hard it was for a woman to raise a child alone. Perhaps this was why he was so sensitive to women's needs. He had always been very protective of Belle, understanding when she was tired, willing to do anything to help her. Now she was having his baby, she knew she could rely on his strength to keep her safe, and on his sense of humour to lift her spirits, and with him beside her she wouldn't be scared of childbirth. Perhaps too he would even help her shake off the memories of Miranda's ordeal. But above all she knew the baby would never want for love and affection. They were going to be a happy family, Jimmy would play cricket and sail boats on the pond with their child, he'd tell him or her bedtime stories, kiss sore knees better, soothe bad dreams; in fact he'd be the kind of father that both she and Jimmy wished they'd had. How lucky she was!

After the bar was closed for the afternoon, Jimmy and Garth joined Mog and Belle in the kitchen for a cup of tea and some cake.

They had hardly sat down at the table when Jimmy blurted

it out. 'We're going to have a baby,' he said, without any lead-up. 'Belle told me just a couple of hours ago.'

Garth's reaction to the news was not as they had both expected. He got up from the table and did a little jig around the room, whooping with delight. For a big man he was light on his feet, but he still looked and sounded a little ridiculous.

'That is the best news ever,' he said, giving Jimmy a slap on the shoulder that would have knocked a smaller man down. 'Not that I've had much dealing with babies. I used to hold you sometimes of course, but that was a long time ago. Hope it's a girl, don't know that we want another carrot-haired man in the family.'

Mog put on a good display of being as surprised as Garth; she got up and hugged Belle and Jimmy and said it was the best news she'd ever had. Then as she poured the tea for everyone, she talked with breathless excitement about making a layette for the baby and getting a crib.

'When will you give up the shop?' Garth asked Belle. 'You shouldn't be on your feet all day.'

'I hadn't really thought that far ahead,' she said.

Garth crossed his arms and looked fierce. 'Well, I think you should wind it up in the next few weeks,' he said, and looked to Jimmy for back-up. 'Don't you agree, son?'

Jimmy smiled at Belle and took her hand. 'I'm sure Belle will do whatever is best for our baby.'

To anyone else that would have sounded as though she had a free choice, but Belle sensed that he meant she should stay at home knitting and sewing till the baby arrived. Clearly some of his uncle's values had rubbed off on him.

Garth didn't hold with female emancipation. Mog loved to challenge him on his views, whether that was women wanting the vote, coming into the bar, or doing a job which was a traditionally male one. Yet however much she teased him, in truth she was his ideal woman, for she washed, cooked and cleaned superbly and let him make all the decisions.

Until now, having a baby was just a rosy daydream. Belle had imagined life going on the way it had been, yet with a plump baby that they'd all adore, cooing in a crib. She hadn't really considered that it also meant her freedom to do as she pleased would end.

'You look very tired, Belle,' Mog said, perhaps sensing what she was thinking. 'Why don't you go and have a lie-down for a bit?'

'Yes, I think I will,' Belle replied. 'But you have a rest too, I bet you've been up since the crack of dawn.'

Belle was still awake when Jimmy came into the bedroom, but she kept her eyes closed and pretended to be asleep. She guessed he had hoped to talk about the baby, but she didn't want that, not now. He took off his shoes and lay beside her, and within a short while his deep breathing told her he had dropped off.

It was very hot, and Belle lay on her back watching dust particles floating in beams of sunlight coming through the white lace curtains. She had chosen everything in the bedroom herself, from the rose-strewn wallpaper to the brass bed with its thick white counterpane and the rosewood dressing table with tiny drawers that held all her jewellery. Garth had once teasingly asked Jimmy how he could bear to be in such a feminine room with all its frills and flounces, and Jimmy had replied that he loved it because Belle did.

That reply had summed up how Jimmy was. He wasn't soft by any means; he could be tough with customers who behaved badly and had little time for the work-shy or those who constantly complained about their lot in life. But he was an uncomplicated man who took things as they came and he didn't care about other people's opinion of him. In fact Belle didn't know anyone who didn't like him, for he was kind, generous, interested in other people and had a great sense of humour. But above all he was honest. If asked for his opinion, he gave it; if he promised something, he kept his word.

There was a silver-framed photograph of them on their wedding day beside the bed. Mog had made Belle's wedding dress of beautiful ivory satin, high-necked and long-sleeved with a pin-tucked bodice and a small train draped to one side to show it off. Jimmy had never looked more handsome to her that day, in a pale grey pin-striped morning suit. In all the other photographs they had looked very stiff and serious. But this one had been taken as they were looking at each other and laughing and it reflected their true personalities. It was a constant reminder to Belle of how lucky she was to have someone who loved her unconditionally despite her past.

Here in this pretty room nothing mattered except the joy they found in lovemaking. Jimmy may have been a virgin on their wedding night, but in his arms she'd found even greater ecstasy than she'd experienced with Serge in New Orleans. Serge had been paid to teach her about the delights of lovemaking, and he'd been a master, but Jimmy taught her that true love and real heart-felt passion were a greater power.

'It's time you proved to him that you can be a real wife. Making and selling hats isn't as important as that,' she thought.

Turning over towards him, she put her arm around him and held him tightly. With a baby on the way it was going to be another new beginning, only this time she would have to remember to take Jimmy's feelings and ideas into account.

Chapter Five

The tinkling of the shop-door bell made Belle put down the net veiling she was attaching to a hat and hurry out into the shop.

'Jimmy!' she exclaimed, surprised that it was him. He only ever came to the shop to walk her home when the weather was bad. But it was only three o'clock on a beautiful October day. 'What brings you here?'

'I came out to get some paint for the window frames,' he said.

Belle frowned. The hardware shop wasn't up this way, and furthermore Jimmy looked a bit shaken. 'Is something wrong?' she asked.

'Does there have to be something wrong for me to visit my wife?' he retorted rather sharply.

Belle went over to him. 'There has to be something wrong for you to snap at me,' she said reproachfully.

'I'm sorry,' he said. 'But a woman came up to me and gave me this.' He reached in his pocket and pulled out a white feather.

Belle gasped. She had read in the newspaper just a day or two ago that there were women going around giving white feathers to men. It was a suggestion they were cowards because they hadn't enlisted. But she had imagined these were isolated cases, a few silly women with nothing better to do with their time than harass hard-working men.

'Take no notice, she'll just be a crank,' she said.

'No, there was a group of about ten of them,' Jimmy said,

looking very disturbed. 'They were stopping all the men. I saw Willie the window cleaner get one, also the man who sells newspapers by the station, and another man just strolling along with his wife. I was so shocked I didn't hang around to see who else got one and came straight up here.'

'It doesn't mean anything,' Belle reassured him. 'No one has to join up if they don't want to.' Yet even as she said this a chill ran down her spine, because only a couple of weeks earlier she'd seen a huge poster put up at the station showing Lord Kitchener in uniform pointing his finger. The poster read, 'Your Country Needs You'. She had thought at the time it sent out a powerful message.

'It might not be compulsory, but maybe it's morally right to do my bit,' Jimmy reflected.

Belle was frightened then. She knew when Jimmy used words like 'morally right' that he was already convinced about what he had to do. 'You can't, not with the baby coming!' she exclaimed.

Jimmy moved to embrace her. 'I wouldn't want our son or daughter to think I was a coward,' he said softly, his lips against her hair. 'And it isn't as if I'd be leaving you alone to fend for yourself, you'll have Uncle Garth and Mog to take care of you.'

Belle stepped back from him angrily. 'But you could be killed! Our baby won't want a dead hero for a father.'

'It won't come to that,' he said, making a pleading gesture with his hands.

'Just go.' Belle pointed to the door. 'And by the time I get home I hope you'll have seen sense.'

He left without another word and Belle returned to her workbench. She was so angry she accidentally tore the veiling she was working on, and picked up the hat and threw it on the ground.

The shop bell tinkled again, and thinking it was Jimmy coming back to apologize, she ignored it.

'Belle!' a tentative female voice called out. 'Are you there?'

It was Miranda. Belle struggled to compose herself and went into the shop. Miranda looked very elegant in a pale mauve costume and a matching small hat trimmed with artificial violets; her cheeks were rosy and she had a glow about her.

'What a lovely surprise,' Belle said, grateful for a diversion from her anger. 'I've thought about you so often.'

Miranda had written her a letter a couple of weeks ago, while she was down at her family's country estate in Sussex. In it she had thanked Belle for her kindness and said she had fully recovered without anyone becoming suspicious.

'It's good to be back in London,' Miranda said. 'I so much wanted to talk to you while I was away. Mama was insufferable, more so than she usually is. She's that desperate to get me married off she kept inviting people with eligible sons to dinner. She couldn't have made her intentions plainer if she had actually put on the invitations that it was to find a husband for me.'

Belle smiled. 'And did anyone nice come?'

Miranda rolled her eyes. 'Awful, all of them. And besides, all they talked about was the war and joining a regiment. I was bored senseless. But how have you been?'

'I was fine until a few minutes ago when Jimmy came in. He thinks he ought to enlist, but I can't bear the thought of him going.'

'Oh dear! I'm sure you can't. But you told me before he had no intention of enlisting until it was compulsory.'

'That's what he said. But a woman gave him a white feather today and now he feels guilty and afraid people will think he's a coward.'

'Mama has joined a group handing out white feathers,' Miranda said, wrinkling her nose in disgust. 'In my opinion it's bad enough for men having their peers push them into it, but now with women humiliating them, the poor dears will feel obliged to go. Women like my mother don't think about how soldiers' wives and children are going to manage. As I understand it, army pay is only a pittance.'

Miranda's sympathy for wives and children seemed like the ideal opportunity for Belle to tell her she was having a baby.

'I'm not so concerned about army pay, but you see, I'm expecting a baby.'

'That's wonderful news,' Miranda said and the warmth of her smile showed she was sincere. 'When is it due?'

'The end of February.'

Miranda looked shocked.

'Yes, I knew I was back then,' Belle said. 'But I couldn't bring myself to tell you that night. Well, you know, it seemed all wrong.'

'How doubly awful of me to inflict my troubles on you at such a time,' Miranda said, moving to embrace Belle. 'But I am very happy for you, and please don't feel you can't mention it for fear you'll upset me. I can understand too why you wouldn't want your husband joining up at such a time. But I'm sure once he's thought it through he'll decide against it.'

'Well, plenty of other men with several children have gone,' Belle sighed. 'We heard just yesterday that a man from Lee Green with five children enlisted. Garth said the men in the bar were joking about it and said he was going to get away from them.'

They spoke for a few more minutes about the war in general and Miranda said that she'd given a lot of thought to getting a job, and ultimately leaving home.

'I've applied for several positions in the last couple of days,' she said. 'I'm not fooling myself, I know I have no experience. The only thing I can do which is in any way remarkable is to drive a motor car.'

'Gosh.' Belle was impressed; she didn't personally know any men who could do that, let alone a woman. When they had first moved to Blackheath motor cars were still quite a rare sight, but in the last two years they had gradually become much more common. It was still only rich people who had them, though, and she couldn't see that changing for a long time.

'I got Papa's chauffeur to teach me while I was in Sussex,' Miranda said airily. 'I thought with so many men going off to the war, there might be an opening for a woman. Motor cars are very hard to start though, you need brute strength to crank that handle. I've been reading up on how they work too. I don't want to look foolish if it breaks down.'

'I'm so pleased you are sounding so organized and optimistic,' Belle said.

'Well, you know who I have to thank for that,' Miranda replied, raising her eyebrows. 'Now you've told me your news, perhaps there's a way I can repay you for all you did for me. I could mind the shop if you wanted a rest or to go somewhere.'

Belle was touched. 'That's very thoughtful of you,' she said. 'But I think I'll be giving up the shop well before the baby arrives.'

'Oh no!' Miranda exclaimed. 'You can't, you are so talented and everyone loves your hats so much. Can't you get a nursemaid in?'

'I'd never do that,' Belle said in horror.

Miranda laughed. 'No, I don't suppose you would. But I fared much better with a nursemaid than I would have done with my mother.'

'There is one thing I must ask,' Belle said. 'Are you really all right? I don't mean ill or anything, but have you got over it?'

Miranda's face clouded over. 'I had a few days when I felt weepy and sorry for myself,' she admitted. 'But it was better when I got down to Sussex. I went on walks, busied myself learning to drive, and visited some of Papa's tenants. I've never done that before; I think what happened to me opened my eyes to the real world. They were probably astonished that I was showing an interest in their gardens, children and whether or not the roof leaked. Some of those people are so desperately poor, it made me realize that I wasn't so badly off.'

They chatted until it was time for Belle to close the shop. As she was locking the door behind them, Miranda put her hand on Belle's arm and squeezed it. 'I hope Jimmy doesn't join up, but if he does, remember you've got a friend in me.'

Belle knew that night as she and Jimmy got into bed that he had made up his mind. The bar had been quiet and he'd been up and down the stairs, sitting for a few minutes with her but saying nothing, then going back down. She guessed by his strained expression that he wanted to talk, but was afraid of it turning into a row. Belle was aching to get it all out in the open, but she knew Jimmy well enough to be aware that he liked time to weigh up situations for himself, and if she pushed him too hard now, she might regret it.

But now, as he curled his body around hers just as he always did, she could almost hear his brain whirling with conflicting emotions.

She knew he wasn't afraid for himself, only of leaving her. She knew too that if she cried and pleaded with him, he could be persuaded out of it. But was it right to do that when he felt it was his duty to go?

69

Belle guessed that he was very aware that the Railway didn't really need both him and Garth to run it, especially now that so many of their once regular customers had already left for France. He probably felt guilty each time he heard that someone else had enlisted when he was young and healthy and had no good excuse to stay home. A baby on the way certainly wouldn't be considered a valid excuse for not enlisting, as most men distanced themselves from the whole thing and left it to their wives' mothers and sisters to offer support.

Belle knew too that Jimmy would make a good soldier; he was brave, strong and intelligent. Other men liked him and she had no doubt he'd soon get promoted because he had the qualities needed for leadership.

However terrified she was that he might be wounded or even killed, one of the things she loved most about him was his honourable nature. She didn't like to see him in turmoil, trying to balance what he perceived as his duty against her reaction. She had no doubt he was afraid she would see it as him deserting her, and that would drive a wedge between them.

She loved him too much to prolong the confusion he was in. She knew she had got to be as brave as he was and let him do what he felt was right.

Taking his hand lying on her hip, she squeezed it. 'I don't want you to go,' she said softly in the darkness. 'I'm not like you, I don't care about King and Country, I'm selfish enough to want everything to stay the same cosy way it is now. But I know you have principles, and if you feel you must go and fight, then I'll support your decision.'

'Really?' he whispered back. 'You see, although I don't want to be apart from you, when your country is at war that isn't a valid excuse for wriggling out of fighting. Almost all the men who've already gone must have had sweethearts or wives they didn't want to leave, but they found the courage for it. That white feather today will be just the first of many if I stay. Some people will say that I'm not only a coward, but I'm profiting from the war. I couldn't live with that.'

Belle clung to him, biting her lip so she wouldn't blurt out that she didn't care if he was called a coward as long as she had him home with her. 'I know, I couldn't bear that either,' she lied.

'I wish I did believe it will all be over by Christmas,' he said, drawing her into his arms. 'I wish I could promise you too that I'll come home safe and sound. But I do believe that as God kept you safe and brought you back to me after all you went through when you were abducted, then he wouldn't be so cruel as to let me be killed in France when we're expecting our first baby.'

Belle wasn't so sure God worked that way. She thought it was more likely that he put some people on this earth to be tested again and again. She and Jimmy had had two years of sublime happiness, and perhaps that was all they could expect.

He moved his right hand down on to her belly, stroking the small curve as if silently trying to tell his child that he loved it and that he intended to be the best of fathers.

'So when will you go to the recruitment place?' she whispered, moved by his sensitivity.

'Tomorrow,' he said. 'No point in prolonging the agony.'

The weather turned suddenly autumnal on the day Jimmy went to the recruitment office. The temperature dropped and it was wet and windy, bringing down showers of golden and russet leaves that until then had been beautiful. To Belle it was an omen that all the happiness they had shared was ending, but she bit back her tears and packed warm thick socks, underwear, soap and some little comforts in a bag, trying hard not to dwell on whether the precious two days they had left together would be the last.

On the morning Jimmy was to take the train to London Bridge to join the other men in the Royal Sussex regiment, the sky was as leaden as Belle's heart and a cold wind whistled under the back door. Garth made jovial remarks over breakfast about how good the send-off had been in the bar the previous night, but it was clear he was also dreading the moment his nephew would leave. Mog's face was wreathed in sadness as she packed sandwiches and cake for Jimmy to take with him, and Belle couldn't trust herself to speak.

At eight the four of them were at Blackheath station and Belle clung to Jimmy while Mog and Garth looked on. When the first of their customers had joined up, they'd both stood outside the pub cheering them on their way, but since then they'd seen casualty lists and the reality of war had set in. Now anxiety was etched in their faces.

'You'll be in my heart every minute of every day and night,' Belle whispered. At London Bridge Jimmy would board a troop train to Dover, then travel by ship to France where he would do his basic training in Etaples.

The platform was crowded with groups of friends and relatives who had come to see their men off. Some were mere boys, being fussed over by tearful mothers and sisters. There were some men already in uniform, perhaps returning from leave, a handful of smartly dressed officers, but far more men of Jimmy's age. Belle guessed that like Jimmy they had thought the initial rush to join up was foolhardy, but now in the wake of white feathers and Kitchener posters felt they had to go.

She noticed that one of the wives was heavily pregnant, and her face was blotchy as if she had been crying all night.

'And you will be in my heart for every second,' Jimmy whispered in her ear. 'Don't get used to taking up the whole bed. I'll probably prove such a bad shot they'll send me straight back to you.'

Belle forced a smile. Jimmy had been making jokes about going ever since he signed up. But his bravado wasn't fooling her; she knew he was scared.

She could hear the train coming, and knowing that meant she had only a minute or so more with him brought the tears to her eyes that she'd been fighting back since she woke a couple of hours earlier with him making love to her. Every caress had been so tender, each kiss so sweet, that it seemed impossible death would ever separate them, but now as the train chugged ever closer that didn't seem so certain.

'Let me come to London Bridge with you,' she begged him.

'No, my darling,' he said, putting his arms around her and holding her tight. 'It's bad enough saying goodbye here. It would be even worse there, and you'd have to come back alone.'

'You will write, won't you?' she asked.

'Of course I will, every day if I can, but the post will probably be slow, so don't get upset if there's a delay.'

The train was coming into the station now, smoke billowing around them as the engine passed. Jimmy kissed her again, then turned to embrace Mog and Garth.

'You keep safe for us,' Mog said in a trembling voice.

'Keep your head down, son,' Garth said gruffly. 'Don't be a hero, leave that to someone else.'

All at once the train doors were open and the guard was blowing his whistle to tell everyone to get in. Belle caught hold of Jimmy and hugged him hard. 'I love you,' she whispered as she stood on tiptoe to kiss him. 'Keep safe for me.'

73

He had to break away and get on the train, but after closing the door he leaned out of the open window, blowing kisses to her. The final whistle went, the train began to move, and Belle walked along beside it, gradually moving faster with it until she was running, tears rolling down her cheeks.

She saw Jimmy wipe his eyes and mouth the words 'I love you', then suddenly she'd run out of platform and had to stop. It was only then she realized she wasn't alone; at least twenty other women had done the same as her. And they all stood crying at the end of the platform until the train was out of sight.

It struck her then that this was the first time she'd ever seen such a public display of emotion, and she turned to a girl even younger than herself who was crying hysterically and put her arms around her.

'I'm sure they'll be all right,' she murmured comfortingly.

'Why did he have to go?' the girl sobbed. 'I begged him not to.'

'Because they believe it's the right thing to do, and we must be strong and admire their conviction and courage,' Belle said.

As she and all the other women turned to go back along the platform, many of them reached out to touch another's shoulder or arm, just a small gesture of shared sorrow and understanding. It reminded Belle of the way it had been with the other girls in Martha's sporting house in New Orleans: silent but deeply felt sisterhood which in its way was more comforting then mere empty words.

Two weeks after Jimmy left for France, Belle was sitting on a chair in the shop late one afternoon, reading once again her first proper letter from him. It was raining hard and growing darker by the minute, another unwelcome reminder that winter wasn't far off, and she got up to turn on the lights.

She had received a postcard the week before. It was a somewhat blurred picture of Boulogne harbour, which she supposed he'd bought as he got off the boat, for he'd written it on his first day in Etaples. It was only a few lines, just to say he'd arrived and was sharing a hut with nine other men. He warned her he wouldn't get much time to write as the days would be long with firing practice, drill and physical training up and down over the dunes on the beaches.

That first week without him had crawled by; she missed his warm body in the bed beside her, his hand on her belly which seemed to have got suddenly bigger since he'd gone. She missed sharing the evening meal with him, his jokes about the customers in the bar, bits of village gossip. Garth and Mog tried to make up for it; Mog would steal into the bedroom at night to kiss her and tuck her in, Garth took to cleaning her shoes, and asked about her day in the shop. But kind and dear as they were, they could not fill the hole Jimmy had left.

They all felt it, the absence of his whistling coming up from the cellar, his light step on the stairs, his infectious laugh and his charm. Mog had been in tears one afternoon when she'd taken some buns out of the oven and put them on a cooling tray and he wasn't there to cheekily snatch one while her back was turned. Garth had grown so used to Jimmy doing the lion's share of the heavy work, moving barrels and hauling in crates of beer, that now he had to do it all, his back ached, and he struggled to get through it before opening the bar.

To finally receive a real letter had been a relief to all three of them. It was good to have a glimpse of what his training entailed, to hear about friends he had made, and to know that he was holding his own.

Jimmy had started the letter on his second night in the

training camp, telling Belle about the men he shared the hut with, the training and even the food. He had palled up with a man called John Dixon who came from Woolwich. He described him as flash, funny and a bit of a rogue, and said he reminded him of some of the men in Seven Dials.

He must have had to stop writing then and restarted the following evening after a long day of rifle practice. 'I was useless,' he wrote. 'We had to fire again and again at the target, then go up to it to see where we'd hit it. I hadn't got anywhere near the target, not even once. The sergeant called me a useless carrot head, with a few extra insults that I won't repeat.'

The day after that it was physical training. Jimmy had managed thirty press-ups before collapsing, but most of the others hadn't got beyond ten. 'I always suspected lifting barrels must be good for something,' he added. At that point, even though he didn't actually say so, it sounded as if he was finding it all very hard and daunting. He said that some of the men were reeling with exhaustion after a long run over the dunes.

Just the fact that he didn't write more than a few lines at a time was evidence that they were kept busy from dawn until late at night, but a couple of days later he wrote with some pride that he'd got scores of seventy hits out of a hundred at target practice and had managed fifty press-ups.

As Belle read on she thought it sounded like the worst kind of nightmare – kit inspections, running at the double for miles with a full pack on his back, crawling on his belly over wet sand dunes, bayonet practice, and rapid loading of his rifle. He also said it kept raining and it was cold.

He mentioned something called the Bull Ring where they did square bashing, and said that the village of Etaples was a godforsaken, rundown place that didn't even have a decent shop. The images he was creating for her were all so grim, yet he sounded surprisingly cheerful, even when he described wearing the boots he'd been issued with as like having a lump of lead on each foot.

But the best thing about his letter was his thoughts about her. 'I imagine you brushing your hair at the dressing table, the way it tumbles over your shoulders as shiny as tar. Or seeing you when you leave for the shop in the mornings, all prim and buttoned up. I think of how you eat apples, the glimpse of little white teeth and your tongue all pink and pointy as you lick your lips.'

She guessed he had been thinking far more personal things about her, but couldn't bring himself to write them because he knew letters were likely to be read by a censor, and that she would read some of the letter to Garth and Mog. But he'd ended it by saying, 'You are on my mind all the time, I wonder what you are doing, if you are lonely without me. I think of our baby growing inside you and pray that I'll be back before he or she is born. I hope you aren't angry with me for going away just when you need me most.'

Belle had written a letter to him every day since he left, posting them as she walked home in the early evening. But she found it hard to think of different things to tell him, as each day for her was much the same as the one before. Trying to make her letters amusing was even harder. Most of her customers were very ordinary and it was rare anyone said anything he would find remotely funny. Sometimes when she read over about what Mog had made them for tea the previous night, or she passed on a message that had come through Garth for him from one of the customers, she felt the letter was barely worth reading. But she always tried to find some old shared memory to make him smile, told him how much she was missing him, and what he meant to her. Then at the bottom of each letter she drew something, a rabbit, a cat or some other pretty small animal, and added a hat.

She picked up the letter she'd written to him earlier, in which she'd told him about a huge spider sitting on her workbench that morning. She had been frightened to death of it, put a glass over it, then ran to the shop next door to ask Mr Stokes the cobbler to come and remove it.

So at the bottom of the page she began to draw a comic, fat spider wearing a top hat, and she chuckled to herself as she drew it, remembering how Jimmy had found it funny that she was so scared of spiders.

The door bell tinkled and she leapt to her feet, placing her writing pad on the counter.

It was a big man wearing a long, very wet mackintosh, and her first thought was to wonder if she could ask him to remove it and leave it by the door because she didn't want it dripping all over the floor.

'Good afternoon, sir,' she said politely. 'Can I help you?'

'I want a hat,' he said very brusquely.

'I don't sell gentlemen's hats, sir,' she replied, assuming that was what he wanted as he wasn't wearing one and his almost bald head was glistening with rain. 'But there is a gentlemen's outfitters just a few doors down the street that does.'

'Did I say I wanted a man's one?' he snapped back.

All at once Belle was scared. While he looked and sounded respectable enough at a distance, there was a musty smell coming from him that reminded her of Sly, one of the men who had abducted her back when she was fifteen. He had a moustache, but it was untrimmed and he had stubble on his chin. As she looked closer, she saw the collar on his shirt was very dirty.

'So you wanted to buy a hat for your wife perhaps?' she asked.

She had never felt frightened in the shop before, but now, as she saw how dark it was out on the street, and deserted too because of the rain, she realized she could seem an easy target to a thief looking through the shop window and seeing she was alone.

'I want money,' he growled, and putting his hand into his pocket he pulled out a short, stout wooden cosh.

Belle stared at it in astonishment and fear. He'd made her feel nervous, but she hadn't expected that. 'I've hardly taken any money today,' she gasped. It was the truth; she'd only sold one hat and that was a cheap felt one costing two shillings. With the odd change she kept in the counter drawer there was perhaps seven or eight shillings in all.

His lip curled back. 'Don't lie to me, I know you do a good trade.'

'Not today. It hasn't stopped raining and it's cold,' she said.

He lunged forward, brandishing the cosh, and Belle cowered back, covering her head with her hands. 'Don't hit me, I'll give you what I have,' she cried.

When the expected blow didn't come she peeped through her fingers. He was already at the counter drawer, scooping out the change in there and putting it in his pocket. That proved to her he had been watching her on some other occasion as the drawer was a tiny one and not immediately obvious.

'Right, where's the rest?' he said, coming towards her again. 'If you don't get it I'll smash the shop up, then you.'

Belle's heart thumped with fear. Desperation was written all over the man's face, and she sensed he meant what he said. 'There isn't any more,' she insisted. 'I've only sold one cheap hat, I don't keep any other money in here.'

'Don't lie to me!' he yelled. 'Get it now.'

If there had been any other money anywhere, Belle would

have run to get it. She'd had enough run-ins with desperate men before to know appeasement was vital.

'I promise you there is no more,' she said frantically. 'If I had any, I would give it to you.'

With that he swung his cosh at her cheval mirror and smashed the glass, shards falling tinkling to the floor.

'Get it or you'll be next,' he yelled at her.

Belle didn't know what to do. The back door was locked and bolted, and even if she tried to reach it she knew he would catch her before she had a chance to open it and escape.

'I can't find something that isn't here,' she cried out. 'You have all there is.'

He gave a kind of angry growl and leapt forward, bringing his cosh down hard on her shoulder. Belle screamed in pain and staggered back, clutching at her shoulder.

'It's in there, isn't it?' He pointed his cosh towards the work room at the back.

Belle's back was to the wall by the back-room door. 'If you can find any money in there you are welcome to it,' she sobbed.

As he moved as if to go into the back room she saw her chance, and flew towards the front door. But as she caught hold of the handle to pull it open, he was there behind her and he grabbed her by the shoulder and hauled her back.

'You aren't going anywhere, bitch!' he yelled at her, and lifting his cosh again he brought it down with such force on her side that she crumpled and fell to the floor. But he wasn't satisfied with that, and swinging his leg back he kicked out at her.

In the split second as his leg moved, she tried to protect her belly with her arms, but it was too late for his boot struck squarely at her abdomen, sending her skidding across the floor to crash against the counter.

The pain was so fierce she didn't attempt to get to her feet.

Instead she curled up, hardly able to see. She heard him lock the front door and pull the blind down over it, and sure he was going to kill her now, her only thought was what that would do to Jimmy.

But he didn't come back to her, he just stepped over her and went into the work room. She heard him crashing about, pulling down the boxes of trimmings on the shelves like someone possessed. She was fairly certain he'd pocketed the key to the door. Trying to reach the telephone was not an option because he'd stop her the moment he heard her. She couldn't fight him, she didn't even dare cry out in pain for fear that would anger him still more. So remaining motionless and seemingly unconscious on the floor seemed the only thing to do, for once he'd satisfied himself there was no more money anywhere, he'd go.

It was so hard to just lie there when she wanted to scream out because she was in so much pain. But somehow she managed to do it. She opened her eyes once on hearing a tin being opened and saw him stuffing the biscuits it contained into the pockets of his coat.

The pain was so bad that the room began to swirl around, and the last thing she remembered thinking was that she was going to be sick.

'Mrs Reilly! Mrs Reilly!'

She heard a man's voice as if from a great distance away, and forced her eyes open.

'Oh, thank heavens!' he exclaimed. 'I thought for a minute . . .' He broke off. 'Now, don't move, there's broken glass everywhere. I'm going to call for help.'

Belle was aware enough to know it was Mr Stokes the cobbler from next door, but she didn't know why she was in such pain or lying on the floor which was covered in glass.

It only came back to her when she heard several other male voices and recognized one as Dr Towle's.

She had thought Dr Towle rather pompous when she called on him about her pregnancy. He was tall and rather handsome with thick black hair and deep blue eyes, and she had felt that perhaps his manner was such because so many women patients doted on him. But now, as she registered the kind and gentle way he examined her as she lay on the shop floor, and his genuine outrage that she could be attacked in such a way, she realized he wasn't just a handsome stuffed shirt, but a compassionate man.

She managed to tell a policeman who was there too about the intruder who had robbed and attacked her, then Garth appeared and with the aid of another man they had put her on a stretcher and carried her home.

'You were subjected to a horrifying attack,' Dr Towle said sympathetically some time later when she was back at home in her own bed. 'But I had you brought back here instead of getting you to hospital as I believe you will recover quicker with Mrs Franklin nursing you.'

Belle wasn't able even to nod to show her appreciation that she was back with Mog and Garth.

'Is the baby all right?' she managed to ask as he used a little silver trumpet-like instrument to listen at her belly.

'His heart is still beating,' Dr Towle replied, patting her hand in sympathy for her anxiety. 'But it is essential you stay in bed, as I suspect you have a couple of cracked ribs. I have strapped them up to enable them to heal. But there is little I can do about your shoulder; it is not broken – the pain you feel is the severe bruising from a heavy blow. You will be in pain for a few days, and it is quite common after such a shock to feel very low for a time. But all this will pass, and I shall be calling to see you every day.'

After giving Mog some further instructions, and some medicine to ease Belle's pain, the doctor left.

'You poor love,' Mog said, bending over the bed and stroking Belle's hair back from her face. 'I just hope they catch that fiend that did this to you. Garth said one of the police told him there was a similar attack on a shopkeeper in Lewisham just last week. They think it was done by the same man.'

'I thought he was going to kill me,' Belle said weakly. 'Did he smash up the whole shop?'

'Garth said it was a mess, but men always exaggerate when they are angry. I'll go up in the morning and see for myself and clean it up. But you won't be going back there, my girl!'

'Mr Stokes found me,' Belle said. 'Did he see the robber?'

'Only a man fleeing up towards the heath,' Mog said. 'Apparently he was shutting up his shop as the man came haring out of yours, and at the same time a policeman came up the street. But Mr Stokes told Garth he thought you were dead at first.'

'Don't let's tell Jimmy about this in our letters,' Belle begged her. 'I don't want him worrying about me.'

'I'll need to talk to Garth about that,' Mog said. 'He's so angry he wants to lash out. But I think you are right, telling Jimmy would serve no useful purpose.'

Belle began to cry and Mog perched on the bed. She couldn't hug Belle for fear of hurting her more, so she just wiped away her tears.

'There, there, ducks, Garth and I are here to look after you,' she said soothingly.

'I feel as if the bad times are coming back again,' Belle sobbed. 'First Jimmy enlisting and now this! I might have known the happiness couldn't last.'

Chapter Six

Belle was woken by a sharp pang. There was nothing unusual in that – in the last two days since the attack she had grown used to being woken by pain. But this was different: it wasn't coming from her ribs or shoulder, it was in her belly and her lower back.

It was still dark and she could see the faint glow around the edges of the curtains coming from the gas light out in the street. But the medicine Mog had given her had made her very groggy, and as the pain subsided she fell asleep again.

She was woken again by another pang. She didn't know how long it had been since the previous one, maybe an hour, maybe minutes, but this time it was even stronger, enough to make her cry out. It seemed to build up to a peak, then slowly subside, and as it faded completely she knew what it was.

The baby was coming.

Lying there on her back, she put her hands on her belly, feeling the curve of it, and cried, knowing a baby couldn't survive being born at a little less than six months.

In her mind's eye she could see Miranda lying on the bed of cushions in the back room of the shop, looking exactly the way she felt now. Was this God's judgment on her for helping Miranda? If so he was a cruel God, for all she had done was act as a nurse, she hadn't made the abortion happen, or even been party to Miranda's decision to have it. Both Jimmy and she had wanted this baby. It would have been loved and nurtured because both of them wanted to give it all they had not had themselves as children.

Or was this punishment for her former life as a whore?

Another pang came and she gripped on to the mattress as it engulfed her. Much as she wanted to stay silent, she couldn't help but cry out, for she had never experienced pain as bad as this before.

Her bedroom door opened and Mog came in carrying a candle.

'What is it, ducks?' she asked.

'It's the baby,' Belle gasped. 'Help me!'

'Oh my giddy aunt,' Mog exclaimed, going over to the bed and setting the candle down. 'How long have you been having pains?'

The pain subsided enough for Belle to tell her, but as the older woman listened she lit the gas light on the wall, got a clean sheet from a chest, folded it over and tucked it beneath Belle.

'I'm just going to wake Garth up and send him for the doctor,' she said, as ever calm even in a crisis. 'I'll dress and come right back to you. Just hold on, I won't be long.'

Belle was vaguely aware of Garth speaking to Mog out on the landing. She heard his heavy step on the stairs and the door downstairs slam shut behind him. Mog came back to her soon after with a jug of hot water and some towels.

'I would swing for that bastard who did this to you,' she said as she washed Belle's hands and face with a flannel. 'But for now we've just got to get through this together.'

The pains came and went, each one stronger and stronger with less time between them. Mog held Belle's hand, bathed her face with cool water and spoke soothingly, telling her the doctor would soon be here.

Belle could not respond, for even between pains she was bracing herself for the next one, and when it came it was white hot, a hideous agony which she thought might kill her.

Dr Towle arrived just as the baby began to come away. Belle saw Mog cover her face with her hands as he pulled back the bedclothes, and though Belle couldn't see what they could, she could feel the warm slippery mass between her legs and the sensation of liquid flooding from her.

From then on everything became blurry and disjointed. The next thing she knew, the doctor was listening to her heart through his stethoscope.

'I'm so sorry, Mrs Reilly,' he said. 'I hoped so much that the injuries you received wouldn't result in this, but these things are out of our hands.'

She didn't have to ask if the baby was dead, she knew it hadn't stood a chance. 'Was it a boy or a girl?' she managed to get out.

'A girl, but she was much too tiny to breathe,' he said and his voice cracked with emotion.

Jimmy had hoped for a girl, he'd wanted to call her Florence. Tears ran down Belle's face unchecked; she felt that everything had been taken from her.

'Mrs Franklin and I will clean you up now and give you something to help you sleep,' the doctor said as he took her pulse. 'I wish it was in my power to take away your sorrow too, but I'm afraid only time will do that.'

Belle felt another rush of blood come from her, and she closed her eyes, not wishing to see the panic on Mog's dear face.

It was ten in the morning when Mog accompanied Dr Towle downstairs to see him out. They were both tottering with exhaustion, Mog's white apron was stained with blood, and the doctor looked less than his usual immaculate self for he had dark stubble on his face and his eyes were bloodshot.

The sky was dark grey and it was very cold. They could

hear Garth moving barrels down in the cellar, as he'd left the door open.

'Is she going to recover?' Mog asked tremulously. Belle had lost a tremendous amount of blood, and at one point it looked as if there was no possible chance of saving her. But the doctor had packed her with gauze and now it was in the hands of God.

'She's young and strong,' Dr Towle said with a deep sigh, as if he was trying to look for positives. 'If she gets through the next twenty-four hours without a further haemorrhage and no infection sets in, then I think she will recover fully. I'm going to arrange for a nurse to be with her. You are admirable, Mrs Franklin, but you are exhausted now and Belle will need specialist care.'

Mog nodded. 'Whatever is best for her. I couldn't bear to lose her.'

'Are you her aunt?' he asked, looking down at her curiously. He knew that Mr Franklin was Jimmy Reilly's uncle, but he'd sensed the deep love this small woman had for his patient, and it seemed much stronger than if they had been related just by marriage.

'I was her mother's housekeeper,' Mog replied. 'But I brought Belle up right from a baby.'

'I see,' he nodded. 'Well, you did a fine job – she is a lovely young woman, and my wife tells me she is a very talented milliner. It is such a shame her husband has recently gone to France. I'm sure his presence here now would be very good for her.'

'Should we try to get him home then?' Mog asked. 'Belle didn't want him to know about the attack on her for fear of it worrying him, and I expect she'd say the same about this.'

'Yes, but from what I've heard about Jimmy I'd say he'd be the kind to want to be here to comfort his wife. Obviously it will take time for him to be contacted and for him to get back here, but I do think it should be done.'

'But how, doctor?' Mog asked, wringing her apron in her hands in agitation. 'I don't know who to go to about it.'

'Just tell me his regiment and other details and leave it with me. I have a little influence which I can use to get him back.'

After giving Mog instructions as to Belle's care until the nurse arrived, and writing down Jimmy's details, Dr Towle left, saying he would come back again in the evening.

Garth came into the kitchen as Mog was putting the soiled linen in the wash tub to soak. He looked over her shoulder at the cold water turning red and paled.

'Is she going to pull through?' he asked.

'I don't know.' Mog turned to her husband and burst into tears.

She had heard him walking up and down the landing during the night, and it had helped her to know that he was as afraid as she was.

Garth put his arms around her and held her tightly. 'Fate couldn't be cruel enough to take her now, like this, not after all she's been through and all she means to Jimmy and us,' he said, his voice trembling with emotion.

'I must get back to her,' Mog said, straightening up and wiping her eyes on her sleeve. 'Will you bring up some coal so I can light the fire in her room? It's grown so chilly, and when the nurse gets here we can't expect her to sit in a cold room.'

'Do you ever think of yourself?' he asked gently, touching her cheek affectionately. 'You only had a couple of hours' sleep before this happened. You look all in.'

'I'll be fine once I know she's on the mend,' Mog said.

He hugged her again and stroked her hair. 'Go on up then and I'll bring you some tea and do the fire for you.'

*

At eight that evening Mog was sitting in the easy chair in Belle's room, watching the flickering flames of the fire.

Dr Towle had called in an hour earlier to repack Belle with gauze, and had been heartened by no further heavy blood loss and her stronger pulse. Because of this he sent Nurse Smethwick home, asking her to come back in the morning to relieve Mog. He also said he'd managed to get a message through to the commanding officer in Etaples and he felt it was likely Jimmy would be on the next ship back to Dover.

Mog could hear the wagons, carriages and the odd motor car pass out on the street. She heard someone with steel blakeys on their boots walk by, but the bar was much quieter than usual. She thought Garth must have told the customers to keep the noise down because of Belle. It had been such a long and distressing day. Smethwick, though clearly a very good nurse, was one of the bossiest women Mog had ever had the misfortune to meet. The first thing she demanded was that Mog remove all of what she called the 'folderols' from the bedroom, which included fancy cushions, lace bed-side tablecloths, the hat stand which held around six pretty hats and innumerable scarves and the frilled counterpane. Mog pointed out that Belle would be shocked to find herself in a room stripped of all the things she loved, but the nurse insisted they harboured germs. And so it went on all day, with Mog being ordered hither and thither to do the woman's bidding. Not once did she suggest Mog catch up on sleep, even though she was rocking on her feet with tiredness.

She even insisted Mog went out to buy some liver, which was to be lightly braised in milk and fed to Belle when she felt able to eat, to enrich her blood. Mog pointed out that Belle hated liver and she thought a glass of Guinness would do the same job in a more palatable way.

'Give a sick woman alcohol?' Nurse Smethwick retorted. 'Whatever next!'

Mog avoided any further confrontation with her, but she planned to give Belle some Guinness next day if she was feeling like it, as it was one of her favourite drinks.

She had intended to catch forty winks by the fire, but now she could rest she couldn't seem to keep her eyes closed. Getting up from her chair, she went over to check on Belle. In just the firelight and with one candle by the bed she couldn't tell whether colour was coming back into her face, but she looked peaceful. Her dark hair was lank and tangled, and her lips looked cracked, but to Mog she was still a beauty. She remembered how she'd nursed her through measles when she was five. Mog had stayed in the darkened room with her constantly for two weeks, sponging her down to reduce the fever, terrified she might lose her sight as so many children did with the disease. Annie only ever came as far as the door to see how she was. She claimed it was because she didn't want to risk spreading the disease, but Annie always had an excuse for not having normal maternal urges.

'I ought to send her a telegram,' Mog thought, feeling guilty that she hadn't thought to do so after the attack and therefore prepared her for what had happened today.

Mog's relationship with Annie had floundered back at the time the brothel had been burned down after Belle was abducted. Two years later, when Belle came back from France, they patched things up for her sake, and Mog had invited Annie to her wedding. She'd come to Belle's too, and helped with the wedding arrangements, but in reality all they had was a shared past. Mog often wondered if she could claim that they were ever really friends. Looking back, it seemed far more of a mistress and servant partnership.

Yet even though Annie was as hard as nails and not given

to showing her feelings, Mog knew she did love her daughter. Belle had said that the last time she visited her and told her she was expecting, Annie had said she hoped she would do better as a grandmother.

A tear rolled down Mog's cheek. When Belle became pregnant she was so excited and thrilled she had entirely forgotten about hoping for her own baby. She'd knitted two little jackets already and made several tiny nightdresses and was just about to start on a shawl.

The clothes didn't matter; she could give them to another young mother. What really hurt was that all those lovely little daydreams she'd had were shattered. She wouldn't be able to walk the baby in a perambulator up on the heath. There would be no family holidays at the seaside, or filling a Christmas stocking and walking a little girl or boy to school. Dr Towle had told her this evening that he thought it would be unwise for Belle to try for another baby as there was a chance she might have been damaged internally and this could happen again.

Jimmy was going to be devastated. He'd told Mog once he'd hoped they'd have at least four children. He wouldn't love Belle any less of course, but she knew he'd want to vent his anger on the man who had robbed and beaten her. He would never care about the stolen money or the damage done to the shop, but that wicked man had robbed Belle and Jimmy of the most precious thing in life.

Belle stirred and opened her eyes. 'Why are you standing there?' she asked, her voice a mere whisper.

'Looking at you, ducks,' Mog said, and sat down on the edge of the bed. 'How are you feeling?'

'I don't know,' she replied. 'Have I been here a long time?'

'Quite a while,' Mog said. 'It's nearly ten o'clock at night. Over twenty-four hours since it began.'

'I've been asleep ever since it happened?'

Mog realized then that because Belle had been slipping in and out of consciousness for most of the day, she wasn't aware how dangerously close she had been to death.

'Yes, most of the time,' she said. 'And you can go back to sleep again, but let me get you a drink first. The doctor said you were to have some warm milk with a drop of brandy in it. I'll go and get it now.'

Mog returned with the milk, laced not only with brandy but with the medicine the doctor had left to help Belle sleep. She put one arm behind her and lifted her carefully so as not to jar her bad shoulder, and held the cup to her lips. 'Drink it all down,' she said, just the way she had when Belle was a little girl. 'It will make you better.'

It was pleasing to see her drink it all, as she'd had nothing but sips of water all day. When she had finished, Mog plumped up her pillows and laid her down again.

'How will I tell Jimmy?' Belle asked, her eyes filling with tears.

'We'll think on that one in the morning,' Mog said. 'I'm going to stay in here with you tonight, just in case you want something.'

'Come in the bed with me.' Belle caught hold of Mog's hand. 'Please. I don't want you sitting in a chair all night, you must be so tired.'

It crossed Mog's mind that Nurse Smethwick would not approve of that. But she and Belle had often shared a bed in the past, it was a comfort in bad times. Besides, what did it matter what Smethwick thought? It was Belle's wishes that were important.

'If you want me to I will,' Mog said. 'I'll just go down and say goodnight to Garth and get myself into my nightdress. You go back to sleep now.'

She bent down and kissed Belle's forehead. It felt warm, but not feverish. Had her prayers been answered?

Throughout the following day Mog was on edge. Belle did appear stable, and had even eaten a few spoonfuls of soup, but that didn't mean she was out of the woods. Mog knew that an infection could set in at any time, and that was what killed women in this situation.

Nurse Smethwick was getting on her nerves with her bossiness and superiority. She had made it clear she didn't want Mog coming in and out of the sickroom and that left her just doing chores and worrying.

Mog had sent a telegram to Annie, and so she could turn up at any time. That would bring more tension into the house. Garth didn't like her much, and if Annie was her usual abrasive self that would be likely to upset him. All Mog really wanted was for Jimmy to turn up. It would comfort Belle and give Garth a male ally, and Jimmy's quiet strength would hold her together.

Then the telegraph boy came, bringing a reply from Annie. 'Tell Belle sorry. Unable to come now. Soon. Annie'.

'What could be more urgent than seeing her sick daughter?' Garth said, his lip curling in the way it always did when he was holding back his real feelings.

As ever, Mog felt compelled to act as peacemaker. 'Maybe she's ill. She could have a difficult guest. Anything.'

'More likely that she doesn't see losing a baby as anything but a good thing,' Garth said churlishly.

'Don't say that,' Mog retorted. 'Belle said she was very happy at the prospect of being a grandmother.'

'The only thing that makes her happy is making money,' Garth said and walked away.

*

93

As soon as Nurse Smethwick had left for the evening, Mog went up to see Belle. She was awake, and it looked as if she'd been crying.

'What's up, ducks?' Mog asked, sitting on the bed beside her.

'Wishing Jimmy was here,' Belle said wistfully. 'And wondering how I'm going to break the news to him.'

'Well, you can stop worrying about that, the doctor got a message through to him and asked that he be sent home. I didn't tell you before because I hoped if he just came through the door it would be a lovely surprise for you.'

'Someone else had to tell him?' Belle looked horrified. 'And why would they let him come home for that? Unless they thought I was dying!'

Mog gulped. She might have known Belle would only think of Jimmy's feelings, not her own needs.

'Dr Towle said he had some influence. He thought you needed Jimmy here.'

'And he thought it was a kind thing to let him travel all the way back home thinking the worst?'

'I'm quite sure Dr Towle would have told the commanding officer that you were recovering, ducks. I also know Jimmy well enough to know he'd have been angry with us if we hadn't at least tried to get a message to him. It would be far crueller to tell him the news in a letter and let him imagine all sorts.'

Belle covered her eyes with her hand and sobbed. 'It's never going to be the same again. All our plans have gone wrong. Jimmy's in the army and now I've lost the baby. There's nothing left.'

'That's plain silly,' Mog said indignantly. 'You and Jimmy have still got one another, the war won't last for ever. And there's the shop too, once you're well again.'

Belle took her hand from her eyes. 'You know perfectly well that neither Garth nor Jimmy will allow me to go back there again. I'll have to be like every other wife in England, a stop-at-home. No chance to be me, just watching the years go by without anything to look forward to, nothing to achieve.'

Mog protested because she thought she must. She insisted Belle was overwrought through losing her baby and looking at things in a distorted manner. Yet she knew Belle was right. Garth and Jimmy wouldn't want her going back to the shop, they'd be afraid for her after what had happened.

If Belle had been like any other ordinary, well-brought-up young woman, she wouldn't be wanting anything more than just to be a very well-loved wife. But Belle wasn't ordinary, she hadn't had a normal childhood with a mother who did the chores while her father went out to work. At her most impressionable age she had been snatched away from her home and learned things on both sides of the Atlantic Ocean that wiped out her innocence and taught her to live on her wits.

Mog knew Belle hated class distinction, yet right from the first day she opened her shop, she'd been compelled to pander to 'nobs' because she couldn't survive without their patronage. At home she was always mimicking the ladies who came into her shop, strutting around with their noses in the air and complaining how exhausted they were after a dress fitting, a luncheon with friends or even a game of bridge.

Mog, Jimmy and Garth had always found her little impersonations very comic, as she vividly portrayed the vacuous dullness of these women's lives. They did little for themselves, and their sole aim appeared to be to see that their daughters married well and lived exactly the same way as they did.

Yet because Belle was such a talented milliner, she had achieved a special status amongst these women and had grown used to being fêted by them. She might not like much of what they stood for, but she took pride in managing to have one foot in their world. If she gave up her shop she would immediately be seen as just the wife of a publican, and those women who once treated her as a friend would drop her.

Belle needed people almost as much as she needed creativity. If she'd had the baby, she would have been a good, loving mother, but she had too much fire, imagination and intelligence to settle into a life of domestic chores.

'It's going to be a little while before you feel yourself again,' Mog said carefully, for she didn't want to go against anything Garth or Jimmy might say. 'Just rest, get better, and talk to Jimmy when he gets home. He's very understanding, you know that. He might not want you to continue with the shop, but I don't think for one moment he'd object to you doing some volunteer war work.'

'Handing out white feathers like Miranda's mother?' Belle said with some bitterness. 'Or maybe you'd like me to join your knitting circle? Can you really see me doing that kind of thing?'

'You know what I think of those stupid women who hand out white feathers,' Mog retorted. 'There are other roles, useful ones. So while you are lying here, instead of feeling sorry for yourself, why don't you think about what you would like to do?'

Chapter Seven

'All right, all right, I'm coming,' Garth grumbled as he made his way up the cellar steps to answer the knock at the door. He knew Mog was in with Belle, Nurse Smethwick hadn't arrived yet, and so he assumed this was Dr Towle coming earlier than usual, as it was only half past seven in the morning.

He shot the bolts back on the side door and turned the key in the lock, to find Jimmy in uniform on the other side.

'Jimmy, my lad,' he exclaimed in surprise and delight. 'There's a sight for sore eyes! Come on in.'

Jimmy took his cap off before going in, and then stopped in the hall, looking up the stairs. 'How is she? The CO only told me she'd lost the baby, but I know there's more.'

Garth had never found it easy to talk about women's matters, and hesitated.

'She's not dead, is she?' Jimmy asked, his eyes wide with alarm.

'No, no.' Garth patted his shoulder. 'Of course not. She was very poorly, but we think she's on the mend now. She'll be all the better for seeing you.'

Jimmy ran up the stairs two at a time. Mog had just taken Belle's breakfast tray from her when he burst into the room.

'Jimmy!' both women exclaimed.

Mog said how good it was to see him and Belle burst into tears.

She was propped up on pillows but in the daylight her face was like yellowing parchment. Mog had brushed her hair for her, but it still looked lank and dull.

Jimmy rushed to embrace her, but Mog stopped him. 'Be careful of her shoulder and ribs, they are still hurting.'

'Why?' he asked, looking puzzled.

'We'll explain that later,' Mog said.

Jimmy shot her a bewildered look, but sat down on the edge of the bed and caressed Belle's cheek. 'Don't cry, sweetheart,' he said. 'I'm here now, and you can tell me all about it when you're ready.'

Mog could hear Nurse Smethwick clomping up the stairs. 'That's the nurse, and she needs to bed-bath Belle and other things. You come on down to the kitchen while she's doing that and I'll get you some breakfast. You must be tired and hungry if you've been travelling all night.'

'I'm not going to be dragged away from my wife because of a nurse,' Jimmy declared indignantly.

Mog looked round to see Nurse Smethwick in the doorway. She was a plain, plump woman with a face like a lump of greying pastry, and she had clearly heard Jimmy's remark.

'Your wife, Mr Reilly, needs a nurse right now,' she said tartly. 'And don't sit on the bed. Heaven only knows what germs that uniform has clinging to it.'

Jimmy's mouth dropped open, but Belle hauled herself up from her pillows. 'Don't you dare talk to my husband like that,' she exclaimed. 'He's travelled all night to get here from France. We are paying you for your nursing services, not to bully my husband or my aunt. Kindly remember that if you wish to work here.'

Mog smirked. She was sure Belle must be getting better if she could stand up to a dragon like Smethwick.

'Leave them for ten minutes, nurse,' Mog suggested. 'Come down to the kitchen and have a cup of tea with me while I make Jimmy some breakfast.'

Jimmy smiled at Belle as Mog and the nurse left. 'Where did you find that ogre?' he asked.

Belle flopped back on to the pillows. 'Mog said the doctor sent her, but I think she just manifested. A punishment for past sins.'

'Now, tell me what happened,' Jimmy said. 'What did Mog mean about your shoulder and ribs? Were you in an accident?'

Belle had been trying to think of some way of watering down what had happened in the shop so that Jimmy would let her go back there, but seeing the deep concern in his eyes, and knowing how fearful he must have been as he travelled home, she realized she must tell the whole truth.

She saw his fists clench and unclench as she told him how it had all come about. Men like him and Garth were not the kind just to sit and wait for the police and the courts to mete out justice. She was fairly certain Garth had already offered a reward to anyone who would tell him the name of her attacker.

'I'm so sorry, Belle,' Jimmy said, putting one hand on her cheek, his eyes brimming with tears. 'I can't bear the thought of anyone hurting you. I'm so sad about our baby too. I can't find the right words to comfort you.'

'You just being here does that,' she said, taking his hand and kissing it. She could see sores and blisters on it, and it was a reminder that where he'd been was no picnic either. 'Go and have some breakfast now, and then have a bath and a sleep. Let the ogre come and see to me. And try and persuade Mog to rest today, I'm sure you can imagine how she's been.'

He smiled glumly. 'All the time in France I only ever imagined you all talking and laughing in the kitchen, everything just the same as it had always been. I thought if anything was to go wrong, it would be to me, never you.'

'I'm on the mend now,' she said. 'Go on, away with you. We'll talk later.'

As soon as Jimmy had eaten his breakfast and drunk three very welcome cups of tea, he went to find Garth. He was polishing glasses in the bar, and looked round anxiously as Jimmy came in and closed the door to the house behind him.

'How was the training?' Garth asked. 'The haircut is a bit severe.'

Jimmy smiled ruefully and ran his hand over the inch-long stubble that had been left by the army barber. 'With luck I won't need another cut till Christmas,' he said. 'Belle told me about the attack. Have you got any information on who did it?'

'Only that there's been quite a few similar attacks in the past few months, in Lewisham, Catford and Greenwich,' Garth said. 'The police think it's the same man, he always preys on people alone in shops, usually at the end of the day. They think he's from Deptford, but you know what it's like down there.'

Jimmy did know: grim, overcrowded tenements, hovels like rabbit warrens and people who weren't going to squeal on one of their own. 'If they think he's from Deptford, do they have a name?'

'If they have, they aren't telling. It's hard to track someone down without a full description. Do you think Belle could draw him? That might help.'

Jimmy thought about this for a moment. Belle was very good at quick sketches of people but he wasn't sure whether sketching a man she'd rather forget would be good for her. He told Garth this.

Garth sighed. 'I know, I haven't said anything because of that. A man who would beat a defenceless woman needs a good kicking himself. It would do me a power of good to be the one to do it.'

'Me too,' Jimmy said. 'But I've only got a couple of days' leave, and I want to spend all of that with Belle.'

'How is it over there?'

'I've got aches in muscles I never knew I had,' Jimmy said wryly. 'But I'm fitter than most of the others. Getting to be a crack shot too – the sergeant has packed in shouting at me and he even said I was doing well the other day. I just hope I can hold my nerve once I'm at the front. Most of the younger men can't wait to get there, but I came back on a ship with the wounded and saw injuries so bad that I felt sick.'

He didn't want to tell Garth that he had got stuck in to helping the nurses. He couldn't do much, just offer water, or hold a cigarette to a soldier's lips. Some of them asked him to write a letter for them to their loved ones at home. These men were all regular soldiers, tough, fearless men some of whom had fought in the South African war, a very different breed from the volunteers Jimmy was training with. If they, with all their knowledge of warfare, could be wounded or killed, what would happen to the novices who still thought war was an adventure?

Two of the men Jimmy wrote letters for died before reaching Dover, but all the same he would go out and post their letters later. It might be a small comfort to the relatives to know they had been thought of right to the end.

Garth gave him one of his hefty pats on the shoulder. Jimmy knew that was his uncle's way of saying he was proud of him and understood his fears.

After a bath, a couple of hours' sleep on the couch and once again dressed in civilian clothes, Jimmy heard the doctor leaving Belle's room and caught him as he was going down the stairs.

'How is she, doctor?' he asked after introducing himself.

'A great deal chirpier now you are home,' the doctor smiled. 'I think she's out of the woods now, but it's going to take a while to build her strength up again. She lost a great deal of blood.'

Jimmy nodded. 'Mrs Franklin will see she gets the right food and plenty of rest. Thank you for all you've done for her. And for seeing I got leave. I really appreciate that.'

'It was nothing.' The doctor put his hand on Jimmy's shoulder, and looked at him with concern. 'But I'm afraid there is something more I must tell you. It would not be advisable for your wife to risk having another baby.'

Jimmy paled. 'Not ever?'

'I cannot say with absolute certainty that the injuries she received will prevent her from ever carrying another baby full term, but it would be risky,' the doctor said gently. 'I know what a blow this will be to you both, and I am so sorry.'

'Have you told Belle yet?' Jimmy asked, his voice quivering with emotion.

'No, I haven't, and for the time being I think it would be advisable to keep it just between you, Mrs Franklin and myself.'

Jimmy swallowed hard and nodded. He didn't trust himself to speak.

Two days later, while Belle was having a nap, Jimmy walked up to her shop.

This morning there had been several kind letters from her customers who had heard what had happened and wanted to offer their sympathy. Belle asked him how she should reply to them, and if she was to tell them she would be closing the shop down.

Jimmy hadn't known how to reply. Garth had made his

feelings on the subject quite plain. He felt it wasn't safe for her there any more and her place was at home. Jimmy agreed with Garth, but he also knew what the shop meant to Belle so was reluctant to say anything just now.

He thought if he just looked around he might be able to clear his head and come to a firm decision. He closed the shop door behind him and stood there for a moment gazing around him. Mog had cleared up the day after the attack, but the cheval mirror without glass in it and the broken chair in the stock room was enough for Jimmy to imagine how bad it had been. There was still a smear of blood on the wall too and the sight of it made his insides contract with anger.

Yet as he walked about the shop, touching the pretty hats Belle made so well, he knew he couldn't bring himself to insist that she gave it up entirely. Without that interest and with him in France, she would feel she had nothing left.

The sound of banging on the shop door interrupted him. Mog had put a notice on it saying 'Closed until further notice', but despite this he could see a young woman outside who was gesturing for him to open up.

Somewhat irritated, Jimmy opened the door. The woman was young, very stylishly dressed in a green hat with a feather which he was sure was one of Belle's. 'I'm sorry, but the shop is closed,' he said, and pointed to the notice.

'I know, I can read,' the young woman said tartly. 'But I've been away for a while. I came round to see Belle, we're friends, you see. My name is Miranda Forbes-Alton. Has something happened to Belle? And who are you?'

Jimmy did recall a mention of someone called Miranda, Mog said she had an overbearing mother, and judging by the daughter's snooty manner she was cut from the same cloth.

'I'm her husband,' he said. 'She was attacked and robbed and as a result she lost the baby she was carrying.'

To his consternation the woman's eyes filled with tears. 'Oh, dear God no,' she said, dabbing at her eyes with a lace-trimmed handkerchief. 'Poor, poor Belle, what a terrible thing to happen! She was so happy to be having a baby. If only I'd known sooner! Is there anything I can do now? I could mind the shop if that would help.'

Jimmy hadn't liked the curt way she had asked who he was. Yet her obvious distress at Belle being hurt made him warm to her.

'That is kind of you,' he said. 'But we've decided to keep it closed for a while. As you can imagine, she's still very weak and sad.'

'Of course she must be. I'm so sorry about speaking sharply to you, Mr Reilly. I didn't expect it to be you as I knew you were in France. Tell me about the attack. What time of day was it?'

Jimmy explained in more detail, including how close Belle had come to dying from blood loss and how the doctor had pulled strings to get him home. Miranda winced and looked horrified.

'But you will have to go back to the army, won't you?' she said. 'Is there anything I can do to help out then? I like Belle so much and I know she'll be even sadder once you are gone.'

Jimmy could see this woman meant what she said, and he was sure he would feel easier about returning to France if he knew Belle had a good friend to talk to.

'I do have to go back tomorrow,' he said. 'I'm sure Belle would be glad of a visit in the afternoon, maybe you could cheer her.'

'I will certainly try,' she said. 'And please tell her that I'm thinking of her, and explain I didn't know about the attack until talking to you.'

'Of course, Miss Forbes-Alton. She will appreciate your

concern, as I do. We have a side door at the Railway; you don't need to go in through the bar.'

'I shall be there around two,' she said. 'And you keep safe back in France. Belle needs you all in one piece.'

Jimmy smiled at her then. He understood now why Belle liked her; she might be a bit snooty at first, but she improved on acquaintance.

At six that evening, Jimmy was trying to persuade Belle to eat a little more. 'Come on, just one more mouthful,' he said, holding out a forkful of fish pie to her.

She sighed, dutifully opened her mouth and let him feed her. Mog made the best fish pie in the world, and under normal circumstances she would have wolfed it down, but she wasn't hungry and had only eaten a couple of mouthfuls before giving up. But as Jimmy was going back to France in the morning, she knew he'd be less anxious if he thought he'd got her eating again.

Having him home with her had made her feel better. Much to Nurse Smethwick's annoyance, he had spent most of the previous two days on the bed beside her, talking and reading the paper to her. She was going to miss him so much when he had to go back.

Dr Towle had told Smethwick the previous evening that she wasn't needed any more. Both Belle and Mog were glad to see the back of her as she had been such a tyrant.

'You see, you were just being lazy,' Jimmy said triumphantly as he spooned yet another mouthful into her mouth. 'Now, if you don't feed yourself I'll tell Mog to get Smethers back.'

'I really have had enough now.' Belle nudged the plate back to him. 'I'm not using up enough energy to be hungry. That will come back once I can get up each day.'

'That won't be for at least another week,' Jimmy said firmly, putting the dinner plate back on the tray. 'And then only for an hour or two to start with.'

'You won't know,' she teased him.

'I bet I will, I feel connected to you even when we're apart. The day that man attacked you I had a strange feeling of foreboding. I just didn't think it could have anything to do with you.'

'Then I'd better be very careful what I get up to,' she said impishly. 'Now, pass me my sketchpad and I'll try and draw that man.'

Jimmy lounged back on the pillows as Belle sketched. It never ceased to amaze him that anyone could capture a likeness of anything with just a pencil. He could only draw like a child – dogs that looked like sausages on sticks and flowers all turning out like daisies.

It grieved him to see Belle look so pale and weak. Her hair needed washing, he'd never seen it so lank and dull, but it couldn't be washed until her shoulder stopped hurting. He knew she was trying hard to convince him she really was on the mend, and physically she was, but however much she tried to laugh and to tease him, he could sense her deep desolation at losing the baby. He just wished there was something he could do or say to make that go away.

When he'd got home earlier and told her that Miranda would be coming the next day, she'd seemed very pleased. 'I'm so glad you met her,' she said. 'She comes across as stuck up at first, but that's just the way she's been brought up. Once you get to know her she's no different to us.'

Now, as he watched Belle sketching and thought about her striking up a friendship with someone as unlikely as Miranda, he wondered whether Belle's father had been a gentleman. Even at fifteen, she had had that polished, refined look about her that was prevalent in the upper classes. Maybe it was partly because they had better nourishment right from infancy, but you only had to look at thoroughbred horses to know blood lines did count. Mog might have nurtured her and taught her good manners, but Belle's black curly hair and her beautiful blue eyes must have been inherited from her father. He thought her poise and charm were likely to have come from him too.

If Annie knew who he was, and in her line of work she probably didn't, she was never likely to tell Belle. Mog didn't know; she said she had paid little attention to Annie until she was in the later stages of her pregnancy, and when she once asked Annie about it she'd been told to mind her own business.

Jimmy knew from Mog that Annie had grown up in a village and that her father was a carpenter. She might put on airs and graces, dress well and have gained a patina of sophistication, but no one would ever be fooled into thinking she was out of the top drawer.

'Well, that's the best I can do,' Belle said, rustling her sketchpad and bringing Jimmy out of his musings with a start.

Jimmy took the pad from her and studied it, but instead of the villainous kind of thug he'd imagined, she'd drawn a very ordinary face which could easily belong to a bank clerk or a station porter.

'Not what you expected?' Belle asked. 'Sorry I couldn't give him a villainous scar, or a patch over one eye, but he was quite run of the mill. He was stocky, almost completely bald, about five feet eleven. He had a rough kind of voice, and it was only once he came closer to me that I noticed his dirty collar and untrimmed beard and could smell a damp, musty odour coming from him. That was when I got scared.'

'I should know from the years in Seven Dials that bad people don't come with warning signs on them,' Jimmy said thoughtfully. 'You are so good at drawing, Belle. Maybe you should take it up, seriously I mean.'

'Instead of the shop?' she said, and he saw that stubborn look in her eyes that he knew so well.

'Not necessarily,' he said carefully. 'Look, I agree with Uncle Garth that it isn't safe for you to work in there alone any more. It's too close to the heath, so easy for any thug looking for easy pickings to rob you and get away unseen. But if you were to take on an assistant, you'd be much safer.'

'Paying someone else would cut down the profits,' she said.

'At first it would. But if you picked the right person, say your friend Miranda, you'd be free to make hats all the time. You could keep your special designs just for your shop, and maybe sell more ordinary ones to other shops, say in Lewisham or Greenwich.'

'So are you saying you'd let me keep the shop?'

Jimmy smiled as he saw her eyes brighten suddenly. 'I'm your husband, not your keeper,' he said. 'I know most men think the two go hand in hand, but then, I grew up with my mother running a dressmaking business, and no man throwing his weight around. She always said that women were really the stronger sex. I've only got to look at you and Mog to see that's true.'

Belle took his hand, lifted it to her mouth and kissed it.

'But you won't go back there until Dr Towle says you are well enough,' he warned her. 'And until you have an assistant.'

Belle looked at him for a moment or two without speaking and a tear trickled down her cheek.

'What is there to cry about?' he asked.

'You just do that to me,' she said. 'It's because you are

always so understanding and thoughtful. I am so lucky to have you.'

Jimmy leaned over and kissed her. 'Well, let's just hope Uncle Garth isn't determined to be lord and master because I think it's time I went and told him our plans. I'll take the sketch down too and ask him to take it to the police tomorrow.'

It was still dark the following morning when the alarm clock went off. Jimmy stopped it and moved to get up.

'One last cuddle,' Belle said sleepily.

He turned back to her and carefully put his arms around her, avoiding her bruised shoulder and ribs. Her warm body seemed to melt into his and he breathed in her lavender smell and wished with all his heart he didn't have to catch that train. Her hair against his cheek was silky, her body beneath her white cotton nightdress was so soft, and he had no idea how long it would be before he could hold her like this again.

'I have to go now,' he whispered. 'You stay here and go back to sleep. I don't want you trying to come downstairs – saying goodbye here is better.'

He kissed her gently, then wriggled away and got out of bed, lighting a candle so he could see to find his clothes.

He sensed she was watching him as he washed his face and cleaned his teeth at the washstand.

'Put on that new vest Mog knitted for you, it will be cold on the ship,' she said as he pulled on his trousers. Mog had sponged and pressed his uniform, and Garth had dubbined his boots for him, their little way of showing how much they cared. Just now he wished there was less evidence of love for him, that Mog wouldn't be downstairs ready with a mug of tea, a packet of sandwiches to take with him, and extra warm socks and a new scarf tucked into his kit bag. Such loving care made it so much harder to leave.

Finally he laced up his boots and went back to kiss Belle one last time. He wanted to tell her that if he shouldn't come back, she was always to remember that having her to love had made him the happiest man in the world. But he couldn't put the idea that he might be killed into her head. Nor must he put it in his own either; he must only ever think of the future they'd share when the war was over.

'I love you,' he said simply, and pulled the covers back over her and tucked her in.

He allowed himself one long last look, a picture that he could hold in his head however bad things got in France: the black storm of curls on the pillow, blue eyes brimming with tears and her soft, full mouth trembling.

'Take great care of yourself and write to me every day,' he said softly before blowing out the candle and then turning to go out of the room.

He had to stop at the top of the stairs to compose himself. In this house he could be just a husband, but once out of the door he had to be a soldier, and put aside fear and sentiment.

The sound of Jimmy's heavy boots on the road outside a little later made Belle cry. She heard the train coming into the station soon after, and then the chugging sound as it left, carrying him away from her.

Meg came upstairs then, and as expected she opened the bedroom door to look in, but Belle pretended to be asleep, knowing that sympathy would just make her feel worse. She cried on and off all morning; now that she'd lost the baby, Jimmy had gone, and knowing there was a possibility he might never make it home again, she felt completely bereft.

It didn't help that Mog was sharp with her for not eating her breakfast or her lunch.

'I understand perfectly that you are feeling down in the

dumps because Jimmy's had to go back,' she snapped. 'But not eating won't bring him back, all it will do is stop you from getting stronger again. I've got better things to do than keep coming up here with trays of food which you won't even try to eat.'

When Belle heard footsteps on the landing around two in the afternoon, she thought Mog was coming back to give her a further lecture, and she buried her face in the pillow to feign sleep again, but as the door opened it was Miranda's voice she heard.

'Oh, my poor Belle,' she exclaimed.

Belle hauled herself up to a sitting position. She had forgotten that Miranda was coming. Had she remembered, she might have asked Mog to put her off. But now she was here, with a large bouquet of hothouse flowers in her arms, Belle couldn't bring herself to be churlish.

'How nice of you to call,' she said weakly, very aware of Mog standing just behind Miranda, poised to say something if Belle didn't show some genuine appreciation.

'I was absolutely horrified when Mr Reilly told me about the attack, and I'm so very sorry for your loss,' Miranda said. 'I've been down in Sussex so I didn't know. I wish there was something I could do or say to make you feel better.'

'I feel better already just seeing you,' Belle said. 'Do come in and sit down. Are those beautiful flowers for me?'

Mog smiled, clearly relieved Belle wasn't going to be awkward. 'Would you both like some tea?' she suggested. 'And I'll take the flowers if you like and put them in water.'

Miranda said she'd love some tea and pulled up a chair to the side of the bed. Mog left the room, taking the flowers with her.

'You've been crying,' Miranda said as the door closed. 'But

that's to be expected, especially now Jimmy's gone back to France. I bet you feel everything's been snatched from you?'

'Yes, that just about covers it,' Belle sighed. 'I don't know what I'd do if I lost Jimmy too. He'll be sent to the front very soon, and though he might have learned how to shoot straight, I doubt there's a way of teaching men how to dodge the enemy bullets.'

'He struck me as very level-headed and intelligent,' Miranda said. 'He also has a lot to come back for. I've an uncle who is a brigadier; he once told me that soldiers who have nothing to lose can be a liability. They are frequently very brave, but also foolhardy. The ones with everything to lose like your Jimmy don't take risks which would endanger them or their fellow men, and they are ultimately the best to command.'

'That's comforting,' Belle smiled weakly. 'But help me out of this wallowing in self-pity. Tell me what you've been doing.'

Miranda flicked back the elegant silky scarf at her neck with a gesture that said she had quite a lot to tell. 'Well, strange as it might sound, I've been helping out in a small hospital down in Sussex,' she said. 'Most of the patients were wounded officers and because I could drive I was taking them on to convalescent homes, or to their own families when they were well enough to travel. But it ended because someone made a fuss about a woman doing men's work.'

'How ridiculous!' Belle exclaimed. 'Surely most men who can drive have enlisted?'

'It doesn't seem so,' Miranda said glumly. 'I was just a volunteer of course, and quite honestly I felt it was churlish of them to refuse my help. It was suggested I could become a VAD and help with the sick and wounded if I wanted something to do. But I do hate this notion that women are only good for washing people and rolling bandages. As you can imagine, my dear mama thinks that a well-brought-up young lady shouldn't even be doing that.'

Miranda launched into telling Belle about a scrape she'd got into while driving. In the dark she had taken the wrong fork on a country lane, and ended up getting stuck in mud in a wood with a patient who couldn't walk.

'It was frightful,' she said. 'I had to leave him in the car and walk to find the nearest farm to get help. It was tipping down with rain and my shoes and coat were quite ruined. When I finally got a farmer to take me in his tractor back to the car to pull it out, the wretched patient took me to task for not checking he had some matches to light his cigarettes before I set off. I ask you! There he was sitting in the warm and dry, complaining that he hadn't been able to smoke, when I'd walked about five miles and looked like a drowned rat!'

Belle spluttered with laughter. Miranda did give the impression of being somewhat callous. The patient probably thought she'd gone off to the nearest hotel to get a bed for the night and had forgotten where she left him. 'So what's next then?' she asked. 'Handing out cups of tea to soldiers while they are waiting for the troop trains?'

'I have been asked to run a tea stall,' Miranda said. 'But it will be hell. I'll be stuck with a bunch of women like my mother all day. Don't know that I could stand that for long.'

'You could come and help me in the shop when I'm better,' Belle said impulsively. 'Jimmy said I could go back as long as I have someone else there. He even suggested you. I'd pay you of course, and you'd be ideal. Look at you, a fashion plate!'

Miranda was wearing a silver-grey costume with a long, slender skirt; around the neck of the fitted jacket she had draped a fringed silk scarf in shades of blue and silver with just a hint of pink. Her plain, grey-brimmed hat had a band of the same material as her scarf.

'You don't mean it, surely?' she said, looking very surprised.

'Of course I do,' Belle insisted. 'I've got to employ an assistant, but it makes far more sense to have someone with a bit of flair and presence than some lumpen shop girl who has only ever cut up cheese.'

Miranda laughed. 'Oh Belle, I'd be in my element as I adore hats. Heaven only knows what Mama will say though.'

'Maybe you could tell her you're just helping me out? Make it seem more like a mission of mercy than a job?'

At that both girls burst into giggles. In Belle's case it was because she could imagine the formidable Mrs Forbes-Alton all puffed up with indignation, airing her views on common shop girls as if they were a species of rodent.

'She'll say, "You can't be serious, Miranda! People will suspect you of being a suffragette,"' Miranda said, imitating her mother's voice. 'She thinks anything slightly subversive is an indication of suffrage.'

'Mog has great sympathies with suffrage,' Belle said. 'And so have I. Why shouldn't women vote?'

'To tell the truth, I agree,' Miranda confided. 'If women were in control there wouldn't be wars. We've got better things to do with our time than digging trenches and shooting people.'

'So what would you be doing with your time if you could do anything you wanted?' Belle asked.

'I wouldn't mind an afternoon with a wonderful lover,' said Miranda.

Her unexpected and saucy reply took Belle right back to lazy days at Martha's sporting house in New Orleans. The girls there had always been warm and open, and she missed that kind of feminine banter. Miranda hadn't been as explicit as the girls there would have been, but the fact that she felt secure enough to speak out showed that she really did see Belle as her friend.

Miranda put her hand over her mouth. 'Oh, that was so tactless of me after all you've been through,' she said, blushing furiously.

'Not at all,' Belle laughed. 'You've cheered me more than you can imagine.'

'Really?'

'Yes, really. It's lovely that you didn't feel you had to pussyfoot around me.'

They were still laughing when Mog came in carrying a tray with the flowers in a vase and tea and cake for them both. 'I heard you laughing from downstairs,' she said. 'Let me in on the joke?'

'It was just something silly about one of Belle's customers,' Miranda said. 'It just tickled us both.'

'Well, it was good to hear,' Mog said. She put the tray down on the dressing table and placed the flowers on the chest of drawers. 'I'll leave you to be mother, Miss Forbes-Alton,' she said as she turned to leave.

Belle spluttered with laughter. 'Miranda, you are as good at lying as I am,' she said.

'Something I learned to keep dear Mama sweet,' she replied. 'She would go up in a puff of smoke if she heard me wishing for an afternoon with a lover.'

All at once Belle saw why Miranda had been so reckless with Frank. She might have been somewhat naive when she met him, but she wasn't the delicate little flower Belle first took her for. She was an adventuress at heart, and it was only her lack of experience with red-blooded men that had caused her to be fooled by her more practised seducer. It seemed they had even more in common than she'd originally thought.

Miranda stayed with her until almost five o'clock, and the time passed in a flash as they talked about anything and everything. It was only as Miranda realized the time and said she must go home that she became serious.

'I know I haven't asked you how you feel about losing your baby,' she said, and she leaned over and caressed Belle's cheek, her pale blue eyes full of sympathy. 'Please don't think it's because I don't care, because I do, deeply. But after what we've been through together, I didn't feel I had the right to ask such a thing because you probably imagine I never felt the loss of my baby.'

Her sincerity touched Belle.

'I know exactly what you mean, Miranda. It was for the same reason that I didn't tell you I was having a baby that night. We've both lost our babies, whether intentionally or accidentally, and the sorrow inside us is the same. I think you were very brave to come and see me; you must have been afraid that I might have turned against you. But you've made me feel better, given me hope that I will get over it in time. That is much more valuable than mere words of sympathy.'

Miranda hastily wiped a tear from her eye. 'May I come to see you again? I can tell you need rest to get your strength back, but how about the day after tomorrow?'

'That would be lovely,' Belle said. 'And I meant it about you working in the shop, so you'd better think of a way of preparing your mother for it.'

That made them both laugh again, and Belle was still smiling as Miranda left the room and went down the stairs.

Chapter Eight

Once in an interview room at Deptford police station, Police Constable Broadhead removed the sketch Mrs Reilly had drawn of her attacker from a folder and showed it to Sergeant Wootton.

Garth Franklin had brought the sketch to Blackheath police station a couple of days earlier, and Broadhead had wasted no time in jumping on his bicycle and pedalling off to call on each of the other victims of similar crimes in the area to show it to them. All but one of them confirmed it was the same man who robbed them.

For the first time since James Broadhead had been turned down by the recruitment board for the army, he actually felt that maybe he could do more for his country by staying in the police force.

At thirty-five, single and as strong as a horse, he'd felt dutybound to enlist. But he'd been turned down because he'd got two fingers missing on his right hand. He'd lost them eleven years earlier when his hand was trapped under a metal girder while he was trying to free a small boy who'd been playing in a derelict building when it collapsed.

The board hadn't believed he could fire a rifle. He would have liked to be given a chance to prove them wrong – after all, the loss of his fingers hadn't affected his police work. Rejection had soured him for a while and made him feel less of a man, but the excitement he felt now he'd got evidence that Mrs Reilly's attacker was responsible for other crimes too had cleared that away.

'What's he done?' Wootton asked, taking the sketch closer to the light and peering at it. He was in his fifties, with heavy jowls and a military-style handlebar moustache.

Broadhead gave him a résumé of the man's crimes, and told him that other victims of similar crime had confirmed this was the face of the man who had robbed them.

'Who drew the picture? Is he in the force?'

'It was sketched by Mrs Reilly, the milliner in Blackheath. She also lost the child she was carrying and came close to death because of it.'

Wootton frowned. 'Then we'd better catch him before he hurts anyone else. His face is familiar, though I can't quite put a name to it. But someone here will know if we've nicked him in the past.'

Broadhead grinned in delight, as this investigation had become personal to him. He was the first officer at the scene of the crime, and had been horrified that a woman he'd admired from a distance for so long could have been treated so badly. The Railway was the pub he drank in, and as he had a great deal of respect for Jimmy Reilly too, he very much wanted to bring his wife's attacker to justice.

'Can you find out now?' he asked Wootton. 'The sooner we get the toe-rag behind bars, the better.'

Wootton went off to consult other officers and was gone some twenty minutes. As Broadhead waited alone in the interview room he was staggered by the noise and rumpus in the building. Except on Saturday nights when fighting drunks were hauled in, Blackheath police station tended to be a very quiet place. But this was noon on a weekday, and a woman was shouting at the top of her lungs, someone else was drumming on a cell door, doors banged incessantly, and every couple of minutes there was an eruption of shouting and swearing. At one point there was a scuffle right outside the door of the interview room, a man protesting loudly that it wasn't him.

Wootton came back into the room looking rather smug. 'Yes, he is here on our patch. Name of Archie Newbold, but with no fixed abode. They say he was invalided out of the army some years ago, and we've had him in here several times for brawling and being drunk and disorderly.'

Broadhead nodded. 'So when can we go after him?'

'There's no "we",' the senior man said sharply. 'He's on our patch, we'll bring him in. You go on back to pleasant Blackheath; we'll contact the nick there when we've got him.'

Broadhead felt as though he'd been slapped. 'But sir, I've done all the legwork on this. I wanted to bring him in.'

Wootton looked hard at him for a moment before replying. 'To capture villains here, you need to know the area. There are scores of narrow dark alleys, old warehouses, opium dens, knocking shops, and tenements with as many as ten people to a room, filthy holes where the women are as bad as the men and the children following suit. You'd be a liability to us. You look tough, but that's not enough here, you need to be as wily as they are.'

Broadhead resented the inference that his police work consisted of finding lost dogs and escorting old ladies across the road, but he knew better than to argue with a senior officer, and Wootton looked as if he could be a nasty piece of work if crossed.

'Well, you know where I am if you want any extra help,' he said. 'I'll take the sketch back with me as it will be needed as evidence.'

Wootton looked at the sketch again. 'It's a good likeness. I wonder if she could draw someone described to her. That would help us track down villains far more easily.'

'I'll pass on the compliment, but I can't imagine her wanting to spend her time in such a way, not after what she's been through,' Broadhead replied. 'I'll be off now; I wish you luck in catching Newbold.'

In the last week of November Belle went to look at her shop for the first time since she was attacked. She had Mog with her and Miranda was due to meet them at any minute too.

'It smells a bit musty,' Mog said as she opened the door and turned on the lights. 'But that will soon go once we get the stove going.'

Belle walked in hesitantly and felt some surprise that everything looked exactly the same as it had before the attack. She knew Mog and Garth had got the cheval mirror glass replaced and removed anything that was broken, but she had expected there still to be some evidence of the events of that last afternoon she was here.

She knew she ought to feel relieved there were no reminders, and even excited to see the place she once loved so much. But the truth was she didn't want to be here at all. Not now, or in the future.

It wasn't that she was afraid. She just felt that whatever it was that had made her want a hat shop so badly, and work so hard to make it a success, had gone. She didn't feel she had it in her any longer to spend hours designing a hat and then working out how to make it. Nor did she want to stand in this shop day after day watching women try on hats and listening to their stories about what they wanted them for.

The irony of this change of heart wasn't lost on her. She'd worked on Mog, Jimmy and Garth to convince them she needed the shop, and now they were convinced, she didn't want it. But she couldn't see a way out now, especially as she'd impulsively offered Miranda a job.

'You'll need to make some new stock and change the window so people can see you are happy to be back,' Mog said.

Belle opened her mouth to say that she would never be happy to be back, but she closed it again, knowing that if she told Mog how she was feeling she'd become worried.

'I can't do it before Christmas,' Belle managed to get out. 'I'll wait till New Year.'

Her body might have healed, but it was as if the vital spark she'd once had inside her had gone out. She often felt so low and melancholic that she took herself off to her bedroom, pretending to Mog that she wanted to read. But she wouldn't attempt to open a book, and just lay in bed staring at the ceiling, feeling hopeless and desperately sad.

'I think that's wise,' Mog said without even looking at Belle. She was straightening up a red velvet hat on a stand as if that was all that mattered. 'You won't have enough time to make more than a few new hats, and you really should make a splash for the re-opening. Besides, Miranda's still helping out on the tea stall.'

Right on cue Miranda arrived, waving at them through the window. Glad of a diversion, Belle opened the door and embraced her friend.

Belle felt that if it hadn't been for Miranda's regular visits she might have fallen apart in the past few weeks. Miranda never probed; if Belle was in a sombre mood she just accepted it. If she was tearful she gave her a hug and offered to do her hair for her, or suggested they went for a walk. Often she told her tales about the ladies she worked with on the tea stall at Charing Cross station which were very funny. It was her ability to make Belle laugh that had got her through so many bad days.

'I'm so excited to come back in here,' Miranda said

breathlessly, then spotting a midnight-blue hat on a stand she darted forward to pick it up.

'Oh, what a darling one,' she gasped, tossing her own brown felt hat aside and replacing it with the blue one. Then, striking a pose in front of the mirror, she sucked in her cheeks and pouted. 'How did I miss this one before? It's just me.'

As always, she made Belle laugh. The blue hat was a bit of nonsense really, all tulle and velvet flowers, a hat for afternoon tea in a smart hotel, and perfect against Miranda's blonde hair. 'I think your mother would say it isn't likely to keep your head warm,' she said.

'Who would care about warmth when something is so pretty and such fun?' Miranda replied. 'You are so clever, Belle. I hope I can learn to make something that resembles a hat while I'm here.'

A stab of guilt ran through Belle as she realized Miranda had taken the offer of a job very seriously. Doubtless she'd get over the disappointment if Belle was to explain how she felt, but in that moment, with her friend looking so pretty in the hat, her cheeks glowing with her excitement at a new start, Belle couldn't bring herself to stick a pin in her balloon.

After Mog left to do some shopping, leaving Belle and Miranda to come back to the pub when they'd finished looking around, Miranda wandered about the shop trying on hats, and with each one she pretended to be a different person talking about what occasion she might wear it for.

Putting on a rather plain navy-blue felt cloche, she became a country girl at an interview for a position as a nursemaid.

'I know's everything about kiddies,' she said in a strong rural accent. 'I'm the oldest of ten, you see, and me mam she likes a drink, so it falls on me to care for 'em. I don't believe in taking a strap to young 'uns, not even when they're being little bleeders, a good hard slap usually does the trick, then locking 'em in the coal shed.'

Belle burst out laughing because the way Miranda screwed up her face to say her piece reminded her very much of a hateful teacher she'd had at school who had regularly whacked her pupils with a cane.

A rap on the shop door startled them both. Miranda snatched off the hat guiltily. 'It's a policeman,' she said.

Belle got to her feet. 'It's Constable Broadhead, the one I've told you about.'

She opened the shop door and invited him in. Although she didn't really remember his role on the day of the attack, since then he'd called to see her at home several times, and she'd grown to like him.

'What brings you here today?' she asked.

'They've found and arrested your attacker,' he beamed. 'It was in the early hours of the morning, in Deptford. He'll be appearing in court tomorrow but will be held in custody until his trial. Whether that will be before Christmas depends very much on how busy the courts are at the moment.'

Belle felt a wave of relief. 'That is good news,' she said. 'Knowing he's out of harm's way will make me and the other shopkeepers in the street feel much safer.'

The policeman nodded. 'I saw Mrs Franklin down the road and she said you were here. Glad to see you up and about again. You've had a rough time of it, especially with your husband away.'

Belle introduced Miranda to him and explained she was going to be her assistant in the shop. 'Jimmy's on a march to the Western Front,' she added. 'At least he was when I last heard from him. Goodness only knows when he'll get home again.'

'And they said it would all be over by Christmas!'

Broadhead said. He looked a little awkward, as if he had something else to say but couldn't get it out.

'Am I expected to be at court tomorrow?' Belle asked, hoping that would prompt him.

'Oh no, it's just a preliminary hearing. A solicitor tells the judge what the case is about.'

'So you'll tell me when I am needed then?' she said.

'Yes, of course,' he said and smiled. 'I'd better be off, but I wanted to tell you that without your sketch of this man, we'd never have got him. You have a rare talent. And your hats are lovely too.'

'Well, thank you, Constable,' she said. 'And I'm very glad you've got your man.'

After he'd gone, Miranda leaned against the wall smirking at Belle.

'What's that look for?' Belle asked.

'He's got a thing for you,' Miranda said.

'Don't be ridiculous,' Belle retorted.

'He couldn't take his eyes off you! I'd bet he's heard that you once lived in Paris and he's hoping for a little ooh-là-là.'

Belle wiggled a finger at Miranda like a school teacher. 'You, Miranda, have a smutty mind and an over-active imagination.'

Miranda was in fact very perceptive because as James Broadhead walked back to the police station, his mind was on Belle. Right from the first day she opened the shop in Tranquil Vale, she had caused a ripple of excitement around the village which had even reached the police station. Her beauty was enough to get her noticed, but there was something about her elegant, totally feminine shop which intrigued everyone, male and female. Every time James passed it while on his beat, he could never resist looking in the window. He had heard the rumour that she was French, and there was an implication of being 'fast' in that. However, that rumour was scotched when it became known she had only trained to be a milliner in France, and that she was going to marry Jimmy Franklin, who co-owned the Railway with his uncle.

But James had never spoken to Belle before the day she was attacked. All he'd had were glimpses of her as he passed the shop window. Sometimes she was serving a customer, at other times sitting on a chair sewing or writing something. But he always got a jolt at the combination of her dark, shiny hair, creamy skin and slender but very shapely figure.

He had been passing by the church on her wedding day just as she was coming out on Jimmy's arm and she took his breath away. Glorious was the only word to describe how she looked, in cream silk with a froth of veil around her lovely face. She was looking up at Jimmy and laughing at something, and James felt a stab of pure envy. No woman had ever looked at him in quite that way.

It was pure chance that he was first on the scene when she was attacked. The direction of his beat had been changed just the day before, and if he'd been on the old one he would have been walking down towards Lee Green instead of coming up Tranquil Vale. And Stokes the cobbler who came running out of the shop shouting for help would have found someone else.

She was lying crumpled on the floor, blood splattered up the wall behind her. He hadn't known until then that she was carrying a child, but the way she had fallen made the curve of her belly obvious, and she still had one hand protectively over it, which he found deeply affecting. Once the doctor arrived, James ran up on to the heath looking for her attacker, and he thought that had he found him, he might have ripped his throat out.

Since that night he'd called on Belle on three more occasions. The first was the day after the attack when he visited her to take a statement. She had looked so pale, drained and battered then, yet she had still made the effort to give him as much detail as possible.

Then he heard that she had lost her baby, and that for a while it was touch and go whether she would pull through. But happily she did, and on each of the subsequent occasions he had had reason to go and speak to her, she looked a little better. Even after all she had been through she didn't whine about it; in fact she had seemed impatient for his questions about it to be over, so she could ask him about himself.

People always looked at his missing fingers, then quickly averted their eyes as if repelled by the sight. But Belle asked him what had happened and how long it had been before he had been able to use his hand again. She asked what injuries the little boy he had rescued had, and said how indebted his mother must feel to him for saving her son. James had left the Railway that day feeling that his missing fingers were a badge of honour rather than something he ought to keep hidden.

He had wanted to say how pleased he was to see her looking so much better now, but he was too struck by the vivid blue of her eyes, the length of her dark eyelashes and the plumpness of her lips. He wished he was better at social chit-chat, then she might have engaged him in conversation a little longer. He would gladly have examined every one of her hats, swept her floor and cleaned the windows, anything to remain with her. But her friend was there, and he couldn't think of anything further to say.

He was thrilled that her attacker had been caught, and he felt proud to be complimented by senior officers on all the legwork he'd done on the case. Maybe he'd even get promoted, which would round things off nicely. But in the meantime he knew he'd have to try to stop daydreaming about Belle. She was after all a married woman.

James Broadhead wasn't alone in thinking about Belle. Jimmy was too – it was the one thing that always managed to make him feel warmer.

The march from the training camp at Etaples through France was tortuous. French roads were cobbled and very hard on the feet, especially as the army-issue heavy Ammos had not been broken in. He'd had his share of blisters – the one on his heel was now the size of a half crown – but other men had it much worse; their feet were bleeding and they hobbled along like old men.

Antwerp had fallen and the roads were a seething mass of people running away from the Germans. Some pushed hand-carts or perambulators loaded high with their belongings. He'd seen one cart piled up with furniture and an old lady perched up on a chair at the top. Other people were bent almost double with the huge loads they carried on their backs. Women with frightened eyes and babies in their arms begged for milk and bread, and there were so many children and old people who looked lost and pitiful. No one seemed to know where they were going or how they would live. Jimmy thought they were like so many hundreds of sheep, following the person in front of them blindly.

From the start of November there had been continuous heavy rain, and now they had to contend with snow too. It wouldn't have been so bad if each night they had had warm shelter and a hot meal, if they could have dried out their clothes properly and start the next day refreshed. But instead, the best they could hope for was a night in a barn – they didn't even have tents as some of the other regiments did.

Many nights they'd spent in the open, shivering with only a waterproof cape over them, and cold bully beef to eat.

Tonight as he thought about Belle, he was in a barn, and as he looked around him at men he had trained with at Etaples trying to sleep, huddled together for warmth in the straw, he wondered how many of them would even make it to fight at the front. Many had terrible coughs, some kept having to get up to go outside as they had the runs, one man had collapsed today and it was said he had pneumonia.

They were in the main bank clerks, shop assistants and factory workers, and there were a couple of school teachers, not men used to the outdoors. The training period at Etaples might have toughened them up to some degree, but this long march was gradually weakening them to the point where dozens more might become seriously ill.

Jimmy felt he was holding his own, but then he'd hauled heavy barrels around from the age of sixteen in all winds and weathers and his working days had always been long too. Plus he had several layers of warm, woolly underwear beneath his uniform. Yet as he lay back on his pack shivering he couldn't help but wonder how much worse it was going to get.

He'd heard the bad weather had brought something of a lull in hostilities at the front, but Captain Brunskill had said they needn't think that meant they were going to be idle, as the trenches and holes the British Expeditionary Force had dug to protect themselves from the German artillery when they'd first got there were rudimentary. Their job would be to improve and extend the trenches to command a satisfactory field of fire.

Jimmy wished he had not been so hasty in enlisting. It was clear to him now that the Germans had a formidable army, and it was said that a huge proportion of BEF had already been decimated at Mons and in what they called the Race to the Sea. Those men were seasoned soldiers, small in numbers perhaps compared to the size of the French army, but tough as old boots and trained to the hilt. Now all England could offer to swell their numbers was Kitchener's Army, a ragbag of young lads who had left their homes in search of glory.

Jimmy couldn't see anything in the darkness of the barn – the fire they'd lit earlier outside had been put out by the rain – but he could hear snuffling, snoring and coughing, and he wondered too how many of the men were crying silently, wishing they hadn't been caught up by patriotism or followed their friends who wanted to join up. But they were here now and in a few days' time they would be at the front. There was no way back except with a serious injury; even the dead got buried here.

Chapter Nine

Constable Broadhead pushed his way through the throng of people in the vestibule of the court at Lewisham to catch Belle and Mog before they left. 'I just wanted to thank you for giving your evidence today,' he said to Belle. 'It can't have been easy for you.'

Belle smiled weakly. It certainly hadn't been easy for her to wait to be called into the court room as a witness surrounded by dirty, bedraggled people who smelled bad and looked at her balefully. She had been cross-examined about the robbery and the injuries she sustained and, even worse, had to tell the court that she'd miscarried too. But Constable Broadhead had been very kind to her, and she didn't want to make him feel he'd added to the distress she had suffered.

'I'm just relieved it's over and that he won't be robbing or hurting anyone else for some years,' she replied. 'And you did very well to bring him to justice.'

Archie Newbold had been found guilty on all seven counts of robbery with violence and had been sentenced to ten years in prison. She was just one of several witnesses, but the judge had singled her out to compliment her on the sketch she'd drawn of Newbold, which had made the man in the dock stare menacingly at her and make her feel fearful.

It was mid-January and snowing outside. Belle felt chilled to the marrow and completely wrung out, but not just by the trial. Yesterday they had read in the newspaper that there had been Zeppelin bomb attacks in Yarmouth and King's Lynn in which twenty-eight people were killed and another sixty injured. Added to that were the ever-lengthening lists of those killed in action. It seemed to Belle that a very dark cloud was hanging over England, which was not going to roll away any time soon.

'May I take you both for a cup of tea to warm you up?' Broadhead asked, as if he sensed how she was feeling.

'That is very kind,' Belle replied. 'But I think with this snow we'd be better to hurry along home.'

'Who is that?' Mog asked the policeman, indicating a tall, thin man wearing a dark coat and trilby hat. He was leaning against the wall by the court exit and looking towards them. 'He seems to be taking a great deal of interest in us. I noticed him in the court room.'

Broadhead glanced at the man. 'I expect he's a reporter. He's probably hoping to speak to you. If you like, I'll come out with you and see you into a cab; that should deter him.'

Belle hadn't noticed the man before, but having no wish to speak to anyone further that day, she took Mog's arm and allowed Broadhead to lead the way to get them a cab.

But as Broadhead started down the steps, the tall man moved right into the path of the two women. 'Miss Cooper, isn't it?' he said, holding out his hand to shake Belle's.

Being called by her maiden name was a jolt. It made Belle falter and look to Mog for help.

'I know you are Mrs Reilly now, but you were Belle Cooper, were you not?' he said, his tone oily and knowing, his eyes a yellowish-brown.

In a flash of intuition Belle felt he must have connected her with the trial of John Kent, the man who had abducted her and sold her into prostitution because she witnessed him murder one of her mother's girls. Kent was hanged before she married Jimmy, and she had believed when she moved to Blackheath that her past was buried and forgotten.

But to deny the name of Cooper would be pointless and make her look as if she had something to hide.

'Yes, my maiden name was Cooper,' she said, trying very hard not to show any anxiety. 'Have we met before?'

'Constable Broadhead has got us a cab,' Mog said, tightening her grip on Belle's arm to indicate they should get away quickly. 'We must go, can't keep him waiting when it's so cold.'

'Blessard,' the man said, still holding out his hand. 'Frank Blessard of the *Chronicle*. No, we haven't met before but . . .'

Belle cut him off by shaking the proffered hand. 'Good to meet you, Mr Blessard, but we must rush now.'

As she and Mog hurried down the steps she was aware he had half pursued her with the intention of asking her something else, but she didn't turn her head, and asked Broadhead if he would like to ride back with them to the village.

'That is very kind of you. I was intending to catch the tram,' he said, his face lighting up at the offer. 'But if I'm not imposing, it would certainly get me back a great deal quicker.'

'That man Blessard who spoke to us said he was with the *Chronicle*,' Belle told Broadhead once the cab was moving. 'I don't know that newspaper. Do you?'

The policeman grimaced. 'A gutter rag. Good job you cut him short, he'd be hoping for more gory details than he got in court. If he approaches you again, just send him on his way. I've got no time for those jackals, they pick over a case and if they can't find any sensational story, they make it up.'

The snow had turned to driving sleet by the time they got back to Blackheath and Belle paid the driver, bade goodbye to the policeman and hurried indoors with Mog.

Garth was in the kitchen. 'Did it go well?' he called out as they took off their outdoor clothes and boots. 'The kettle's on. How long did the rat get?'

The two women joined Garth in the kitchen, going over to the stove to warm their hands. Mog told Garth the verdict. 'But Belle's a bit shaken, a journalist there knew her as Cooper.'

'You don't want to put no mind to that,' Garth said, going over to Belle and putting one big paw on her shoulder. 'Your maiden name's no secret. Plenty of people round here know it, you was living here for months afore you was wed to our Jimmy.'

'That's all very true, but why would he use the name of Cooper when I'd only been called Reilly in the court? And there was something slimy about him,' Belle said, leaning against Garth's big chest for comfort. 'I think he was at Kent's trial.'

Garth hugged her to him. 'There now, don't you be worried about that. They never brought up nothing bad about you in that trial. I'd say he got a bit excited cos you've been a victim of a bad man again. That's like human interest, ain't it?'

'Course it is,' Mog said stoutly. 'You being so pretty 'n' all, your hubby off at the war and you being so clever as to do that picture of that villain. Noah would tell you there was a time he'd bite off anyone's hand to get such a good meaty story.'

'Maybe I should telephone Noah,' Belle said, looking from Garth to Mog. 'You know, get his advice. Somehow I don't think I've seen the last of that man, and I need to know how to deal with him if he turns up again.'

'As if you haven't got enough to worry about with Jimmy,' Mog said.

Belle was well aware that Mog was susceptible to extreme anxiety where Belle's well-being was concerned, and so she felt it best to reassure her.

'I'm not too worried about him, he's fine really, just grousing in his letters cos he's missing us all and fed up with being cold and wet all the time,' she said lightly. 'He said his feet aren't nearly as bad as most of the other men's. And if he can't grouse to us about it, who can he grouse to?'

Belle was in fact very worried about Jimmy as she could sense the misery between the lines in his last letter. He had said he'd been to see the MO about trench foot, but then added his wasn't anywhere near bad enough to get him sent to hospital like some of the other men. He'd said it was lucky Mog had knitted him so many pairs of warm woollen socks as he'd been able to change them frequently, but drying them out was the problem.

Belle knew trench foot was caused by standing in water for long periods. It made her shudder to think of the conditions the soldiers lived and fought in over there.

There was so much about a soldier's life that was unfair. If they were wounded in battle they would get an army pension, but those who became disabled in some other way or just became sick through the conditions they lived in, got nothing.

Jimmy had made what passed for a joke in his letter about how the only way to get home was on a Blighty ticket. By that he meant a serious wound or an ailment that couldn't be treated at the front. He'd said that one man in his regiment had shot himself in the foot, and claimed it was an accident while he was cleaning his gun. Another soldier was seen waving his arm above the trench, clearly hoping the Boche, as the soldiers called the Germans, would shoot him.

Belle didn't think he'd mention such things unless he too

had toyed with the idea of doing something similar. He'd also told her about being part of a patrol sent over into No Man's Land at night to reconnoitre, and how one night the Germans had sent up flares and he described himself like a rabbit stunned motionless by a bright light when he should have dropped to the ground. He'd gone on to joke that it seemed the Boche couldn't be bothered to shoot him.

But Belle realized that there was nothing funny about it; he'd clearly frozen with terror. Bad as it was to imagine him that way, somehow it seemed worse to think he didn't dare admit it for fear of being seen as a coward.

Belle was horrified by the way most people were glorifying the war. She wondered if they'd still feel the same if they lost a family member. The newspapers veered between reporting German atrocities – everything from killing babies and raping women to torturing prisoners of war – and jubilantly encouraging everyone to believe the Allied armies were winning, regardless of the already horrific losses. As soldiers weren't allowed to say exactly where they were, and wouldn't be able to tell the truth about how the war was going, even if they knew, no one could be sure what was really happening there.

'Are you all right, Belle?'

Mog's voice cut through her reverie, and she looked up with a faint smile. 'Yes, I'm fine. I think I'll go up and light the fire in the living room and write to Jimmy. He'll want to know how it was today.'

'Don't give that reporter another thought,' Mog replied. 'By the time he's sat through the rest of the cases tried today he'll have forgotten all about you.'

Belle wrote her letter to Jimmy. She told him nothing about Blessard, only about the other witnesses and the outcome of the trial. She mentioned that it had been snowing, which had now turned to sleet, and that she was opening the shop again in a week's time. She had found a source of stylish fur hats and matching muffs which should sell well and give her time to design and make hats for the spring.

But as always, most of her letter was filled with little details of home life, how concerned she, Mog and Garth were about him, and how much she missed him.

The picture she drew at the bottom was of a pig wearing a judge's wig, as she'd noticed that morning that the judge resembled a pig, with very small dark eyes and a nose more like a snout.

On a separate piece of paper she sketched Blessard as she remembered him. A bony face, bad skin, thin lips and a small, light brown moustache, but she found she couldn't remember the shape of his eyes, only the cunning in them.

Was her past about to come back and haunt her?

Six weeks after the trial at nearly four in the afternoon Belle wrapped up warmly in her brown fur hat, brown tweed coat and a thick blue scarf Mog had knitted for her, to go up to the shop. As it was snowing hard that morning, Belle had remained at home to work on some new designs and left Miranda to open the shop. In the dark the snow looked very pretty; there had been so little traffic all day that even the road was covered in a good two inches. Mog had said it was daft to go up there as there wouldn't have been any customers in this weather, but Belle needed some fresh air, and she wanted to see Miranda.

The bowed shop window always looked inviting in the dark as the light from the shop streamed out on to the pavement. Belle paused for a moment, looking at the display of the fur hats and muffs in the window.

Beyond the window display she could see Miranda standing on a stool, rearranging hat boxes on a shelf. She looked elegant as always in a plum-coloured wool dress with a matching small jacket trimmed with velvet and her blonde hair plaited and wound around her head.

She jumped down from the stool as the shop bell tinkled and Belle came in. 'I didn't expect you to come up today,' she said, looking both surprised and pleased. 'But I'm very glad you have because I've had some hideous people in here today and I wanted to share the experience with you.'

Belle smiled. Miranda liked dramatic words; hideous was one of her favourites.

'In what way hideous? Ugly, rude, badly dressed?'

'Hideously boring mostly. One woman regaled me about her precious cat who had just passed on. I ask you! How can anyone expect me to listen to the virtues of a ginger tom for over an hour without yawning? Then there was that woman that wears a kind of turban and sniffs all the time.'

Belle laughed. She knew exactly who Miranda was referring to, the woman came in all the time but had never once taken off the curious turban to try on a real hat. Belle had always suspected she might be bald. 'I take it business has been hideous then?'

'On the contrary, I've sold four fur hats and three muffs,' Miranda said gleefully. 'Also, that ghastly Miss Orwell who looks like she has a permanent bad smell under her nose came in with her mother to see if you would make her a headdress for her wedding in April. She also wants something for her bridesmaids. I said you'd telephone her and arrange an appointment to discuss what she wants.'

'That's marvellous,' Belle said. 'We must endeavour to try and like the ghastly Miss Orwell. Fortunately she is quite pretty, so one of my stunning designs won't look out of place on her.'

They both laughed. One of their delights was to ridicule the customers they didn't like, even though they were always charm itself to the women's faces. Belle went through to the work room to check on the little stove that kept the shop warm and banked it up for the night. 'Shall we have a cup of tea before we shut up?' she called back.

Belle often wondered what she would do without Miranda as her friend. They had a similar sense of humour, conversation never dried up between them and she trusted her completely. Much as she loved Mog and Garth, they were rather limited as they had little interest in, or knowledge about, anything beyond the pub and family. Miranda on the other hand had travelled; she was interested in all kinds of things, and had a joyous nature that even her overbearing mother had not been able to subdue.

'Or we could shut up the shop and have a glass of that sherry left over from Christmas,' Miranda called back.

'I knew I hired you for more than your good looks,' Belle said, taking the bottle down from the shelf. 'Lock the door and pull down the blind.'

A few minutes later they were both in the work room, sitting by the stove with a glass of sherry in their hands.

Belle had admitted to Miranda a few days earlier that her heart wasn't in the shop any more. Miranda hadn't taken her seriously then, assuming she was just having a bad day. Belle knew she had to make her see that it was more than that.

'I wish I didn't have to bring this up again, Miranda,' she said. 'But I really don't want to carry on with the shop. I know you love it, and that you think I'll get my enthusiasm back, but I won't. I'd sooner do something for the war effort.'

'But it's such a success!' Miranda protested. 'I can run it for you. You just stay at home and make the hats.'

'I don't even feel the same about the hats either,' Belle

admitted. 'And the lease will be up for renewal soon. They are bound to put the rent up and I really can't bear to commit myself for another three years. Especially if the war drags on.'

Miranda looked at her appraisingly for a moment. 'Even when we re-opened at New Year I did notice a slump in your flair and your enthusiasm. I didn't remark on it because I hoped it would come back eventually.' She paused for a moment, as if thinking what to say. 'But if you feel it is never going to, I can see why you would want to give up. But war work! I know they want people in munitions, but I can't see you doing that. They need nurses too, but you aren't one. I suppose you could volunteer as an orderly, but do you really want to do the mucky jobs?'

'I wouldn't mind.'

Miranda looked shocked. 'You're completely serious, aren't you?'

'Yes, I am. I don't want to do you out of a job, but my heart really isn't in this any more. I used to love designing and making the hats, but now it's a real chore. Maybe if I volunteered at the hospital and gained some experience, in a few months I could join the Red Cross.'

'You mean go to France?'

Belle hadn't actually thought of that, but suddenly that seemed to be exactly what she did want. 'Yes, I think I do.'

Miranda stared at her. 'And what would Jimmy have to say about that?'

Belle pulled a face. 'He'd be horrified. And so would Mog and Garth. There would be hell to pay. But it's my life and they need every pair of hands they can get over there. You can't tell me I wouldn't be more useful than some of those dopey society women who've never even dressed themselves or drawn their own bath water. Someone like me wouldn't faint at the sight of lice or a man's naked body.'

'Like me, you mean?' Miranda grinned. 'Mind you, I wouldn't faint at a naked male body.'

Belle giggled. 'I didn't mean like you, and you know it. But we've both read in the paper about such women becoming VADs and assisting trained nurses. If they can do it, why not me?'

'Well, for a start you have to be twenty-three and I doubt they'd take you as you are married.'

'I could lie about that,' Belle said.

Miranda tutted and waved a finger disapprovingly. 'What is it in your past?' she asked. 'Whenever you say something like that I always get the feeling you've done so much, seen so much. We're friends; you can trust me, so why don't you tell me about it?'

Belle half smiled. 'You might not want to be friends if I told you the whole story.'

Miranda reached out and took Belle's hand. 'There's nothing you could tell me which would stop me liking you. Besides, I can't fall out with you, you know far too much about me. So tell me, and I promise I'll join you in this mad idea of going to France.'

'You wouldn't want to do that surely?' Belle exclaimed. 'Cleaning up vomit, cutting blood-soaked uniforms off wounded men?'

'I'm not too wild about any of that.' Miranda winced. 'But God knows I could do with some excitement, and I can't think of anyone I'd rather throw my lot in with. I could drive an ambulance maybe? My father has all sorts of connections, and as you said we could get experience at a local hospital, maybe do a first aid course?'

Belle felt a warm glow spreading through her. She didn't think it was quite as simple as Miranda made it sound, but the possibility of doing something different and reckless was thrilling and drove away the melancholy that seemed to have settled on her for so long.

'You'd really join me?'

'Yes, I would. What have I got to lose? You helped me when no one else would. In truth I know now that you are the only true friend I have, or have ever had, the rest are mere acquaintances. You are inspiring, funny, kind and you have a core of steel that makes me feel braver and better for being with you.'

Belle's eyes prickled with tears at such a sincere compliment. 'It could be the greatest adventure,' she said in a low voice. 'Maybe a bigger and far more worthwhile one than anything that's ever happened to me before.'

'Now, about that "before".' Miranda picked up the bottle of sherry and poured them both another glass. 'Tell me about that.'

Belle recalled how one afternoon just before Christmas she had been feeling desperately low and had told Mog that if Miranda called round she was to say she had gone out. Miranda did call, but she wouldn't be fobbed off and insisted on seeing her. All she did was come into the living room, plonk herself down on the couch by Belle and put her arms around her.

In that hug was a wealth of understanding. She hadn't listed all the things Belle had to live for, no platitudes, no pep talks, she just offered herself as a prop, a listening ear, and a true friend, the kind that asks for nothing in return. Belle felt that perhaps she did owe her the truth about herself.

'All right then, if we are getting into this together, then it is best you know. To start with, I was born and brought up in a brothel.'

Belle told her story as simply and concisely as she could: Millie's murder, and how she was abducted by her killer and sold into prostitution in France. She was aware as she continued on to how Etienne took her to Martha's sporting house in New Orleans, that Miranda's eyes were wide with shock, but she did not falter.

'I decided there that as there was no way I could get back to England I might as well accept it and be the best of whores,' she said plainly. 'I was the top girl, and at times I even enjoyed it.'

It was only when she got to the part about Pascal, who had locked her in the attic room in his house in Montmartre, that Miranda gasped.

'If it was anyone else telling me this I'd think they were making it up,' she said.

Belle continued with how Etienne rescued her, and finished off the story with her being a witness at Kent's trial.

'That is some story,' Miranda exclaimed. 'But it explains lots of things about you which have puzzled me. I'm so glad you felt able to tell me.'

'I am too,' Belle admitted. 'You see, I really wanted to confide in you about something that happened at the court on the day of Newbold's trial. I couldn't tell you about it, not when you didn't know about my past. But a reporter spoke to me. He knew my maiden name, and I think he was at the trial of Kent, the man who abducted me, so he'd know a huge amount of my past. Part of the reason I want to give up the shop is because of him. I've got a feeling he might approach me again.'

'You mean you think he might try to blackmail you?'

Belle shrugged. 'You are quick, that's one of the things I like about you. Mog just thought he was after a story about the robbery, but I've met a few maggots in my time, and I think he's one. Call it gut instinct.'

'But everyone you care about already knows all this,'

Miranda said. 'You can't blackmail someone unless they are hiding stuff from their nearest and dearest.'

'That's true, but what he may have realized, if he's been poking around up here, is that I'm very respectable now. Imagine how people in the village, my customers, would react if they knew the truth about me!'

'But he can't possibly know the whole story! Only that you were sold into a brothel as a very young girl, and people would be very sympathetic about that.'

Belle raised one eyebrow. 'Round here? No one would ever buy a hat from me again. Can you imagine what your mother would say?'

Miranda nodded. 'Yes, I can, but not everyone's like her.'

'Enough are,' Belle said sadly. 'Mog and I have been so careful to fit in, to be respectable. That man could shatter all that. I don't mind so much for myself as for poor Mog. She and Garth are so happy, she loves being well respected in the community. I brought her so much pain when I was abducted, I don't want to bring disgrace down on her now she's so settled.'

'Running away to France isn't going to stop that happening if Blessard does want to expose you,' Miranda said.

'True. But I suspect money is all that man wants. He's probably looked at this shop and thinks I've got plenty and I'm a soft target because my husband is away at the war. If the shop goes and I'm a volunteer nurse's aide, what's in it for him?'

'Ummm.' Miranda looked thoughtful. 'He could try Garth?'

Belle sniggered. 'Would anyone in their right mind attempt to blackmail Garth? He'd wring his neck as soon as look at him.'

They both fell silent for a while, sipping their sherry and looking into the fire.

'About this man Etienne.' Miranda cocked one perfectly shaped eyebrow quizzically. 'I sense something there. Was he a lover?'

Belle shook her head. 'No, but I loved him.'

Miranda smirked. 'That couldn't be another of France's attractions, could it?'

Belle's eyes widened. 'No, of course not. He didn't even cross my mind. I just want to do something worthwhile, to feel alive again, not just marking time till Jimmy comes home.'

'Well, you've made me want to join you in this mad idea,' Miranda said. 'So we'd better make some plans and work out how we're going to go about it.'

Chapter Ten

The Railway bar lights were off when Belle got home at midnight after her first day at The Royal Herbert Military Hospital. She let herself in very quietly through the side door, and was just taking off her coat in the dark hall when the kitchen door opened and in the stream of light she saw Mog.

'You startled me. I thought you'd gone to bed,' Belle said.

'Do you think I'd go to bed with you out roaming the streets?' Mog snapped. 'I had your tea on, but it's ruined now. I suppose you've been living the high life with Miss Toffee Nose?'

Belle was swaying with exhaustion and in no mood for a row. 'I've only just left the hospital,' she said. 'The only high life I've had today was the stink of gangrene.'

'I take it you won't be bothering to go again tomorrow then?'

Mog had her arms folded across her chest, and she was puffed up with anger and indignation. All the way home Belle had told herself she couldn't possibly continue being a nurse's aide; she had never worked so hard in her life or seen so many distressing sights. But Mog's scorn banished that thought.

'Have you ever known me give up on something I wanted to do?' she asked.

It was the end of April, and for the past month since she'd told Mog and Garth that she wasn't going to renew the lease on the shop and had been accepted at the hospital as a volunteer,

Mog had ridiculed her plans. At times she had been so nasty about it that Belle had been tempted to find a room somewhere and move out. But knowing that would upset Jimmy, she'd resolved to stay in the hope Mog would come round.

'Then you must have a screw missing to work a sixteen-hour day for nothing,' Mog retorted.

'You think it's nothing to help save soldiers' lives?' Belle sighed. 'To me it's far more rewarding than making hats for vain women with more money than sense.'

'What about making some money for when Jimmy comes home? You'll soon fritter away everything you made at the shop with nothing more coming in.'

'That's my business,' Belle said.

'Maybe it is, but I'll bet you'll talk it over with Miss Toffee Nose and she'll come up with another hare-brained scheme even more ridiculous than this one.'

Belle felt hurt and saddened by the jealousy and spite in that remark. 'I've already told you dozens of times that this was my idea and not Miranda's, and don't call her Miss Toffee Nose, she isn't, and she's been a very good friend to me. I'm going to bed now. I just hope by tomorrow night you have found a way of accepting that this is what I want to do.'

Mog snorted her disapproval. 'It's all women of her sort who are rushing off to make nuisances of themselves in France. That'll be her next plan, I expect.'

'Those women are not making nuisances of themselves in France. They are doing a marvellous job.'

Mog flounced back to the kitchen and slammed the door behind her. Belle was too tired to pursue her and try to talk her round, so wearily she went on up the stairs to her bed.

She knew that the real cause of Mog's disapproval was fear that Belle was forgetting she was a married woman. Mog saw marriage as a finality; that once the vows were made a wife shouldn't want or need a life beyond serving her husband and keeping him happy. While she appreciated it couldn't be quite that way for Belle as Jimmy was away, she still wanted to see her centring her life round him, sitting at home at nights knitting him socks, writing him letters and making plans for when he returned.

Belle certainly hadn't forgotten she was married; she wished more than anything that the war would end soon and Jimmy would come home so they could settle down together again. But it was clear the war wasn't going to end any time soon, and she couldn't even be certain Jimmy would survive it. It was not in her nature just to sit around indefinitely twiddling her thumbs.

Jimmy was right behind her too. The letter he'd written in reply to hers about doing voluntary work had made his views quite clear.

'I'll be proud to think you are doing your bit for wounded soldiers,' he wrote. 'God knows, the wounded men I've seen here need all the help they can get to recover from their injuries. Uncle Garth and Mog will probably disapprove of you doing anything that takes you out of their sight, but pay no heed to them, they've got fixed ideas because of what life has dealt them.

'I think when I do come back that we should get a home of our own. We've both spent too long having our lives arranged by others. I often daydream about us living by the sea, maybe running a guest house instead of a public house, I'd give anything to be somewhere quiet and clean. Even when we're sent back from the line the gunfire never lets up, but the way I deal with all the horrors here is imagining lying between soft, clean sheets with you, windows open, a soft breeze wafting in and complete silence, or sitting by a roaring fire eating anything that isn't bully beef.'

Jimmy always mentioned the constant noise of gunfire and his longing for silence in his letters, and Belle was well aware that the man she married might not be the same man when the war was over. Maybe it wouldn't be possible to go to France, but at least working at the hospital would give her a better understanding of what he was going through.

Once Belle was in bed, she lay there thinking over the long day she'd just had. Matron, a slender and severe-looking woman, had looked her up and down when she arrived on the ward in the morning. Belle was wearing the regulation high-necked, ankle-length navy blue dress, white cuffs, collar, apron and cap but it didn't appear that she had the woman's approval.

'All your hair must be secured back under your cap,' Matron said archly. 'You will do exactly as you are ordered and if I find you incompetent I will ask you to leave immediately.'

'Yes, Matron,' Belle said as she tucked back the couple of stray curls which had escaped her cap. She was a little shaken by the chilly reception, for although she hadn't expected to be thanked for volunteering to help out, she certainly hadn't anticipated being treated like a schoolgirl.

Her first impression of the forty-bed ward to which she had been allocated was surprise that it was so orderly and peaceful, even if rather gloomy as the window at the far end of the ward was high up and narrow. Most of the patients were lying down, and their counterpanes were smoothed out, snowy-white sheets turned neatly back, but there was no groaning or thrashing about in pain as she'd expected. Almost all of the patients' eyes turned to look at her; some of the men even managed a cheeky grin. There were two Queen Alexandra's Sisters on duty, and two other women who she assumed were either civilian nurses or volunteers like her.

The first task she was given was to go outside the ward to scrub down a bed a soldier had died in the night before. The disinfectant was so strong it stung her hands and the smell took her back to New Orleans and the stuff they used to wash the clients' private parts with. It made her smile to herself to imagine how Matron would react if she was to reveal that.

When she had finished that job Sister Adams, a plain and very skinny woman in her late thirties, who Belle assumed was the most senior of the nursing staff, told her to observe while Sister May did the dressings.

It was like a baptism of fire. The first patient had been hit by a grenade. He'd had what was left of his right arm amputated just below the shoulder at a field hospital, but his whole chest and right side was a vivid mass of torn and burnt flesh.

Belle didn't feel sickened, just appalled at such a hideous wound, and had she been left to clean it with the saline solution herself she wouldn't have known where to start and would have been frightened of hurting the man even more. But Private Lomax didn't cry out as Sister May gently dabbed the wound; he kept his eyes on Belle and even tried to hold a conversation.

'Your first day?' he asked.

Belle told him it was.

'You watch Sister May carefully, she's the best and the gentlest. I see you're wearing a wedding ring. Is your husband in France?'

As Miranda had said, married women couldn't be accepted for nursing training. Belle had lied about her age and said she was twenty-three, but she had admitted she was married. At her interview they had made it quite plain they were only prepared to accept her as a volunteer because her husband was on active service.

'Yes, I think he must be near Ypres. He can't say of course, but there've been little hints.'

'We've had a great many men in here who were wounded there,' Sister May said. 'I do hope your husband stays safe.'

'Thank you, Sister,' Belle replied, then turned her attention to Lomax again. 'What will you do now?' she asked. He was so young, no more than nineteen; although his good arm was muscular, his body had the wiriness of a young boy.

'Go on back to Sussex and help Dad on the farm,' he said. 'It's lucky I'm left-handed. So I'll still be able to do most things.'

His courage and lack of self-pity brought a lump to Belle's throat.

By the time she and Sister May had worked their way round one side of the ward, Belle realized that it must be a sort of code of honour among the wounded not to show distress at their injuries, as not one of them complained or cried out as their wounds were dressed. One man had lost both legs, one had to lie on his stomach because his back was one huge open wound. Another man had been told that morning that his leg had to come off above the knee as he had gangrene.

The smell from his wound was the only thing that had made Belle gag during the day. She'd emptied countless bedpans, three times she'd had to clean up a man with dysentery. She had dealt with vomit and blood, and helped lay out a man who had finally died from a terrible stomach wound. Yet it was only the smell of the gangrene that really sickened her.

Sister May was around twenty-eight, tall and well-built, with the rosy cheeks of a country girl. She was firm and professional, but Belle sensed her innate kindness as she worked quickly and efficiently without any fuss. She was a good person to learn from as she gave Belle a little information about each patient and explained what each of them needed. She said she and the other nurses were very glad of volunteer help, and that she thought Belle was made of the right stuff to be very useful.

During the afternoon a convoy of ambulances arrived at the hospital with over a hundred more wounded on stretchers. Belle went out with Sister May and Sister Adams to receive them, and to show the stretcher bearers which ward they were to take them to.

At least half of the new arrivals were in a very bad way. They might have been stripped of their uniforms and their wounds dressed in a hospital in France, but now they were going to have operations in an attempt to save their lives.

Belle had never felt quite so inadequate. All she could do was watch and learn from the nurses as they spoke to the patients and reassured them. Sister May directed her to which of the men could be given a drink, or to light and hold a cigarette to the lips of those who wanted one, and at one point she took Belle aside and asked if she would write a letter home for one man who had been blinded.

'His name is Albert Fellows, and he probably won't last the night,' she said quietly. 'He has a terrible chest wound along with his facial injuries. He said he was eighteen to join up, but I'd say he's only seventeen, and he wants his mother to know he was thinking of her at the end.'

Albert Fellows had his head and eyes bandaged, and what was showing of the rest of his face was a shocking mess of torn tissue. Belle took his hand as she sat beside his bed ready with a notepad and pencil. 'Hello, Albert, I'm Mrs Reilly,' she said. 'I'm not a nurse, just a volunteer, but Sister said you wanted to send a letter to your mother. Can you tell me what you want to say?'

It was impossible to picture what he'd looked like before he was blown up, but the hand in hers, though calloused and rough, was small, reminding her he was just a boy.

'I never did much letter-writing,' he croaked out. 'Sarge used to do it for me, so you write what's best.'

'Dear Mother then,' Belle suggested.

'I calls her Ma,' he said.

'Dear Ma, I'm in the Royal Herbert Hospital in Woolwich now,' she began. 'Does that sound right?'

'Yes, tell her I'm poorly but I'm in good hands. Tell her I wasn't windy when I went over the top, and I'm sorry that I was such a worry to her.' He stopped then, and it was clear from his laboured breathing that he found talking very difficult.

Belle had heard the expression 'windy' several times already that day. It meant being afraid. She was sure all the men must have been afraid, but like not complaining about their injuries, it was considered honourable to hide fear. She wondered how they could possibly be brave enough to leap out of the trenches, knowing full well they were likely to be gunned down.

'Have you got any brothers and sisters I should mention?' she asked.

'I'm her only one, Pa died a few years back,' he wheezed. 'Tell her to pat Whisky for me, that's my dog. I don't know what else.'

'You could say you love her,' Belle suggested.

'We never said soppy stuff,' he croaked.

Belle squeezed his hand gently, glad he couldn't see the tears in her eyes. 'Now's a good time to be soppy. I know I'd like to hear such a thing from my brave son.'

'OK then. And tell her to look after herself and not work so hard.'

Sister May had suggested Belle scribble it down as he dictated and write it up properly later. 'And I'll sign it from your loving son Albert,' Belle said.

'You'll post it for me?' he asked.

'Of course I will, Albert,' she said. 'Now, you go to sleep until the doctor comes to see you.'

'Are you young?' he asked. 'You sound as if you are and your hands are nice and soft.'

'Yes, I'm young,' she replied, trying hard to control the quaver in her voice. 'I haven't been helping here long enough to get rough hands. But I expect I will.'

'I never even kissed a girl,' he rasped out. 'Some of the blokes told me all sorts they did with girls. Reckon they were lying to look big?'

'Yes, I'm sure they were,' she said, wishing she could reassure him he'd get to do all that too one day. But she couldn't, he already knew he wasn't going to make it. 'I have to go now, but I'll come and see you again later.'

Albert died just an hour later but Sister May was with him, holding his hand. Belle struggled to hold back tears and Sister put one steadying hand on her arm. 'It was for the best, Reilly,' she said softly. 'His pain is gone, and what kind of life would he have with no sight and his face disfigured? Better too that his mother didn't get here in time to see him like that. She can be proud of his courage and remember him as he was.'

'Will it always be like this?' Belle asked, thinking that she didn't know if she would be capable of holding herself together if scenes like this were a regular occurrence.

'We have to take heart from the ones who recover,' Sister said. 'Not dwell on those who don't. We do our best for all of them, and even if all you could do for Albert was to write to his mother, that gave him more comfort than the morphine.'

As Belle began to drift off to sleep she wondered how Miranda had fared today. They had gone to the hospital together that morning, but Miranda had been sent off to a different ward, and Belle hadn't caught sight of her again, not even when the convoy of wounded arrived.

Three days passed before Belle met up with Miranda again. From her second day Belle had reported for duty at six in the morning, and left at six in the evening, and for all she knew Miranda might have been given different times.

But on her third day she was walking up Shooters Hill when the tinkle of a bicycle bell made her look round. Miranda was pedalling laboriously up towards her.

'Now, that's a good idea,' Belle said. 'An awful lot quicker than walking.'

'Papa got it for me,' Miranda panted as she dismounted and walked beside Belle, pushing the bicycle. 'How are you getting on?'

'Becoming very aware nursing isn't for the faint-hearted,' Belle said. 'How are you finding it? I'd begun to think you'd given up as I hadn't seen you.'

'I'm in the officers' ward,' Miranda said. 'I nearly did turn tail and run. It's pretty hideous! Just because they're all gentlemen doesn't make their injuries any more palatable than in the other ranks. But I won't give up; if I do my mother will crow with delight.'

Belle laughed. 'I feel the same. Mog's waiting for me to give up. She's been rather nasty too.'

They chatted about the two older women's attitude as they walked.

'I think we'll have enough experience to be able to apply to go to France in September,' Miranda said. 'I haven't told them at home that's the plan. Have you?'

'No, I daren't, I'll only tell them at the last minute,' Belle said.

'It might be a good idea for you to get a bicycle too,' Miranda said as she pushed hers into the shed. 'I could teach you to ride one.'

'Could you?' Belle asked eagerly. 'I'm off on Sunday, are you going to be off too?'

Miranda said she was, and suggested they meet up in the afternoon for a lesson. 'We could do it in Greenwich Park.'

After arranging to meet at three in the afternoon they both rushed off to their respective wards.

Belle's first job of the morning was to scrub down a couple of beds outside. As she worked she smiled to herself at the thought of Miranda teaching her to ride a bicycle. It would make it much quicker to get to and from the hospital.

On Sunday afternoon Miranda was waiting with her bicycle by the church when Belle met her at three. It was a sunny day, and the heath was full of families flying kites, walking to the pond with boats to sail, exercising dogs and playing ball games.

'Mama said I shouldn't be out riding a bicycle on a Sunday,' Miranda said. 'She said it was ungodly!'

Belle giggled. She'd had the misfortune to meet Mrs Forbes-Alton again just before she closed down the shop. The woman had cross-examined her about volunteering, and made it quite plain she held Belle responsible for giving her daughter what she called 'peculiar ideas'. Belle had been tempted to say that if she didn't spend her time handing out white feathers, perhaps there would be fewer men needing nursing back to health. But she didn't quite dare, the woman was too formidable and it would only come back on Miranda.

The girls walked with the bicycle to a quiet part of the

park. 'Get on then,' Miranda said once they'd found a deserted path. 'I'll hold you upright until you get your balance.'

Belle got on, and with Miranda holding the saddle, she pushed off and began to pedal. Miranda ran along beside her, steadying her. Then she let go, and Belle toppled over.

This happened many times. Belle got her skirt caught on the chain, she hurt her wrist when she fell on it, and bruised her knee, but she was determined she was going to master it.

'How long did it take you to learn?' she asked Miranda breathlessly.

'Ages, and I learned wearing knickerbockers which makes it easier,' she replied.

'I haven't got ages,' Belle said. 'I've got to learn today so I can ask Garth to buy me a bicycle tomorrow and ride it to the hospital on Tuesday.'

She gritted her teeth and got on again. This time she managed to stay on for about ten yards before losing concentration and toppling over.

'You've got it now,' Miranda called out to her. 'On again and keep pedalling.'

Belle managed to keep going. She wobbled, didn't steer straight, but she was really riding it.

'Well done!' Miranda yelled from a long way behind her. 'Keep going till you find somewhere wide enough to turn round without getting off and come back to me.'

Belle did it. She not only stayed on but turned round and rode back with ever-increasing confidence. Miranda clapped her hands with delight.

'You learned a lot quicker than me,' she said. 'Now, let's go and have a cup of tea, then you can ride all the way home.'

Over tea and a cake in the park tea room, once Belle had got over her excitement at learning to ride, they discussed their first week at the hospital.

'I'm not really cut out for it,' Miranda admitted. 'Emptying bedpans makes me heave and I don't think I could ever dress a wound, but luckily the real nurses do that. Sister MacDonald is on at me all the time. I don't think she likes me at all. But I keep reminding myself that I'm going to be an ambulance driver, I only need to know basic first aid, and that gets me through it.'

From what Miranda said about her work on her ward, she really was only being given the cleaning-up kind of jobs. Belle did those too, mopping the floor, giving out and taking away bedpans, feeding patients who couldn't feed themselves and making beds. But she was also entrusted with washing and shaving patients, and she had dressed less serious wounds too.

But neither of them dwelt for long on the hardships of the job. There were too many funny stories for them to laugh about.

'A new volunteer started on Friday,' Miranda said. 'Sister told her to take a bedpan to a patient who had the curtains pulled round his bed. The nurse in with him was giving him a bed-bath so he was naked except for his dressings. You should've seen her as she came out, face as red as a letter box and quivering like a blancmange. She told me afterwards she'd never seen a naked man before, she hadn't even got any brothers.'

Belle laughed. The nurses on her ward had told similar stories, in fact they'd said she was the first volunteer not to look embarrassed. She'd thought it was lucky they knew she was married or they might have wondered about her. 'It's just as bad for the men,' she said. 'We had a very young lad in yesterday and I had to wash him. He kept his eyes tight shut, I think he imagined if he couldn't see me, I couldn't see him either. I don't suppose anyone but his mother has ever seen him naked. He was still blushing and trying not to meet my eyes when I had to feed him later.'

'How did you get on when you were doing, umm, well, you know? In New Orleans,' Miranda asked.

'After the first half dozen men the embarrassment goes,' Belle sighed. 'I got to know too much about men. I tried to wipe it all from my mind when I got back from Paris, but I didn't succeed.'

'I often wonder how it will be for me when and if I meet another man I really like,' said Miranda. 'I tell myself I'll never do that again, not until I'm married, but I wonder if I'll be strong enough.'

Belle looked at her friend appraisingly. She guessed that what she really meant was that she thought about making love often, and missed it. All the other women Belle had met of a similar age and background were prim and strait-laced, but she thought Miranda had been born with a wanton streak. The more she'd got to know her, the more she felt Miranda was unlikely ever to conform to the strict rules society laid down for young women. Perhaps it was just that similarity between them which had made them become such close friends.

'Then just make sure you fall for a man who is worthy of you,' Belle said warningly. 'You don't want to go through all that pain and heartache again. The war might be opening things up a bit more for women, with more choices and opportunities, but some things will remain the same.'

'I know,' Miranda sighed. 'My mother for one. She is such a crashing snob. I expect she thinks officers' shit doesn't smell as bad as enlisted men's.'

Belle laughed. 'If you really hate it at the hospital, give up. I bet you could get a job driving someone about. There must be people whose chauffeur has joined up. You could put an advertisement in the paper.'

Miranda pulled a face. 'I need to do this, Belle. I want to be able to prove to myself and the family that I can stick at something, be useful and independent. Sister Crooke told me yesterday that she thought I wouldn't even finish the first day. She isn't the kind to praise anyone but I think she was trying to say I had surprised her and I was doing all right. That must mean something.'

Belle lifted her tea cup and clinked it against Miranda's. 'To France,' she said.

'To France,' Miranda said. 'Do you really think we'll get there?'

'You can do anything if you're determined enough,' Belle replied. 'And I'm going to prove it by riding your bicycle home.'

Belle rode confidently all the way back to the church on the heath and then waited for Miranda to catch up with her.

'Well done,' Miranda said. 'I was just thinking that if that Blessard creature should try and contact you again, at least once you've got a bicycle you can ride off in a hurry.'

'I'm hoping he'll give up now the shop is closed down,' Belle said. 'He's so creepy, I really don't know what it is he wants from me. It doesn't seem to be just a story for his newspaper.'

'I think it's you he wants,' Miranda said. 'He knows enough about you to be stimulated by your past. I'd say he is aroused by that.'

'Oh, don't say that, it reminds me of the way that man in Paris was about me,' Belle said in some alarm.

'He'll be a lot less stimulated by you if he spots you in your uniform.' Miranda grimaced and then laughed. 'Go on home and don't worry about him, he's just an idiot. Good luck in talking Garth into getting a bicycle for you.'

As Belle walked down Tranquil Vale she couldn't help but think about Blessard.

After Newbold's trial she was never alone in the shop, and as time passed she almost forgot him. But one day when Miranda had just popped out to the stationer's he walked in, giving her a real shock. It seemed to Belle he must have been watching the shop and seized the opportunity when she was alone.

But she didn't let her alarm show. He said that he'd just dropped by to ask if he could interview her for an article he was writing about different ways the police identified criminals. His interest in her was that she had drawn a sketch of her attacker.

She just said that she was sorry, but she didn't wish to be interviewed, not then or at any time in the future. Fortunately the telephone rang at just the right moment, so she showed him out.

Because he went so easily, it seemed to her then that she might have been mistaken about his intentions. But two weeks later he turned up again, on the one day when she had opened the shop to give Miranda a break.

He was far more pushy this time, sitting down uninvited and being far too personal, calling her Belle as if he was an old friend.

'It's Mrs Reilly,' she reproved him. 'On your last visit I told you that I didn't wish to be interviewed. Now, if you'll excuse me, I have a lot of work to do, and a gentleman sitting in the shop is off-putting to my lady customers.'

He got up and went towards the door. When he turned she thought he was going to apologize. But she was mistaken.

'You wouldn't have been so hoity-toity when you were over in Paris,' he said. 'I know a great deal about you, Belle, it would pay you to remember that.'

'It would pay you to remember that I am not intimidated easily,' she said. 'If you call here again I will call the police and tell them you are harassing me.'

But after he'd gone she had to go into the back room and sit down because she was so shaken.

During Kent's murder trial it had been raised that she was taken by him to Paris and sold to a brothel. However, Belle was sure Blessard wasn't referring to that time, but to the period two years later when she returned to Paris and worked as a prostitute. She couldn't imagine how he had managed to find that out when her friends in Paris had succeeded in concealing it from the gendarmes. But she knew from Noah that reporters with a hunger for a big scoop could and did dig and dig until they found what they were looking for.

Blessard hadn't been back since that day, but she had made sure she was never again alone in the shop. Garth had said he'd wring the man's neck if he came to the Railway. Yet Miranda's remark about him being stimulated by her past niggled at Belle. She knew what it was to have men becoming obsessive about her. However, as Miranda had pointed out, now she could ride a bicycle she could whizz past him if he tried to waylay her.

Chapter Eleven
1916

Etienne leaned back against a tree stump, lit a cigarette, closed his eyes and savoured the warm May sun on his face. It was so good to have a few days away from the front line at Verdun, to be able to sleep, eat, and mend his tattered uniform and his frayed spirits. The stench of dead bodies lying in No Man's Land had become ever more sickening since the weather grew warmer, men were going down with dysentery, supplies of drinking water got held up, often they had no time during the endless assaults even to eat their rations.

For now all he wanted was to imagine he was at home on his small farm near Marseille, but the constant sound of gunfire in the distance prevented that.

He had first come to Verdun when he was twenty. It had been a jewel of a place then. The medieval city with its narrow, winding streets had enchanted him, and when he stood on the old city walls and looked down, there was the sparkling River Meuse meandering through fertile green pastures and woods. When he saw the ring of stone forts on the surrounding hills, twenty small ones and four big ones, the history lessons he'd had as a small boy came back to him. It was the last place to fall in the Franco-Prussian war, and had held out for ten long weeks before surrendering.

Because of its history and the courage of the people who fought so savagely to keep it in French hands, it held a special place in the heart of every Frenchman. This of course was exactly why the Germans wanted to take it. They knew the French generals would send every man they could to defend the city, and then with their formidable army and firepower they could bleed France dry, thereby knocking Britain's 'Best Sword' out of its hand.

Those green pastures he remembered were now barren wasteland, peppered with bomb craters, the trees uprooted by enemy fire or cut down for fires and trench props. No birds sang there, and whether that was because of lack of trees for cover, the sound of guns, or soil that must be soaked in soldiers' blood, he didn't know. But if he had been a bird he wouldn't want to stay in such a sorry place either.

Dotted all around him were other French soldiers, doing exactly the same as he was, savouring a few days' rest and respite from the front. Back behind him in what once had been a small village, still more men were getting a meal and a few drinks at an *estaminet*, a simple café with rough wooden tables and benches.

There was also the sound of splashing and raucous laughter coming from somewhere close by. Whether it was at a pond, stream or merely a crater full of rainwater, he didn't know, but he thought he might go and join them in a while. The opportunity to strip off his filthy clothes and wash all over was not to be missed.

When Etienne had marched here as a raw recruit back in October 1914, it was believed Verdun was invincible, as it was virtually surrounded by hills and ridges on both banks of the Meuse and guarded by rings of forts, Fort Douaumont being the strongest and most dominating. And so it seemed right up to the New Year of 1916, as they had held their ground despite heavy bombardment from the enemy. Fort Douaumont could and should have held fast, but General Joffre in his wisdom removed most of the guns to use them elsewhere on the front.

Etienne still winced with horror when he thought back to

dawn on 21 February, when the Germans attacked again, this time with unbelievable force. It transpired they had been secretly bringing in men and heavy guns for some time, but their reconnaissance planes had intercepted any English or French aircraft that might have reported back on the intense activity.

Along the entire eight-mile front, fire rained down on the French, uprooting trees, tossing them into the air, and killing and wounding many thousands of men. The German guns destroyed French communication lines and effectively blocked reinforcements coming in.

Etienne was one of Lieutenant-Colonel Driant's Chasseurs, and under his command they offered stubborn resistance, but it was to no avail. Gallant Driant was killed later that afternoon as he was attempting to pull back to Beaumont with the remnants of his battalion. A substantial part of the front line had caved in, and the French losses were horrific, but Etienne felt they had managed to give the enemy a bloody nose as their casualties were very high too, especially amongst their valuable storm troops.

On 24 February Samongneux fell to the Germans before dawn. The 51st and the 72nd Divisions lost two thirds of their men and were at breaking point. Beaumont was next, and the Moroccan Trailleurs and Algerian Zouaves who had only recently arrived were fed piecemeal into the battle without any prepared defences against either the bitter cold or the relentless German bombardment, and soon Fort Douaumont fell too.

Every Frenchman here could appreciate that the fall of Fort Douaumont would send shock waves all over France, not only because it was a source of national pride, but because it left the way clear for the enemy to take the city of Verdun.

Yet abandonment of the city so dear to France was unthinkable, and it was General Pétain who prevented it. Maybe this hard-headed man would have opted for controlled withdrawal if he had had the choice, but knowing he had not, he became set on defence. Pétain had two priceless qualities: a real grasp of the nature of modern firepower, and command of the respect and trust of front-line soldiers.

Etienne remembered how his appearance at Verdun had immediately restored confidence and boosted morale. He played the Germans at their own game by ordering his artillery to inflict the maximum casualties on them. As the rail links to Verdun had already been severed, he took care to ensure supplies were brought in on a single-track road, which had now become known as the Voie Sacrée, or Sacred Way. Daily this road was one constant stream of vehicles bringing in reinforcements and supplies.

Yet even before Pétain had made a real impact on the battlefield, it seemed that the Germans were running out of steam. Etienne, like so many others, relished watching their struggle to haul their guns forward over shell-cratered ground, and enjoyed even more gunning them down remorselessly.

The battles had raged on and on, both sides never getting a moment's respite from awesome artillery fire. Each enemy attack was followed by a French counter-attack, and by the end of March it was said that the German casualties were almost as high as their own. But 88,000 French casualties were far too many.

Now, in May, things were looking even worse, for General Pétain had been promoted and General Nivelle had taken over command, with General Mangin as divisional commander. Mangin was said to be one of the old school officers, all for attack without regard for the cost to his men. Already he had been dubbed 'The Butcher', or 'The Eater of Men', and Etienne could only see more misery ahead.

He had lost every single friend he'd made when he first joined the army. As he was moved along the line, new soldiers had taken their place and become friends, but he had lost most of them too. Now he was reluctant to get to know anything personal about the men he fought with. In quiet times he would play cards and drink and joke with them, but he knew that if he got to know about their wives, children, family background, what they believed in, what their dreams were, their deaths would hurt far more.

Each day he was in the front line he knew that it might be his last, and his only prayer was that he should be killed outright. He knew he couldn't live the rest of his life with the terrible injuries he'd seen inflicted on other men.

Sometimes he asked himself why his luck had held out this long. Was it because he'd learned survival skills at an early age? Or because he was quick, decisive and fearless, as Capitaine Beaudin had said when he promoted him to Caporal back in January? He'd also stated at the time that he was a fine soldier, a born leader and an asset to the regiment. Etienne had smiled to himself, wondering whether the Capitaine would have put so much faith in him if he knew how he'd once lived.

Etienne was roused from the reverie he'd sunk into by the sound of raised voices and got up to look back towards the village *estaminet*. He could see a truck and four men in English army khaki, in the midst of a bunch of French soldiers. Even from a distance of some 500 yards he could tell by the Englishmen's demeanour that this was a situation which could turn into a fight.

Relatively few English soldiers came this way, as they were busy defending the front line up around Ypres. Etienne thought they must be asking for directions to wherever they were bound for, but as the French soldiers were probably drunk, and few, if any of them, would be able to speak English, they had probably resorted to baiting them.

Etienne didn't want to see any bloodshed, so he felt he must intervene.

As he got closer and could hear what was being said, he knew he was right about the situation. The Tommies were trying to get directions to the French army headquarters, and the French clearly did understand that much, but because they were so drunk they were enjoying being deliberately obstructive and making insulting remarks.

Etienne was around a hundred yards from the *estaminet* when one of the Tommies strode up to the most vocal of the French soldiers and caught hold of his shoulders. It was clear he was about to punch him.

'Don't hit him, he's just a drunken idiot,' Etienne called out. 'I can help you.'

The English looked round in surprise. Etienne addressed the French soldiers then, saying they should be ashamed of themselves for not helping their Allies, at which they all shuffled back off into the *estaminet*.

'Can I buy you all a drink?' Etienne asked the English soldiers. 'I'd like to make amends for my countrymen's rudeness. I can give you directions and draw you a map.'

The four men looked at one another, then the small, dark-haired corporal thanked him and said they'd like that.

As the men weren't keen to go inside with the men who had been insulting them, they sat down on the ground outside and Etienne bought a bottle of wine and shared it with them.

'No beer here,' he said as he handed round the glasses. 'And the wine isn't too good either.'

He asked them where they were from, and explained roughly where the French headquarters was.

The men referred to the short, wiry corporal as 'Corp'. A fair-haired lad of no more than nineteen was called 'Donkey', for reasons Etienne could only guess at, and the big man who had been about to punch the French soldier was nicknamed 'Bin'. The fourth man, whom they called 'Red' on account of his red hair, laughingly told him Bin had got his name because he'd always 'Bin' everywhere.

As Etienne made a sketch of the route they needed to take, they asked him a few questions about Verdun, and how long he'd been at the front. In his reply he told them something of the horrors there. They had their own horror stories of Ypres too, but said that lately it had been fairly quiet, and they spent most days improving the conditions in the trenches.

'You speak bloody good English,' Red remarked. 'Have you lived in England?'

'I did once for nearly two years,' Etienne replied. 'I was in London, and you are from there too, aren't you? I recognize the accent.'

'I thought us Tommies all sounded the same to you Frenchies?'

'Not once you get your ear in. If you lived in France for a while, you'd get to know the difference between someone from Paris and someone from the south,' he said, looking hard at the Londoner. He seemed familiar, but Etienne couldn't think why. He didn't think he'd ever spoken to a red-headed Englishman, not here or anywhere else.

'How are your lot holding up?' the corporal asked. 'We heard it's been a massacre, over eighty thousand dead.'

'So it has been said, perhaps even more,' Etienne sighed. 'But then the Boche have lost almost as many. What are you going to French headquarters for?'

He noted the way they all exchanged glances.

'You don't have to tell me just because I bought you a drink,' he said. 'Only curious.'

'Actually we're picking up a couple of our men,' Red said. 'It's not clear whether they deserted or just got lost. Your lot picked them up.'

'But you're not Red Caps, are you?' Etienne despised military police and if he'd known these men were that he wouldn't have bothered to help them.

'Hell, no. This isn't an official trip. Our captain's a good man, and these two that went missing are old hands and good soldiers. We all thought they were on the wire when they didn't get back after going over the top; we lost so many that night and some of the bodies just got buried in the mud. But then Captain got the message they'd been picked up and he remembered that there'd been thick fog on the night in question. It's easy to lose all sense of direction in that. So he felt they should be brought back for him to question. If he'd sent the Red Caps after them they wouldn't have a prayer.'

Etienne raised one eyebrow. He'd never before heard of any officer, French or English, giving anyone the benefit of the doubt where desertion was concerned. He'd been told French soldiers were shot as they ran away at Ypres, but they weren't deserting, just trying to escape poison gas. 'Then they are very lucky,' he said.

'I don't think deserters, whether intentional or accidental, should be shot,' the red-headed man said heatedly. 'It's a waste of life. If they're windy, they should be given jobs as base rats – they need men there just as badly as in the trenches.'

'Our Little Red Reilly would stick up for the rights of a rat if it was about to bite him in the balls,' the corporal said with a wry grin. 'Good job we know he's not a windy bastard.'

The name Reilly gave Etienne a jolt. All four Tommies laughed, but he could only stare at Red in astonishment.

It couldn't be Jimmy, surely? Not just because he was a Londoner, called Reilly and had red hair. It was too much of an outlandish coincidence. Besides, Belle's Jimmy was a publican, he wouldn't have enlisted, not until it was compulsory. And even if he had, was it likely that fate would bring two men who loved the same woman together at a wayside *estaminet* in France?

He had only seen Jimmy once, that day he went to Blackheath, and fleetingly and from a distance. All he really remembered about the man was that he was tall and had red hair; he hadn't got a good look at his face. As for thinking he looked familiar, it could be that his mind was playing tricks on him and all these months of hell were finally making him crack. Reilly was a common enough English name; there must be hundreds in London alone.

'What's up, mate? You look like you've seen a ghost!'

Etienne was jolted again by the corporal's remark and forced a smile. 'Just thinking how I'd react if a rat bit my balls,' he said.

Conversation resumed about the poison gas attacks. 'We was lucky we'd been stood down that day,' Bin said. 'Their faces went black, they was coming out of the trenches tearing at their throats, 'orrible it was.'

The corporal spoke of how they were told to cover their mouths and noses with a cloth soaked in water or their own urine, and said their captain had told them that the men who had died from it had actually drowned from the foam in their lungs.

'You had any of it here?' he asked.

Etienne was just about to say that he hadn't experienced it himself, but he'd heard a great deal about it from men who had, when the corporal's attention was diverted by the sight of a man just inside the door of the *estaminet* with a plate of food.

'They've got egg and chips,' he exclaimed. 'Gotta have some of that!'

The corporal leapt to his feet, quickly followed by Bin and Donkey. Red asked them to get some for him too, and stayed with Etienne.

Being suddenly alone with Red seemed the perfect time for Etienne to scotch his daft idea.

'Were you called Red back home, or did you get the name here?' he asked.

The man grinned. 'At Etaples the drill sergeant called me carrot head. Once he saw I could shoot straight it became Red. It stuck with the other blokes, but my name is really James, known always as Jimmy.'

Etienne felt a chill run down his spine and his mouth went dry. 'What did you do before enlisting?' he managed to ask.

'Ran a public house with my uncle,' Jimmy said. 'Mostly I think I must've had a screw loose to join up. My wife was expecting, and I was still at Etaples when I got the news she'd lost the baby. I got sent home because she was so ill, and I can tell you, I was tempted not to come back.'

'Is that why you are sympathetic to deserters?'

'Maybe. Belle was in a bad way, she'd been attacked and robbed in the shop she ran, and I felt I shouldn't have left her when I did. But she pulled through, even went back to her shop for a while. But she's given that up now and she's doing voluntary work at the Military Hospital.'

Etienne wished he'd stayed sitting against the tree stump and hadn't intervened with these men. That way he could have gone on believing that Belle was living the kind of happy life she deserved.

'Nursing?'

'Well, she's the ward dogsbody, but she's made of the right stuff to nurse. She's got the crazy idea that if she gets some experience at the hospital, she can join the Red Cross after a bit and come out here and drive an ambulance.'

'That's no job for a woman,' Etienne said. He'd only seen a couple of female ambulance drivers, and they'd been hatchet-faced women with nerves of steel. 'It's dangerous, they often come in quite close to the front line. Don't let her do it.'

Jimmy grimaced. 'If my Belle gets an idea into her head, there's no shaking it,' he said. 'But the hospital is so busy now with wounded, they depend on her, so I'm hoping she's given up the idea. She hasn't mentioned it in her letters for a long while now.'

Etienne's whole being wanted to say he was aware how stubborn and hot-headed Belle was, but he knew he must not. If he admitted who he was, he might also reveal his feelings for her by accident. He couldn't let the man go back to the battlefield with that on his mind.

'I must go now, I'm due back,' he said, getting to his feet. 'It was good to meet you. Keep your head down, and keep that wife of yours safe at home for when you get back.'

'I'm very glad we met you,' Jimmy said, getting up too and shaking Etienne's hand. 'You keep safe too. And thanks for the wine and the directions.'

Etienne walked away swiftly. He heard Jimmy call out that he hadn't told him his name, but he pretended he hadn't heard and kept on going.

'Where's the French bloke gone?' the corporal asked Red as he came out with two plates of egg and chips. 'I got him some too.'

172

'He had to go back,' Red replied. 'Shame, he was a good sort. I meant to ask him for a few phrases to help when we get to the French HQ.'

'Looked like a tough bastard,' Bin remarked as he came out, also carrying two plates of food. 'Did you see his cold eyes? No wonder the Frenchies backed off when he shouted at them. Before we got 'ere I thought the French were a load of nancy boys.'

'Why? Had you "Bin" with one?' Donkey asked teasingly and all the men roared with laughter.

'I'll have the Frog's chips then,' Bin responded. 'And you lot can whistle for a share-out.'

As Etienne walked back to the camp he felt shaky. He'd managed to put Belle to the back of his mind after he left England in 1914, but today's events had brought her right back into the front of it.

He might have spent less than half an hour with Jimmy, but that was long enough to see what he was. It might have been satisfying to find he was a dull weakling. But he was a strong, principled and forthright man, with that quiet steadiness which made a first-class soldier and the best kind of friend.

Would Belle come out here? Most women, he thought, would be far too scared even to consider going to a country in the grip of war, but Belle had more courage than was good for her. She was also single-minded when she wanted something, whether that was escaping from Martha's in New Orleans, or getting her own hat shop.

Chapter Twelve
1 July 1916

'That's a bleedin' lark!' Donkey remarked, looking upwards at the clear blue sky, trying to spot the singing bird as he drank his rum ration. ''Ere, Red, reckon that's a good omen, or is 'e just 'appy that the guns have stopped at last?'

It was seven thirty in the morning, already very warm, and after five days of constant and deafening bombardment of the enemy lines the guns had suddenly cut off. Now it was eerily quiet apart from the birdsong. Even the German guns had fallen silent.

Jimmy and his regiment had marched here to the Somme from Ypres two weeks earlier to join what had looked like the whole British army camped out for miles behind the lines. As always, no one had seen fit to tell them why this part of the Western Front was important to the generals. They had just been told that there were no major roads or rail centres close behind the German lines, and up till now it had been a quiet sector. Yet whatever the reasons for this being chosen for a major push, the men's first reaction was mainly delight, as it wasn't marshy ground like Ypres. Chalky soil meant trenches wouldn't get flooded, and it was pretty, verdant farmland with the river Somme meandering through it.

Only yesterday Jimmy finally learned that this battle was to draw the Germans away from Verdun and ease the pressure on the French army still fighting there. His captain had said that the five-day bombardment had smashed the enemy's barbed wire defences and wiped out all the men and guns in the first line. Now as they waited for the whistle to signal the first wave of men to go over the top, they all believed it would be like a walk in the park across No Man's Land, and the fighting would only start once they reached the second line.

'The lark is a good omen,' Jimmy said, gulping his rum ration down in one. He wasn't entirely convinced it was going to be as easy as everyone thought. But it was good to have the heavy guns silenced, and to enjoy the warm sunshine.

The peace was short-lived. All at once the British guns started up again, this time trained on the enemy's second line of defence. At the signal the soldiers who were lying in position out on No Man's Land rose up and set off with their officers at a steady, well-rehearsed pace towards the enemy.

Then it was time for the first wave of men to go over the top. Jimmy and his chums were in the second wave, and they held back, watching the officers running along the parapet shouting encouragement and leaning in to give a hand to over-burdened men laden with full packs on their backs to pull them up and over. From Jimmy's position he couldn't see what was happening elsewhere on the line, but he knew it would be identical to here. Once down on the other side there was their own barbed wire to go through, but sections had been cut the previous night, or duckboards would make a bridge over it.

'Us next,' Bin said cheerfully, stamping out his cigarette almost gleefully. 'By God, I'm ready for this.'

It was then they heard enemy machine-gun fire. Not just a few guns, but hundreds of them, all firing at once. Bin's grin vanished and Donkey turned to Jimmy with a look that said, 'I thought we'd knocked them out.'

'It sounds worse than it is,' Jimmy said, but his insides were turning to water as he stepped forward and urged the others to do the same and take their places ready for their turn to go over.

The waiting, vision obscured by the high trench walls, was the worst. The sound of machine-gun fire ringing in their ears, the weight of their heavy packs on their shoulders and the sick feeling they might not even make it across to No Man's Land was terrible. Men who had been laughing a short while ago were now pale and twitchy, and Jimmy saw one young lad vomiting further along the trench.

But all too quickly the order came. As they reached the parapet Jimmy saw the enemy front line was fully manned, and the Germans were focusing some of their guns on the gaps in the British barbed wire. It was like shooting fish in a barrel. Men were lying dead on the wire with their comrades being forced to climb over them.

Yet further ahead was even worse. Jimmy thought more than half of that first wave were already dead or lying wounded on the ground and in the second before he too jumped down he saw still more of the remainder fall.

He got through the wire, waited a second to regroup as they'd been instructed, and with Donkey to his right and Bin to his left set off at a purposeful plod into a rain of bullets.

Donkey was hit within ten yards. His body jerked forward as if he'd got an electric shock, then fell back motionless. Just one glance told Jimmy he was dead; he'd been hit in the chest and blood was pouring out of a gaping hole.

'Come on, Red,' Bin urged him when he hesitated. 'You can't do anything for him. We'll make it.'

On they went through the enemy fire. Jimmy offered up a silent prayer for his own safety as he saw more men he knew well stagger and fall all around him. The smoke, the rapid rat-a-tat-tat of gunfire and the screams of the wounded were terrifying, but he couldn't falter, they had to reach the enemy lines at all cost.

A sudden searing pain in his upper right arm alerted

Jimmy that he too had been hit. He looked down in horror and saw blood pumping out. He went on, but his arm felt as if it was on fire, the pain so bad he was lurching from side to side. He could barely hold his rifle – firing it would be impossible.

'I've been hit, Bin,' he yelled. 'Go on, hold your nerve and join the others.'

Bin turned his head, hesitating for just a second, but then, signalling with his hand, went on. Jimmy took a few more steps, then, seeing a shell hole, dropped into it.

He must have passed out. When he came to, there were two other men from his regiment in there as well, both groaning with pain. Jimmy still had his pack on his back, and wincing from the pain in his arm, he gingerly took it off. It was very hot, though still early in the morning. He knew by the men rushing past above him, all intent on reaching the German lines, that he could expect no rescue until sunset. He looked up at the sides of the hole and realized he wouldn't be able to climb out of it unaided.

Loss of blood was making him feel light-headed. Or maybe that was just the rum he'd had such a short while ago.

'How bad are you two hurt?' he asked the other men. 'Can I do anything to help?'

It was the longest, most painful and worst day of his life, and since joining the army he'd had plenty of bad ones. He took off his tunic and put a dressing over his wound in an attempt to keep infection out, and did what he could for the other two men, but they both had serious chest wounds and passed out by eleven in the morning. He tried to eke out the water he was carrying, but it was so hot his thirst got the better of him.

All he could see from the hole was the blue, cloudless sky above him, and a never-ending stream of soldiers rushing by. Machine-gun fire rattled out just as endlessly and remorselessly, and above it he heard screams and the moaning of men dying just a few yards from his hole. By the time the sun was directly overhead burning down on him, he had no water left and the pain in his arm made him want to scream too.

He tried to think of Belle, and imagine the coolness of the kitchen back home. But although he could hold those images for a second or two, the noise and carnage all around him soon brought him back to reality.

A rat appeared, running over one of the unconscious men, and Jimmy shuddered and threw a stone at it to chase it away. The rat disappeared, but it was obvious that it and others would soon be back, attracted by the smell of blood. He tried to stand up then, with the intention of trying to get out and get back to the line. But whether it was the vast number of bodies he could see all around his shell hole, his wound or just the heat, his legs gave way under him and he had no choice but to slump back down. He checked on both the other men and found they were dead.

It was anger he felt then. How could the generals send so many men to certain death? If what he'd seen from his hole was happening all along the length of the line, then surely half the British army must be wiped out.

Dusk was falling when they finally got him out. He must have been unconscious for most of the afternoon. As they held a water bottle to his lips he could barely swallow as his tongue and the whole of his face was swollen.

Belle got a note from Jimmy telling her he had been wounded a week after it had happened.

'I got shot in the upper arm, but don't worry, it isn't a really bad wound. They've patched me up and they'll be sending me home on leave soon. I'm one of the lucky ones, my pal Donkey bought it, and so many more men I liked. But I expect you've heard how many casualties there were on 1 July.'

Belle did know. The first of them began trickling into the Herbert by 4 July and by the next day it was a flood of wounded. An officer on Miranda's ward had said he thought there were over 18,000 killed and 30,000 wounded just on the first day of the battle of the Somme. Belle didn't know then that Jimmy was in the battle, but she was afraid he might be as he'd written a while ago to say he was on a march to a new place. So each day until she got his letter she had been bracing herself for the dreaded telegram.

She was joyful he was only wounded, but at the same time she was afraid. Many of the wounded men she saw were withdrawn and had terrible nightmares. From things they said, often just in passing, she knew that they'd seen hell that day in France.

Jimmy returned home the last week in July. His arm was in a sling and the skin on his face was peeling, but his smile was as bright as ever.

'Don't fuss,' he said when she rushed around trying to make him comfortable, offering to cut up his food and undress him. 'I'm fine. Never been so pleased to see you and home. But I'm fit to fight another day.'

He had been lucky, compared with so many men at the Herbert. The wound had remained clean and it was healing well. He pointed out that the sling was only to prevent him straining his wound; all his fingers worked, which he demonstrated by playing a little tune on the piano in the bar. 'I think I'll keep the sling on for other people though,' he said with a smirk. 'I quite like being treated as a hero.'

It was twenty months since he'd enlisted, and he made love to Belle that first night home as if he thought he'd never have the chance again. 'This was worth getting wounded for,' he said at one point. 'I couldn't think of anything else while I was in hospital; the nurses kept asking me what I was smiling about.'

He admitted a day or two later that he was so relieved they'd given him a Blighty ticket. He hadn't expected to get one; wounds like his were usually patched up over there, and then it was back to the front. He said he thought his CO had intervened on his behalf.

Yet however lovely it was to have him home, knowing he'd got to go back to the front frightened Belle. She couldn't take the view that he did, that this wound was his lot and he'd be safe from now on. Each time she bathed and dressed his arm wound she couldn't help but think what it must be like for wives who got a telegram to say their husband was dead.

Even in the sweetness of their lovemaking, her mind flitted between dreading his leaving again and guilt that she'd managed so well without him all this time.

Mog boasting to Jimmy how they valued Belle at the hospital, and Garth saying how much he and Mog depended on her, made her sound like a paragon of virtue. It was difficult to believe Mog had once been so against both the work and Miranda, and changed her tune about both, even encouraging Belle to spend her off-duty days with her friend. Just a few weeks earlier they had ridden their bicycles out into the countryside beyond Eltham, and on many evenings they went to concerts and the theatre together.

Now Jimmy had come home after such a close shave, Belle felt torn between being the perfect stay-at-home wife and pursuing her own dream. She still really wanted to go to France with Miranda. They had applied to drive ambulances twice, and been turned down. Miranda was sure it was only because they weren't considered experienced enough yet, and insisted they had to try again.

The weather was good, and Belle managed to get a couple of days off so that she and Jimmy could spend some time together. They took a picnic to Greenwich Park and sat under a tree and talked. Jimmy told her about his army friends, about the conditions he'd fought under, and groused about the generals, who he felt were mainly stupid and ill-equipped to lead men. 'That five-day bombardment at the Somme was a waste of time and effort,' he said with some anger. 'Half the shells were duds as it turned out, and those that weren't didn't smash the barbed wire at all, or send the Boche running back to their second lot of trenches. One man I saw in hospital was stuck on the wire for hours; he was shot in four different places during the day and torn to pieces, and he was one of hundreds. Our men found out afterwards that the Boche had really dug themselves in there too. They had safe concrete shelters and far better and bigger guns than us. We didn't stand a chance.'

As the days passed Belle realized Jimmy was a little ashamed that he'd gone into the shell hole and stayed there all day. He had no reason to feel that way; she could see by the wound that he could never have fired his gun, and would probably have passed out through loss of blood anyway, which meant he might have been hit again, fatally. She told him this, then drew him away from the subject by describing the many strikes around the country, the rising cost of living and the shortages of food.

She was a little ashamed of herself too for not telling him she still wanted to go to France, and that Miranda was giving her driving lessons whenever she could borrow her uncle's car. But Belle reasoned with herself that they might never get accepted anyway. Besides, the war might be over soon, even though Jimmy thought not. She was relieved he had not been badly hurt and she wanted him to go back to France remembering the park in summer, their lovemaking, good meals and laughter. Not a wife who always seemed to have something else up her sleeve.

Chapter Thirteen
1917

Belle reached the bicycle shed and before pulling the cycle out, she hitched up the skirt of her uniform dress a couple of inches and tightened her belt to secure it.

It was a mild April evening, and after a long day in a stuffy, somewhat gloomy ward it was good to be out in the fresh air. The ride home over the heath always invigorated her and she was looking forward to it.

But as she pulled her bicycle out, she saw that yet again both tyres were flat. There was no point in trying to pump them up; like all the other times this had happened, she knew it had been done intentionally. As she spun the wheels round, sure enough, there was a flat-headed tack in both of them.

Belle was adept now at mending punctures, in fact since learning to ride she had become expert at all kinds of repairs. But not here – she would have to walk home with the bicycle and fix it there.

As she began walking, pushing her bicycle, several nurses, other volunteers and orderlies on their way home or just arriving for the night shift waved or said goodnight. She had become quite well known at the Herbert and had made many friends. She was going to miss them when she left for France with Miranda in two weeks' time.

This business with the flat tyres was one thing she wasn't going to miss though. Everyone else thought it was a stupid and random practical joke. But Belle wasn't so sure about that; it felt as if she was being maliciously singled out.

There was no regularity to it. Sometimes it would be once

in a fortnight, then nothing for weeks, and once there was a gap of three months, long enough for her to think whoever was doing it had grown tired of it.

But the culprit always came back. She had tried leaving her bicycle somewhere else, risking a telling off for doing so, but it still happened. Sister Adams had suggested it was done out of jealousy, because she was pretty and popular with staff and patients alike. Everyone agreed it must be someone who worked at the hospital.

The last year had been exacting for everyone in England. At the start of the war there was excitement and patriotic fervour to carry people along. But when it didn't end as quickly as everyone had believed it would, and the casualty lists grew ever longer, along with the terror induced by air raids, and shortages of food, weariness and doubt had set in.

The war had brought some changes that Belle welcomed. Young women had gained more freedom, taking on jobs which just five years earlier would have been unthinkable for a woman. There were female bus conductresses and taxi drivers, postwomen, and women working in munitions factories and farming. Chaperones had become a thing of the past; as with so many young men off in France they were deemed unnecessary.

Yet Belle often smiled at angry letters written to the newspapers by staid matrons about the breaking down of morality. They claimed that young women were behaving recklessly, going out dancing, walking out after dark with men in uniform and drinking in public houses. All this was true, and Belle thought it was totally understandable that the young should seize the moment when they believed that death could strike at any time.

The last year had been good for her, though, apart from missing and worrying about Jimmy. The melancholy which followed the loss of her baby had gone, leaving just sadness which she knew she must live with. She had her close friendship with Miranda, and Mog and Garth not only accepted her work at the hospital now but were proud of her. Sometimes Mog said she hoped when the war was over that Belle would go back to millinery, but agreed that she had been right to volunteer at the hospital.

It was very hard work, with no let-up from the moment she got to the ward in the morning until she left at six. There was a constant stream of wounded every day, though never again as many as there had been after the battle of the Somme last July.

In the last year Belle had seen injuries so appalling that she could not believe the human body could withstand so much – loss of sight, arms and legs blown off, hideous burns and abdominal wounds. She hated the facial and head wounds most. People treated men on crutches or in a wheelchair as heroes, heaping admiration and respect on them. But those who were terribly disfigured found people averted their eyes from them, and even some of their own families found it difficult to deal with.

It was the colossal numbers of casualties in 1916 which had finally made it possible for Miranda and Belle to be accepted as ambulance drivers. The hellish battles at Verdun had resulted in 87,000 French casualties, and the battle of the Somme, which continued until November, chalked up over 400,000 among the Allies, finally changing the outlook of the Red Cross. On top of this many American ambulance drivers had left to join the army, as at long last America had agreed to come in on the Allies' side. With German submarines attacking shipping mercilessly from February and just recently the battle in Arras commencing, creating even higher casualties, the authorities were glad of any help they could get.

Both girls had glowing references from ward sisters and Matron, plus they could drive. But Belle thought what had really tipped the balance in their favour was that they both spoke a little French, and kept coming back to apply, showing determination.

Matron, who rarely praised even highly experienced nurses, let alone lowly volunteers, had surprised Belle. 'I thought at first that you were a foolish, giddy young woman,' she said, fixing her sharp eyes that missed nothing on Belle. 'But you have proved yourself to be reliable, conscientious and steady. Had you not been married, I would have asked you to train as a nurse. I don't wish to lose your help here, but I know that the quicker wounded men can be got from the dressing stations to hospitals, the more likely they are to survive. I shall be stating to the Red Cross that I believe you have the necessary resourcefulness and pluck, and that you have had enough experience here to be suitable for the task.'

Belle was excited to be going, but scared too. She and Miranda had talked about it for such a long time, but now it was really going to happen, they both had doubts about their abilities. It was one thing changing dressings under Sister's watchful eye, quite another to be responsible for getting badly wounded men in terrible pain to the safety of a hospital. They were worried they might get lost, that the ambulance might break down, and that they might not be able to stay calm in an emergency.

But Belle wasn't thinking about what might happen to her in France as she walked home pushing her bicycle; her thoughts were with Jimmy. He was lucky to have got off so lightly with his wound when so many of his regiment had died on that first day at the Somme, and she would never forget how passionately he'd spoken of what he called 'the butchery' there. Yet for all his insistence that his wound was nothing and he was fine, during that time he'd spent at home she'd fleetingly seen the same haunted look in his eyes shared by so many of the wounded at the hospital.

On his final day before returning to France he'd suddenly blurted out how the Germans had used liquid fire against them at Ypres. He described how suddenly all along the trenches to his right there was a wall of fire bursting up into the night sky, and he heard the men screaming and the smell of roasting flesh as they tried to climb out of the trenches and get away. The fire didn't reach to where he was, but that night around fifty men he knew well died, and many more who did survive would live the rest of their lives with pain and terrible scarring.

He was one of the men sent to remove the bodies for burial. He said some of them were still stuck like crabs to the wall of the trench, caught by the flames while trying to climb out. Others had fallen back on to the bodies of other men, all of them black and charred, their uniforms burned to ash. He had vomited at the sight, and couldn't eat anything for several days afterwards.

Almost immediately he apologized for burdening Belle with those images. She told him it was better to talk about it than keep it inside him, but it was obvious to her he felt really bad about divulging it. Perhaps he thought real men must keep such memories to themselves.

Since he'd gone back his letters were brief but cheerful, telling her funny little anecdotes about other soldiers. There were the ones who were good at scavenging, who would disappear for a while and come back with a bottle of brandy, or a rabbit they'd trapped. Some wrote poetry or could sing, some made everyone laugh, and others could tell a good tale. Anyone else reading his letters would think he was at a Scouts' camp, sitting around all day telling jokes. But Belle had grown adept at reading between the lines. She knew he was afraid most of the time he was sent up to the front line, but he felt his fate was preordained and there was nothing he could do to change it.

Belle knew too that once she was driving an ambulance she would be experiencing sights as bad as any of those Jimmy had seen. The wounded brought into the Herbert had been cleaned up and had their wounds dressed. She hoped she would be able to deal with far worse horrors without falling apart.

'Hello Belle, got a puncture?'

Belle jumped at the man's voice behind her, and even without looking round she knew it was Blessard. In that instant her instinct told her he was responsible for the punctures and had been lying in wait for her to come past, standing just inside a garden gate.

She guessed too that he'd done this often before, but on many of the occasions she'd had a puncture she'd been given a lift home by a doctor who happened to be leaving at the same time, or by Mr Eldredge, the greengrocer who supplied the hospital and always stopped at the Railway for a drink.

'Mrs Reilly to you,' she said, and continued to walk on without looking round.

He came up behind her, grabbing the saddle to stop her. 'Don't be like that. I only wanted to say hello.'

She turned to face him then. He was wearing a tailored checked jacket and grey flannel trousers, the smartness of his clothes suggesting he hoped to impress her. 'Well, you've said hello now, so let go of my bicycle, please.'

He did so, but as she walked on he fell in beside her. 'It must be hard work at the hospital. I really admire you ladies volunteering to work there, can't be easy.'

'It isn't easy for the wounded soldiers either,' she said crisply. 'I'm surprised you aren't in uniform, why's that?'

Conscription had been brought in the previous year, and he had no obvious disability.

'I've got a heart complaint,' he said. 'If it wasn't for that I'd be over there doing my bit.'

She gave him a withering glance. He could of course be telling the truth but it was far more likely he'd bribed a doctor to exempt him. 'Look, Mr Blessard, I don't wish to be rude, but I have nothing to say to you and I have no wish to be in your company. So kindly go about your business and leave me alone.'

With that he grabbed hold of her arm, squeezing it so tightly it hurt. 'How did a whore like you get to be so snooty?' he said. 'I know all about you. Every last thing. See, I make it my business to find out about people who interest me. You may have convinced folk in Blackheath that you were in Paris learning millinery but I know what you were really doing. You might have got a couple of influential friends to cover it up for you, but a reporter can always get at the truth.'

Belle let go of her bicycle and as it clanged to the ground, she wheeled round sharply, and bringing her knee up fast, she drove it into his genitals with all the force she could muster. He reeled back in agony.

'I learned a lot of things in Paris,' she snarled at him. 'And one of them was how to deal with weasels like you. If you come anywhere near me again you will live to regret it.'

Picking up her bicycle, she moved on swiftly. In a quick glance over her shoulder she saw he was doubled up in pain. He was in no condition to follow her.

When she got home, Garth and Mog were just about to have their dinner. They remarked on her flushed face and she told them what had happened.

'I'll go out now and get that blackguard,' Garth exclaimed, rising from the table.

'He'll have gone now,' Belle said. 'Crawled back to what-ever hole he came out of.'

'But what if he comes after you again?' Mog said, her eyes wide with fear.

'I'll be off to France in two weeks. I doubt if he'll have ral-lied himself before that,' Belle said.

'You shouldn't have done that to him,' Mog said. 'It will only make him want to make trouble for you.'

'Mog! He deserved it,' Garth exclaimed, looking astounded that his wife wasn't backing Belle up. 'What was she sup-posed to have done? Let him have his way with her?'

'Well no, but violence just begets more violence,' Mog said timidly.

'My arse, fight fire with fire, that's what I say,' Garth responded. 'Good for you, girl, and meanwhile I'll have a word with that policeman Broadhead. He'll find out where the man comes from and I'll deal with him.'

Mog shook her head. 'You can't tell Broadhead what the man said to Belle!'

'No, you can't,' Belle agreed. She liked PC Broadhead, who was a good man, but she knew that he was sweet on her and would be likely to rush to arrest Blessard. A man like him would if cornered shout her past from the rooftops. She couldn't risk that. 'Best to let it go. He won't be able to bother me again if I'm not here.'

Yet despite what she'd said, that evening as she wrote her usual letter to Jimmy she felt very anxious. As Blessard hadn't tried to contact her for so long, she had believed he'd lost interest in her. Today's encounter proved that was not the case, and she was just fortunate not to have been waylaid by him any of the other times he'd punctured her tyres. But by reacting the way she had this evening, she had shown her true colours, and that was likely to make him even more determined to expose her.

She didn't really care about herself. If nothing else, this war and the sights she'd seen had taught her that bad things happen, and nothing stays the same. She and Jimmy could move away when it was all over, but as always it was Mog and Garth she was concerned for. They were very happy here, they were liked and respected by everyone. In the last year Mog had become a leading light in the village fund-raising events for the war effort; she cooked, sewed, knitted, manned stalls, made costumes for pageants and parades. For the first time in her life she was looked up to and people counted on her.

Belle knew that if her past should come out, Mog would suffer. Even if Mog's previous employment never became known, as Belle's aunt she'd be shunned just because of the association.

But there was nothing Belle could do to prevent Blessard exposing her if that was his intention. All she could hope for was that any damage would be limited to her.

Two weeks later, Belle and Miranda were finally on the train heading for Dover. It was packed with soldiers returning to France, but they had the Ladies Only compartment to themselves.

'Thank heavens that's over,' Miranda said jubilantly as she turned away from waving out of the window and flopped down on to the seat. Her parents had come to the station to see her off, and her mother had embarrassed her by sobbing loudly and acting as if she would never see her daughter again.

Belle pulled up the window, and surreptitiously wiped the

tears from her eyes before sitting down. Mog had remained quiet and calm at the station, but Belle knew she would go back with Garth and break down and cry in the privacy of her home, and her tears would be genuine. It was a timely reminder to Belle of how fortunate she was to be loved. Miranda might have all the advantages that came with wealthy and well-connected parents, but her family would disown her the moment she put a foot wrong. She had no doubt that Mrs Forbes-Alton would boast to her friends that Miranda was off to do vital war work, but this morning's tears weren't real, heartfelt ones, and in truth she was glad to get her troublesome daughter out of the way.

'Mama is such a fraud,' Miranda exclaimed. 'Even before we left this morning I heard her telling the maid to pack my stuff up and put it in the cellar and get my room ready for her sister who's coming to stay. I'm never going back there, you know. Today is the first one of my new independent life.'

'My mother is as bad,' Belle admitted. 'I wrote and told her two weeks ago that I was leaving and asked if she'd come over on Sunday to see me before I left. She sent the briefest note back saying she couldn't spare the time but wished me well. I don't feel inclined to bother with her any more either.'

'How can she be like that?' Miranda asked.

Belle had asked herself the same question countless times. Annie had never comforted her about losing her baby, nor had she shown any concern for Jimmy's safety, or interest in Belle's work at the hospital. All she could talk about was how well her guest house was doing, and how many charming officers came to stay. She didn't even appear to be overly concerned at how many of these guests' names had appeared later on casualty lists.

'She was never a real mother to me,' Belle sighed. 'She's a

cold, self-centred woman. The best thing she did for me was to put me in Mog's care.'

'Mine is as bad. When we were little she only ever saw us for about ten minutes before we went to bed. She's such a fraud, she makes out to other people she did everything for us. But the truth is we were brought up by the servants. Papa did stuff some money in my hand this morning though,' Miranda grinned. 'A hundred pounds! Not sure whether that was to ensure I didn't return or an attempt to show he cared.'

Belle thought of the new clothes Mog had made for her, the fruit cake she'd baked and packed in her case. The time and trouble she took with such things made her love visible, and it meant so much more than a wad of money. As for Jimmy, he showed his love by being glad she'd got the opportunity to do something she wanted to do. He said he would be proud of her doing something so important, and maybe he'd get some time off to come and see her.

'Well, it's just us now,' Belle said. 'Let's hope we can actually drive those ambulances. And remember some French.'

'Of course we will, we'll be brilliant. Now, do we have to stay in this Ladies Only carriage? I'm sure it would be much more fun with all the soldiers.'

'Miss Forbes-Alton, you aren't here for fun,' Belle replied in an imitation of Matron at the Herbert. 'Besides, the train is packed. We're extremely lucky to have a seat, let alone a whole compartment to ourselves.'

'We could sit on someone's knee,' Miranda said impishly.

'Just make the most of the comfort here, the boat will be packed with soldiers. I expect by the time we arrive at Calais even you will have got tired of flirting.'

'I can't believe it's against the rules for VADs to be seen socially with soldiers,' Miranda said, taking a compact from her bag and powdering her nose. 'I had hoped to find a gallant officer to squire us around when we're off duty.'

Belle laughed. 'I suspect we'll be too exhausted to do anything off duty but sleep.'

'I wonder if you'll get to see Jimmy, or even the Frenchman,' Miranda said thoughtfully.

'I certainly hope we don't see either of them in an ambulance,' Belle replied. She wished Miranda wouldn't refer to 'the Frenchman' so often. Belle had no way of knowing if Etienne was still alive, and it worried her somewhat that he crept into her thoughts so often. 'But what about your brothers? Where are they?' She knew they only joined up just before conscription forced them to, and they were both officers, but Miranda hadn't said where they were in France.

Miranda looked a little embarrassed. 'They've both got desk jobs in London. How I don't know, probably dear Mama pulling strings.'

Belle couldn't help but smirk. Mrs Forbes-Alton was a piece of work, hounding other men into joining up while her own sons remained safe. She wondered how the woman could hold her head up.

It was late at night when the girls finally arrived at Camiers, the base depot of the British army. Belle knew it was just north of Etaples where Jimmy did his training and close to the sea, but she hadn't expected such a vast place. There were row after row of what looked like big tin sheds on both sides of the road, with just a dim light above each door, and behind them they could glimpse rows of large bell tents.

Ten nursing VADs were in the back of the truck with her and Miranda, plus a couple of older women who were with the Red Cross but were evasive about their role. It had been a very cold and bumpy ride from Calais as the lorry had canvas sides which billowed in the wind, and the road appeared to be full of pot holes.

'I hope we aren't expected to sleep in a tent,' remarked one of the nursing VADs in a very plummy voice.

Belle looked anxiously at Miranda. She didn't relish the thought of that either.

'Those buildings which resemble sheds are mainly wards,' one of the older women volunteered. 'They are a lot better inside than you'd imagine from this view. They have a long skylight on the top so they are quite bright, especially on a sunny day. Between them are theatres, kitchens and suchlike. I'm quite sure you will all be housed in a hut; the tents are mainly occupied by men working here, and used as extra wards when there is a large influx of wounded. Last year during the battle of the Somme every one of them had to be pressed into service.'

The nursing VADs were shown into one hut, much smaller than the ones they'd been told were wards. Belle and Miranda were shown to a different one close to where rows of ambulances were lined up.

'One of the women in there will explain everything to you,' the lorry driver said. 'Good luck, you'll need it, this place can be hell on earth.'

A big woman of about thirty with very short hair and wearing blue flannel pyjamas got up from her bed as the girls walked into the small hut. 'You must be Reilly and Forbes,' she said, holding out her hand to shake. 'Sally Parsons. I stayed up to welcome you; the others wanted to but sleep overcame them.'

'That was kind of you,' Miranda said. 'But don't let us stop you going to bed. We're sorry we're so late.'

As Miranda spoke for them, Belle was looking around. There were six beds, three of which were occupied, and

Sally's was clearly the one with a small light by it. There were no comforts. It was just a shed, with a bare wooden floor, a couple of windows on either side and a stove in the middle with a table at the far end with two benches to sit on. Beside each bed was a small locker.

'The lavatory is through that door.' Sally pointed to a door at the far end of the hut. 'There's a couple of washbasins too, but only cold water I'm afraid. And we hang up our overalls and leave our boots out there as well. I'll show you where to go for a bath tomorrow. Now, if you don't mind I'll lock the door and get my head down.'

As soon as Miranda switched on the light between her and Belle's beds, Sally turned hers off and got into bed. The two friends looked at each other, not knowing whether to laugh or cry. They hadn't expected luxury, but this was very Spartan, and cold too.

Miranda prodded her bed and winced. 'Like a concrete slab,' she whispered.

'At least we've got one another,' Belle whispered back.

They were in their beds within ten minutes and though Belle had laughed when Mog packed a wool comforter she'd knitted, now as she cuddled it around her she was very grateful, as the sheets on the bed were rough and cold, and the blankets smelled strange.

There was a little light coming through the small windows, and she could hear men talking in low voices close by. Every now and then someone walked along the pathway they'd driven in on, and there would be the occasional bang of a door.

'Sleep tight,' she whispered to Miranda. 'It will all look better in the morning.'

Chapter Fourteen

They woke to a grey, damp morning and Sally introduced them to the other three girls, Maud Smith, Honor Wilkins and Vera Reid. 'Maud and I went to school together in Cheltenham,' she said. 'Honor is from Sussex, Vera from New Zealand. We're the only female drivers here, and we get teased by the men, but we stick together and rise above it.'

Sally, Maud and Honor were three of a kind, probably around thirty, plain, buxom and with plummy voices. They put Belle in mind of schoolmistresses, sensible and good-hearted but almost certainly dull company.

Vera on the other hand looked like fun. She was younger, and had a freckled, open face, duck-egg blue eyes and a wide, warm smile. 'My only excuse for being here is that I'm mad,' she said. 'Well, that's how it seems most days.'

Belle had never met anyone from New Zealand before and Vera's accent sounded very odd to her.

There was no time for further conversation. Sally handed Belle and Miranda a khaki overall each to put over their clothes and suggested they shortened their skirts a few inches or they'd be trailing them through mud. Then, with their hair tied firmly back under a peaked khaki cap, they left for a breakfast in the canteen of slices of bread with a couple of rashers of fatty bacon, and a mug of tea, then went to meet Captain Taylor of the RAMC who was in charge of the ambulance drivers.

'We wait in there.' Sally indicated a further hut in which through the open door they could see about thirty men sitting around. 'They ring a bell when a train of wounded is coming in, then we dash down to the station. Everyone tries to get up front, as they unload the sitting patients first.'

Captain Taylor was elderly and looked the girls up and down with the kind of bemused expression that said he was not convinced any woman was strong enough to handle stretchers. He said very little, just that he expected them to keep themselves and their ambulance clean, and that they must obey the rules posted up on the wall in the ambulance drivers' hut. He then paired both of them with a stretcher bearer who would ride in the ambulance with them.

Miranda got Alf, who was around fifty and very short, with notably bandy legs but massive shoulders.

'I won't be dreaming of him tonight,' she whispered to Belle behind her hand.

Belle got David Parks, from Sheffield. He was only about twenty-five, fresh-faced, fair-haired and with sticking-out ears. He told Belle he'd been invalided out of the army because of a leg wound he received at Ypres back in 1915, but he'd asked to stay on here to help with the wounded. As he walked away to speak to someone she saw he limped badly, and she wondered whether he was really up to carrying heavy loads.

Within the hour Belle was very glad she'd got David. He not only knew exactly where to go and what to do when they got to the station, but also understood the ambulance's little foibles and didn't appear horrified to be paired with a female driver. He had a very thick Northern accent, but a gentle, rather shy manner which she liked. He said he couldn't drive an ambulance himself because his injury wouldn't let him put enough pressure on the clutch.

'Why didn't you just go home after you were wounded?' she asked him as they drove out in a convoy of ambulances making the first trip of the day to the station. She was struggling with the gears and the heavy steering, but David guided her through it and gave her confidence. 'Surely you'd had enough of war after being wounded?'

'What's at home for a cripple like me?' He shrugged. 'No one's gunner give me a job, me mam don't want another mouth to feed, not with the house full up with little 'uns, and me mates are all out here.'

His words echoed ones she'd heard before from other soldiers at the Herbert. Many of them had come from poor families in cities like Leeds, Manchester and Birmingham. They had joined up to escape poverty and grim surroundings and lack of opportunities. Sadly a large proportion of the wounded would return home embittered, to an even worse life than before.

Yet Belle had also talked to men who felt the army had improved their lot in life. Regular meals and muscle-building exercise during their training had turned them from scrawny lads into men. The close friendships they'd made with men from different backgrounds and the guidance from their officers had often opened their minds and given them new skills. She was certain David fell into this camp.

'Maybe you can get a job in a hospital when the war is over,' she suggested.

He smiled shyly. 'I've been reading up on physiotherapy. I'd like to do that. I reckon it's one field where they wouldn't turn you down because you was lame.'

By the time they had moved up in the line of ambulances close enough to see the station platform, the sitting patients had already been driven off to the hospital, and there were only lying patients left. Although the station was crowded with nurses, men on stretchers and other army personnel, Belle was surprised by the organization and the calm. At each carriage door an army nurse in a crisp white apron and cap stood with the notes of the men under her care and directed the stretcher bearers in which order they were to be taken. Each patient had his Dorothy bag of personal possessions tucked in beside him, but few were wearing the hospital blues Belle was used to seeing at the Herbert. Most were in under-shirts, some torn and bloody. She saw bandaged stumps of arms, heads swathed in dressings, raw, burnt faces and in some cases no legs were visible beneath the covering blanket. She could hear groaning and the occasional shriek of pain, but in the main the wounded were quiet, some so still they appeared lifeless.

'Move on forward, it's our turn now,' David said as the ambulance in front of them pulled away after being loaded with six stretcher cases in the racks made for that purpose. 'When we start the loading, try not to let the men see you haven't done it before or show horror at their injuries.'

Belle might have thought she was used to seeing appalling injuries, and to helping to lift patients into bed, but she had never lifted a stretcher before; the orderlies at the Herbert had always done that. As she and David picked up the first stretcher, carrying a man with abdominal wounds, she staggered momentarily as it was so heavy, and his pain-filled eyes pleaded with her not to hurt him further. 'It will all be better soon,' she said soothingly. 'You won't be moved again once we get you to the hospital.'

As they lifted and slid him into the ambulance her arms felt as though they were being pulled from their sockets, but she reassured the wounded man again and wiped his brow with a damp cloth.

'You're doing all right,' David said in a low voice as they fetched the second man. 'You're made for this – a smile and a comforting word do almost as much as the morphine.'

Once they were fully loaded, notes attached to each stretcher, Belle drove away, trying to avoid the jarring pot holes in the road. She was damp with sweat, her arms felt as if they'd been stretched on a medieval rack, and she knew the same procedure would be repeated in reverse at the hospital. It was just after nine in the morning, and she'd be doing this again and again until six. She wondered if it would be possible to complete the day.

If it hadn't been for David, she thought she might have thrown in the towel by midday. But he said the first day was always the worst and urged her not to give up. 'I know it seems impossible to lift another one,' he said as he gave her a mug of tea to wash down a couple of aspirin. 'But muscles soon get stronger, and you don't want to give Captain Taylor the pleasure of seeing a girl not up to the job.'

At six in the evening when Miranda and Belle returned to their hut, they both sank on to their beds with a groan. They had been back and forth to the station so many times they had lost count. Every muscle in their bodies had been strained to the limit; the terrible sights, evil smells and cries of pain which assaulted their senses over and over again had taken them to the edge of endurance.

'I didn't expect it to be like this,' Miranda said, her voice weak with exhaustion.

'Nor me,' Belle agreed. 'I doubt I can even lift my arms to undress and brush my hair.'

'Enough of your moaning,' Vera piped up from across the room. She had stripped off to a lace-trimmed petticoat, rushed off to wash and was now putting on a blue dress as if she was off to a party. 'Go and have a hot bath, that will revive you.'

Belle managed to sit up. 'Was today especially busy?' she asked hopefully.

'It's about average for when the fighting is going on,' Vera said. 'It was fairly quiet until Easter, but then the fighting in Arras began and we got some two thousand casualties in soon after, British, French, Australian and Canadian. They say it's going to get even worse soon.'

'I don't think I can face another day like today,' Miranda admitted, voicing what Belle had been thinking.

'You can,' Vera said firmly. 'I thought the same on my first day, but you do get used to it. Go and have a bath, get some food and then go to bed. You'll sleep like babies and when you wake up tomorrow it won't seem as bad. Give me your skirts and I'll take up the hems for you tonight.'

'You'd do that for us?' Belle asked. Her long skirt had hindered her all day but she hadn't the strength to shorten it herself tonight.

'Of course, we're all in this together,' Vera said. 'Helping each other is how we get by.'

'But aren't you going out somewhere?' Miranda asked. Vera had taken the pins out of her hair and was brushing it vigorously.

'Only to get some supper, but we always change when we get back. As Sally would say, "Us gals must keep up appearances." '

Belle was to discover in the days that followed that Vera's philosophy about helping one another was what made the job easier, and it created camaraderie. It didn't take that much extra effort to help another driver load their ambulance, and it was invariably reciprocated, especially when a patient was particularly heavy. It had rained almost constantly since they got here, and one day Miranda's ambulance got stuck in mud. Men came running to help immediately, bringing sacks to put under the wheels. Another day David stumbled with a stretcher, and suddenly there was a helping hand to steady him.

In periods when there were few trains, she and Miranda got to know the other drivers and stretcher bearers. They were from all walks of life. A few were like David, invalided out of the army but wanting to stay on to help others. Some had been turned down by the army because of a minor health problem. But still more had come for similar reasons to her and Miranda, to do their bit or wanting a change from what they did at home. Whatever their backgrounds, they all mucked in, there was a great deal of laughter and leg-pulling, and even though the work was extremely hard, she and Miranda felt liberated by being accepted in a predominantly male world.

One of the older drivers, whom they had both considered to be totally prejudiced against women ambulance drivers, roared with laughter one day on overhearing her and Miranda impersonating two nursing sisters who were real battleaxes. A day later when the fan belt broke on Belle's ambulance, he came to her rescue and showed her how to put a new one on. He said as she thanked him that it was nothing, that she and Miranda were rays of sunshine and he was glad they'd joined the team. Belle was elated to have his approval, and in that moment she felt that however hard the work was, or how primitive the living conditions, they had made the right decision in signing up to come here.

Even Captain Taylor nodded approval at them from time to time. David said he'd overheard him telling another RAMC officer that 'Those two new girls are made of the right stuff.'

It kept on raining remorselessly. By the end of each day they were often soaked through and chilled to the bone. The hut looked more like a laundry room at night, with clothes hung up to dry and soggy boots stuffed with newspaper all around the stove. Yet despite this, Belle seemed to have more energy than she'd ever had at home. Instead of going back to the hut straight after supper to play cards or read and write letters, she liked to go into the wards for an hour or so and check on the progress of the men she'd brought in.

She often offered a little help to the nurses, writing letters for men who couldn't hold a pen, reading to someone who was blinded, or just feeding those who couldn't manage it themselves. Miranda teased her about it; she said she saw enough gore during the day without looking for more.

Because Belle was kept so busy, her letters to Jimmy were now often as brief as his to her. She tried to write to Mog and Garth every week too, but it proved difficult to respond to Mog's gossip about people in the village, the shortages of food, and who had been at the weekly sewing circle meeting. It all seemed so trivial in the face of what she saw here daily.

She understood now why Jimmy had always said so little about his day-to-day life. There was the censor looking over his shoulder of course, but it was more likely he felt that what he saw daily could not be understood by people who hadn't experienced it. She felt the same: she couldn't explain the black humour they all used as a way of dealing with the horror they saw, or why she had become so attached to every-one she worked with. She knew now that a soldier's life wasn't anything like the way the newspapers at home portrayed it.

Until she got here, Belle had imagined Jimmy cowering in a trench being fired on constantly. Now, thanks to David who had been at the front, she knew that soldiers only spent four days at a time in the front line before being sent back behind the lines.

Jimmy had gone back to the front after his wound healed, but to a different regiment, and up until his last letter they were still in reserve. Yet David had told her that even if he was in the front line that didn't mean he was in constant danger of being shot. Apparently the men endured long periods of utter boredom, when all they did was keep watch for enemy activity. Furthermore, some places on the line saw very little action; David said there was often a 'live and let live' attitude on both sides. Of course, even in these quiet spots, men could get killed by a sniper or a thrown grenade, and the real danger periods came when the generals ordered an assault, or when the men were sent out into No Man's Land on patrols to see what the enemy were doing.

Belle had also imagined that being 'in reserve' meant resting up, but according to David that wasn't so. They were kept very busy, training, moving supplies around, improving trenches, burying the dead, repairing the barbed wire, taking ammunition to where it was needed, along with washing and mending their uniforms.

Jimmy had touched lightly on things like lice, mud, soaking uniforms, rats and the state of the latrines ever since he finished his training back in 1915, but it had always been in a casual way, as if these things didn't bother him that much. But the drivers here who had all done a stint at some time collecting the wounded from dressing stations were more graphic about these horrors. One described to Belle how the men were almost driven mad by lice and would run a lighted candle down the seams of their uniforms to burn them off. He said their bodies were covered in bites which often became infected. She heard how the thick mud the soldiers had to wade through was often mixed with excrement from the latrines and even body parts from men who had died there. Rats were said to be as big as cats and overran the trenches, and so even a fairly minor injury could easily become gangrenous and result in amputation.

On Easter Monday, 9 April, when the battle at Arras had begun, there had been the further trials of sleet and snow to contend with. The wounded who were coming in daily spoke of tanks being bogged down in the thick mud, of pack mules falling over and drowning in it, and many of the wounded often couldn't drag themselves out of the mud so they died there too.

Jimmy was billeted in a barn and wrote more about having a drink or a plate of egg and chips in an *estaminet* than about the conditions out there in low-lying marshy ground, but it was clearly only a matter of time before his regiment would be sent into the battle. Knowing now what that would entail, Belle found it hard to pen bright, cheerful letters to him, as day after day she was seeing what could well happen to him.

Vera was excited by the imminent arrival of her two brothers who had joined the Anzacs and were on their way here from New Zealand. They were called Tony and 'Spud' and she just laughed when Belle asked her about the nickname. But along with the excitement that she might get a chance to see them, even if only briefly, she was also afraid they would be sent directly to the front as Canadians and Australians had been.

Sally, Maud and Honor all had brothers or cousins here, and Belle had noticed that although they said little about them, they discreetly checked the casualty lists every day. There appeared to be an unspoken agreement amongst everyone that you controlled your anxiety about relatives at the front. Henry, one of the drivers, saw his nephew posted as missing, presumed dead soon after she and Miranda arrived here. Belle had seen Henry standing behind the hut, head bowed and shoulders heaving, yet he jumped into his ambulance when the bell rang and continued to work all day as normal. Sally said in her usual practical manner that remaining busy was the best way to deal with grief.

But even if all the nurses, drivers, orderlies, doctors and other personnel at the hospital managed to hold themselves in check, the relatives who arrived from England to see sons or husbands who weren't expected to live could not control their grief. Day after day the girls saw these people arrive at the hospital. They stood out from the work force not only by their civilian clothes, but by their strained and bewildered expressions. Most of them had never been out of England before, they couldn't speak any French, and they knew too that their son or husband was going to die. Often they arrived too late and he was already dead. The nursing staff were always sympathetic and did their best to offer some comfort, but it seemed even more tragic that those poor people had come so far yet had no chance to say a proper goodbye. Almost every day there were burials; Belle's blood ran cold each time she heard the haunting sound of the bugle playing the Last Post.

David was very philosophical about the grieving relatives. He said that at least they knew where their loved one's body lay, and had heard the prayers, unlike the relatives of thousands of other men who had been committed to a communal grave near the battlefields. And some bodies were never found; they were blown to pieces and scattered in the mud. For the families of those men it had to be torture, hoping against hope that they'd been taken prisoner, or that they were lying in a hospital bed somewhere and would one day return home.

At the end of May, when the girls had been in France for over a month, they were told they could have the following day off. Up until then they had only had the odd half day, usually on a Sunday when fewer trains came in. But as the nearest village had nothing much to offer, and it was a long walk too, they always just stayed in the hut or did their laundry.

Not having to get up early was a real treat in itself, and when they eventually woke to find the sun shining, Miranda suggested they got a lift into Calais that afternoon to look around.

Trucks went to and from Calais daily to pick up supplies from the docks, and they knew it would be easy enough to persuade one of the drivers to let them go with him. They had a bath, washed their hair, and put on their best dresses. They had been told before they left England to bring only sensible, everyday wear as space would be limited in their accommodation. But neither had been able to resist packing something slightly fancier in case a special occasion should arise. Miranda's dress was blue crêpe-de-chine, and Belle's was a mauve floral print.

'I wish I had a prettier hat,' Miranda said as she put on the navy-blue felt one she'd worn to come here.

'If we left here looking like we were off to a garden party that would arouse too much attention,' Belle said, skewering on her own light brown hat which she'd made to go with her winter coat. She wasn't sure if going into Calais was even allowed. One of the nurses had told Belle that neither the nurses nor the VADs were allowed to fraternize with soldiers, and they could be sent home if they were suspected of doing so. The same nurse said that one of her colleagues was refused permission to go out of the hospital grounds with her father, who was a serving officer. That seemed utterly ridiculous, but then, Matron at the Herbert had been equally tough on her nurses.

'Maybe we could buy another hat each in Calais,' Belle said. 'We can't wear these all summer.'

'Don't you just ache to have a long soak in a bath and then

dress up in something frilly and go somewhere elegant?' Miranda asked, pinching her cheeks to make them pink.

'I ache for lots of things,' Belle admitted. 'Mog's cooking, a comfy bed, and Jimmy cuddling me at night. The only time I've ever been to elegant places was in Paris, and I don't like to think about why I was in them.'

'Maybe we could go to Paris one day?' Miranda said hopefully. 'You could look up that friend you had there that owned restaurants. I bet he'd show us a good time.'

'That part of my life is dead and buried. I never think about it,' Belle said a little sharply. This wasn't strictly true; she had thought about Etienne and Philippe, the restaurateur Miranda had mentioned, far more since she'd been here. Each time she heard a French accent she was jolted back to the past. But admitting that to Miranda would open a floodgate of memories she'd have to share with her.

'Sorry I spoke,' Miranda said, pulling a face. 'All I want is a bit of fun.'

The truck driver they picked to ask for a lift was a Frenchman in his fifties. He didn't know much English, but he managed to tell them he was returning at six, and if they weren't there to meet him he'd have to come back without them.

'Calais not a good place for *jolies filles*,' he added reprovingly. 'Many soldiers!'

The driver was right about there being many soldiers. They were everywhere, in the cafés, bars, in trucks, and milling around the streets. There were French, English, Australians and even a few Scots Guards in kilts. The girls were gawped at, whistled at, and one young soldier began singing 'If You Were the Only Girl in the World' very loudly, and his friends with him all joined in.

Both girls put their noses in the air and kept on walking, even though they wanted to laugh, for they were mindful that someone from the hospital might see them here and if they appeared to be encouraging the men they'd be on the carpet the next day.

It was intoxicating to be out in the sunshine, to see shops, cafés and ordinary people going about their business, and to be free of the sights, sounds and smells of the hospital. They found a dusty little hat shop in a back street and bought a straw boater each, putting them on immediately and relegating their old hats to the shopping bag. They bought some new stockings, had a cup of chocolate in a café, and then went for a walk along the beach.

The English Channel was bristling with ships, a reminder that the war wasn't only being fought on land. The Germans held Zeebrugge and Ostend just up the coast, and their U-boats were constantly targeting British ships.

Miranda looked up at an aeroplane flying overhead. 'It's odd how we just accept them now,' she said thoughtfully. 'Papa showed me a picture of one a few years back, he was so excited about flight. But I couldn't understand how they could stay up in the air and I thought it was just a fad that would die out.'

'I still don't really understand how they fly,' Belle said. 'And motor cars! I was about thirteen when I saw my first one in the Strand, and I ran along beside it. People said they would never catch on. But they did, and now even people like us can drive them. Imagine when we've got children and we tell them things like that! They won't be able to imagine life before these things were invented.'

'I can't even imagine what life will be like when the war ends,' Miranda said. 'I mean, how can I go back to how it was before?'

Belle was surprised at the bleakness in that remark. 'It won't be the same,' she assured her. 'How can it be when the war has changed everything?'

'So many thousands of men have died already, even more will be left crippled,' Miranda said. 'There will be even less chance of me falling in love and getting married than there was before it started. You'll have Jimmy, and I'll be the spinster growing old still living with my parents.'

'That's such a defeatist attitude,' Belle said indignantly. 'You will meet someone and fall in love, I'm sure of that. Besides, you said you were never going home, that this was the start of your independent life. You've managed so well in this job, so when the war's over you'll be able to do anything you put your mind to.'

'Then why can't I ever imagine it?' Miranda asked, picking up a pebble and skimming it into the sea. 'I bet you can.'

'Well, yes, I can,' Belle admitted. 'But imagining is only thinking what you want to happen. I like to picture Jimmy and me living by the sea, perhaps running a guest house or something. I doubt it will really happen, but unless you have a dream and work towards it, nothing will change.'

They walked back into the town then, and went into a café for something to eat before getting their lift back.

It was small and scruffy, with plain wood tables that needed a scrub, but other cafés that were nicer had been full of soldiers. Two elderly men were tucking into a plate of what looked like beef stew, and it smelled delicious, so when the waitress came over to them for their order they pointed at it and asked for some wine too.

They were eating their food when two American soldiers came in. They were young, perhaps twenty-three or -four, tall with sunburnt faces, and in comparison to their English counterparts, their tan uniforms looked very smart.

Miranda beamed at them, and Belle shot her a warning glance.

Both men removed their hats and paused at the girls' table, looking not just at them but their food too. 'That looks good, mam,' the dark-haired one said. He had a sergeant's three chevrons on his sleeve. 'Would you recommend it?'

'It's very tasty,' Miranda said, blushing a little.

'Then I guess we'll settle for that too,' he said. 'We don't know our way round here yet, only arrived a few days ago. May we share your table?'

'By all means,' Miranda said, not looking at Belle, who she clearly knew would not approve. 'I'm Miranda Forbes-Alton, this is Belle Reilly. We don't know our way around either, this is the first time we've come into Calais.'

'I'm Will Fergus,' the dark-haired sergeant said, offering his hand. 'And this is Patrick Mehler,' he added, nodding at his fair-haired companion. 'Are you sure we aren't intruding?'

'We have to leave soon for a lift back,' Belle said, hoping that was enough of a hint for Miranda not to get too carried away by two such handsome men.

'Back to where, mam?' the sergeant asked as both men sat down.

'Camiers. The hospital,' Miranda said. 'We're ambulance drivers. And you don't have to call us mam, we're Miranda and Belle. In England only royal ladies are called mam.'

Will laughed, showing beautiful white teeth. 'Well, ladies, may I call you Belle and Miranda? I can't believe two such pretty girls can do such a job. It would be worth being wounded to be driven by one of you.'

Belle knew in that instant that Miranda was going to fall for this man. He was handsome, charming and able-bodied. Furthermore, he didn't have that war-weary look that most of the staff at the hospital had.

The men ordered their meal, and they all made smalltalk. Will came from Philadelphia, Patrick from Boston, and they were here as part of an advance party to get things ready for the American troops who would be arriving at the end of the year.

Belle quickly established that she was married; Patrick was too, and she sensed that he felt much the same as she did, a little anxious that he might be dragged into something by Will. So she talked to him about Jimmy, and why she and Miranda were here, and asked him about his wife, making it quite clear where she stood.

Within a very short time it was quite obvious to Belle that Will was as taken with Miranda as she was with him. They were laughing like old friends, talking nineteen to the dozen and leaning closer to each other over the table. If it hadn't been against the rules to fraternize with soldiers Belle would have been delighted for her, but she knew her friend well enough to be sure that she would be prepared to risk anything for a man she liked.

When Belle began reminding Miranda they had to leave to get their lift back Will was quick to offer to drive them. 'I've got a staff car,' he said. 'Stay a while longer. We're only just getting to know one another.'

Belle knew if she insisted they left now Miranda would be cross with her. But more than that, she could see the first signs of a budding romance there, and she couldn't begrudge her friend that. So she smiled and accepted another drink.

Will was as good as his word. After a walk around the town and then several more drinks, he took them back. At least, Patrick drove and Will and Miranda sat in the back, kissing the whole way.

'You don't approve,' Patrick had said in the last bar they went into. Miranda and Will were a little way off, standing so

213

close together, gazing into each other's eyes, that they looked like one person.

'It's not that. They make a lovely couple,' Belle sighed. 'I just don't want her to be hurt, or get into trouble at the hospital.'

'I've never seen him like this with a girl before,' Patrick said. 'He's got it bad, I'd say. Hell, why shouldn't they have fun? I'm sure it's the same for you in England, folks saying do this, don't do that. We're here in France, there's a war on, and any of us could get killed any day. You and I are married, Belle, but we've had that same crazy feeling ourselves. Shouldn't we be glad they will have it too?'

'Yes, you're right,' she admitted. 'But this has come on too fast. Miranda's headstrong.'

'And Will's a good guy.' Patrick put his hand on her shoulder. 'You don't choose to fall in love, it chooses you. Besides, you are too young and pretty to worry your head about what could go wrong.'

Will and Patrick dropped them at the hospital gates. It was nearly eleven and Belle realized as she began to walk with Miranda to the hut that she was tipsy.

'Isn't Will just wonderful?' Miranda said breathlessly, linking arms with Belle.

Belle glanced sideways at her friend. Even in the dim light on each ward door, she could see her eyes shining. 'Yes, he is,' she replied, shivering with the cold. 'But right now I'm just afraid we might be in serious trouble.'

'I'm meeting him again tomorrow,' Miranda said in a tone that implied she wasn't prepared to be argued with. 'I've met the man I want to spend the rest of my life with, and I don't care about anything else.'

Vera was reading in bed when they got in and put her

214

finger to her lips to remind them the other three girls were asleep.

'You're late,' she whispered. 'I was getting worried. Did you have a good time?'

'The very best,' Miranda whispered back and did a pirouetting dance right down the hut to the lavatory.

Belle sat on Vera's bed. 'Did anyone ask about us? Are we in trouble?'

'No, only with me for making me worry,' Vera smiled. 'So tell me, what happened?'

'The full story in the morning,' Belle said. 'But let's just say Miranda's fallen in love. Don't say anything to the others; we don't want Captain Taylor hearing about it.'

Belle looked over at Miranda before she turned off her light. She wasn't asleep, just lying there with a smile on her face. She'd never looked so radiant.

Chapter Fifteen

Belle found the change in Miranda since she'd met Will remarkable. Even though she was slipping off to meet him almost every night, and not getting back until after twelve, she was up like a lark in the morning, singing, laughing and being sweet to everyone.

Sally disapproved. She said cattily that Miranda was being 'fast', but snooty and jealous as she was, she wasn't the kind to tell tales. Belle found it hard not to be jealous herself. To see her friend with shining eyes and a dreamy expression reminded her of the way she used to feel about Etienne, and she guiltily wondered why it was she was remembering her feelings for him, and not for Jimmy.

'What's this bloke of Miranda's like then?' David asked Belle one morning as they were taking their first trip to the station to collect new patients.

'What do you mean?' Belle said cagily. She hadn't told a soul about Miranda's man, and she didn't think the other girls would have told anyone about it either.

'Don't be daft, I could see something had happened the day after you slipped out to Calais,' he grinned. 'You looked troubled and she was skipping about like a new lamb. It don't take much to put two and two together.'

Belle saw no point in lying to David. He was a good sort and he was always discreet. 'Well, keep it under your cap. American, very handsome, a nice man. He's a sergeant.'

'A Dough Boy, eh?' he said. 'Well, tell him from me to get the rest of the Yanks in and help us end this bloody war.'

'They are coming, or so it is said,' Belle said. 'He won't get so much free time to see Miranda then.'

'Why are you so troubled about it if he's decent?'

'Well, she *has* gone rather overboard,' Belle sighed; she was rather glad to have someone to confide in. 'I'm scared she'll get sent home or it won't work out for them.'

'No good being a worry-wart about it,' he shrugged. 'If I met a girl that made me glow the way Miranda does, I'd walk over hot coals to be with her. Besides, isn't the reason you came here to be closer to your old man?'

Belle nodded agreement, but she felt a stab of shame that it wasn't true. She hadn't even thought to ask Captain Taylor if it was possible to have a couple of days off to meet Jimmy somewhere. Why hadn't she?

A couple of nights later, Miranda was doing her hair in readiness for going out to meet Will, when Belle came into the hut, her oilskin coat dripping with rain. She said nothing, just took off her coat, hung it on a peg by the door and then bent down to take off her boots.

The other four girls were clustered up at the other end of the hut. They looked up and gave Belle a wave, which she returned, and then she got her towel to dry her wet hair. It seemed to Miranda that Belle was deliberately ignoring her.

'Are you cross with me?' she asked when Belle finally sat down on her bed.

'Of course I'm not,' she replied, looking surprised at the question. 'Why would I be?'

'I thought perhaps it was because I'm always going out with Will these days and leaving you on your own.'

'I don't mind that, Vera is good company too,' Belle said. 'We've become quite close.'

Miranda felt that was a snub. 'I don't want to lose you as a friend,' she said.

Belle laughed. 'It will take more than a man to shake me off,' she said.

Miranda breathed a sigh of relief. Belle wouldn't make a joke of it if she was cross.

'You see, we have to make the most of it now. He could be sent off somewhere else at any time.' Miranda felt she had to explain herself.

Ever since she was about sixteen she'd longed for the kind of love she'd read about in books. She'd been a bridesmaid three times and all of those marriages had been more about the bride finding a suitable partner her family approved of than being ecstatically in love. By the time she met Frank she had begun to believe love might not even exist.

But after all the hurt Frank caused her she had begun to think maybe it was best just to settle for a kind, decent man who she could trust and rely on. But then Will came along, just when she least expected to find romance, and all at once she knew with utter certainty that he was the man she'd always hoped for.

Everything was so right with him; they could talk about anything, laughed at the same things. He made her heart soar, he was on her mind from first thing in the morning till she fell asleep at night. But best of all, she knew he felt just the same about her. The war made the future uncertain, but she was certain of Will. This was the love she had always hoped for.

Yet however much he dominated her thoughts and dreams, she never wanted to lose Belle's friendship. She was far too special, and Miranda was ashamed that she might have been neglecting her.

Belle leaned over and put a cold, damp hand on Miranda's

arm. 'I understand, and I'm happy for you,' she said. 'Just be careful. Keep something in reserve.'

Miranda glanced around the room to check no one was listening, but Sally was reading, Vera was darning some socks and Honor and Maud were playing chess.

'We haven't done it yet,' she whispered. 'Is that what you're worried about?'

Belle sniggered. 'That wasn't what I meant. I'm hardly the right person to come all moral on you. I'm just afraid you are going too fast, too soon.'

'It might be a bit late to warn me of that. Captain Taylor said I could have this Sunday off and Will's taking me some-where overnight.'

When Belle didn't respond, Miranda caught hold of her hand. 'I know you think I'm being reckless, but I love him, Belle. Really love him. He loves me too.'

Belle smiled at her. 'I do understand, and I'm certainly not sitting in judgment. If I were in your shoes I'd probably do just the same,' she said. 'But why are you loitering here if he's waiting for you now? And you'd better put my coat on, you'll get soaked through otherwise.'

Miranda left the hut a few minutes later, the oilskin coat over her head. She took the road out of the hospital grounds, then, as usual, some hundred yards before the main gates she slipped down a path between two wards until she came to the fence and climbed through a hole in it.

She had found this way out some time ago, knowing that if she used the main gates the sentry there was likely to report her. Will waited in the car close by, shielded by some thick bushes. As always when she met him she was fizzing with excitement. Even when she was having the affair with Frank she hadn't felt quite this way, but then she'd never felt as if she really knew him.

Will was quite different. He was warm, open and dependable, always there at the arranged time, and he hadn't pushed her to have sex with him, even though he said that every time they kissed it was like the 4th of July. She really liked that description, it felt like fireworks exploding to her too; she had only to touch his hand and she wanted him. In truth it was only the fear of getting pregnant again which had held her back so far.

Her mother wasn't likely to approve of any man unless he had blue blood or was very rich. And Will's family in Philadelphia were totally undistinguished. His father had been one of thousands of poor Irish who had emigrated to America in the late 1800s and had married the daughter of Italian immigrants a couple of years later and produced five children of whom Will was the eldest. His father had a small building company, and he'd wanted Will to work with him, but although Will had for a few years, he'd joined the regular army when his younger brother was old enough to take over. Will had said he had his eye on a bigger horizon than just bricklaying.

But although from humble origins, Will was a gentleman. He treated Miranda with great tenderness and respect and he seemed to like everything about her. No one had ever done that before, not even her own family. She wanted to spend her life with him in America after the war was over, to embrace his life and forget her old one. She really didn't care if she never saw her own family again.

Will opened the car door as Miranda rushed over. 'Hi, beautiful,' he said, his teeth very white in the darkness.

She scrunched up the wet coat, pushed it over into the back seat and got in, turning to him eagerly.

'Hmmm,' he said after the longest, deepest kiss. 'That was

worth waiting for. I hope you can get away this weekend, I've found a place for us to stay.'

'Yes, I've fixed it,' she said, leaning into his shoulder. 'But you will be careful, you know what I mean?'

'Sure, honey, I'll keep it covered,' he chuckled. 'I don't want you having a baby, not till we've been married a respectable time.'

'Married?' Miranda exclaimed.

He laughed. 'I guess I should've asked you properly. l had planned to at the weekend, but it just slipped out. But what d'you say? Will you marry me when all this war madness is over?'

Miranda threw her arms around his neck. 'I'd marry you tomorrow, even in this madness,' she said, covering his face with kisses.

He took her hands and held them, kissing her fingers. 'I can't offer no guarantees about where we'll fetch up,' he said. 'I could be posted anywhere, but I know I want you to be with me wherever that is.'

'I wouldn't mind if we had to live in a desert, on top of a mountain or on the moon, as long as you are with me,' she said, and tears of joy ran down her cheeks.

'Hey, don't cry, honey,' he said, wiping the tears away with his thumb. 'I already told my folks about you in a letter and I know they are going to love you as much as I do. What'll your folks have to say?'

'I wish I could say they'd be overjoyed,' Miranda said sadly. 'But I've already told you what my mother's like. I don't care though, my life will be with you and they'll have to lump it.'

'They'll think I'm not good enough for you?'

'Nobody would be, not unless Mother knew the family and they were close to royalty,' she sighed regretfully. 'But don't concern yourself with that. You'll be marrying me, not my mother.'

Belle was asleep when Miranda crept into the hut well after twelve that night. She was so excited that she just had to wake her friend.

'Surely it's not morning yet?' Belle muttered groggily as Miranda shook her.

'No, it's not, but I have something to tell you that can't wait till morning.'

There was just enough moonlight for Miranda to see Belle rubbing her eyes. 'This had better be good,' she said.

'It is. Will proposed. I'll go back with him to America when the war's over. Isn't it wonderful? I'm so happy!'

Belle sat up then and groped for Miranda's hand to squeeze it. 'It is wonderful news, I'm really glad for you. But will you get married here?' she whispered.

'We haven't decided that yet. I'd like to, but he wants his family to be there. We'll talk about it more at the weekend.'

'Are you going to tell your parents?'

'No, Mama will just be horrid about it. I shall present them with a fait accompli.'

'I hope the wedding's here, then I can be with you,' Belle said. 'But can I go back to sleep now?'

'It's "may" I go back to sleep,' Miranda said with a giggle. She was always correcting Belle's speech – it was a long-standing joke between them that she was her grammar coach.

'May you bugger off then,' Belle said. 'And don't forget I'm to be matron of honour.'

On Saturday it was dry for once, though still chilly. Just that afternoon one of the French ambulance drivers had said that this was the wettest summer he could remember. There were huge puddles all around the hospital grounds, which gave everyone a clear idea of how appalling the conditions were for the men at the front.

Miranda met Will at six o'clock in the usual place for their night away. It was the first time since the night they met that she'd seen him in daylight and she could see the car had been washed and polished. So was he; Miranda could smell lemon soap on him as she kissed him, and though he was in his uniform as always, it was freshly pressed, his boots gleaming with polish.

'I thought tonight would never come,' he said, nuzzling his face into her neck. 'I took a lot of stick from the other guys; they said I was watching the clock all day.'

'I was too,' she admitted. 'We were very busy, and the gears kept sticking in my ambulance, so my arm aches from trying to whack it in. I hoped I'd have time for a bath before meeting you, but no such luck. And you look so smart and spruced up.'

He had never looked quite so handsome. His skin was golden, his eyes were shining and his dark hair was so neat and well cut. Her heart was thumping with anticipation at the night ahead, but she wished she'd had time to make herself beautiful for him.

'You look gorgeous to me, good enough to eat,' he said. 'I'd better whisk you away before you change your mind.'

Despite France being a war zone and all the destruction caused by it, battlefields where no tree or bush was left standing, the mass graves, hastily built hospitals, supply dumps, and roads teeming with lorries, gun carriages, horse-driven carts and marching soldiers, just a few miles away from this ugliness it was still a rural idyll. People often commented on this, and as Will drove Miranda away from the hospital in the direction of Rouen, she saw this for herself. The countryside here was still pretty, fields with green crops, pastures with grazing cows and old people carefully tending vegetable patches.

'It's lovely,' she said as they made their way down the narrow country lanes. 'I can smell new-mown hay and damp earth, and so many wild flowers. It's like being back in Sussex, so different from around Camiers.'

Will smiled at her. 'Just don't expect the Waldorf, honey. The French officer who told me about it spoke English as bad as my French; he might have been telling me it was a dump for all I know. But he did say he took his lady friend here, and contacted them for me.'

'I'm impressed that you can find your way, I haven't seen any signposts,' she said.

'Don't praise me yet, we might never find it,' he laughed.

'Here we are,' he said a little later, pulling up by a picturesque but crumbling old stone house with peeling shutters. The sun was a big fiery ball, just sinking down behind the house, giving it a pinkish glow.

The faded sign said 'Le Faisan Doré'. Miranda knew *doré* meant golden, but she didn't understand the other word. The place might look a bit shabby, but compared to a chilly hut with a tin roof, surrounded by mud, it was a palace.

The inside was equally shabby, but quaint, the way so many old country houses were in England. The front door led straight into one large, low-ceilinged room. To the right of the front room was a bar and sitting area; some of the chairs and couches had stuffing coming out of them, and the rugs over the stone floor were threadbare. To the left was a dining area with scrubbed plain wood tables which were being laid for dinner by a skinny young lad of about fourteen. There was a roaring fire on each side of the room, and a plump, smiling-faced elderly woman came forward to greet them, immediately offering them a glass of red wine.

She said in rapid French that if they wanted dinner they must order it now, as they were always busy on Saturday nights. It seemed there was just one dish on offer, and Miranda only recognized the word '*boeuf*' in her description. She translated this for Will and he nodded agreement.

They sat by the fire to warm up while they drank their wine, and when he'd finished laying the tables the young lad showed them to their room which was up the staircase at the back of the bar.

Miranda gasped with delight as the lad opened the door at the back of the house. It was as shabby as downstairs, yet it was the kind of comfortable, faded grandeur she remembered in her grandparents' home when she was small. There was an old and beautiful walnut bed with a matching armoire and dressing table and by the window overlooking fields was a small round table with a vase of pink roses sitting on it.

Will had to duck his head to avoid the beams on the ceiling, and as the boy backed out grinning at them, Miranda prodded the bed and thought it must have a feather mattress as it was very soft.

'What d'you think, honey?' Will said, looking anxious.

'I think it's lovely,' she said truthfully. She might have stayed in far more beautiful rooms in the past, but this one looked romantic and cosy. 'Just the perfect place to spend our first night together.'

She pulled back the faded chintz counterpane and to her surprise the bed was made up with lace-trimmed linen. It was a little creamy with age, but ironed smooth, and she could smell lavender. When she opened a second door it led to a small room with a bath and a bidet. On turning on the tap it was an even bigger surprise to find the water was piping hot.

Back at the hospital they were lucky to get more than three inches of hot water in the bath before it ran cold. Sally had said they'd fixed it that way so no one would linger in there, and no one did as the bathroom was a stark, draughty place. She looked round at Will in delight.

He put his arms around her and kissed her. 'I can see by the look on your face that you are dying to get in the bath, so I'll go down to the bar and have a drink and wait for you there. Come down when you're ready.'

Once again Miranda was touched by his sensitivity. She had fully expected him to leap on her as soon as the bedroom door was closed, and though she wanted him badly, she also wanted everything to be right.

She had come wearing a blouse and skirt so as not to attract any attention to herself when leaving the hospital. But she'd packed a dark red velvet dress which she hadn't even told Belle she had brought from England. Once she'd seen how they were to live at the hospital it looked ridiculously unsuitable. All these weeks it had remained in the tissue paper she'd packed it in at home, and she'd thought she would never get the opportunity to wear it.

While the bath was running she took it out, and to her joy found it had remained uncreased.

Will was on his second brandy, watching the place fill up with French officers in their grey uniforms who had come for a meal, when he saw them all turn to look at the stairs.

Miranda was coming down and she looked sensational. She'd twisted her blonde hair up and secured it with a couple of tortoiseshell combs, and her dark red dress clung to her curves and flattered her pale English complexion. The neckline was cut to expose her creamy shoulders, and the skirt flowed out behind her as she swept down into the dining room. With a sparkly necklace, matching ear bobs and dainty shoes, she could have stepped out of a fashion magazine. Will felt a surge of pride that she was his girl.

'Will I do?' she whispered to him as she reached him.

A lump came up in his throat. She looked what she was, a high-class girl from a privileged background, and he could hardly believe she would love him.

'You're kidding! You'd do for the President himself, let alone a humble sergeant.'

'I have to own up to something,' he said later as they sat at a table by the window. The place was crowded now, and the young lad who had shown them to their room was playing an accordion. The meal was steak and frites, the steak bloody but very tender, and the wine fruity and heady.

There were four or five other women around the room. They were well dressed, but drab compared with Miranda. She had already remarked that she believed them to be wives rather than girlfriends, as they looked very comfortable and weren't talking to their men much.

'I hope it isn't that you have a wife already,' Miranda said. 'If it is, I might throw this glass of wine over you.'

'Certainly not,' he laughed. 'It's an embarrassing confession.'

'You have an artificial leg?' she suggested with twinkling eyes. 'That's fine, I can cope with that.'

'I think you would've guessed that some time ago,' he said. 'No, it's my name.'

'What's wrong with Will?' she asked.

'You think it's short for William?'

Miranda nodded. 'Isn't it?'

'No, it's Wilbur.'

She spluttered with laughter. 'Wilbur?'

'I'm afraid so. Can you live with that?'

'Well, I really don't know. It is rather grim. Belle will have hysterics if she comes to our wedding.'

'Then we'd better get married in secret. And soon too, because after tonight I'll need to make an honest woman of you.'

She just looked at him, her sparkling eyes saying all he needed to know. His father had once told him that when he met his mother he felt a pang in his heart, and he knew then it was true love. Will felt that same pang now; everything he wanted in life was right here in front of him.

'I'd marry you tomorrow if it was possible,' she said softly.

As dawn broke and the first rays of light came through the edges of the curtains, Miranda leaned up on one elbow to look at Will. He had fallen asleep, one strong tanned arm over her, his face squashed into the pillow. She could hardly believe how wonderful his lovemaking had been. It had wiped out everything that had gone before, the humiliation that Frank had made her feel, the knowledge that her mother didn't care much for her, and the sense that she wasn't worth much.

He had kissed every inch of her, even places that made her blush to think about, caresses of such tenderness that he'd made her cry. Lovemaking with Frank had been hot and steamy, but she knew now what had been missing; he'd never made her feel like a goddess the way Will had. There had never been such joy and sweetness, or unhurried delight in pleasing each other.

She ran her hand lightly over his back, revelling in his smooth, silky skin and taut, muscular buttocks. Looking at his perfection, she felt a pang of fear that he might be wounded when he had to go into battle with his regiment.

Daily she felt horror at all those young men maimed and disfigured, but the thought that it might happen to Will was unbearable and tears started up in her eyes just at the thought of it.

During the night she'd voiced her anxiety for him. 'I'll keep safe for you,' he'd said cheerfully, as if he felt love alone was a kind of armour. 'I don't believe that God would let me meet a girl like you, make me love you with all my heart, then allow me to be killed or seriously wounded.'

He had made her believe it too, then. It surely wasn't possible to love so much and then have it snatched away by a shell or bullet. But now, watching him sleeping, she was afraid again.

It struck her that Belle had never voiced any such fears for Jimmy. Was that because she had convinced herself that her man was invincible? Or was she in fact terrified and felt that if she talked about her worst fears they might come true?

'Why are you watching me?' Will said sleepily, wrapping his arm around her more tightly and drawing her down to him.

'Because you're so beautiful,' she whispered.

It was almost eleven when they finally went downstairs, sated with love. They would have liked to spend all day sleeping in each other's arms, but they had to vacate the room.

There were just one couple and three French soldiers in the bar. They had seen the couple the night before, but the soldiers were different ones, enlisted men who appeared just to have come in for coffee.

The woman owner of the hotel asked Will in French if they'd like coffee, and smiled knowingly as if she understood how their night had been spent.

Miranda replied for them both in halting French, saying that would be very nice.

'I suppose she sees people like us all the time,' she whispered to Will. 'In England they wouldn't approve of such behaviour.'

'Americans can be very righteous too,' Will said. 'You'd have to pretend to be married to be given a hotel room.'

The woman brought them a pot of coffee and some warm croissants in a basket. As she turned away, she said something to the French soldiers which Miranda didn't catch, but whatever it was, she was sure it was about them because the men looked over and smiled.

'Do you think this is a place only the French know about?' Miranda asked.

'Possibly. It is in the French army area,' he replied. 'It would be too far for most English officers to get to anyway, and from what I hear not many of them have their wives coming over here to see them.'

One of the two corporals called out to Will. He spoke too fast even for Miranda to understand. Will looked at him, puzzled.

'He asked you when the Americans are going to get here and help us,' the sergeant translated for them in perfect English.

'They are on their way,' Will said.

The man then asked Will about where he was based and how long he thought it would be before the troops would be ready to fight.

Will told him he was based in Calais and that he'd been told the troops would be ready in early 1918. Then he asked about Verdun and the battle of the Somme and how shocked he'd been when he heard about the enormous number of casualties, both English and French. The sergeant translated what he was saying back to his companions.

Will had told Miranda a few nights earlier that it was difficult to learn the truth about conditions at the front and even more importantly how the French and Allied troops viewed the arrival of American soldiers. If there was hostility, it was something that needed to be overcome. Miranda realized that Will saw this chance meeting with some French soldiers as a golden opportunity to find out how they felt.

Miranda left him to it and drank her coffee and ate a croissant, but all the time she was looking at the French sergeant, not just because he spoke such good English, or that he and Will appeared to be getting on well, discussing weaponry, the pros and cons of tanks and the use of cavalry.

Everything about the man was fascinating, his steely blue eyes, the sharpness of his cheekbones, including an old scar that looked as if it had been inflicted with a knife. Even his hair was unique as it was a very light brown with streaks of pure blond amongst it. She would not describe him as handsome, not in Will's polished, healthy-looking way; he looked too tough for that. But he had that élan for which French officers were noted, along with a warm laugh and excellent English, and she felt there was far more to him than in an ordinary soldier.

'I've been remiss in not introducing myself,' Will said. 'Sergeant Will Fergus, and this is my fiancée, Miranda Forbes-Alton from England. Miranda is an ambulance driver at Camiers.'

'You are much too beautiful for such work,' the sergeant said gallantly, instantly making himself even more appealing to her. 'This is Caporal Pierre Armel and Caporal Deguire, and I am Etienne Carrera. We are all enchanted to meet you.'

The name Etienne jolted Miranda. For all she knew, it could be one of the most common names in France, but somehow everything Belle had ever told her about her

Etienne seemed to fit with this man. She had never mentioned his surname or described what he looked like; she'd only said that he had a dark past and spoke very good English. How odd it would be if it was him!

Will moved on to ask about the recent mutiny in the French army. He said he'd heard large numbers of men had deserted their posts and he wanted to know if it was just a baseless rumour.

'Yes, it was true, though none of us three were involved,' Etienne said. 'But I wouldn't blame those who were, for taking a stand. Our men were always prepared to defend their positions on the line, but it was insanity to keep sending them on assaults which meant certain death. The men involved were not deserting, whatever you may have heard. They were exhausted, badly fed and poorly equipped; they knew they were vastly outnumbered and had far fewer big guns than the Boche. They protested in the only way they could. And it worked, because at last the situation is improved, and we are getting better food and more rest.'

This conversation went on for some time, the two corporals asking questions in French, and the sergeant translating for Will. Miranda just watched Etienne. The more she looked at him, the more she felt she had to find out if he was the man Belle had loved.

She waited for a lull in the conversation before speaking. 'Sergeant Carrera, are you by any chance from Marseille?' she asked.

'Yes, I am,' he said, looking very surprised at her question. 'Do you know it?'

'No, but a friend of mine knew someone called Etienne from there,' she said. 'I just wondered if it could be you.'

He looked guarded then, his eyes narrowing. 'What is your friend's name?' he asked.

'Belle Reilly.'

He looked stunned. 'Yes, you do have the right man. I do know Belle.'

Will looked at Miranda in surprise. 'Small world,' he said.

'She's here in France,' Miranda said. 'She works with me at the hospital.'

It was interesting to see how much that news affected him. He didn't respond immediately but she could almost see his thought processes, wanting to ask questions, but also concerned by just how much she knew about him.

'She is an ambulance driver too?'

'Yes, we came here together. We have been friends for some time; we live in the same part of London.'

He was leaning towards her now, clearly eager to know more, and all at once it occurred to her that Belle might not appreciate it if he turned up at the hospital.

'Of course her husband is somewhere in Belgium, she thinks at Ypres,' she said. 'He was wounded at the Somme, fortunately not badly. Have you been wounded at all?'

He smiled at her, his eyes softening in a way that was devastatingly attractive. 'Only minor injuries. You can tell Belle my luck is still holding out.'

There was something so intimate about his reply that she felt unnerved, and she suggested to Will that it was time they left. She really wished she'd thought it through before she'd asked him if he knew Belle. She'd be to blame if he did come to the hospital and put her friend in an awkward position.

Later Miranda and Will drove to another small village and took a walk by a river before finding somewhere to have lunch.

'Tell me how Belle knows the French sergeant,' Will asked. 'He sure looked surprised to hear she was in France.'

Miranda wanted to tell him the whole story but she couldn't, not without revealing a great deal about Belle's past.

'She met him when she was in Paris before the war,' she said carefully. 'It was long before we met and became friends.'

'I'd say he must have meant something to her if she told you about him,' Will replied. 'And she sure meant something to him – he nearly jumped out of his seat when you said her name.'

'Maybe there was something. But she went home and married Jimmy. He'd been her childhood sweetheart.'

'Jimmy must be one helluva man then.'

Miranda knew exactly what he meant. Even in that short meeting she had been aware that Etienne's two friends and Will too were admiring of him. It wasn't anything he'd said or done, he just had that inborn superiority that some people have. Being able to speak another language fluently was part of it, but his looks and his manner did the rest.

'Jimmy is a very good man,' Miranda said. 'Loving, dependable, and just as charismatic in his own way. They are very happy together, and they are right for each other.'

'So maybe you shouldn't tell her you met her old friend?' Will said.

Miranda thought he was very perceptive. She didn't think many men would weigh up the situation as quickly as that. 'Yes, I think you might be right. But it will be hard to keep it to myself.'

The other three girls were already asleep when Miranda got back at eleven that night, but Belle was sitting up in her bed reading and waiting for her.

'How was it?' she whispered, putting her book down and patting her bed for Miranda to come and sit on it.

'So wonderful I don't think I can even explain,' Miranda said.

234

'Well, suppose you tell me first what the place was like where you stayed?'

'Old, faded but cosy, and bliss after this place. This is the real thing, Belle, every bit of me knows it, not even a tiny little sprinkle of doubt. I didn't think I would ever be this happy.'

'Did you decide when the wedding is going to be?' She had never seen her friend look so lovely, happiness had made her beautiful, and all Belle's previous worries about the rightness of this love affair vanished in the face of it.

'We thought we'd have it here, but Will said he'll have to ask his CO's permission. He might refuse of course, what with all the American troops due. And I haven't a clue about where we will live, if I should stay on here, or anything really.'

'It'll all work out, things always do,' Belle said comfortingly. 'Maybe you'll have to be patient for a little longer. But that's not such a bad thing.'

'Easy for you to say,' Miranda grinned impishly. 'Now I've had my wicked way with him I'm going to want him even more, it's going to be agonizing waiting. I shall have to get a new dress for the wedding; do you think I'll find a dressmaker in Calais?'

'I'm sure you will, but you'd better get into bed now. We heard today that there's a great many wounded on their way. No peace for the wicked!'

Miranda lay awake long after Belle had fallen asleep, reliving her night with Will. Just thinking about it aroused her and made her heart beat faster. To try to get to sleep she imagined the war being over and boarding a ship with Will for America. He had said his parents' home was small, a 'row house', he called it, which she assumed was like a terraced house in England. But they would only be there for a while until Will got a new posting; after that they would live in married quarters.

When Belle had come up with the plan to volunteer at the Herbert, Miranda hadn't really wanted to do it. She was just carried away by her friend's enthusiasm. Dozens of times she was on the point of walking out because it was such hard work and she couldn't stand being bossed around. She only stayed, if truth were told, because she knew her mother would say, 'I told you so.' She came up with the idea of driving ambulances as it seemed an easier and rather more glamorous job. She could laugh at that silly idea now, as there was absolutely no glamour in it and it was even harder work.

But now it looked as if it had been her destiny to come here and meet Will. Ahead was a new beginning in a country she'd always wanted to see. He had told her so much about it today, the struggles his parents had when they first arrived as immigrants, the crowded, tough neighbourhood they lived in when he was younger, and the beauty of the country away from the big cities.

He said he was going to get a book about America for her, so she could form a better idea of what life was like there. Tomorrow she would start asking Belle things too. She'd never thought to ask her before.

It was strange to think she had Frank to thank for all this. If not for the affair with him and the abortion, she'd never have got to know Belle, and her life would have been completely different. Her parents would probably have married her off by now, and she'd undoubtedly be spending her days knitting socks and scarves for soldiers, growing more like her mother every day.

Belle was the only person she was going to miss when she began her new life. Her friendship had meant so much, all the shared secrets, the laughs and the joy of being with someone who knew all about her, but loved her just the same. And she thought that knowing Belle had made her a better person.

It was going to be very hard to say goodbye to her.

She glanced over at Belle's bed. It was too dark tonight to see her, but she was making soft little snuffling noises in her sleep. Miranda wished she could tell her about meeting Etienne, but Will was right, it might disturb her serenity to know he was so close.

Miranda smiled to herself. He was the kind of man who would disturb any woman. His steely blue eyes, sharp cheekbones and French accent were enough, but there was something more about him. Belle had said once that another friend had described him as a tiger, and Miranda thought that was an apt simile. He could be a hunter, strong, ruthless perhaps, and dangerous if you got on the wrong side of him.

Yet there was no doubt in her mind that he had cared and still did care deeply for Belle.

'Time to get up, girls,' Sally called out at six the next morning.

Belle groaned, rubbed her eyes and wearily pushed back the bedcovers. 'It can't be morning already, it seems only minutes since we went to bed,' she said.

'For some it probably was,' Sally said archly, looking across at Miranda who was still fast asleep.

'No need for sarcasm, Sally,' Vera piped up. 'You're only jealous.'

'For the record, she came in at eleven. I spoke to her,' Belle said, and reached out to shake her friend's arm to wake her.

The rain was back. When they left the hut to go and get their breakfast, they squelched through puddles once again. Fifteen minutes later Belle was running over to her ambulance, her coat over her head, and she saw David was already sitting in it with the engine running. As she got in, she saw Miranda standing beside hers, with Alf, and she seemed to be angry about something.

'I wonder what's wrong?' Belle said to David as she prepared to drive off.

'I think she's cross that she's got to drive that one again,' David said. 'You remember on Saturday she was moaning about the gears sticking?'

Belle did remember. Miranda had said it made her arm ache trying to change the gears. 'I suppose she was in so much of a hurry to get off on Saturday she forgot to report it,' she said.

The two girls always tried to drive one behind the other as it meant if there was a delay at the station they could chat to each other, so Belle waited a moment to see if Miranda was able to drive the ambulance. When she saw it move, she set off and Miranda fell in behind.

'It seems to be all right,' David said, looking in the wing mirror. 'Maybe it was fixed after all. Did she have a good weekend?'

'The best,' Belle grinned. 'She looked like she was on cloud nine when she got back. Today should bring her down to earth with a bump though, if it's true there's going to be even more casualties than usual.'

David began telling her about an argument that had broken out last night between two men in his hut about a missing fruit cake sent from home. Dan, whose cake it was, thought the other man, Ernie, had taken it and scoffed it all.

'And had he?' Belle asked.

'No, it turned out Dan had squirrelled it away for safe-keeping in his suitcase, and he'd forgotten about it. He got his case out for something else, and there it was. There was nothing Dan could do but share it out then, and Ernie made him give him a really big piece to apologize.'

Belle laughed. There were always arguments about such things in the men's hut. The girls she shared with were far more civilized; when any of them got stuff from home they always shared it.

'This damned rain, do you think it's going to last for the whole summer?' she said, leaning forward to peer through the windscreen as the wipers weren't clearing it very well. The level crossing was up ahead, but as Belle reached the box where the man sat who waved a warning flag if a train was approaching, she noticed he wasn't in it.

'I wonder where he is?' she said to David. She often had a chat with the man if they had to wait for a train to pass.

'Perhaps there's no train expected after all,' David said hopefully. 'Or it's already gone through.'

Belle drove on over the tracks, and glanced in her mirror to see if Miranda was right behind, but she'd fallen back some four hundred yards, so clearly she was still having trouble with the gears.

Belle slowed down for her to catch up, and at that moment she heard a shrill train whistle.

'Bloody hell, there's a train coming!' she shouted in alarm. She pulled up, and both she and David jumped out to warn Miranda. But by the time they'd got to the back of the ambulance, they could see she was already right on the crossing and appeared to have stalled.

'God in heaven!' David exclaimed. 'What is she doing?'

They started to run the six or seven hundred yards towards her, waving their arms in warning, but she wasn't moving, and even at that distance they could sense she couldn't get the vehicle to go back or forward.

The hospital trains were slow, but the line curved round

near the crossing and the driver wouldn't see the ambulance in time to stop.

'Get out!' both David and Belle yelled at the top of their voices. 'Get out now!'

The train was nearly there, hidden from view by trees, but they could see the steam and hear it lumbering ever closer.

Belle was screaming in terror; she was close enough to the crossing now to see Miranda's white, panicked face, and the train bearing down on her. Alf in the passenger seat was gesticulating, clearly shouting to Miranda to get out, then his door opened and he leapt out and ran full tilt towards Belle.

Everything seemed to slow right down then. The train driver had clearly seen the ambulance because they could hear the shriek of the brakes, Miranda turned her head towards the train, her arm moving as if still trying to wrestle with the gears. Then all at once the train was right there, slamming into the ambulance and pushing it sideways along the track like a piece of cardboard.

They saw Miranda's arms come up and cover her head just as the ambulance was swept over on to its side, and the train went right on to it before it finally came to a halt.

Chapter Sixteen

David tried to hold Belle back, but she pushed him off and ran to the mangled ambulance. Even as she ran she knew there was very little chance of Miranda not being seriously hurt; the train had crushed the cab.

The train driver and the fireman both jumped out of the engine, and all along the train nurses were looking out of the windows, trying to see what had happened.

Alf sank down on to his knees in the road, wailing that he'd tried to make Miranda get out. Belle yelled back to David to see to him.

The fireman from the train tried to block Belle's way. 'That's not going to be any sight for a girl,' he said, grabbing hold of her arms.

'She's my friend and I see wounded men daily,' Belle sobbed. 'Just let me see if I can get into the cab to find out if there's any hope.'

She threw him off and ran the last few yards. The train engine's front wheels were embedded in what had been the driving seat and as Miranda wasn't visible it seemed she had been flung over on to the passenger side. The windscreen was shattered, shards of glass all over the track, all of them splattered with blood.

Belle almost lost her nerve then. People were shouting and steam was belching out from the train engine, but she had to look, and kneeling down she peered into what remained of the crushed cab.

Right down at the bottom, against the passenger door,

Miranda's blonde hair showed up in the gloom, but her body was hanging upside down and it was twisted grotesquely, both her legs trapped beneath the train engine's wheel.

There was so much blood that Belle retched. 'Miranda, can you hear me?' she called out. 'It's Belle, I'm here, please speak if you can.'

There was no sound or movement. Belle could just make out her friend's hand, still raised to her head the way it had been as the train hit. She reached in and caught hold of it, feeling her wrist for a pulse.

But there was none. She was already dead.

'I loved you, Miranda,' Belle whispered, rain mingling with her tears and running down her face. 'I never had a real friend before you and I don't know how I'm going to manage without you.'

The train driver came and lifted her up and she fell against his chest, sobbing.

'Come away now, sweetheart, there's people coming to move the ambulance. There's nothing more you can do. We've got to get the wounded men on the train off to hospital too.'

It was the very worst of days. Railway men arrived with heavy machinery to back up the train engine and remove the ambulance from the tracks. The engine wheels were buckled and they had to be fixed before it could continue to the station. Meanwhile, all the ambulances which were on the station side of the track had to drive a circuitous route to the other side so they could take the wounded off the train.

All of them were distressed further by the delay and the job of lifting them from the train was far harder without the height of a station platform. Tempers were short, and the extra jolting was painful for the wounded. With all the drivers and stretcher bearers shocked and deeply upset by the terrible accident, they were not at their best.

Belle had to carry on; with so many seriously wounded men in grave need of operations and treatment, she couldn't do otherwise. But the spectre of what she'd seen and what she'd lost was impossible to put aside. Alf was in deep shock; he'd been taken back to the hospital but he kept haranguing everyone who knew Miranda, clearly desperate for them all to tell him he couldn't have done more to get her out. One thing was clear from what he said: she hadn't frozen with horror – right until the last minute she was bravely trying to get the ambulance off the tracks because she was afraid it would derail the train.

It was late in the afternoon before soldiers got Miranda's body out of the ambulance. As the rain was still pouring down everyone became soaked to the skin and that added another dimension of misery to a terrible day.

When Belle and David drove back to the hospital at nearly eight in the evening with their last load of wounded, a message was waiting for them that they were to report to Captain Taylor.

'That's all we need,' David groaned. He had been strong for Belle all day. He'd got her hot, sweet tea, comforted her, dried her tears, and fended off all those who clamoured to ask her questions. But he had liked Miranda too, and had also witnessed the horrific accident; his face was so pale he looked as if he could pass out at any minute.

Captain Taylor was an excellent organizer, but he could be brusque with those under his command, and it was generally known that he had not approved of women being taken on as drivers. Both Belle and David expected that he would take a hard line about Miranda's death if she hadn't reported the problem with the gearbox.

He was speaking to someone on the telephone as they went into his office. He indicated they were to wait. Their overalls were soaking wet, water was dripping from them on to the floor, and they were very cold, possibly more as the result of shock than the temperature.

Captain Taylor was short and stout, with grey hair and a handlebar moustache. His uniform was always impeccable, as if he pressed it daily, and it was common knowledge that in civilian life he'd been a bank manager. As he talked, he was looking Belle up and down, as if appalled by her drowned-rat appearance.

'You are very wet,' he said as he put the telephone down. 'I won't keep you long but I need to hear your version of what occurred today.'

'There was no one manning the level crossing, sir,' Belle said. 'I noticed that as we went through. We both assumed this was because no train was due.'

She felt she had to get that in first, as it was the reason for the accident. The faulty gearbox was incidental.

'Parks!' said Captain Taylor, looking at David. 'Tell me what happened. In full.'

David began by confirming the crossing had been unmanned, then explained how they had noticed just after they passed over it that Miranda had fallen well behind them in the convoy, so they pulled up. 'I intended to suggest she left her ambulance and came to the station with us, sir,' he said. Then he went on to describe the events which occurred when they heard the train coming. 'The ambulance was stalled right on the crossing. We could see her trying to get it into gear. When we heard the train coming we ran and shouted for her and Alf Dodds to get out. There is a bend on the line just before the crossing and we knew by the time the train driver saw the ambulance and braked, there wouldn't be enough time to stop it.'

'Did Forbes-Alton tell either of you there was a problem with the gearbox before she set out?'

'She said it was hard to change gear on Saturday, sir,' Belle said.

'But she didn't report it?'

'I don't know, sir,' Belle said. 'I didn't speak to her on Saturday evening as she was going away for the night.'

Suddenly her anger flared up. Her friend was dead, and now this pompous little man who sat in his office all day and never lifted a stretcher or even came down to the station to see the wounded, was implying the fault was all Miranda's.

'Surely this shouldn't be about what was wrong with the ambulance?' she snapped at him. 'There should've been a man on the level crossing. Even if Miranda had managed to cross it safely, the next ambulance might have been hit. She's dead, through no fault of her own, a hideous death just as she was planning to get married. And what about her parents? Have you contacted them yet?'

He had the grace to look faintly embarrassed. 'No, I haven't, Reilly, but I will send a telegram.'

'Can't you telephone them?' she implored him, moving closer to his desk. 'Imagine their reaction to getting a telegram saying she'd been hit by a train!'

'The correct procedure is a telegram,' he said woodenly.

'I'm sorry if I'm speaking out of turn, sir,' Belle said, tears welling up in her eyes. 'But surely the army and Red Cross owe her parents a personal call and an explanation as to why their daughter is dead?'

'I realize you are upset, but army protocol has to be followed. A telegram is the way we inform relatives.'

'But she wasn't a soldier, she was a volunteer. And who is going to break the news to her fiancé? Or are you just going to wait until he comes here looking for her?'

'I wasn't even aware she had a fiancé,' he said.

'Well, she has, and he's a sergeant in the American army. His name is Fergus; at present he's organizing the billets for the expected troops.'

Taylor made a note of the name on his jotter, then looked back at Belle. 'I will contact his CO. In this instance I will put your lack of respect down to the shock of losing a close friend. You may go now, get into some dry clothes.'

David saluted the captain and turned to go, but Belle stood her ground.

'Please, sir. Miranda worked hard here, and she has influential parents,' she pleaded. 'You really should telephone them tonight and break the news to them of their daughter's death. You have to give them the opportunity to arrange for her body to be taken home. Or were you planning to put her into a mass grave with the soldiers who will die of their injuries tonight?'

He looked hard at her for a moment, then dropped his eyes. 'All right, Reilly, you've made your point. Give me the number and I will put a call through to them now. Now, go and get into dry clothes. Both of you may have tomorrow off, I appreciate you need some rest to get over this.'

Belle stepped forward, picked up a pencil from his desk and wrote the Forbes-Altons' telephone number on his jotter. 'Thank you, sir,' she said, and turned away before he could see she was crying.

Outside, David put his arms round her. 'That was brave,' he said, holding her tightly against his shoulder. 'For a moment I thought you would hit him if he didn't give in.'

'It was only me saying her parents were influential that

persuaded him,' she sobbed against his shoulder. 'After all we see here daily you'd think you'd get hardened to it, wouldn't you? I could just about deal with those two men with stomach wounds who were dead on arrival at the hospital today, death was better than life for them. But Miranda had everything to live for. She wanted love so badly and at last she'd found it. It is just so cruel she had to be taken like this.'

He held her for some little time to comfort her. 'Come on, I'll take you back to your hut,' he said eventually.

'I'm worried about Will,' she said, allowing herself to be led away. 'Miranda had arranged to meet him tomorrow night. What if Captain Taylor doesn't get in touch with him?'

'I think he will; after what you said he wouldn't dare do otherwise. But what about you? Will you go home for her funeral?'

Belle just looked at him dumbly; she couldn't see beyond the pain inside her.

David appeared to understand. He didn't press her further, just led her to her hut, opened the door and nudged her in. 'Ask one of the girls to make you a hot water bottle,' he said. 'And stay in bed tomorrow.'

The following day it had stopped raining and the sun came out. Belle remained in the hut alternately crying, thinking about all that she had loved about Miranda, and staring blankly at the ceiling. When the other girls came back in the early evening, their kindly questioning about whether she'd eaten and how she was feeling made her want to cry again. Using the excuse that she needed some fresh air, she went outside and sat on the step.

The big puddles of the day before were far smaller now, it was warm and everywhere looked cleaner and fresher. She felt curiously numb, and she thought that must be nature's way of dealing with grief. She knew she should pack Miranda's things, and write her parents a letter, but she couldn't do that yet. She couldn't even write to Jimmy or Mog.

So many memories of Miranda still kept flitting through her mind, but they were the happier ones now. She could see her in the shop trying on hats and pulling faces in the mirror, and recalled the laughter they shared when she was teaching Belle to drive her father's car, and the comfort she'd given her when she lost her baby. She remembered her friend's gift for mimicking people, and her sarcastic little asides about them that were always so acute and funny. Yet Miranda had never been deliberately unkind, she had been generous, affectionate, and loyal too. Belle had always imagined they would still be friends when they were old ladies. They knew all about each other, good and bad. Miranda was the one person Belle felt she could always be her true self with. She didn't believe it was possible to find another friend like that.

'Tell me to go away if you'd rather be alone.'

Belle started at Vera's voice. She hadn't heard her open the hut door.

Vera was a very bouncy, happy person, renowned for her jollity. Even the most dour drivers and stretcher bearers remarked that she was a tonic with her ready smiles and the way she was always ready to help anyone.

Her pretty, elfin, freckled face, red, curly hair and slender shape belied how strong she was. She joked that she'd built up muscle even as a child helping her father knead dough in his bakery.

'No, stay,' Belle said, remembering that it had been Vera who had kept her company all the time Miranda had been seeing Will. 'I thought I wanted to be alone, but I don't think I really do.'

'You two were so close I don't suppose you can imagine life without her,' Vera said, sitting down beside her.

'That just about sums it up,' Belle said glumly. 'Mostly I thought I was the one who held her up; I had the ideas, she followed me. But now without her I feel I'll never have another idea or plan again. I was thinking earlier how odd it is that I think that; after all, if she'd run off with Will, or decided to go home, I'd have been fine without her.'

'But you didn't see this coming, and it's final, that's why it hurts so much,' Vera said. 'None of the rest of us got really close to her, but it's still knocked all of us for six. Every single one of the drivers and stretcher bearers feel it too.'

'I don't know if I can stay here now,' Belle said sadly. 'I'd give anything to be at home with Mog and Garth, yet at the same time I know if I was to go home I'd feel just as empty there.'

'Would it make you feel better to go and see Miranda's mother?'

Belle shook her head. 'She's the last person I want to see. She'd put on a big display of grief, but I'd be thinking how false it is because she wasn't very kind to Miranda.'

'What about Will? He'll need someone to talk to.'

'Yes, that's true. Poor man, they had made so many plans. Miranda didn't even have time to tell me them all, but I don't think I could talk to him, not yet.'

'You can talk to me any time,' Vera said, and put her hand on Belle's arm.

They sat there together for some time in companionable silence. Every now and then a couple of nurses or orderlies would come past, and there were a number of civilians too, perhaps relatives of patients. Further down the path, there were some men well enough to leave the wards, some on crutches, an arm in a sling, or a bandage around their head.

Birds were chirping nearby, but behind that they could hear the muffled boom of guns miles away at the front.

Belle broke the silence. 'The guns must be very loud if we can hear them all this way away,' she said. 'It must be like hell there. Three years of war now and we're still no closer to ending it. How many more men have to die before they are satisfied?'

Vera took Belle's hand and squeezed it, a way of saying she shared Belle's anger. 'You know, I sometimes wonder what it was that made me come all this way. I can remember thinking it was my duty to help, but I had no real understanding of the destruction, the sheer brutality of war.'

'Miranda and I saw it as an adventure,' Belle confessed. 'That seems so stupid now, after all, we'd worked in a hospital back home and knew the horror of it. But we thought we were being brave and noble.' Her laugh was hollow.

Vera nodded in understanding. 'I suppose I thought I was being noble and self-sacrificing too. But the real truth is that I was so bored working in the bakery. I'd listen to customers telling Mother about their problems, trivial things like a child who'd broken good china, or the dress material they'd sent for that hadn't arrived, and I wanted to scream at the dullness of my life.

'I used to daydream of living in a big city, going dancing, having enough money to buy anything I wanted. But I wasn't qualified to do anything other than serve in a shop. When I heard they needed volunteers here, it seemed the answer to everything. I would see more of the world; I'd learn things I never could at home.'

'Well, you've certainly done that,' Belle said. 'But didn't you get some hospital experience before you came?'

'Only a month in Auckland, but because I could drive they put me on collecting and taking old people home, so I didn't learn anything much. That's why I got put on driving an ambulance here. But my first day collecting the wounded from the train shocked me to the core.'

'I should think it did,' Belle agreed. She'd found it shocking too and she was already used to seeing gory sights.

'I wanted to go home,' Vera went on. 'The tranquil life I had back there seemed like heaven when I was surrounded by blood and guts and young soldiers crying for their mothers. I'm so used to it now that I've started to worry that I'll never fit in again back home.'

'I sometimes feel like that too,' Belle said. 'It's hard to write home because I know they can't imagine what we do, or maybe it's that I don't want to put those pictures in their heads. So tell me about New Zealand. That would be a far more pleasant thing to describe to them. Is it very hot?'

'It can be in the North Island where I come from,' Vera replied. 'It's sub-tropical, you see. But down in the South Island it can be very cold and often very wet. It's a beautiful country, with mountains covered in snow in winter, lakes and fast-flowing rivers. There's lots of sheep, many more of them than people, there's so much space, you can go miles without seeing a single house.

'But I live in a little place called Russell. It's in the Bay of Islands. The sea is turquoise, with little islands dotted about in it covered in trees, and it's very quiet and beautiful. Yet once it was a very wicked place, which they called the Hell Hole of the Pacific because the whalers used to come there to get drunk and find women.'

Belle half smiled because that made her think of New Orleans, but she wasn't going to tell Vera that. 'It sounds lovely. Have you ever seen a whale?'

'Lots of times. I used to go out fishing with my father and brothers and we often saw them, dolphins too, they are exciting to watch, so playful and beautiful. But I guess no one ever appreciates where they grew up, not until they go away from it.'

'It sounds heavenly to me,' Belle sighed. 'Jimmy and I used to think we'd like to live by the sea when the war is over, but the longer I'm here, the less I think about the future. I can't imagine doing ordinary things like washing clothes or baking a cake any more. Maybe you are right and we won't fit in when we go home.'

Just then they saw Captain Taylor walking towards them. 'He's coming to speak to you,' Vera said. 'I'll go in and leave you to it.'

'Thank you for the chat, Vera,' Belle said as the girl got up. 'You've cheered me, I'm very grateful for that.'

'Good evening, Reilly,' the captain said as he drew closer. 'I just came over to tell you that I've managed to contact Mr and Mrs Forbes-Alton. They are arranging for their daughter's body to be taken home to them. It will be tomorrow morning.'

'And did you manage to contact Sergeant Fergus?'

'Not personally,' he said. 'I spoke to his CO this morning and he will have told him by now. It's a bad business, we are all sadly accustomed to informing relatives of servicemen killed in action, and now and then we have to inform men here too of deaths in their family back home, but I never expected to have to relay the news of a death of one of our female volunteers.'

'May I go home with Miranda?' Belle asked. 'I mean, on the same train and boat. She would have wanted me to.'

She saw by the way his face tightened that this wasn't possible. 'Or just so I get back in time for the funeral,' she said. 'I know it must be difficult with one driver gone, without a second one asking for leave.'

'I'm sorry, Reilly. But Mrs Forbes-Alton has insisted that you are not to attend their daughter's funeral,' he said.

Belle was stunned. 'But why? How could she say that? I was Miranda's closest friend. She would want me there.'

The captain looked uneasy and made a helpless gesture with his hands. 'She was adamant, extremely forceful. I'm sure it was grief, it does make people say irrational things sometimes. She appears to blame you for her daughter's death.'

'Me!' Belle was incredulous. 'How could I be blamed for it?'

The captain shrugged. 'She said you persuaded her to come here, that she hadn't been the same girl since she met you. But as I said, people do say foolish things at such times.'

'That woman is such a witch,' Belle gasped. 'Miranda was older than me, she had a mind of her own, I didn't force her to come, she wanted to. How dare her mother say such a thing?'

'I have to admit I was rather shocked at her outburst,' he said. 'I pointed out that her daughter had been happy here, that she was a valued member of our team and that I'd found you to be a steadying influence on her. But it was to no avail. I'm sorry, Reilly.'

'Did you tell her that she was going to marry Sergeant Fergus?'

'No, I didn't, it wasn't an appropriate thing to say under the circumstances.'

'I'm a volunteer. If I want to go home on leave tomorrow, can you prevent me?'

He looked at her for a moment, as if weighing up the situation. 'No, I can't prevent you. But I would urge you to think it through. We need you here, and Mrs Forbes-Alton has connections in high places and is likely to use them if you go against her wishes. Please think it over calmly. I'm sure your friend would not have wanted you to jeopardize your future just to attend her funeral.'

Belle was just about to make an angry retort when an American staff car drove past. She saw a familiar face glance at her and the captain, then the driver stopped the car and reversed back towards them.

'That's Sergeant Fergus,' Belle gasped. 'I hope to God he's been told already, I don't want to have to break the news.'

Belle could see by Will's face as he got out of the car that he had been told. He seemed to have shrunk a couple of inches and the glossy appearance he'd had the day they first met had vanished.

He saluted the captain, then looked at Belle with such pain in his eyes that a lump rose in her throat.

'Will, this is Captain Taylor, who runs the ambulance unit,' she said. 'Captain Taylor, this is Will Fergus, Miranda's fiancé.'

The captain offered his condolences and explained that Miranda's body was being taken back to England in the morning. Then, perhaps realizing it was Belle that the man wished to speak to, he said that if Fergus had any further questions of him, he would be in his office.

'Oh Will, I'm so very sorry,' Belle said once the captain had gone. 'How much did they tell you?'

'The minimum,' he said. 'A train hit her ambulance. Was she killed instantly, Belle? I can't bear to think of her suffering.'

He sat on the hut steps next to her and Belle told him exactly how it came about and assured him it was instantaneous. 'I ran to her, and she was already dead, Will. She didn't stand a chance.'

'She told me on Saturday night that her arm was aching from the stiff gears,' he said. 'If only she'd refused to drive it again.'

He told her then how they had discussed getting married, and although he would have liked it to be back in Philadelphia with all his family there, they had decided that if they got married in France it would be far easier to take her home with him when the war was over.

'Another reason was that she wanted you there,' he said. 'She joked that she was going to make you wear something so ugly you wouldn't outshine her.'

That brought tears to Belle's eyes because she could imagine Miranda saying it.

'I never thought for one moment when I left the States that I would find love here in France,' he said. 'Me and the other guys had the idea that the French girls would be queuing up for us, we talked about little else on the way out here. If anyone had told me I was going to fall for a classy English girl I would've laughed at them. I was so proud of her I felt I could burst with it. I'd written home and told my folks all about her. I had my whole future planned around her, all I was scared of was that I might die here. It never crossed my mind it would be her.'

Belle told him then what Captain Taylor had said, how she wasn't welcome at Miranda's funeral, and that made her cry. 'At least you were spared that overbearing ogre of a woman as a mother-in-law,' she sobbed. 'I can't believe she would blame me.'

'Hey, don't take it to heart,' he said, putting his arm around her, tears running down his face too. 'Miranda said she didn't care if she never saw her mother again. I thought at the time they'd just had a bit of a tiff, but I guess she was on the level about her. Don't put yourself through going over there just to make a point.'

'All I wanted was to be with Miranda on that final journey,' Belle sobbed. 'We meant so much to one another it seems awful that she'll be going alone. How could anyone be so cruel and nasty?'

'Beats me,' he said sadly. 'No wonder Miranda said she wasn't even going to tell her folks about us until after we were married. But I tell you what, suppose I come tomorrow night with flowers and we go down to the level crossing and say our goodbyes to Miranda there?'

Belle sniffed back her tears. 'That would be good,' she said.

'She loved you like a sister,' Will said, hugging her to his shoulder. 'She said that meeting you was the best thing that ever happened to her, well, up till meeting me. We've both got broken hearts now, I can't see mine ever mending, but I know she'd want you to laugh again, to be happy with your old man. So you gotta do it for her.'

'I'll try,' Belle said, deeply touched that he was soothing her when he was hurting so badly. 'I suppose I ought to go in now. I know Captain Taylor kind of gave us permission to talk, but it will still be frowned on, me being out here with you.'

'Can you meet me tomorrow? I'll wait outside the fence where I used to meet Miranda.'

Belle nodded. 'I'm glad you came, I was so worried about you. It was me who told Captain Taylor he had to inform you. If it had been left up to him even her parents would only have got a telegram.'

'Thank you for saying I was her fiancé,' Will said. 'That made me feel like I had a real claim on her, y'know what I mean? And if you give me her folks' address tomorrow, I'll write them and make them see Miranda was very special.'

Belle gave him a watery smile. She thought he was one of the nicest men she'd ever met, all that Miranda had claimed.

'And I'll tell 'em what a gem you are,' he added. 'We'll stay in touch, yeah? Maybe when we're all done here I'll come to England and meet your folks and your old man. He's lucky he's got you to come home to.'

After Will had gone, Belle went into the hut and with help from Vera packed up Miranda's things. She found her friend's copy of the photograph they'd had taken together before they left England. They were wearing dresses of a similar style, with loose frills down the bodice and a wide sash at the waist. Belle's was green washed silk, and Miranda's blue-and-cream-striped crêpe, and they both wore pretty little hats that Belle had made. The sepia colouring of the picture didn't do the dresses or the hats justice, but their smiles were real, because they were excited about going to France. She thought she would give it to Will as she still had her own copy she would never want to part with.

When she found the dark red velvet dress she guessed that was what Miranda had worn on her last evening with Will, and she hugged it to her, breathing in her perfume that still lingered on it. It was tempting to keep it, but it looked as if it had cost a small fortune and Mrs Forbes-Alton might claim she had stolen it.

She kept a silver bracelet for herself as a keepsake, though, and the fluffy pink shawl that Miranda used to wrap around her shoulders when sitting up in bed. It still smelled of her lavender toilet water.

'Why don't you give her diary to Will too?' Vera suggested when she found the small blue leather book in her locker. 'I bet she's written all sorts of things about him in it. And she wouldn't want her mother reading it.'

Belle agreed. Then they folded up all the clothes and put them in the suitcase. A little later Belle carried it over to Captain Taylor's office.

In bed later, she read the diary, and for the first time since the accident she found something to smile about. The writing was as irrational and flippant as Miranda had been. One day she wrote a whole page very neatly, on others she scrawled just one line. There was one entry which made Belle splutter with laughter. It was 19 January. 'Sister Fogget might be an excellent nurse and a good example to a know-nothing idiot like me, but I'd like to tie her to the bedsteads she makes me scrub, and beat her with a wet towel.'

On the day they'd left England she'd written, 'Poor Belle, struggling not to cry at leaving Mog. But I'll convert her to being as uncaring as I am.'

A few days later the entry read: 'Belle was made for this, she has a smile that would make a blind man see, and a lame man walk. She's even turned me into a half decent person.'

Will was there too. The day she met him she'd written, 'Met Will, a Yank, in Calais. I am fast. I took one look at him and knew he was the one I'd been waiting for. Kisses that made me weak with longing. I hope I had the same effect on him.'

Belle closed the diary then. She'd skimmed through it quickly and seen all the later entries were about Will, and she felt it should only be read by him. She hoped it would make him smile and see how meeting him had changed Miranda for the better. And above all it would comfort him to know that he was in her heart right up to the moment she died.

Chapter Seventeen

Sally walked past Belle as she was cleaning out her ambulance at the end of the day. 'Captain Taylor asked me to inform you there's someone waiting to see you in the drivers' room,' she said curtly.

Belle assumed it was Will. It was two weeks since the evening they went down to the level crossing and placed flowers for Miranda there. That evening had been particularly painful because the crushed ambulance had still been there, lying on its side by the track. The cab looked as if it had been opened with a giant tin opener to get Miranda's body out, but although the heavy rain had washed away her blood, the horror of the moment when Belle saw the train crash into it came back to her anew. For Will it must have been simply devastating to see how Miranda met her end. He broke down, sobbing so hard that Belle wished she'd never agreed to show him where the accident happened.

'I had so many plans for us,' he said through his tears. 'I was going to take her to the Waldorf in New York and have a picnic in Central Park. My folks would've loved her, and even if I could never keep her like her own folks did, we would've had a good life together.'

All Belle could do was hold him and tell him all the lovely things Miranda had said about him. That she'd been waiting all her life for love like his, and how she couldn't wait to marry him.

They sat on an old tree trunk and cried together, then Belle gave him the diary and the photograph.

'I haven't read the entries since she met you,' she told him. 'That's just for your eyes. But I hope it will give you some comfort to read the funny things she said, and help you understand more about her. Try and remember her as she was on your last night together, not how her life ended. She'll be looking down on you and wanting you to be happy with someone else one day.'

The memory of that painful evening with Will was still imprinted on Belle's mind, and she hoped he'd called today to tell her that he'd heard from Miranda's parents because she didn't feel she could cope with any further emotional scenes.

'You'll be in trouble if you get any more male visitors,' Sally added waspishly. 'But then, I suppose you've wormed your way round Captain Taylor.'

Sally often sniped at Belle. It reminded her uncomfortably of the cattiness of some of the girls in Martha's sporting house in New Orleans. She didn't know what Sally had to be jealous about; it wasn't as if they were in competition here, and Sally was a far better driver and a really good mechanic too.

'Well, no one could ever accuse you of worming your way round anyone,' Belle retorted. 'You're more of a cobra, you spit venom to paralyse your victims.'

Sally flounced away without responding. Vera, who had heard the exchange, grinned at Belle and put one thumb up in approval.

Vera had been such a comfort to Belle. She had moved into Miranda's old bed, perhaps understanding that it would be at night that Belle would miss her old friend the most. The other girls didn't speak about Miranda at all, it was as if she'd never been there, but Vera got Belle to talk about her, and that had helped a great deal.

As Belle didn't want Will seeing evidence of the nature of her job, she quickly ran back to the hut, took off her blood-stained overall, washed her face and hands and brushed her hair before going over to meet him.

The drivers' hut door was open, and she walked in ready to greet Will with a smile, but when she saw who was waiting there she froze in shock.

It was Etienne.

Whenever she pictured him in her mind it was always as he'd looked in Paris at the Gare du Nord, with a trilby hat, a dark suit and striped waistcoat, his eyes like blue glass. But now he was dashing in the French grey-blue uniform, his boots polished to a mirror shine and sergeant's chevrons on his sleeve. Yet his blue eyes were just the same and made her heart flip.

When she first got to France, she had scrutinized the French soldiers, half hoping to see him. She had always checked the names of any French wounded brought in too. But she certainly hadn't expected him to turn up here to see her.

'Etienne!' she exclaimed. 'What? How?' She paused, so shocked she couldn't get any sensible words out.

'I ran into Will Fergus at the American base when I collected some supplies from there,' he said. 'He told me what happened to his girl. I felt I had to come and see how you were; I knew you must be taking it just as badly as he is.'

Belle felt a bit faint with the shock and had to sit down. 'But how do you know I knew her?' she asked.

Etienne frowned and sat down too. 'Didn't Miranda tell you that we met when she was staying at the Faisan Doré?'

'No, she didn't,' Belle said. 'But she got back late that night and it was the next morning she was killed.' She paused, looking at him in puzzlement. 'But how on earth did she connect you with me?'

Etienne shrugged. 'I was in there with a couple of men from my company. Will spoke to us and I translated what he said to the other two. At one point we exchanged names. I can only suppose she recognized mine because of something you'd said to her, because she inquired if I was from Marseille. When I said I was, she asked if I knew someone called Belle. I was like you are now, stunned. She said you came here together.'

'But she never told me this,' Belle gasped.

'That may have been because she thought it best not to,' he said. 'It struck me afterwards that you must have told her a great deal about me for her to remember my name. That touched me. Then to hear she'd been killed in such a terrible way! Will could hardly bring himself to tell me about it.'

'Yes, it was terrible,' Belle said. 'I still can't really believe it. We were such good friends and I thought we always would be. I'm lost without her.'

'I thought that would be the case, that's why I had to come,' he said. 'But I have to admit that finding you'd told her about me made me glad you hadn't forgotten me entirely.'

The hut door was open, they were sitting opposite each other, and should anyone look in they would see nothing to suggest the French sergeant and she were anything other than casual acquaintances. Yet Belle suddenly felt very nervous.

'Oh, we had one of those you-tell-me-your-story-and-I'll-tell-you-mine conversations once,' she said lightly, as if it was of no real importance. 'She was the only person I ever told about New Orleans and Paris and your part in it. But Miranda was a romantic, and a great one for reading more into things than was really there.'

'She must have meant a great deal to you if you felt able to confide in her about that time.' He looked straight at Belle, one eyebrow raised questioningly. 'How did you meet her?'

'In my shop,' she said. 'She lived nearby, and yes, she did come to mean a great deal to me. Her death has knocked me sideways. It was just so awful, as it wouldn't have happened if the crossing had been manned like it's supposed to be.'

'It's hard losing good friends,' he said. 'I've lost so many since the war started I avoid getting friendly with anyone now.'

'I'd never had a real friend before, not someone you can confide in and talk about anything. I don't think she had either. We might have come from very different backgrounds but we had a great deal in common.'

'So what happened to the shop?'

'Jimmy joined up, I lost the baby I was carrying, and I grew disenchanted with making and selling hats, it seemed so frivolous when men were dying at the front.'

'I am very sorry about the baby,' he said. 'I can see that would change everything for you, especially with your husband away. But what made you and Miranda come here?'

Belle felt that his line of questioning was to discover if thoughts of him had prompted her choices. She knew she must make it clear they had not, but the feelings she had had for him and believed were dead and buried were bubbling up again inside her. His French accent was so attractive, and it brought back many good memories of the time they shared together.

'That was pure chance,' she said, not meeting his eyes because she was afraid he'd read in hers that she wasn't being entirely truthful. 'We decided to do our bit for the war by volunteering at the military hospital and in the year we were there Miranda taught me to drive. Then we were told ambulance drivers were desperately needed here. I thought I'd get the chance to see Jimmy more often too.'

'Have you seen much of him since you've been here?'

As before, when asked about meeting up with Jimmy she

felt a twinge of guilt that she hadn't even attempted to do so. 'No, unfortunately it's too busy here to get away.'

'Miranda managed it,' he said.

Belle blushed. She might have known he would pick up on that. 'It was easier for her. Will isn't tied down by regular duties and anyway, he was close by.'

'I'm not close by, and I have regular duties too, but when I knew you were here I wanted to come and see you straight away. The only thing that stopped me was not the difficulties, but fear you wouldn't want to see me.'

She felt he was pushing her into a corner, trying to get her to admit her feelings for him. The easiest way out of it would be to say she hadn't wanted to see him, but she couldn't bring herself to say that.

'I didn't expect to see Will ever again,' he went on. 'But fate intervened and I was sent to the depot he was at in Calais. When he told me how upset you were about Miranda's death, I felt you needed an old friend. But if I'm unsettling you, then perhaps I should go?'

'You unsettled me last time you turned up,' she said. 'Why do you do that?'

'Why do I turn up? Or why do I unsettle you?' he asked. His clear blue eyes seemed to be looking right into her soul. 'I turn up because I can't stay away. Only you can say why that unsettles you.'

'Then why didn't you come to England and see me after I left Paris?' she blurted out. 'You must have known I was hoping you would.'

He sighed deeply. 'I thought you needed time to get over all you'd been through.'

'That one letter you sent me could have come from an uncle asking after my health,' she said indignantly.

He got up from his seat and came over to her to take her hands. 'I told you I wasn't good at writing in English,' he said reproachfully. 'The letter you sent was full of Jimmy this and Jimmy that, you were living under the same roof as him too. Noah wrote to me and said he thought you would marry him. I wanted you to be happy and I thought it best to bow out of your life.'

'How could I tell you how I felt when you'd never given me any encouragement to believe you thought of me as anything but a friend?' she asked, his closeness to her and his hands holding hers making her tremble.

'Surely coming to your aid so quickly and staying near you as you recovered in Paris was enough evidence of my feelings for you?' he said. 'After what you'd been through I didn't dare even to kiss you.' He cupped her face in his hands, then kissed her.

It was the gentlest and most tender of kisses, lingering just long enough to make her heart race.

'I am a married woman,' she said, but she didn't move away and she knew she hadn't even sounded indignant.

'All is fair in love and war, so they say,' and his smile was mischievous and boyish. 'None of us know if we will survive this war. I wouldn't want to die knowing I failed to tell you my true feelings for you.'

'That is a cheap shot,' she said, and now she did feel indignant. 'I suppose you came here thinking that I'd fall into your arms because I'm lonely without my friend and because Jimmy is at the front? Well, you thought wrong. You had your chance to express your feelings back in Paris.'

'If I had, would you have stayed with me?'

Belle recalled the last few minutes with him at the Gare du Nord and the ache in her heart from wanting him so badly.

'At the station I asked you to say something in French. I didn't understand what you said, but I know it wasn't that you loved me.'

'I said that I'd walk through fire, flood and face any peril for you,' he said, looking right into her eyes. 'If that wasn't telling you I loved you, I don't know what it was. I would still do all that, even face your displeasure for coming here now you are a married woman.'

Tears started up in Belle's eyes. She felt as if something was melting inside her, and although she knew she ought to tell him such words were too late now and walk away from him, she couldn't.

He lifted his hand and silently wiped her tears away with his thumb, then his mouth came down on hers and he was kissing her the way she'd hoped for back in Paris.

Her arms went round him involuntarily. His tongue was teasing hers, his body pressing against her, and passion flared up between them like a forest fire. She forgot that the door was open and she could be seen by anyone passing; she forgot too that she had a husband whose heart would break if he got to hear about this.

She was lost, and she knew it. There was no breaking away now and pretending it meant nothing to her. She wanted him to possess her, the feeling was too strong to fight off.

'Come with me,' he said as his lips finally released her, but he still held her tightly in his arms. 'I know a place we can be together.'

'It's wrong, Etienne,' she said weakly.

'How can it be wrong when I found the girl I love, by pure chance in a country torn apart by war? I could be killed in the next battle, Jimmy could too. We have to seize what we have now, we don't know what tomorrow will bring.'

She'd heard these words so many times since she'd been

in France, and she had always agreed with the sentiment, but a small voice inside her was trying to remind her it didn't apply to her situation because she was married. However, a much louder voice was shouting it down, telling her that it was now or never with Etienne, and to hell with the consequences.

She heard herself telling him to drive out of the hospital grounds and wait for her by the same bit of broken fence that Miranda had climbed through to meet Will.

One more kiss sealed it. Etienne drove off and she ran back to the hut to change her clothes and pack an overnight bag.

As luck would have it, Vera was alone in the hut, lying on her bed reading. She said the others had gone to play a game of tennis. 'Will you cover for me?' Belle asked her, after only telling her that she was going out with an old friend. 'Be vague, imply you think it was my husband who called to see me. I'll be back in time for work in the morning.'

'But it isn't Jimmy?' Vera asked. She looked surprised but not horrified; she never seemed to suffer from that rigidity the English had. She had also said many times that she thought any chance of happiness should be grabbed with both hands.

Belle shook her head. 'I'll explain tomorrow. And pray for my soul because I know I really shouldn't be doing this.'

After only the quickest wash and changing into fresh underwear and her one good dress, and stuffing her working clothes into a bag for the morning, Belle rushed off down through the rows of wards and out on to the road where Etienne was waiting.

Her pulse was racing and her heart was doing somersaults, but as she jumped up into the lorry he was driving, one look at his face, alight with joy, told her that whatever came later, it would be worth the risk.

'It's only a café with some rooms above where I'm taking you,' he said. 'But I know other men who've taken their wives there and they said the rooms were clean. I promise I'll get you back to the hospital well before six, that's if you haven't changed your mind about it?'

Belle could only shake her head, smile and reach over to kiss his cheek. For tonight she would pretend she was as free as a bird. The reckoning could come later.

The café was around fifteen miles away down winding lanes. It was in a place that couldn't even be called a village, it was so small, just a handful of small houses, a general shop and the café which rented out rooms above.

They ate egg and chips with a glass of red wine so rough that Belle had a job to drink it without wincing. There were a few French soldiers in there too, but Etienne got them a table at the back, and if he knew any of them he didn't say. He had spoken to the man behind the counter about a room when they arrived, a fast interchange peppered with shrugging shoulders and waving hands. When Belle asked him what had been said he just laughed and claimed the man had remarked that she was a beauty and he'd give them the bridal suite.

'So this is the bridal suite,' Belle said when they went upstairs later. It was a very small room at the back of the building, with scarcely room to walk round the double bed, and the flowery wallpaper was peeling off in places.

'Well, it's got a double bed,' Etienne said as he prodded it. 'And there is a bathroom next door – I expected a latrine out the back.'

Belle felt awkward when he moved to look out of the window. She was neither a whore expected to take the initiative, nor a wife who usually got into bed first and waited to see her husband's mood. She was bashful about taking off her clothes in front of him, which, considering at sixteen she'd got into his bunk on the ship to New Orleans and blatantly offered herself to him, seemed ridiculous.

He turned from the window and smiled at her. The evening sun was coming through the window and it turned his hair to a golden halo. 'Scared?'

She nodded, not trusting herself to speak. He squeezed around the edge of the bed and put his arms around her. 'I have the remedy for that,' he said softly, and kissed her.

As his lips covered hers and his tongue darted into her mouth she was instantly aroused and it blotted out all fear or shame.

He moved her back until she fell on to the bed, and carried on kissing and kissing her until she was writhing against him and pulling at his uniform to get it off.

'You first,' he whispered, pushing her hands away and turning her over so he could unbutton her dress. He kissed and licked her back as each button came undone, then slid the sleeve down over one arm, kissing all the way till it went over her wrist, and did the same on the other arm. Then he pulled the dress down and rolled her over to kiss her breasts, which were barely covered by her camisole.

'They are bigger now than they were at sixteen,' he whispered. 'Beautiful, womanly breasts, just as I imagined they would become.'

He continued to kiss them as he unbuttoned the waist of her petticoat and tossed it to the floor, then peeled off her stockings, drawers and finally the camisole, leaving her naked.

The rough serge of his uniform against her naked flesh heightened her arousal, and he seemed in no hurry to shed it. He pressed his upper leg between her legs and moved it against her, all the time kissing and sucking at her breasts.

Impatiently she unbuttoned his tunic, pulling at it roughly

in her desire to feel his skin against her. He had braces beneath over a blue cotton shirt and she clawed them off him. 'What's the hurry, little one?' he whispered. 'We've got all night.'

She had seen his bare chest dozens of times on the way to America, and marvelled at his broad, muscular shoulders and the slimness of his waist, but as she got the undershirt off him she saw he had a vivid scar on his shoulder and down his side.

'You've been wounded!' she exclaimed, touching it gently. It was far more extensive than the one Jimmy had, but she wished she hadn't been reminded of him now.

'It's fine,' he said. 'As a young boy I always wanted a fearsome scar. I thought it would make me look tough.'

'You look tough enough without that,' she said, running one finger over it.

He pulled her back to him, silencing her with a kiss and running his fingers through her hair.

Belle stopped hearing the sound of soldiers laughing and talking down in the café, she didn't notice day turn to night, and she didn't care what trouble she might bring down on herself for this one night of bliss. Etienne's scar was a poignant reminder of what he'd said earlier, that there were no guarantees of surviving this war. It had never crossed Belle's mind that either she or Miranda would lose their lives, yet her friend was gone now, and although Jimmy and Etienne were more likely to fall in combat than she was to die in some freak accident too, she couldn't be certain.

All she was sure of was that fate had stepped in and brought Etienne back to her. There had to be a good reason for that. She had loved him at sixteen. He'd been the one who enabled her to get beyond what she had been subjected to after she was abducted, and he gave her the strength and determination to cope with all that New Orleans threw at her.

Two years on from that time, he was the one who rescued her from Pascal in Paris and he'd sat by her bedside as she recovered. The rest of the world might think she was just another faithless married woman who gave in to the temptation of taking a lover because she was far from home and lonely, but to her Etienne had first claim on her heart.

Each caress, kiss, stroke and murmured endearment swept her up higher and higher to ecstasy. He was in no hurry to enter her and seemed only to think of her pleasure, lapping at her until she cried out as she climaxed and begged him to come inside her.

Long, slow thrusts into her followed until they were both dripping with perspiration, such tenderness one minute, then ferocity the next. She came again and in the throes of bliss she wasn't even aware that he had withdrawn from her. When she felt the stickiness on her belly she realized that even in his own passion he was thinking of her and not risking a pregnancy.

'My beautiful English rose,' he said as he propped himself up on one elbow, looking down at her, and gently wiped the tears from her face. 'That was all I ever dreamed of and more.'

'If only,' she said, more tears springing to her eyes.

He put one finger, which smelled of her, on her lips. 'Don't say that. We must just believe that as fate brought us together again, it has more plans for us. I love you, Belle, not just for tonight but for ever. Love always finds a way.'

'Are you going back to the front?' she asked.

'Yes, very soon. But I will write to you, and I will come to you when I can. Will you keep faith that one day this war will be over and we can be together?'

'Yes, because I love you.' It wasn't the time to speak of the obstacles that would prevent it. 'And I think it's time I repaid all that pleasure you gave me, something to keep you awake in the trenches.'

She played with him then with her mouth and tongue. Each time he tried to pleasure her she slapped his hands away and continued working on him until he gave in and accepted this was just for him.

Memories of Martha's in New Orleans came back to her as she heard his moans of pleasure. When she was first told she had to take a man's sex in her mouth she thought it the most disgusting thing she'd ever heard of. And it had remained something she would avoid. But there was nothing repellent about doing it to Etienne, it felt like the most natural thing in the world. She felt pleasure herself at pleasing him so much.

It was just before six and raining again when he dropped her back at the hospital. She had her working clothes on and a clean overall, her dress in her bag so she could go straight to her ambulance. Her lips felt swollen from kissing, she was sore down below, tired through lack of sleep, and heavy-hearted because she had no idea when she'd see him again.

'Take this and keep it safe,' he said, pressing a piece of paper into her hands. 'It's addresses where I can be contacted if something unexpected happens to you, or I can't get to you here.'

She glanced at it: his regiment details, and an address in Marseille and one in Paris. 'I will try to write better in English,' he said with a sad smile, and wound a strand of her hair around his finger. 'But if I fail to make a good job of it, remember that I love you, and that I'd go through fire, flood and any peril to be with you.'

Belle could feel tears welling up. 'Keep safe for me,' she

said, her voice cracking with emotion. 'But if you should be wounded, ask that they bring you here.'

'I have every reason to keep safe now,' he said, leaning to kiss her one last time. 'Now go, I don't want you getting into trouble.'

Belle stood for a moment or two watching him drive away. Suddenly the enormity of what she'd done came crashing down on her. How would she ever be able to face Jimmy again? Why had she given into temptation? Was one night of passion worth the guilt she was now going to be forced to live with?

Vera came up to Belle as she was starting up her ambulance. David had gone into the store room to collect some more blankets. 'Sally was a bit nasty after you'd gone last night,' Vera whispered. 'She thought it was Will you'd gone off with, and she said it was time you let him stand on his own feet. I didn't tell her it wasn't Will, so don't let on otherwise if she says anything to you.'

Belle looked at Vera in horror. 'She thought I was with him all night?'

Vera half smiled. 'No, she and the others were all in bed asleep by nine, so they don't know you didn't come back. I got up before they woke this morning, ruffled up your bed and unlocked the door.'

'Thank heavens for that,' Belle exclaimed. 'I couldn't bear them to think I'd snatched Miranda's man. I feel bad enough already.'

Vera took her hand and squeezed it in understanding. 'You may have been a bit feckless,' she said soothingly, 'but not bad. You've reached out for a bit of comfort, that's all.'

Belle was touched by her understanding. 'Thank you for covering for me. I'll try and explain it all to you later.'

*

By ten that morning Belle had completed three runs to the station. As hers had been the second ambulance to leave the hospital, the first run had been all sitting cases which were far easier than the stretcher cases. But the second and third were mainly Canadians, big, heavy men, all with terrible injuries.

'You are very quiet and dreamy today,' David remarked as they swabbed out the ambulance where one of the wounded had been sick. 'Any special reason?'

The truth was that she had been reliving her night with Etienne, so much so that she felt herself grow hot and aroused again and wondered how long it would be before she saw him again.

She confided in David about most things; they'd become good friends even before Miranda's death, but that had drawn them closer still. However, she couldn't confide in him about Etienne – he would be horrified at a married woman with a husband at the front meeting another man.

It was only then that she fully appreciated her situation. Jimmy was a good man, and he loved her. It was going to break his heart if she told him she wanted to leave him. And if she did, she would lose Mog too, as Mog couldn't take her side when she was married to Garth.

'It's just the same old thing, dwelling too much on the casualties of war,' she said quickly. 'Life is very precarious, isn't it?'

'Have you heard from your husband since you wrote to him about Miranda?' he asked.

'No, nor from Mog and Garth either,' she said. 'I keep wondering if Mog went to Miranda's funeral. Mrs Forbes-Alton would have made sure the whole world knew about it, and Mog must've been very shocked that I didn't come home

274

for it. Of course I explained why in my letter, but I doubt she got that in time.'

'Let's hope she didn't lay into Mog with that stuff about you being responsible,' David said. 'That's a terrible thing to say of anyone.'

'Maybe Mrs Forbes-Alton is unhappily married,' Belle suggested. 'I suppose that could turn you sour.'

'Yes, I think so. I had an aunt who was a real dragon to everyone and I found out eventually that she hadn't been allowed to marry the man she loved. The man she was pushed into marrying was a decent sort, but spineless. That was what made her such a bully.

'I often wonder how some of the wives of the very badly wounded men cope when their husbands get home,' he went on. 'However happy they were before he was wounded, living on only a small pension with a man who needs constant care could become a living nightmare.'

Those words pulled Belle up sharply. Etienne had spoken as if they would be able to find a way to be together. Was he hoping that Jimmy would be killed?

Chapter Eighteen

A few days after her night with Etienne, Belle went into the mail room before starting work to see if there were any letters for her. When she was passed one, her heart leapt, thinking it was from Etienne. Her disappointment on seeing Jimmy's familiar writing on the envelope was quickly followed by deep shame that she should react that way.

'*My dearest love,*' she read.

I am so sorry to hear about Miranda. I can hardly believe that she should have been taken in such a tragic and preventable accident. Terrible that you witnessed it too, seeing a friend killed is a hundred times worse than hearing about their death later.

I wish that I had been there to hold you and comfort you, you must have felt, and are probably still feeling, so very alone. I was furious at her mother saying you weren't welcome at the funeral. What sort of a mother can she be to deny her daughter's best friend the chance to say her last goodbyes? But don't grieve about it, sweetheart, bear in mind that Mog will send the story all around Blackheath and it will reveal Mrs Forbes-Alton to be the heartless witch everyone always suspected.

I feel so sorry for Will too. I know if I was to lose you then I'd have no reason to carry on. If you should see him again, give him our address and maybe when the war is over he could come and stay for a while. You could show him Miranda's favourite places. It might help him in his loss to be able to picture where she came from, what her life was like before the war. Though it would be prudent not to introduce him to her mother!

As for me, I am bearing up, though the constant rain in an already swampy area hardly bodes well for the big offensive we are waiting for. We haven't been told yet what's planned, there are rumours that Haig has made too many blunders, and that General Plumer will take over. Whether that will prove better for us soldiers remains to be seen. Our mob has been lucky for some time, no front line stint, but I think by the training we're getting now this is going to end soon. We're all sick and tired of this place, how many more battles will there be over a few hundred yards of land? We're sick and tired of the mud, filth and destruction, not to mention the loss of life. If only there was some way of knowing when it will all end! To me it doesn't look as if we're getting anywhere. The Boche don't show any sign of flagging, and they've got concrete bunkers so they are better protected and more comfortable than us.

But here I am grumbling when you have to deal with the end result of all this madness. God willing it can't be much longer. I dream all the time of being at home again with you, of clean clothes, hot baths, walks in Greenwich Park, a pint of beer, and no more gunfire. I did ask if I could have some leave to come and see you, but it was refused. They said maybe in the autumn, but that seems such a long way off.

Mog said in her last letter that your letters to her and Garth are very short now. I suppose that's because you have to work so hard. I know she wishes you'd pack it in and go home, she misses you so much. Maybe now without Miranda for company you'll want that too. I know I'd much rather you were safe at home.

You said in the letter before the one about Miranda that there were a lot of Canadians in the hospital. I've met quite a few here. They did really well gaining Vimy Ridge, they are good, brave men. If the Americans are half as good maybe we can polish the Boche off by Christmas and all come home. But then we've been hoping for that for three years now.

A million kisses,
Your everloving Jimmy

Belle wiped her damp eyes with the back of her hand. The letter said everything about what Jimmy was, a kind, loving man who cared more about others than himself. He hadn't said exactly where he was because of the censor, in fact it was surprising he dared mention Haig and Plumer, but his description of the conditions told her he was near Ypres; she knew from those who had been wounded there that they were atrocious.

Ever since the night with Etienne she'd been in a kind of bubble which prevented her from thinking too deeply about the future. Somehow she'd just allowed herself to believe that some kind of miracle would happen so she wouldn't have to make a choice between the two men.

But now with Jimmy's letter in her hand she knew she'd been burying her head in the sand. What on earth was she going to do? If he was to turn up here any time she knew she wouldn't be able to face him. It would kill him if he found out she'd been unfaithful, and he had done nothing to deserve it.

She would feel justified if he'd been neglectful, if he'd been a drunk or a wife beater. She did love him too. That hadn't stopped because of Etienne, yet surely it wasn't possible to love two men at the same time?

'Bad news?' David asked.

Belle was a bit taken aback by the question. She hadn't seen or heard David coming towards her, and she guessed he'd been watching her as she read her letter and dried her eyes.

'No, not bad news, Jimmy's letters always make me feel weepy,' she said hastily. 'It's so long since I last saw him, and I get to thinking it will all be so different between us when the war ends. We aren't the same people any more.'

David put his arm around her shoulders, and gave her a

half hug in sympathy. 'At least you've been over here too; you understand what it's been like for him. That's got to give you a better chance than those with wives who've been at home throughout.'

'Perhaps,' she sighed. She folded the letter up and put it in her overall pocket. 'We'd best get going now.'

They had gone some distance down the road towards the station when David spoke again. 'There's something troubling you, I can feel it. You can tell me. I won't say a word to anyone.'

Belle tried to smile. David was another good man, never grumpy, always reliable and loyal. He was also very intuitive, so she knew she had to say something which would stop him probing. 'I've just been floored by Miranda's death. I'm all right one minute, then down the next. I'm tempted to pack up and go home.'

'You can't do that! What would I do without you?' he exclaimed. 'I'm called a lucky bugger because I work with the prettiest girl in the whole hospital; it's really good for my ego.'

Belle laughed despite herself. 'You could ask to be paired with Vera, she's a lovely girl and unattached too.'

'Now there's a thought!' he grinned. 'But it's more likely they'll stick me with Sally, and she's so posh she scares me. Did I ever tell you about the driver I was with before you? He was an American know-all who complained the whole time, by the name of Buck. I couldn't stand him. Luckily he buggered off just as my patience was running out. But speaking of Vera, I was talking to her last night, and she won't want you to go either. She said that getting to know you was one of the best things about coming here.'

Belle was touched by that; she liked Vera too. She was sunny, warm and often very funny. She had no side to her, in fact Belle often had to explain Sally's snobby remarks because Vera had been brought up in a classless society and had no experience of that side of Englishness. Vera had understood Belle's dilemma with Etienne and Jimmy, neither approving nor disapproving. She said in her usual calm and rational way that she believed Belle had only turned to Etienne for comfort after Miranda's death, and that she mustn't do or say anything in haste as she was likely to regret it later.

The following morning a brief letter came from Etienne. He just said that he'd moved up. He couldn't tell her where to, and he hadn't mentioned whether his regiment was in reserve or at the front line. 'I just want you to know you are in my thoughts constantly,' he wrote. He was right about his written English being bad; he used the right words but mostly couldn't spell them correctly.

I am hurting because I know I have put you in an impossible situation. Sometimes I think I should not have come to see you because now I am here, with so many Tommies close by, I feel ashamed of myself for wanting another man's wife.

Yet that hasn't stopped me making plans in my head. One which seemed perfect, though now I see as only desperation on my part, was that you should disappear from the hospital and go to my place in Marseille to wait for me. How could I suggest such a thing? You would lose all those you hold dear, and they would grieve for you again, just as they did when you disappeared before. I couldn't find happiness by causing so much pain to others, and you would never be able to forgive yourself.

The only real way is the honest one, to face Jimmy together and tell him the truth. I tell myself that if he loves you, he will want your happiness. But I know only too well that few men are that noble. Not when they know they will lose the person most precious to them.

Belle began to cry then. Etienne's first idea was one she'd considered and discarded for much the same reasons. The second, however honourable, was one she knew she could never agree to. She just wasn't brave enough to see Jimmy devastated.

She almost wished Etienne had been merely playing with her and would soon grow tired of the game. But the rest of his letter was an outpouring of love for her and it was clear he had no intention of letting her go.

During the last week of June the number of hospital trains coming in with wounded dropped considerably. All the staff who had been here for a year or more said this was just a lull before the storm. It looked as if Jimmy had been right and another big assault was coming soon, because when Belle went to the wards, she could see the doctors and nurses striving to clear them of everyone well enough to be moved. It was clear the hospital was gearing up for another huge intake of casualties.

With fewer hospital trains coming in, Belle and some of the other drivers stopped meeting the trains and instead took recovering wounded to Calais and the hospital ships. Belle was glad of the change; the patients were delighted finally to have their Blighty ticket and were in good spirits, and it was good to see what was going on in the busy port.

The streets of Calais were full of soldiers, Australians, New Zealanders, Canadians and new recruits from England on their way either to training camps or to the front. There were more Americans now too, just a relatively small advance party of professionals who would train the conscripts yet to come.

A couple of these men were at the wharf to help Belle and David with the wounded, but while they were glad to have assistance with the heavy lifting, Belle found the soldiers' manner a little irritating. They were overly jovial and made it clear they considered the American army vastly superior to the British. Given that the United States had sat on their hands for three years, and had only finally agreed to come in to help when their ships had been torpedoed, Belle thought they had no right to act as though they were the saviours.

The big, fresh-faced blond who looked as if he was straight off a farm, kept making disparaging quips about the Tommies looking weary and bedraggled. 'What's up with them all?' he asked. 'They act like they already lost the war. So cynical too, we ask them things and all they say is, "You'll find out for yourself soon, mate." The Frogs are even worse, most of them look like hobos, filthy uniforms and they don't even shave. They sure as hell don't look like soldiers.'

'They're exhausted, they've been ground down to their knees,' Belle retorted. 'They don't want to tell you what it's like because almost all of them have seen friends they came out here with killed. They've had bad food, little rest, they eat, sleep and live in the most horrible conditions, most haven't had any leave since they got here. But don't you for one moment doubt their courage, they rally round when that whistle blows to go over the top, they've all got hearts like lions. As for some of the French not shaving, don't think because you've got smarter uniforms and neat hair-cuts that will keep you safe! What counts on the front is guts, shooting fast and straight, and the ability to crawl to a shell hole when you are wounded, or you'll die out there.'

'Well, mam, that told us,' he replied, clearly taken aback that a young woman could speak with such passion. 'I guess we're in for a bit of a shock then.'

'You certainly are,' she said. 'I just hope you two make it home again. There's hardly a woman left in England that hasn't shed tears over her husband, son or brother. Today you are seeing the luckier men who are going home. They are maimed and broken, but at least they are alive. They all arrived here as keen as you are, buying into the valiant cause for King and Country. Now most will admit that war is the ugliest, cruellest thing they've ever seen, and they'll be having nightmares about it for years to come.'

'Hellfire, Belle!' David exclaimed once they were back in the ambulance. 'You really laid into them.'

Belle blushed. 'Well, they needed telling. Who do they think they are, implying they are God's gift?'

'Not like you to be so crabby,' he said. 'Maybe you really do need to go home.'

She had only told him she was considering going home to put him off questioning her further as to why she seemed withdrawn. Yet in the days that followed she found herself thinking that maybe it was the solution to her problems.

It didn't seem right to be here in France with the two men she was torn between so near. For all she knew, they could even be close to each other. That was unlikely, after all, even if they were both at Ypres, the front line stretched for miles with tens of thousands of soldiers along its length. But that didn't matter, they were there, she was here. And she felt she must distance herself from them both.

Etienne was certain to turn up here again. He wasn't the kind to care about getting permission, he'd spent his entire life bending rules and living on his wits. But if Belle wasn't here she couldn't be tempted again. Back home in the ordered normality of life with Mog and Garth she'd be able to think straight again and put aside this madness.

And it *was* madness. How could she even think of leaving Jimmy? He was the kind of husband all women dreamed of.

What did she really know about Etienne? He might have saved her life back in Paris, but when she first met him he was no more than a hired thug.

In the cold light of day it seemed to her that by the time the war was over and Jimmy came home, she might very well find he was the man she wanted after all. Perhaps Vera was right and the fling with Etienne was only a moment of madness brought on by Miranda's death.

But if she still wanted Etienne at the end of the war, then at least she'd be able to spare Jimmy the pain of her faithlessness. She would just say she'd found she didn't love him any more, and leave. He need never be hurt further by knowing the truth.

In the days that followed she went about her work with the same care as always. In the early evening she continued to go into the wards and read to men who had been blinded, or write letters for those who couldn't manage it themselves. Later on she and Vera would sit and chat over a mug of cocoa. Belle didn't want to discuss her dilemma. Vera was not as strait-laced as most English women, and she found it understandable that Belle would turn to an old friend while she was grieving, but even she would be shocked to hear the whole truth.

So they talked about patients they had got to know and like, about what a mixed bunch the other drivers were, and their lives back home. Belle loved to hear about New Zealand and Vera had the knack of painting pictures with words. Belle could almost see her home, a white-painted clapboard double-fronted shop close to the sea, where her parents made bread and cakes in the bakery behind. She could imagine the heat of the ovens, the smell of baking bread, and the small bedroom up in the eaves with a view of the sea that was Vera's.

'My brothers had the room at the back, and they some-times climbed out the window at night, down on to the bakery roof to go out and meet their friends without Ma and Pa knowing,' she told Belle. 'They always got caught out, someone would tell Ma the next day they'd seen them. I never understood why they did it; nothing ever happens in Russell, well, other than men getting drunk in the pub. But they were too young then to be going in there.'

Her brothers Spud and Tony were somewhere here in France. Vera got only the standard postcard from them, which told her even less than Jimmy's letters to Belle did. Vera was very glad they were in the Engineers, laying tele-phone wires, tunnelling and doing other jobs which kept the army going. Though from what Belle knew such duties could be just as dangerous, as telephone lines went right to the front line and needed repairing there all the time.

It was three weeks after her night with Etienne. Belle had made the decision she was going home, and she told Vera before she did anything further about it. 'I have to go,' she said. 'I know it's not right to be cheating on Jimmy, but if I stay here Etienne will come back and I can't trust myself with him.'

Vera's face crumpled. 'I don't want you to go,' she said. 'I'll miss you so much.'

Belle was very touched and was reminded of just how much she had leant on Vera in the past few weeks. 'Then come with me? I could show you London, we could get jobs together. Mog would love to have you stay, and so would I.'

Vera sighed and pulled a glum face. 'I wish I could, but with Miranda gone and now you, when the next big assault starts they are going to be hard-pressed for drivers. Besides, I'd feel bad about not being here for my brothers if they need me. They might think they are big tough men, but to me they are just my little brothers.'

'I can't see any way out except to go home,' Belle said sadly. 'All I do is think about Etienne. He's on my mind from the moment I wake up till I fall asleep at night. Everything here reminds me of him. I have to try and save my marriage and I stand a better chance of doing that at home.'

Vera nodded. 'Then you must go home, Belle. I'm no expert in such things, I haven't even been in love, so my opinion is worthless really. But from what you've said about Jimmy he sounds a good man, and you were happy with him before Etienne turned up. I'm sure once you're home everything will fall into place again. Just promise me you'll keep in touch. I don't want to lose you.'

The next morning Belle had planned to do her usual duties, then go and see Captain Taylor around five in the afternoon. But as always before she began work in the morning, she went to see if there were any letters for her, and there was one from Mog.

Just seeing the familiar writing on the envelope lifted her spirits a little. She hadn't had a reply about Miranda's death, and aside from wanting to know if Mog had gone to the funeral, she also needed the comfort of her motherly words.

The letter began just as she had expected, saying how shocked and sorry Mog was to hear about Miranda's death; that everyone in the village was horrified too. But then, just as she was expecting Mog to suggest she came home, the letter suddenly took on a very different tone which made Belle feel faint with shock.

If I didn't think you might be intending to come home because you've lost your friend, I wouldn't tell you about what has happened here. So I must tell you how it is so you stay away.

That Blessard man has been spilling the beans about you. It's all over the village. He must have found out that Miranda went to France with you, then when he heard about her death, wormed his way into interviewing her mother.

Miranda's death was reported in the newspaper before I got your letter. It was just like any other news story, how the accident happened, and then about her grieving family and the date and time of the funeral. I was horrified of course to read it like that, but I knew you would've written straight away and that the letter telling me more about it would soon arrive.

So I went to the funeral. There were a great many people there and I didn't get a chance to speak to Mrs Forbes-Alton. But a couple of her cronies gave me sharp looks which made me feel very uncomfortable, as if I had no right to be there. It was my intention to write to the family and offer my condolences once I'd heard from you.

Then a couple of days later, the same day I got your letter, someone brought that rag of a paper Blessard writes in into the bar and showed it to Garth. He'd written an article about Miranda's accident, and that she'd gone to France with you. He quoted her mother as saying, 'I was never happy about her going off there, but she was persuaded to do so by Mrs Belle Reilly. I couldn't think why a married woman would be wanting to go to France to drive an ambulance. It was all very suspicious.'

Just that was bad enough, Belle, but then he dug up all the old stuff about Kent's trial, all of it slanted to make you look bad. Then finally he said that there was evidence that you continued to work as a 'lady of the night' in Paris right up until you came home to England and married Jimmy.

He was implying, though he didn't say it in so many words, that this was why you wanted to go back to France.

Garth of course ripped up the paper and informed the man who had brought it in that it was pure fantasy. We telephoned Noah, and he said we can't sue Blessard and his newspaper for slander because *he hasn't made it up, it's true, all he's done is tell it in a way which isn't sympathetic towards you.*

Noah said we must maintain a dignified silence and then it will all blow over, but though the regulars in the bar don't appear to believe a word of it, I've been cold-shouldered by women in the sewing circle, and I don't feel able to go there any more.

I've hardly been out the door because of it. I can't bear to think people are whispering about you. I think we may have to sell up and move away. But we can't do that now, not with the war on, things are tight everywhere, and Garth says if we go that will make us look guilty. We both agree though that you should stay away for now. You could go to Annie's, I suppose. I went to see her to tell her about it but she was her usual chilly self, more concerned with her business than about you.

Oh dear, Belle. This is such an awful thing to have to tell you, so unfair too when you are far away and I can't hug you and promise you it will all turn right soon. That man Blessard needs stringing up, but Garth can't touch him without further trouble coming our way. That nice policeman Mr Broadhead is on our side, he's already told a couple of gossips that it's vindictive rubbish and they should be ashamed of themselves for believing it. If only there were more people like him.

Write soon, and keep safe. You and Jimmy are in our hearts and thoughts all the time. I'm sorry to be the bearer of bad news when you must already be so sad. I can't bring myself to tell Jimmy about this, he's got more than enough to deal with just now.

Your loving Mog

Belle felt as if a trapdoor had opened beneath her and she was falling into a dark pit. She had put Blessard out of her mind when she left England, and she hadn't for one moment thought he would trouble her again. How stupid was she? He'd just been biding his time and waiting for an opportunity to present itself. And Mrs Forbes-Alton had given him that opportunity.

Bad as it was that people were talking about her, it was Mog she was really concerned for. She had worked so hard to gain respect in the village and now she was afraid and demoralized.

Belle felt that this was a punishment for her wrongdoing.

Somehow she managed to get through the day without breaking down, but when she got back to the hut that evening, Vera was waiting expectantly.

'Was Captain Taylor cross with you?' she asked.

'I didn't go and see him. I'm not going home,' Belle said.

'Why? Is it Jimmy?'

Sally and the other two girls were changing, and they all looked round at her.

Belle inclined her head towards the door. She could barely contain her tears and she didn't want the other girls to see her break down.

Vera came out with her and they went and sat on a bench by one of the wards.

'Well, come on, tell me,' Vera said impatiently. 'Is it because Etienne's coming to see you?'

'No, it's nothing to do with him,' Belle said. 'Mog said I must stay away because of some nasty gossip about me.'

Vera looked puzzled and that made Belle see she'd blundered. She should have made out that Mog was ill, anything other than the truth, because now she would have to explain.

'I was involved in something awful when I was much younger,' she said. 'Someone has dug it up and spread it around.'

It had been easy enough to tell Miranda about her previous life because of what they'd been through together, but although Vera had travelled all the way from New Zealand to work here, she wasn't exactly worldly. Belle told her only an abbreviated version of the story but she couldn't prevent herself crying.

'I don't suppose you'll want me as a friend any more,' she sobbed. 'I thought it was all behind me, and I'd made up for it by working in the hospital back home and coming here. But I was wrong, wasn't I? Fallen women can't be repaired; I suppose that's why I couldn't resist Etienne.'

Vera put her arms around her and held her tightly. 'I am shocked,' she admitted. 'I'd be lying if I said otherwise. But what astounds me is that you've been through all that, and yet you somehow managed to remain such a good person. And of course I'll still want you as a friend; all this has done is reveal more depth to you. A weak person would just have crumpled up, let themselves become a victim for ever more. You fought back and I admire that.'

The sun was setting and it was growing chilly, but Vera didn't suggest they went inside, she just continued to hold Belle and let her cry.

'I understand about Etienne now,' Vera said softly. 'And other things about you that I've often wondered about. When you first arrived with Miranda I thought you were two of a kind, girls from good families who wanted to experience something outside your pampered little world. Sally made a couple of sarcastic remarks about you that suggested you weren't out of the top drawer. Not being English, I wouldn't recognize that straight away. But what I did see, very early on, was that you were the one with the heart, the guts and the drive. I liked Miranda, but you were the one I really wanted to get to know. You remind me of some of the women my mother knows, the pioneers who came out to New Zealand and built a good life for themselves on nothing but hard work and determination. You'll be all right, Belle. You are made of the right stuff. Whatever life throws at you you'll deal with it.'

'That's a nice thing to say.' Belle sniffed back her tears. 'But thanks to my past I've messed up Mog and Garth's life. And what about Jimmy? What will I do to him?'

'You can't be responsible for everyone's happiness,' Vera said. 'My mother said that a few years ago when her sister was having a hard time and expected Ma to sort it for her. Maybe you will discover Jimmy is the only man for you, maybe you won't. Mog and Garth might find they've got to move somewhere else, or it might all blow over. One thing we ought to have learned from this war is that we can't predict anything. It's just destiny.'

'You are very wise,' Belle said.

'I'm also very cold,' Vera said. 'So let's go and see if there's anything to eat in the canteen and get some cocoa.'

Chapter Nineteen

'The one good thing about being really busy is that there's no chance to brood on things,' Belle said to Vera as they snatched tea and a sandwich between runs to the station.

It was the middle of the night. The hospital trains ran at night now because of fear of them being bombed. German bomber planes targeted railways to break service and communication lines, and they had no scruples about blowing up the sick and wounded. So now the ambulances went out in the darkness, without lights, which made the job even harder on the bad winding roads.

It was also raining yet again. People were saying it was the wettest, coldest summer on record, and Belle, who remembered stifling summer nights in Seven Dials as a child, and the steamy heat of New Orleans, wouldn't argue with them.

Vera's freckled face broke into a grin. 'Hard work might suit you, but I'd like time to wash my hair and write letters home,' she said. 'I know I look a fright, and Ma will be getting frantic if she doesn't hear from me soon.'

Belle guessed she looked a fright too; she had long since stopped caring about her appearance. 'I don't know what to say in letters any more,' she sighed. 'I can't bring myself to write that it's raining again and we wade through puddles to reach our ambulance. I've said that all too often before. The food here is as bad as ever, we never get time off, that's also as dull as ditchwater and another repeat. The only difference with the wounded now is that there's more mud on them. They might like to know at home that the death toll at

Ypres isn't as high as at the Somme, but I can't bring myself to even think of men drowning in shell holes, let alone write about it.'

The third battle of Ypres had begun on 31 July, preceded by a fifteen-day bombardment in which four million shells were fired. The noise of the guns was so loud it was said they could be heard in England, and at the hospital it sounded as if they were being fired only a few miles away.

News got through that on the morning of the 31st the weather was dry, although the ground was churned and pockmarked by two years of shelling. By all accounts the infantry, along with a hundred and thirty tanks, made good progress towards the Gheluvelt Plateau, south-east of Ypres. It was considered important to gain this ground from the Germans because its slight elevation gave good observation over all the surrounding lowland.

But then during the afternoon the Germans counter-attacked with such heavy fire that the leading BEF troops had to flee, and in addition there was a sudden torrential downpour which turned the already soggy ground to the con-sistency of porridge. More divisions continued the assault, but it rained solidly for the next three days. Lines of communi-cation were broken, men drowned in shell holes, tanks sank into the mud, horses and mules floundered, and at that point General Haig called a halt to the offensive.

The total casualties, including the French soldiers, were guessed to be around 35,000, and it was reckoned that the Germans had suffered a similar number.

The first wave of wounded arrived on 1 August, and each day since the numbers had steadily risen. Belle couldn't be sure whether Jimmy and Etienne were still alive, just as Vera didn't know about her brothers. They had to make them-selves believe that no news was good news.

But the stories the wounded were telling about the conditions at Ypres were the stuff of nightmares. These wounded were the lucky ones who had managed to stay out of the water-filled shell holes until they were picked up by stretcher bearers. Some of the badly injured told how they had tried to pull a friend out of the mud, only to see him slither back deeper into it and disappear.

While Belle, Vera and the other drivers had no real understanding of the bigger picture and what Haig's battle plan was, it appeared to be as pointless as the battle of the Somme: enormous casualties to gain a few yards, only to lose those yards later in a German counter-attack.

At the field stations and in the hospital trains, the nurses had made huge efforts to clean the mud off the wounded and get them into hospital blues, but even so, many men were still caked in mud on arrival at the train station. This was why Belle and Vera had no time for washing their own hair or writing letters, because as soon as they got the last of the wounded to the hospital, they went to the wards to help out there too. The regular wards were full to capacity and dozens of large tents had been erected for the overflow. Many of the doctors and nurses had stayed on duty for forty-eight hours at a stretch.

'Captain Taylor wants us both driving the men with Blighty tickets to Calais tomorrow,' Vera said as she gulped down her sandwich. 'Reckon that means there's even greater numbers coming in on the trains.'

'Well, I expect we'll be the last to know. But we'd better get back to the station now. No peace for the wicked.'

'You haven't mentioned you know who lately,' Vera said as they walked back to their ambulances.

'I try not to think about him,' Belle replied. 'But I'm not very successful.'

Vera put her hand on Belle's arm and squeezed it, her way of saying she sympathized. 'Let's buy a bottle of something in Calais tomorrow and get roaring drunk when we get back. It might take our minds off the people we love for an hour or two.'

Belle thought about Vera's suggestion as she drove to the station. David was half asleep; like so many of them he too was helping out in the wards during the day. Everyone at the hospital was worn out, not just from the long hours they worked, but from the unremitting horror they saw daily and to which no end was in sight. She and Vera weren't alone in having people they cared for at the front; almost everyone had someone there they were concerned about. Then there were their families back home struggling with food short-ages and being bombed, anxiety for those in France and wondering if life would ever return to how it had been before the war.

Mog's letters had become very different since Blessard's remarks about Belle in the press. There was no gossip in them any more, instead she wrote about making jam and bottling fruit, or going out on a Sunday with Garth to the country. She tried so hard to sound cheerful, but it was quite apparent that she had withdrawn into herself.

Guilt ate away at Belle, for her past which had cast such a cloud over Mog, and for her infidelity to Jimmy. He wrote as often as he could, but there was weariness in his letters too. As for Etienne's, his unfailing optimism that one day they could be happy together was often frightening because Belle knew any happiness with him would only cause others mis-ery. She had said in all her letters back to him that it could never be as simple as he believed it was. All he would say in reply to that was that he was prepared to wait, however long it took.

It seemed to Belle she was always waiting. Waiting in a queue of ambulances to get loaded up, waiting for letters, for a war that seemed interminable to end, and waiting for a morning to break when she didn't wake wanting Etienne so badly that it hurt.

As Etienne sat cleaning his gun early in the morning, sheltering from the rain in a makeshift bivouac, the sound of English voices wafted over to him. This was the first battle in which his regiment would be fighting alongside the Tommies. He had the greatest respect for the ability of the British to endure all that was thrown at them; they fought doggedly and bravely, and showed far fewer signs of the apathy and weariness that was affecting so many of the French.

He had thought he'd caught a glimpse of Jimmy Reilly last night carrying a stretcher to a dressing station, but told himself his mind was playing tricks on him as there had to be many tall, red-headed men amongst their number. Yet the thought persisted and he found himself pricking up his ears in an attempt to hear what the Englishmen were saying.

The odd word he did catch meant nothing to him, just banter between soldiers, and he asked himself what good would come of knowing Jimmy was close by. The answer to that was that it would be a distraction he didn't need. Belle was enough of a distraction already; thoughts of her dogged him constantly and if he closed his eyes just for a second he would see her dark curls framing her lovely face, clear blue eyes smiling at him and soft plump lips waiting to be kissed.

There were times when he regretted seeking her out at the hospital; if he hadn't had that one night with her she wouldn't be burdened with guilt now. He hated himself for putting her in such an impossible position, yet he wanted her so badly that he felt compelled to keep the pressure on.

He stood up, draped his waterproof cape around his shoulders and surveyed the scene around him. Thick, glutinous mud surrounded every waterlogged tent. The misery of it was reflected in every face as the men dragged on a cigarette, tried to shave, drank lukewarm coffee, wrote a letter or cleaned a gun. They had all but forgotten what it was like to be clean and dry, to eat a hot meal at a table and sleep in a warm bed. Etienne and all these men would be moving forward later today, off out on to that hellish No Man's Land where the heavy guns would churn up bodies from both sides that had sunk beneath the mud on previous assaults. The stench of death, the ear-splitting barrage of gunfire, and the terror that today might be your last – that was the soldier's lot.

In his twenties Etienne had always relished a fight. But smashing a fist into the face or belly of a man you had a grievance with was one thing; here it was kill or be killed. He'd seen enough Germans at close quarters now to know they were just boys, like the men under him. There was no satisfaction in seeing a man scream out in agony as a bullet hit home. On the occasions they'd got to a German bunker and been faced with terrified boys screaming 'Nicht schiessen' he'd felt sick to his stomach. How many of the soldiers here would revisit these grotesque images again and again in their minds after the war was over?

At two in the afternoon the whistle blew, and Etienne and his squad leapt out of their trench into No Man's Land, protected to some extent by the heavy guns behind them firing over their heads at the enemy lines ahead. It was tortuous from the outset. The pack on each of their backs weighed around eighty pounds, some men had a shovel on their back too, and the extra weight made them sink into the mud up to their knees. Each step required great effort to pull out the foot which was being sucked down by the mud, and the driving rain made it impossible to see further than a few yards ahead. Etienne knew that there were supposed to be ten men to every yard of front, and in theory, after such a prolonged bombardment, if they were able to trek straight across to the enemy lines their numbers would be sufficient to take and hold that position.

But the theory hadn't taken into account that a distance of one mile became four or five when the men had to wind their way around huge water-filled craters. Then the shelling began before they were thirty yards in. There was nowhere to take shelter, not a tree or building was left in this godforsaken place, just the odd gaunt tree trunk stripped of bark and leaves standing like a monument to devastation.

As shells hit the mud they sprayed muddy water thirty or more feet up into the air like huge geysers, making the visibility even worse. It was virtually impossible to keep his bearings; he could see Tommies who had strayed over with his men and doubtless just as many French had found themselves among the Tommies.

Etienne paused to signal to those lagging behind to keep up, and he hoped as they floundered in the mud that they had taken note of his last order before they moved, which was to make sure they kept their matches dry. Some of the newer recruits had looked puzzled at this order, but they would discover the reason for it later. The only thing worse than being trapped and wounded in a shell hole was finding yourself there and unable to light a cigarette.

As he was looking back for his men, the number of Tommies coming towards Etienne made him realize that by the time they all reached the German lines the two armies would be mixed up together. Another shell exploded and he saw two of his men thrown into the air and dismembered before falling back into a soupy hole in the ground. Then another shell exploded, and a Tommy went the same way.

No longer entirely sure that he was keeping to a straight line, but able to see through the rain that two Germans manning a howitzer were picking off men like fish in a tank, he paused momentarily to fire at them. He had a few seconds of grim satisfaction at seeing them slump forward over their gun. Then, looking around him again, he could no longer see any of his men behind him, only Tommies plodding determinedly towards the German lines.

Etienne had survived the horror of Verdun and been at the later stages of the Somme too, and it was because of what was cited at the time as 'conspicuous gallantry', in rescuing his wounded captain, that he was promoted to sergeant. Yet hideous as those battles had been, he thought this was far worse. The combination of slippery, sodden ground, torrential rain and the hellish shell holes filled with stinking water, often with bodies in there too, made it hard to make any real headway. Finding himself alone with shells bursting all around him, he paused in the shelter of a half-sunken tank, hoping that his squad would catch up with him and they could go on together. As he waited he fired his gun, picking off Germans who were firing relentlessly at the men running towards them. A stray bullet caught him on his lower arm, but he carried on shooting until he'd either killed them or they'd ducked back down under cover.

A Tommie ran past, so close to him that Etienne had to pause firing in order not to hit him. The soldier was slipping in the mud, then he fell, and as he did so his helmet fell off to reveal red hair.

Instinct told Etienne this was the same man he'd seen last night and thought was Jimmy. As he stared, considering going to his aid, a shell exploded in the space on the ground between them.

For a moment Etienne thought he'd been blinded by the blast as he couldn't see anything. But though he could feel the wound in his arm, there was no pain in his face. He touched it gingerly, and recognized it was just covered in thick mud thrown up from the shell. He groped for his canteen of water in his pack and splashed it into his eyes. To his great relief he could see again.

But the red-headed man had not fared so well. He was writhing on the edge of a shell hole, his left leg and arm a bloody pulp. As he tried to move, Etienne saw his face. It was Jimmy Reilly.

This man had crept into his dreams many a night. It was always the same, Jimmy on one side of him, Belle on the other. He would look from one imploring face to the other, and he didn't know what to do. He would try to run from them, only to find he couldn't move.

The dream seemed prophetic now. And just like in the dream, he didn't know what to do.

He had liked Jimmy when he met him in Verdun and his instinct was to run and help him. But then Belle flashed through his mind and he knew this could be the answer to her dilemma. Left here, the man would die of blood loss; maybe another shell would finish him off before that. Nothing and no one would stand between them.

But as he watched, Jimmy slithered over the edge of the shell hole and down into the fetid water. His hand was held up, fingers moving as he desperately tried to find something to cling on to.

It was something about the hand that got to Etienne. He'd shaken it that day near Verdun. He couldn't let a man drown in front of him, especially one he'd liked.

Another shell exploded nearby, and Etienne darted out from behind his shelter and grabbed the man's hand, hauling him out of the hole. Jimmy's face was covered in mud, and he was so caught up in his pain he didn't appear to realize anyone else was near. Etienne looked around him. It seemed the last of the troops had gone forward; there was no sign of any of his men. There were many others, both English and French, lying either dead or wounded, but as yet the shelling was still too heavy for the stretcher bearers to come and carry the wounded away.

One of the army rules was that no soldier was allowed to break off from an assault to rescue another man; they were supposed to press on to the German line and do their job. Jimmy would not drown now, but he could be hit by another shell.

Etienne was torn. As a sergeant, his duty was to find his men and lead them on, yet the image of Belle's distress was too strong for him to leave Jimmy. He could imagine her tear-filled eyes, and knew that even if it meant that the way would be clear for him to have her for himself, he just couldn't have it on his conscience that he'd left her husband here to die.

Frantically scanning all around for a stretcher bearer he could signal to come, but seeing none, he knelt down beside Jimmy and wiped the worst of the mud from his face. 'I've got you now, Jimmy,' he said. 'You're badly hurt but I reckon I can carry you back to the line.'

Jimmy looked up at him, tawny eyes full of pain. 'You can't help me,' he croaked. 'You'll get into trouble and I'm not going to make it anyway.'

'Allow me to be the judge of that,' Etienne said. 'It's going to hurt like hell while I carry you, but I can't leave you here.'

Etienne put down his pack, then hoisted Jimmy upright

till he was standing on his one good leg. He was close to passing out, so Etienne put his shoulder into the man's belly and let him fall forward across his shoulders. He managed to grab his rifle as he straightened up and then set off back towards the line.

It had been hard enough getting that far out into No Man's Land on his own, but bent double with a dead weight on his back, making his way through thick mud, with shells exploding all around him, it was almost impossible. He plodded on, however, every muscle and sinew aching with the effort. At one point, when he almost fell sideways into a water-filled shell hole, he wondered why he was doing it.

A couple of hundred yards from the line French stretcher bearers appeared. 'You'll be all right now, Jimmy,' he said as they drew closer. 'I'll leave you now, got to get back and join my men.'

The stretcher bearers lifted Jimmy down from his back and on to their stretcher. 'Prenez bien soin de lui. Son nom est James Reilly,' he said.

As the stretcher bearers reached the line and other men came forward to help, they turned to look at the Englishman's rescuer. They knew he was wounded too, he'd had a gash in his tunic sleeve and fresh blood was running down his hand. But he was running at full tilt, leaping over shell holes and around obstacles towards the German line. They shook their heads in wonderment. 'Il doit être fou,' one said.

'What was the name of the man who carried me back here?' Jimmy asked some time later, after he'd been given morphine for the pain. He could only remember fragments of what had happened earlier. But he felt he knew the man's face and that he'd called him Jimmy.

'Je suis française,' the nurse said, and shrugged as if that was the end of the matter.

'He was French,' Jimmy said. The man might have spoken to him in English but he knew he'd been wearing the French blue uniform. It was too hard to make any further attempt to make the nurse understand him because his mind was growing cloudy.

They moved him again later. He heard someone say Hôpital de Campagne, which sounded like a field hospital. The pain came back from ruts in the road as he was being driven in an ambulance with other men, and he intended to ask about his injuries, but they gave him another injection before he could and then he felt too sleepy to care.

It was daylight when Jimmy woke again, and he was in a place that looked like a barn with rough stone walls. In the light that came through two small windows, he saw there were perhaps twenty or more other men in there with him.

He was thirsty and tried to sit up, but to his horror his left arm was gone; there was just a heavily bandaged stump above where his elbow had been. A nurse saw him trying to move and she came over, putting her finger to her lips to tell him to be quiet. She helped him to sit up and drink some water, and it was only when he looked down at the bed that he saw just one mound instead of two beneath the covers.

'They've taken my leg and my arm off?' he blurted out, pointing to where they had been.

She nodded, and patted his remaining hand.

He lay down again after his drink, closed his eyes and tried to tell himself this was just a nightmare. Both his leg and his arm felt as if they were still there, he could even wiggle his toes and fingers. But when he slid his hand down under the covers there was only one leg on the right. And he couldn't make his left arm move either.

Biting back tears, he lay there listening to the low moans and groans from the other wounded. There was no gunfire; whether that was a ceasefire or because he'd been taken far behind the lines, he had no idea. He could hear rain splashing down outside. It seemed to have been raining for weeks. He would get a Blighty ticket now, but how could he go home like this, a cripple?

He'd be no use to his uncle in the bar. With an arm gone or even just his leg he might have been able to adjust, but with them both gone, what chance was there for him? And what of Belle? Would she want him like this?

Chapter Twenty

Belle and David were washing out their ambulance at the end of the day when Captain Taylor came towards them.

'Reilly!' he barked. 'Come to my office when you've finished that.'

Belle looked at David as the officer walked away. 'What have I done now?' she asked.

'Maybe he's going to give you some leave,' David suggested.

'I can't see that, there's plenty of other people been here longer than me,' she said. 'Besides, they need every pair of hands just now.'

'Well then, you'd better go and find out what he wants. I'll finish up here.'

Belle hurried over to the office, taking off her overall and cap as she went. Through the open office door she could see the captain sitting at his desk, but she hesitated, not knowing whether it was right just to go in.

Fortunately he looked round. 'Come on in and take a seat,' he said. 'Best close that door behind you.'

He didn't sound angry, but he seemed flustered as he straightened up his blotting pad, put the top back on his ink bottle and tweaked his collar.

'I won't beat around the bush,' he said eventually. 'I'm sorry, but this is bad news. I got a call earlier to say your husband was wounded several days ago at Ypres.'

Belle gasped and turned pale. That was the last thing she had expected.

'How bad is he hurt?' she asked.

'I'm afraid he's lost both an arm and a leg.' The captain's voice softened in sympathy and he leaned nearer to her.

Belle's eyes filled with tears. She must have seen a hundred or more men with such injuries, and felt for them all. But this was her Jimmy, not just a stranger passing through.

'I am so very sorry, Mrs Reilly, breaking news like this is never easy, but to a member of my team it is even worse,' he went on. 'Furthermore, I have to warn you that in the next day or two you will get a letter informing you your husband is missing, presumed dead. You must disregard this, as it was sent before it was known he was in hospital.'

Belle just looked at him, not knowing what to say.

'You see, it transpired that he was rescued by a French soldier during an assault,' the captain explained. 'He carried your husband back to the French lines on his back, almost certainly saving his life. But the French field hospital he was taken to didn't pass on the information he was with them straight away. Hence the mix-up. However, earlier today, when it became known what had happened, the CO telephoned me to explain and ask me to prepare you.'

'A Frenchman rescued him?' Belle wiped her eyes on a handkerchief.

'Yes. Strange, really, the French are known for gallantry in battle, but not for rescuing our fallen men. Your husband's regiment was next to the French line, and I'm told that in the confusion of battle it is quite common for men to stray into another regiment's patch.'

'So will my husband be brought here?'

'I would think so, but that isn't certain. I did of course ask that he should be.'

'Thank you for that.' Belle got up. She wanted to get away from Captain Taylor before she broke down completely.

'I will tell you which ward he's put in when he arrives here. I am so very sorry, Mrs Reilly.'

Taylor was by nature cold and starchy, but just the way he addressed her as Mrs Reilly instead of his usual mere Reilly was evidence he did feel for her and wished to convey his sympathy.

'Thank you, sir,' she said, and left his office.

Once outside Belle felt completely dazed. When Jimmy had first joined up she'd worried all the time about him, but after he was wounded at the Somme she supposed she had bought into his view that nothing further would happen to him. Besides, as far as she knew he hadn't been at the front since then. It just didn't seem possible that he'd lost a leg and an arm; it was too horrific to imagine.

Stunned and feeling quite faint with shock, she wandered down a passage between two wards towards the hospital fence.

Jimmy's soldiering was over now, but this wasn't how it was supposed to end. In so many of their letters they'd both written about what might come next. There had been the rosy little plan for a guest house by the seaside, and Jimmy often mentioned other places in England he'd like to see – the Lake District, the Norfolk Broads and Devon – usually because he'd met someone from one of those places.

They couldn't do any of those things now. Once he was fit to travel he'd be sent back to England, and she assumed she would go with him. She couldn't even begin to imagine how they would live back at the Railway; he'd never be able to manage the stairs, let alone work in the pub again. She might have dressed wounds, washed and fed patients and given them bedpans at the Herbert, but she'd never been in sole charge of someone with two missing limbs.

She had so wished that something would happen which

would solve her dilemma about whether it was to be Jimmy or Etienne she should be with after the war. Her dilemma was solved now, of course, as she certainly couldn't even think of leaving Jimmy with such severe wounds. But fate was so cruel – why did it have to be something like this? Jimmy had done nothing to warrant such a catastrophic fate, or was this the ultimate punishment for her faithlessness?

It was bad enough that she would have to go home and face the gossip about her; she felt certain Mrs Forbes-Alton had continued to spread her poison. Now added to that she would have to take care of Jimmy and live with all the problems that would bring, as well as her huge burden of guilt.

But she knew this wasn't a time for thinking about herself. Jimmy was her husband, she'd promised before God that she'd love him in sickness and in health. She must remember too that he'd never given up his search for her when she was snatched from the streets of Seven Dials. She must make up for her adultery by standing by him, loving and protecting him.

It began to rain again, and in the distance she could hear the rumble of heavy guns, another reminder of what Jimmy had been through. Her thoughts turned to all those wounded she'd seen caked with mud, their haunted eyes reflecting the hideous nature of war, and her tears for Jimmy flowed.

All the girls in the hut were full of sympathy for her when she eventually went back in, soaked to the skin. Even Sally's eyes filled with tears as Belle told them her distressing news. But it was Vera who took charge, peeled off Belle's damp clothes and helped her into her nightdress, then hugged her tightly and let her cry.

'He will be able to get about eventually,' she said soothingly. 'He can have an artificial leg fitted. I've seen people with them and they manage just fine. You said he's a patient man, and that's all it takes.'

Sally brought her a mug of tea and a slice of a cake she'd been sent from home. 'My grandfather lost a leg in the Crimean War,' she said. 'He had a wooden one made, and he could get about as quickly as I could. But they make really good ones now, and while Jimmy's convalescing they'll teach him to use crutches and all kinds of things to help him look after himself.'

Belle didn't point out that Jimmy wouldn't be able to use crutches with only one arm; she couldn't when they were all being so kind and well-meaning.

In the early hours of the morning, and unable to sleep, Belle wrote Etienne a final letter. She told him about Jimmy and said she knew he'd understand that it had changed everything and that her duty lay with her husband.

There was so much more she wanted to tell him, that her heart felt as if it had been torn in two, that she would hold an image of him in her head till her dying day, but she knew it wasn't right to say such things. So instead she finished up by saying she hoped he'd stay safe, and wished him happiness and good fortune when the war was over.

It was a week later that Jimmy came in on the hospital train. Sally was the driver who picked him up at the station, and she gave Belle the message during the afternoon as they passed on the road.

'He seemed cheerful and not in too much pain,' she called out of the window. 'Can't wait to see you of course. I took him to Ward K.'

Belle ran towards Ward K as soon as they'd finished work for the evening, without washing and changing first. She needed to get it over as she was scared. She might have seen count-less men with monstrous injuries before, but this was different, it was her Jimmy.

'He's over in the corner.' Sister Swales waved her hand towards the end of the ward. 'But I'll warn you now, he's very low.'

Sister Swales was not Belle's favourite nurse. In her forties, she was stout, with sprouting hair on her chin, and she treated all the VADs and auxiliary staff with disdain. Belle had only helped on her ward once, and she was so dismissive that Belle had vowed never to go back. She even dreaded bring-ing new patients to Sister Swales's ward as she was invariably rude. But it was said by the other senior nurses and doctors that she was one of the best sisters in the whole hospital.

'Do you know if there is any reason for him being low?' Belle asked.

The Sister looked down her nose at Belle. 'If you had lost two limbs I'm sure you wouldn't be joyful,' she said.

'Of course not.' Belle curbed her irritation as she needed the woman's approval. 'What I meant was, my husband is usually a very cheerful, stoic man, I wondered if there was a medical reason for the way he is.'

'None whatsoever,' she said. 'Perhaps he'll tell you what is troubling him. But don't stay long, he needs rest.'

Jimmy was lying in the bed in the corner staring at the ceil-ing. He didn't turn his head as Belle approached. He had his right arm in the sleeve of his hospital pyjamas which were buttoned up, with the bandaged stump on the left inside the jacket. There was a cage under the bedcovers to protect the stump of his leg, and he had a still livid scar on his left cheek.

'My darling,' she said, her voice cracking with emotion, 'I don't know what to say. It's so awful and I'm so sorry.'

He turned to look at her and attempted a smile. 'No reason for you to be sorry, it's the lottery of war. But I'll be no use to you now, it would've been better if I'd died from the injuries.'

'Don't say that,' she said reprovingly and bent to kiss him. 'I love you and need you and I can only be glad you are alive. This is a terrible shock to you and it's no wonder you feel that way, but it's early days yet.'

'What does early days mean? You think I'm going to sprout a new leg?'

His sarcasm was hurtful, yet she knew what she'd said must have sounded trite. But she couldn't think of anything to say that expressed what she thought and might soothe him. What could anyone say to a loved one who had lost two limbs?

'Of course not. Oh Jimmy, I can't find the right words,' she said despairingly. 'It's awful, horrible, but I know we will get used to it in time. Remember, I see injured men all the time. It's surprising how some of them learn to cope.'

'Spare me the pep talk,' he said curtly and turned his head away.

'Now look here, Jimmy Reilly,' she said firmly. 'This has happened, we can't make it go away, so we've both got to learn to live with it. Don't turn on me, I didn't make you join up.'

He didn't answer, just stared at the ceiling.

'If you aren't going to talk to me and tell me all about it, then I might as well go,' she said after a little while. 'I've been working since seven this morning and I haven't had anything to eat since midday.'

He sighed. 'I'm sorry, sweetheart,' he said very quietly. 'I always thought I was one of the lucky ones who were going to go home intact. I wasn't even scared that day. I ran out thinking, get this over with and tomorrow I'll be back behind the lines safe and sound. Then bang, a shell exploded. The force of it blew me off my feet.'

She reached out and stroked his cheek. 'Captain Taylor said a Frenchman rescued you,' she said.

'Yes, he did. He got me on his back and carried me. Strange, I could swear he called me by my name, but maybe I imagined that 'cos I was hurting like hell.'

'You didn't know him then?' she asked.

'No. At least I don't think so. It was all hazy, I can't imagine why he picked me up, we're supposed to keep going on an assault. And I'd already seen a few Frogs hit and lying there in the mud. I wondered today why he helped me and not one of his own.'

'Well, I'm very glad he did,' she said and kissed his cheek. 'You've got to get yourself stronger and then we can go home.'

'Nothing will ever be the same again,' he said and his voice cracked and tears sprang up in his eyes. 'I won't even be able to wheel myself round in a chair as I've lost my arm too. I'm helpless now, Belle.'

'Not helpless. Your right arm is fine, and depending on where they amputated your left one, you might be able to get around on crutches after a bit. Your mind, eyes, ears and voice all work, your internal organs are all fine. I've seen men much worse off than you.'

'But how long will it be before you get tired of looking after me?' he said. 'I'm not trying to gain your sympathy, Belle, I'm just being realistic. I'm not a man any more, I can't work and keep you. You're young and beautiful, you shouldn't be saddled with a cripple.'

'I married you for better or worse, in sickness and in health,' she said soothingly. 'If it was me in that bed with those injuries, I know you'd take care of me. So why would you think I'll grow tired of looking after you?'

He just looked at her, his eyes which were usually so expressive now as cold as amber glass. 'Go and have your supper,' he said. 'I'm glad I'm here now near you, and maybe tomorrow I'll be more cheerful about everything.'

Belle stroked his hair back from his forehead. She didn't know what more she could say to him to reassure him they still had a future together. It all looked so bleak to her too. But she did know she intended to care for him, whatever that took.

In the days that followed, if it hadn't been for Vera and David, Belle felt she might just have fallen apart. Physically Jimmy was recovering well, there was no sign of infection in either of his stumps, but he swung from being withdrawn to the point where he didn't want to speak to anyone, to being so angry he even shouted at the nurses. She was also told he was suffering from nightmares.

'All that's to be expected,' David shrugged when she told him about it. 'If you weren't here I'll bet he'd be as nice as pie to everyone and be looking forward to going home to be with you. He's been through hell, it's hardly surprising he's having nightmares. But he probably doesn't realize yet what huge strides they've made in medicine since this war started. They've learned to do blood transfusions, skin grafts for burns, stuff that we couldn't have dreamed of before. I'll bet there's one of those clever blokes working on good artificial limbs right now. He'll get a pension, he's not going to be destitute, and he's got you, lucky devil.'

David was right about the enormous progress that had been made in medical science since the war began. In fact just about everything had moved on in leaps and bounds, from motor cars to aeroplanes. As a small child Belle remembered how they only had candles and oil lamps, most people had privies in the back yard, and until a few years ago omnibuses and cabs were all horse-drawn. Now electricity was commonplace, more and more people were using motor cars, and they not only had indoor lavatories but proper bathrooms too. So it did seem reasonable to believe that all this progress would mean that Jimmy might well get an artificial leg that would enable him to walk again.

David was the one with the practical knowledge, but Vera was the one Belle could confide her more personal fears to.

'It's going to be so hard. We're going home to where people will be talking about me and my past. I'm certain Miranda's mother will do her best to keep the gossip going for as long as possible,' she told her friend. 'If Jimmy keeps up being grumpy and angry I don't know if I'm going to be able to stand looking after him. And everyone will expect me to find myself a fancy man because of his injuries, so they'll be watching me like hawks. I want to do the right thing, but I never claimed to be a saint.'

'Take it one day at a time,' Vera said. 'The talk about you will stop if there's nothing further to keep it going. Jimmy will probably be much calmer when he can't hear guns in the distance and he's in his own home. He will find ways to do things for himself, and you won't be alone with him, you'll have Mog and Garth around too. But you keep in touch with me, won't you? I'd love to come to England before I go home to New Zealand. I'll help you jolly Jimmy along too.'

There was one thing though that Belle couldn't talk to anyone about. Jimmy had said he wasn't a man any more. She knew by this, although he wouldn't say it in so many words, that he believed he could never make love again. As far as she knew there was no physical reason why this should be so.

In her opinion, as soon as his wounds had healed up completely and he no longer had any pain, if they were in bed together he'd find it all worked the same as it always had. But she also knew that when men developed a fixation about such a thing, it often became a fact.

If Jimmy couldn't talk about this to her, he would never ask the doctor about it either. And she could hardly ask the doctor on his behalf.

On top of this her mind kept turning to Etienne. By day when these thoughts came to her she would stifle them, force herself to think of something else. But she would wake in the night from steamy dreams where he was making love to her, aroused and wanting him, and that made her feel ashamed of herself.

Then right at the end of August a letter came from him. She felt she ought to tear it up without reading it, but she couldn't. And as she started to read she couldn't hold back her tears.

My dearest, darling Belle,

I am so very sorry to hear Jimmy is so badly wounded, and I understand why you feel you must stay with him. He is a very lucky man to have you, I would willingly change places with him just to be near you.

Even as I write this I know you will not back down from your decision. I admire your conviction and selflessness, and knowing that there is always the possibility that I might be killed before this madness ends, I have made a will leaving my little farm and whatever money I have left, to you. I have made Noah my next of kin, being the one person I know in England who can be trusted with passing it over to you.

Should this arise, Jimmy does not need to find it strange or suspicious. He will know that I was your friend and rescuer back in Paris, and that I have no family to leave the farm to.

Of course I don't intend to get myself killed. I want to be back at my farm after the war, and live out my days growing lemons and rearing chickens. There will never be another woman now, as no one could fill the special place you have in my heart.

I pray that you and Jimmy can be happy together, and I wish too that I spoke of what was in my heart back in Paris, and kept you with me. I will not write again. Nor will I come and find you. I know I must leave you to repair your life and I'm sorry if I caused you sadness; that was never my intention.

My love always,
Etienne

Belle read the letter over and over again and cried at his nobility. That same evening she folded it up small and then unpicked some stitches in the lining of a little Dorothy bag she used to keep sewing items in, put the letter inside the lining and stitched it up again. She had burned all Etienne's old letters. But she couldn't bring herself to part with this one.

Chapter Twenty-One

Vera sat on her bed and watched Belle packing her suitcase. 'I'm going to miss you so much,' she blurted out, her lip quivering.

'Not as much as I'll miss you,' Belle said glumly. 'I haven't got any friends at home now Miranda's gone and if I run into her mother I'm likely to slap her.'

'What about your mother? Will you see her?' Vera asked.

Belle pulled a face. 'I doubt it, she hasn't even bothered to reply to the letter I sent telling her about Jimmy. Thank heavens for Mog; at least she'll be pleased to see me.'

'So are you taking Jimmy straight home?' Sally called from the other end of the hut.

Sally had been much nicer since Jimmy was wounded, often making tea for Belle when she got back from visiting him, and she always wanted to know how he was getting on.

'No, he's going to a convalescent home in Sevenoaks. I'll go there with him to settle him in, and then go on home.'

It was October now, and Jimmy's wounds were healing well. On days when it wasn't pouring with rain, she often took him for a walk in a wheelchair in the late afternoon. But she couldn't honestly say his spirits had lifted. He was cheerful enough with the other patients and the staff on his ward, but alone with Belle he was tetchy and gloomy.

The battle at Ypres was still raging. Recently there had been a three-week bombardment in which the 1st and 2nd Australian divisions joined the British 23rd and 41st, and attacked up the Menin Road east of Ypres. The Germans fell back under the devastating fire, and the Gheluvelt Plateau was finally taken by the Allies. But it was reported that there could be no decisive victory at the half-drowned, blasted and blighted battlefield that was Ypres. The Allies would gain a few hundred yards and move to the new ground, only for the Germans to retaliate and claim it back. Many said it was a wholly futile exercise and General Haig should call a halt to it.

But it seemed that Haig cared nothing for loss of life, or even common sense. With the British army fought out now, he planned to rely on the Anzac and Canadian troops to take what was left of the village of Passchendaele. Everyone at the hospital feared the casualties would be enormous, and for Vera, with her two brothers in the Anzacs, this was very frightening.

'Take this, it will keep you warm this winter.' Belle handed Vera the knitted comforter Mog had made for her to bring out here. 'I'd like to imagine you snuggled up in it, I was very glad of it when I first got here and I was so cold at night.'

Belle felt she should be happy to be going home, but she was dreading it. She might have had to work terribly hard here, but she'd experienced freedom from all the petty little restrictions and niceties that were so much a part of life at home. The male drivers treated her as an equal, her skirts had grown shorter for practicality, she could be herself without anyone making judgments. She loved helping out on the wards too, where she felt valued and needed.

It seemed a lifetime ago that she and Mog moved to Blackheath and spent their days watching and listening to how the middle classes spoke and behaved so they would fit in. Now that seemed as pointless as this war; all they'd done was set themselves up to be knocked down by snobbish, narrow-minded people who were cloistered in their privileged life.

Yet Belle was proud that she'd made her dream of opening her own hat shop happen. When she looked back on those days, marrying Jimmy and the happiness they'd shared, she saw it as a golden period when she'd thought all the bad things in the past were banished for ever.

But it was not to be. War broke out, Jimmy went off to France, and she lost her baby.

Yet working at the Herbert and then coming here had made her feel fulfilled again. She had come to believe that when the war ended, all the experiences she and Jimmy had gained would enable them to build a new life together that would be even better than their first year of marriage.

That hope looked forlorn now. Her once strong, steadfast Jimmy was a broken man and would be reliant on her for everything. Thanks to Blessard, her shameful past was common knowledge. Instead of the respect and admiration she'd once had, people would whisper about her and exclude her. On top of that money would be tight too, so they'd be unable to move somewhere else and start afresh.

'What's wrong?' Vera asked. 'You look like you are going to burst into tears.'

'Just thinking how much I'll miss all this.' Belle managed a weak smile and sank down beside her friend on her bed. She wasn't going to upset Vera by telling her what was really bothering her. 'I'll miss the chats, the laughs and the bad food. I know I'll have my comfortable bed, Mog's cooking and all that to look forward to, but I'm a bit scared really.'

Vera put her arms around her and hugged her tightly. She was very intuitive and probably realized the real cause of Belle's reluctance to go home. 'It will come right, I'm sure of that. Jimmy will become his old self again, and the people where you live will forget about those things they read in the press. Maybe you'll have a baby – think how good that will be! And the Americans will be ready to fight in the New Year, and the war will soon end then.'

Privately Belle thought that the only certainty in that list was that the Americans would be fighting by January. But Vera had enough worries about her brothers' safety without being given cause to worry about her English friend too.

'I'll be fine the minute I see the White Cliffs of Dover,' Belle said. 'But just make sure you come and see me before you go back to New Zealand.'

'Look, Jimmy, how lovely it is,' Belle said excitedly as the car that met them from Sevenoaks station turned into a long drive with a beautiful Georgian country mansion at the end of it.

An avenue of trees just beginning to take on autumn colouring lined the drive. Beyond railings to the right, sheep grazed in a meadow. To the left was a garden, a large, lush green lawn with borders still bright with chrysanthemums and asters. After the bleakness of France it was good to see the English countryside unchanged.

'It's one of the best convalescent homes around here,' Mr Gayle, their driver, informed them. He was in his fifties, a dapper man with a bald head and a thin moustache. He'd already told Belle he was a solicitor, but he had volunteered to drive wounded soldiers to and from here because his eldest son had been killed at the Somme. 'Around the side of the house is a delightful orangery; it's warm in there even in the depth of winter, and the men love it. They have physiotherapists come in a couple of times a week, they'll get you moving around in no time, son. The ladies in the surrounding villages bake cakes and pies for the men, they have visiting concert parties and all sorts. The owners have been very generous, moving into the Dower House to make extra room.

I think it's wonderful that anyone would give up their home like that.'

'What nice people they sound, Jimmy. Fancy giving up their house for the wounded,' Belle said from the back seat. She wished he would just show some appreciation and enthusiasm. They had left the hospital in an ambulance early that morning along with five other men with Blighty tickets. All five of them had been excited about going home, even the ones with worse injuries than Jimmy. But he'd ignored their jokes and refused to talk. On the ship from Calais he'd insisted that Belle move his wheelchair away from them and just sat in sullen silence.

'If they've got a Dower House they're hardly roughing it,' he said.

Belle was mortified. Jimmy never used to have a chip on his shoulder about the wealthy upper classes, but he seemed to have developed one now. He didn't appear to see that he was lucky to be sent to a place like this, which was usually for officers.

Two hours later Belle found Mr Gayle waiting in his car by the front door to drive her back to the station. It was dark now and very chilly.

'Did your husband settle in well?' he asked as he started the car.

'I can't really say, he hardly said a word,' she said. 'I must apologize for him, he isn't normally rude to anyone, but he's down in the dumps.'

'It affects men in different ways, as I'm sure you know as you've been working in France,' he said. 'I have met men so badly injured they really have no quality of life left, yet they are optimistic and cheerful, while others with quite minor injuries rage about everything. But once away from the sound of guns and all the pressure of war, even the most difficult of men usually come round. He's a lucky man having such a pretty and devoted wife. He has a lot to be thankful for. It's the ones who have been gassed, blinded and paralysed that I feel most sorry for. They don't have much of a future.'

Belle had thought Haddon Hall simply wonderful and was so grateful to Captain Taylor who had pulled strings to get Jimmy in here. He was helped into a wheelchair when they arrived and wheeled to the dormitory he would share with five other men on the ground floor. It was a lovely room, very light and bright, with a whole wall lined with books because it had been the library. They were shown the bathroom, newly built on the ground floor with a hoist to help those who needed it to get into the bath. There was a billiards room, a drawing room complete with piano and comfortable chairs and couches, the dining room, and finally the orangery Mr Gayle had already mentioned. There were board games, jigsaw puzzles, water-colours for those who could paint, and one man who had lost both legs was building a model ship.

They'd had afternoon tea in there too, scones, sandwiches and cake, all of which were delicious, but Jimmy barely said a word.

'Now, when you're coming back to visit him again, telephone and I'll either come and pick you up myself or get someone else to do it,' Mr Gayle said, handing her his card. 'We all appreciate how difficult it can be for the wives and mothers of the wounded boys, especially those who have small children and live a long way away.'

'I wondered about getting digs here to make it easier to visit,' Belle said. 'Do you think that's possible?'

'I can put out a few feelers for that,' he said. 'As you've

been an ambulance driver, would you be willing to do some driving here?'

'By all means. I worked at the Royal Herbert as a nursing aide too before going to France,' she volunteered. 'I'd be happy to do that again as well.'

'You are a very plucky young lady,' he said, glancing sideways at her. 'I do so hope your husband will rally round while he's here. He needs to take advantage of all the help and advice on offer.'

'I'm sure he will,' Belle said. 'I'll leave him for a couple of days to get used to it all. He seems to be gloomier when I am around.'

'I expect he's afraid of losing you,' Mr Gayle said. 'Men can be very stupid, they often lash out at the very one they should be cherishing.'

Belle paused for a moment as she came out of Blackheath station. It felt like years since she'd left that April morning with Miranda, yet it was only six months ago. She remembered how they had tried to behave like sensible, responsible adults because Miranda's parents, along with Mog and Garth, were seeing them off, yet in reality they were dizzy with excitement, intoxicated with the thrill of freedom. They had laughed all the way to Dover, unaware then that they had signed up for something that would test them in every possible way, and with no glamour at all.

Within three months they had developed muscles in their arms that a prize fighter would be proud of, they'd found lice in their hair, they'd slipped over in mud so often that it hardly registered. They rarely had time to arrange their hair, the most they could do was wash it and scrape it back into a bun. Some days they got drenched to the skin in the rain, other days they were soaked in sweat. They lived in a hut Miranda said was barely fit for cattle, and they ate food that at home they would have baulked at. They knew they were only one small link in the great chain of wartime administration, but they took pride in getting the wounded to the hospital as quickly yet as gently as possible, and offering what comfort they could.

Miranda had found the love she'd dreamed of. She might only have had a few short weeks with Will, but at least she didn't die never experiencing the bliss of true passion.

As Belle looked across the street at the welcoming lights of the Railway, she knew she must guard against ever letting Mog know that she too had found that bliss. While she doubted Mog would condemn her for it, confiding in her would make it harder to wipe Etienne from her mind. And she must do that.

She looked up and down the street; everything looked exactly the way it always had in the gas lights. The welcome from Mog and Garth would be warm, she knew they would envelop her in their arms and promise her that she and Jimmy would always have a home with them. But elsewhere in the village Belle was going to face scorn. And for now she'd have to live with it.

Picking up her suitcase, she resolutely put her shoulders back and crossed the road.

'Belle! I thought you'd never get here,' Mog exclaimed when she opened the side door to her. 'You must be exhausted. What time did you leave France? How is Jimmy?'

The quickfire questions were as Belle expected and she let herself be drawn into the narrow hall to be embraced.

'Jimmy's fine, Haddon Hall is lovely, and yes, I'm exhausted and it's wonderful to be home,' she said, burying her face in

Mog's neck and breathing in the familiar smell of lavender cologne and baking.

'Come on in and I'll make you a cup of tea,' Mog said. 'Your bed is all made up with a hot water bottle to make it cosy. Garth will be out to see you when he's closed the bar. It's never that busy these days.'

As Mog made a pot of tea and put ham, cheese and bread on a plate, Belle noticed her face was drawn, her hair had far more grey in it and she had aged considerably. She was wearing a navy-blue dress which, though not old, was very drab, like the ones she used to wear back in Seven Dials. It was appalling that Blessard's revelations and Mrs Forbes-Alton's spite had made her revert back to the little mouse she used to be.

'Save telling me about Jimmy until Garth comes through,' she said, putting the plate of food in front of Belle. 'Just tell me how you are. You said in your last letter he was very low, and I'm guessing that can't have been easy for you to cope with. I'm sure you won't like to tell me any of that while Garth is around.'

Belle half smiled at how perceptive Mog was. 'No, it's not easy, mostly he's so grumpy I feel quite defeated. But a few good nights' sleep will put me right. I feel easier now he's at Haddon Hall, and I'll just deal with things as they come along.'

'It's not going to be easy for you in the village either,' Mog sighed. 'People still look the other way when I go into a shop, and I'm afraid they may say nasty things to you.'

'I shall just ignore them,' Belle said more bravely than she felt. 'The only thing that upsets me is to see you looking so careworn and sad.'

Mog shrugged. 'Garth said he'll sell up when the war ends

and we'll move to Folkestone or Hastings. But he doesn't really understand what it's like for me; as you can imagine, no one dares say anything to him about it. So he gets cross with me as he thinks I'm imagining the slights and whispers. You'll also find he's got no real understanding of how Jimmy is feeling either. To Garth he's a wounded hero and a missing leg and arm are a badge of honour. The stupid man thinks Jimmy can sit in a chair all day in the bar and be as happy as a pig in clover.'

Belle winced because that was exactly how Jimmy had predicted Garth would react. But she could hear the hurt in Mog's voice about not being believed about how the neighbours were treating her. 'I'll soon put Garth right on all counts,' she said. 'The way Jimmy is now, we'll be lucky if we can even persuade him to come downstairs. To be honest, Mog, he's very bitter and withdrawn.'

'He's not loving towards you?'

'No, not really. Well, he apologizes when he's said something sharp, and I know he doesn't really mean to be that way. But he's got quite a chip on his shoulder.'

'Oh dear.' Mog slumped down on to a chair. 'I can't imagine him being like that. He was always so kind and thoughtful. It sounds as though you've had a tough time with him.'

'Maybe I haven't been sympathetic enough, after all, I've grown very used to bad injuries. I think he'd have been better in another hospital really, they tended to give him special treatment because of me. I think he resented too that I was off working during the day,' Belle replied. 'Oh, I don't know, Mog, maybe all the men are like that with their wives at first. Please don't tell Garth any of this. Jimmy may change back to his old self at Haddon Hall.'

As Belle ate her supper she asked Mog questions about

how she and Garth were, how the pub was doing and whether she'd heard anything from Noah.

'We had a letter from him to say how sorry he was about Jimmy,' Mog said. 'You can take it to Jimmy when you go to visit him. Of course, he's away most of the time as a war correspondent. Lisette has her hands full with Rose, the baby, and Jean-Philippe. Noah said he'll visit Jimmy as soon as he can. And you must go and see Lisette. Noah said she wanted to know all about your work in France.'

Belle smiled. She would be glad to go and see Lisette, who was the one person she didn't need to hide her past from, Lisette's being so similar. As for Noah, Belle would always have a special affection for him. He'd done as much as Etienne in rescuing her in Paris, and he was the one person who had known she loved Etienne back then, yet he'd never divulged it.

'What about the pub?' Belle asked. She felt Mog was avoiding that subject.

'Not too good, ducks. Well, there's not that many of the younger regulars left here. We get the old ones in still, but they'll nurse a pint for hours. Money is tight for everyone, people are weary of the war now too. All in all, it means a big drop in takings.'

Garth came into the kitchen later, and he beamed on seeing Belle and embraced her in a bear hug. 'Good to have you back,' he said. 'We've both been lost without you.'

He at least looked reassuringly the same as he always had, with his fiery hair and beard, and shoulders like a barn door.

'Tell me about the wounded hero,' he said. 'Can they give him a peg leg?'

Belle told them details of what Jimmy remembered about how he got his injuries, the treatment he'd received, and the

327

possibilities of an artificial limb. She also made it clear how lucky he was to have been sent to Haddon Hall. 'He'll be there for at least two months. I thought I might try and get some digs down there, but I'll leave him to settle in first.'

'He should be back here with us,' Garth said in indignation. 'You and Mog can see to him.'

Belle bristled. Garth meant well, and it was good that he wanted to look after Jimmy, but he didn't have any idea how difficult it would be to take care of an amputee, especially here where there were stairs and narrow doorways.

'He has to learn to do some things for himself before he can come home,' Belle said. 'He also has to come to terms with what's happened to him.'

Garth made a disapproving snort and Belle saw red.

'Mog and I aren't strong enough to lift him up to the lavatory, and he isn't in the best of spirits either. You might imagine he'll be happy sitting in the bar all day with you while people tell him what a brave man he is, but he won't be, and anyway, that is the worst possible thing for him. At Haddon Hall he's with men with similar disabilities and people who can teach him how to deal with them. At present he's bitter; he needs to get that out of his system.'

'We can make that store room into a room for him,' Garth said, pointing to the room off the kitchen as if he hadn't heard a word she'd said. 'I can put a ramp down the back step for his wheelchair so he can use the outside lavatory. You won't need to lift him then.'

'He can't wheel himself around with only one arm,' Belle said through gritted teeth. 'He can't even pull his trousers down himself yet. For goodness' sake, Garth, hold back your plans until you've seen and talked to him. I know you mean well, but Haddon Hall is the right place for him now.'

Garth stared at her for a moment, then suddenly looked stricken. 'It's that bad, eh?'

Belle could only nod, all at once realizing he hadn't quite grasped how disabled Jimmy was.

'I didn't think,' he admitted. 'I just wanted him here with me.'

'I know,' she said, her irritation wiped out by his affection for his nephew. 'But we'll all have to be patient a little longer till we can be a proper family again.'

He moved towards her and drew her to his big chest. 'At least we've got you back,' he said gruffly. 'You look worn out and much too thin, but Mog and me will soon put that right.'

Belle leaned into him, reassured that however bad some things were, Garth was still his strong, dependable self. Whatever difficulties lay ahead, she felt the three of them could tackle them together.

For the first week of being home Belle felt completely lost. She had no role; Mog cooked and cleaned, Garth ran the pub, and there was nothing left for her to do. She dug out her old clothes and tried them on, finding they were all too loose because she'd lost weight. But even her old favourites seemed too colourful and fancy now and made her look like the scarlet woman people believed she was.

On her first morning home she was shunned in the baker's. Two women she knew slightly pointedly turned away as she walked in, as if she was suffering from an infectious disease. She bought the bread Mog wanted and as she was leaving she heard them talking about her. 'The brass neck of her, coming back here,' one said. 'It's her poor aunt I feel sorry for,' the other added.

She went back to the Railway immediately, trying hard to

walk with her head held high, but inside she was crying. She stayed indoors for the rest of the day, making out to Mog that she was very tired rather than admit what had happened.

Later Belle sat by the window of her bedroom remembering how happy she and Jimmy had been when they decorated the room together just before their wedding. Neither of them had put up wallpaper before, and they ruined a whole roll by putting their hands through it, hanging it crookedly or tearing it, before they got the hang of it. But they had laughed so much, delighting in the idea of creating their own little haven. She could see the flaws – parts where the pattern didn't match up, little places where the paper had come away from the wall, the odd bubble which had never been smoothed out. But it hadn't mattered to them, or that the furniture was second-hand. Belle had made the lace-covered counterpane and the curtains, and Jimmy had rubbed down the scarred, battered dressing table and wardrobe and re-varnished them.

Their wedding photograph was now back in its place on the small table by the bed, a further reminder of how they'd both believed that day it would be happy-ever-after. Belle was only twenty-three, and the prospect of living in a place for years where people shunned her and pitied Jimmy was just too awful to contemplate.

A week after taking Jimmy to Haddon Hall, Belle went back to visit him for the first time. She had made a real effort with her appearance because she thought it would please him. She had washed her hair the day before, and she'd put it up the way he liked it, with a few loose curls around her face. She'd painstakingly altered the red wool costume he'd bought her for their first Christmas together, so it fitted better, and shortened the skirt so it was just at ankle height as she'd seen in fashion magazines. Her red and navy-blue hat was one he'd always loved too; it perched on the side of her head at a rakish angle and needed a lot of securing. Over her outfit she wore her navy-blue cape with a fur collar because it had turned very cold.

'You look very lovely today,' Mr Gayle said as he opened the car door for her outside the station. 'That should give your husband a real boost. Is it good to be back with your family?'

'Yes, it is,' she said. 'Though it's strange to have so little to do. I find the time drags. But that will change when Jimmy comes home.'

The wind was whipping the leaves off the trees, leaving a thick carpet on the country lanes as they drove out to Haddon Hall. Belle was cold and couldn't help thinking of Etienne back in France and wondering how he was coping with the cold on top of all the other miseries soldiers had to face.

'I spoke to your husband briefly yesterday,' Mr Gayle said, bringing her guiltily back to her visit to Jimmy. 'He seemed much more relaxed and was looking forward to seeing you. I'm sorry I can't take you back to the station today, but there's someone calling for Mrs Cooling, the wife of another patient, at four thirty, and he'll take you too.'

Belle thanked him and asked how he and his wife had coped with the loss of their son.

'Not very well at first,' he said thoughtfully. 'We were angry, bitter, we thought, "Why us?", but then, so many have lost sons, brothers and husbands, we aren't alone in our grief. In our village there is one widow who has lost all three of her sons. We are lucky to have two daughters and another son who is too young to be called up. Doing our bit for the wounded helps us. We've grown very fond of several young men who have passed through Haddon. Sometimes when I see the terrible wounds some of them have, and how difficult their lives will be because of them, I'm almost glad our John was killed outright.'

'Yes, it's cruel,' Belle agreed. 'I saw so many like that both in France and at the Herbert. I used to wonder how their families would manage to look after them.'

'But your husband will improve.' Mr Gayle reached out his hand and touched her arm. 'Trust in that. Life won't be the same for you as it was before the war, but you will be happy again, both of you.'

'Yes, of course we will.' His kindness prompted tears, but she bit them back. 'We have a lot to be grateful for, and at least I've got some experience of the problems Jimmy will have to face.'

'He told me you used to make hats. Maybe you could do that again at home, to give you an interest and bring in a bit of extra money?'

'Yes, that's a possibility,' Belle smiled at him. She liked this man, for his warmth, kindness and practicality. She silently told herself she wasn't going to wallow in self-pity any longer.

Jimmy was in much better spirits. He beamed at Belle as she walked into the orangery and introduced her to his three companions with obvious pride.

Fred, just nineteen, had lost both his legs, Henry just one leg, and Ernest had been blinded and was partially paralysed due to a spine injury. Belle spoke to each of them, asking where they were from and how long they'd been at Haddon Hall. They were all from South London, but only Ernest had been there for over three months.

'My folks can't cope with me at home,' he said remarkably cheerfully. 'But I don't want to go home anyway. I like it here.'

Belle wheeled Jimmy into the drawing room a little later so they could have some privacy. She knelt down beside his chair and kissed him, and for the first time he responded with enthusiasm.

'That's better,' she said, sitting back on her heels. 'I'd begun to think that bit of Jimmy was left at Ypres.'

He smiled sheepishly. 'I've been a bit of an idiot, too busy feeling sorry for myself.'

'You had every right to feel sorry for yourself,' she said. 'Now, tell me about it here.'

As Belle listened to him describing how it had been, she realized that it was the peace and quiet, warmth and comfort rather than any treatment which had improved his spirits. The only sounds outside the house were of the wind, bird-song and occasionally of someone chopping wood, unlike in the hospital back in France where the heavy guns in the distance and airplanes overhead could be heard constantly.

The other patients were helping Jimmy too, as some, like Ernest, were far worse off than him and had no family visitors. Belle was pleased to hear Jimmy express admiration for his new friend. He seemed more optimistic about coping with his own disability as he'd been told that once the stump of his arm was completely healed he could be fitted with an artificial one, which he could use to support himself on crutches or to manoeuvre a wheelchair for short distances.

He had been reading, learned to play chess, and laughingly said he'd found he could hop out of the wheelchair on his good leg to the dining table, lavatory or bed.

'Only trouble is, I've got to learn to balance myself,' he said ruefully. 'I forgot last night and fell over and couldn't get back up. One of the lads suggested I hang weights on my left-hand side.'

Belle felt her heart lighten to hear him joke about it. She had been afraid that would never happen.

'Would you like it if I got digs down here?' she asked him a little later. 'I could come and see you every day then, and Mr Gayle said I could do some driving.'

'I don't think that's such a good idea,' he said, surprising her by the sudden sharpness of his tone. 'You've been away from home for long enough, and anyway, they wouldn't want you coming here every day.'

On the train going home, Belle kept thinking about what he'd said. She doubted it was true that she wouldn't be welcome at Haddon Hall every day; Mr Gayle would have told her if that was the case. 'You've been away from home for long enough' was more telling. He wanted Mog and Garth to keep an eye on her; he didn't trust her any more!

She couldn't be angry, as she knew she wasn't worthy of trust, but she was saddened that he thought she'd find another man because of his injuries. Didn't he understand she had suggested moving down here to show him she wanted to be close to him?

November came in with relentless heavy rain, making it impossible even to go for a walk to relieve the boredom. Mog was wrapped up in her household chores and didn't want to share them however much Belle begged her to.

'I like things done my way,' she said fiercely. 'You go and read a book or do some drawing. You just get under my feet.'

Belle offered to help Garth in the cellar, but he wouldn't allow her down there because that was 'men's work'. She could see his back was aching with carrying heavy crates of beer, and she reminded him she'd grown used to lifting stretchers with heavier loads than that, but he still refused her help.

She tried sketching, but the only images which came into her mind were those of the station in France and the wounded being lifted off the hospital train. She did a few of them, but then put her sketchbook away. Drawing such pictures depressed her, and also made her think too much of the good friends she'd made in France.

On the second Sunday after Jimmy got back, Garth and Mog went with Belle to see him, and that was a good day. Mog had baked cake and made preserves to take with them, and both she and Garth were very happy to see for themselves that Haddon Hall was everything Belle had said. Mog cried when she saw Jimmy, and even Garth's eyes were swimming. As it was a dry and sunny day, they took Jimmy out for a walk in his wheelchair, and all four of them enjoyed seeing the pretty countryside in all its glorious autumn colours.

Jimmy was in very good spirits. When they got back to the Hall he even demonstrated his hopping technique to get from the wheelchair to the table in the orangery. Yet when Garth asked when he was coming home, he said point-blank that he was in no hurry.

'I'm better off here,' he said, looking as though he felt cornered. 'I like the quiet and the company when I want it. I'll be no use to you in the pub.'

Thankfully Garth didn't argue with him, perhaps he could see for himself that his nephew was better off where he was, but later, on the train journey home, Mog voiced her opinion.

'He's afraid of people staring at him and asking him questions about the war,' she said. 'How can we make him realize that London is full of wounded men? Most people have lost a relative or close friend, so they aren't going to ask him anything.'

Although Belle hadn't been out much since she got back from France, she knew Mog was right. Almost every man under fifty she'd seen was either in uniform or wounded. On her first day home she'd seen the pitiful sight of a man who'd lost both legs, begging outside the station. Mog had said such sights were even more common in Lewisham.

'Well, he can't stay at Haddon Hall for ever,' Garth said.

As Christmas approached Belle took her courage in both hands, and without consulting Jimmy first arranged to see the doctor at his surgery in Sevenoaks before going to Haddon Hall.

Dr Cook's surgery was in the front room of his house, a double-fronted villa quite close to the station. Belle had seen him twice before while visiting Jimmy, but never to speak to. He drove out to Haddon Hall in a pony and trap, a man of about sixty, portly and with white hair.

Once seated opposite him across his desk Belle noted his kindly, bright blue eyes and clear, rosy skin, and felt she could confide in him.

'Isn't it time my husband came home?' she asked. 'I know he doesn't want to, but you've fitted him with an arm now and he's doing quite well on his crutches. I feel he ought to be home with me, I'm living in a kind of limbo.'

'You want him home?' He sounded surprised.

'Of course I do, and so do his uncle and his wife whom we live with. Did he tell you we didn't?'

'Not in so many words, but I got the distinct impression it was felt there were too many difficulties running a busy public house. I had planned to ask you to come and talk to me about it. We do need his bed at Haddon Hall, but you pre-empted that by coming today.'

Belle frowned. 'His uncle runs the pub, his wife does all the housekeeping. I don't have any role there. I am free to look after Jimmy. The only difficulty is the stairs, but I know

336

he can get up and down the ones at Haddon Hall, even if he does manage it on his backside.'

Dr Cook smiled. 'Yes, I've seen him do it, and very quickly too. Tell me, Mrs Reilly, why do you think he is reluctant to go home?'

'His uncle and wife believe it's because he feels people will stare at him, but I don't agree. I think he's afraid of . . .' She stopped short, not knowing how to put it.

'Afraid of husbandly things?' he prompted.

Belle blushed. 'Yes. He did say something once back in France. At the time he was still so badly hurt that I was surprised he had even thought about that! I've tried to talk to him about it a few times, but he always clams up.'

'This kind of problem often crops up with amputees,' he said. 'They can feel they are only a half man, and it's easier to push away the woman they love than expose themselves to possible ridicule or contempt.'

'He surely knows I wouldn't ridicule him or be contemptuous! I've been taking care of wounded men for most of the war.'

'Reason doesn't prevail for men who have been through what he has. It's all trapped up here,' he explained, tapping his head. 'The horrors they've seen, their terror during assaults, the sound of the guns, even guilt that they survived when so many of their comrades didn't. Add a badly damaged body and you have a man who feels worthless.'

'So what can I do to give him back some self-worth?' she asked.

'I will tell him we need his bed and that he's well enough to go home. That may well frighten him, so you and your family mustn't make too much of it. No welcome home party, no people dropping by to see him. Just try to keep everything calm and normal. He may ask to sleep in a separate

337

room from you; I've had men who insisted on sleeping on the floor. You must nip this in the bud, without making too much of it. If he gets his way, he's likely to stay away from you. He will almost certainly have more nightmares, he might even be aggressive towards you sometimes. But if you can remain affectionate, without expecting much of a response, he will gradually revert back to the man he was before all this.'

'What if he doesn't?' she said in a small voice.

Dr Cook smiled at her. 'I have every faith that a beautiful, brave and loving woman like you can do whatever she sets her mind to. Go home today and make plans for Jimmy being there with you for Christmas.'

Chapter Twenty-Two

Belle stood at the living-room window upstairs watching out anxiously for Mr Gayle's car. It was the afternoon of 23 December and he was due to bring Jimmy home at eleven that morning, but there was thick fog all over London and it was very cold.

Unpleasant as the fog was, at least it would prevent any further bombing raids. Just three days earlier it was reported that German planes had come in over the Kent and Essex coast, and more than sixteen people had been killed by bombs they'd dropped.

Belle had been to see Jimmy the previous week to take him civilian clothes, but he had shown no enthusiasm for going home. She wasn't sure now whether she hoped Haddon Hall had decided to keep him there, or that they were just delayed by the fog. If he'd been stuck in a car for several hours in freezing conditions he was going to be very grumpy when he got here. Yet after all the effort she and Mog had made for Christmas they were going to feel very let down without him.

They had spent the last couple of days trimming a Christmas tree and decorating the living room and kitchen with holly tied with red ribbons. It all looked very festive and welcoming. Belle just hoped that Garth had understood what she'd told him about Jimmy, and that he wouldn't undermine her by bringing people in to meet him, or plying him with drink.

The Christmas tree in the corner of the room looked

lovely with the wrapped presents beneath. Belle had dug out the pretty glass baubles they'd bought together for their first Christmas here, and she'd made dozens of little angels from pipe cleaners with white netting dresses and finished each one with gold paper wings and a tiny halo. She felt that when she lit the red candles on Christmas Eve it would look even more beautiful.

Everything was ready: a large turkey in the pantry waiting to be cooked, Christmas pudding and cake made with great care by Mog, and dozens of other special treats which Belle had to queue for hours to buy.

On the previous three Christmases they hadn't made much of an effort because Jimmy wasn't there to share it with them, and Belle remembered how they'd discussed what he would be doing on Christmas Day, and what he would get to eat.

In his letter after the first Christmas he'd said that there was plenty of food and extra rum rations as people in England had sent so much out to France for the troops. He'd even got a parcel with socks, a balaclava, chocolate and cigarettes. He'd been very cheerful about the conditions they'd spent the day in, but at that time he'd been billeted in a barn some way back from the front line.

In the subsequent two years there were still parcels and extra rations, but noticeably less cheer from Jimmy. Belle hoped that on Christmas Day this year he'd feel a sense of peace, knowing he would never have to go through such experiences again.

This morning she'd read in the newspapers that all the hospitals were making huge efforts to give wounded soldiers an extra special Christmas. A great many men at the front had got leave this year too; Garth had been run off his feet in the bar last night, and he expected it to be even busier tonight and tomorrow. She had peeped round the bar door last night and it had been a sea of khaki – she thought most of the men must have woken this morning with sore heads. Garth said they were drinking like there was no tomorrow.

Her head ached from the tension and she felt slightly queasy with nervousness as she glanced yet again in the mirror above the mantelpiece to check her appearance.

Garth had said she looked pretty earlier today, but she didn't agree. The events of the past months had erased the sparkle she once had, she'd become too thin, her dark eyes looked too big for her face and she was very pale because she didn't go out much any more.

Her dark blue wool dress, high-necked and with long sleeves, was an old one which she'd altered, shortening the skirt and taking it in to fit her better. She'd added a lace collar and cuffs to pep it up, but it hadn't really worked. It looked what it was – an old dress pretending to be a new one.

There would be no new clothes for the foreseeable future. She would have to watch every penny now as Jimmy's army pension wouldn't go far. She still had a few pounds left from when she wound up her shop, but she needed to hold on to that for the future.

It was busy out on the street, despite the thick fog. She could hear people talking, babies crying and children chattering and the ring of boots on the pavements, but it was only now and then that she caught a glimpse of someone coming through the swirling fog. Earlier, when she'd gone out to buy vegetables, there had been queues in all the shops, and she knew they were still there, hidden in the gloom. The greengrocer's had looked very festive, with a display of polished red apples, oranges and nuts, but all she could see of it now was an orange glow from the lights. At the butcher's a few doors down from the Railway, she'd stopped to admire the turkeys, geese and chickens hanging above the white marble slab where big joints of beef, pork and lamb were arranged. She'd overheard women complaining how all the prices had gone up, yet in the newspaper this morning it said the government had claimed they were going to fine those profiteering from food shortages. Perhaps they would in poorer parts of London, but she doubted it would be enforced in more affluent areas like Blackheath.

As she stood there she watched a motor car crawl up the hill at a snail's pace, disappearing into the fog. Motor cars were so common now they were rarely remarked on, and although the baker, milkman and coal merchant still did their delivery rounds with a horse and cart, she supposed that in another ten years horse-drawn transport would have disappeared. She just hoped that by that time she and Jimmy would be living somewhere else.

Garth was wearing her down with his prejudice against women. She knew he hadn't really become any worse, it was she who had a different perspective through going to France, but his disparaging remarks and refusal to do anything he considered a female role were irritating. Mog might be happy to be subservient to him, but Belle didn't intend to follow her lead, not even for a quiet life.

Finally she saw Mr Gayle's motor car, and she ran out of the room and down the stairs. 'Put the kettle on, Mog, he's here,' she called as she passed the kitchen door where Mog and Garth were sitting by the stove.

Belle opened the car door for Jimmy. It was a long time since she'd seen him in anything other than his uniform or hospital blues and he looked so different in his old tweed jacket, a white shirt and the brown pullover Mog had knitted for him. 'Welcome home, Jimmy,' she said, reaching out to take his arm, but suddenly remembering it was the artificial one withdrew her hand, and instead opened the back door to get out his crutches.

He had learned techniques of manoeuvring himself and she'd already discovered he didn't take kindly to anyone interfering. By the time she had the crutches he had turned on the seat and had his remaining leg on the ground.

'Pass me one,' he said, and taking the crutch and tucking it under his right arm, he managed without any help to pull himself upright, balancing on the one leg. As always, Belle felt a pang of pity at the sight of the tucked-up empty trouser leg, and knew they'd all got to get used to the sight.

'Now, if you would tuck that under my arm,' he said, indicating the second crutch. Then, hooking the false fingers around a bar on the crutch, he hopped nimbly towards the side door of the pub.

It was very tempting to praise him for his skill on crutches, but Belle knew he hated anyone remarking on it, so she just followed him, resisting the desire to put her hand out in case he should topple. 'Come on in, Mr Gayle,' she called back, once she'd seen Jimmy had made it to the hall. 'You must be dying for a cup of tea.'

Garth took over in the hallway, and despite everything he'd been told he was grabbing Jimmy's arm.

'Let me be,' Jimmy said tersely. 'You're just in the way.'

'How's he been on the way home?' Belle whispered to Mr Gayle.

'Quiet, didn't say much,' he whispered back. 'Hard for him to leave his friends, but that was to be expected. Having to go so slowly once we hit the fog didn't help, I could see him getting more tense with every mile.'

In the kitchen Jimmy took the armed Windsor chair by the stove, propping his crutches up beside him. He seemed agitated, looking around him as if he'd never been there before.

'It's so good to have you home,' Belle said, bending to kiss and hug him, disappointed that he hadn't said how good it was to be home with her. 'We're all excited to see you, but tell us if we are annoying you and we'll stop it.'

'How could you annoy me?' he said, but there was no laughter or even a grin to show it was meant as a compliment.

'You know what I mean, if we're being too bossy, talking too much or you want to be alone,' she said.

They all had tea and a slice of fruit cake and made conversation about Haddon Hall and the journey from there. It was stilted with awkward silences which Mog tried to fill with chatter.

Mr Gayle did his best to steer the conversation on to something more general. 'I heard this morning that the ponds at Keston and Chislehurst have ice thick enough for skating. I can't ever remember them freezing that hard before January,' he said. 'But it says in the paper that up north they've got snow. That's going to please a lot of children, even if us older people view it with horror.'

'With the price of coal so high, a lot of people won't be able to keep a fire going,' Garth said indignantly. 'The government claims it's going to bring down the price, but I'll believe that when I see it. It's a scandal that people are making a packet from it.'

'I couldn't believe the price of nuts this Christmas,' Mog said. 'Brazils are two shillings a pound. And there's a shortage of dried fruit. I'm glad I got mine back in the summer or there'd have been no cake or Christmas pudding.'

'I must go now,' Mr Gayle said, almost as soon as he'd finished his tea. 'Mrs Gayle has invited some people round this evening and she'll be cross if I'm late.'

Belle went out to the car with him after he'd said his good-byes.

'He will be all right,' he said, patting her cheek. 'I can see how anxious you are – it's frightening when you think he might fall over. But he's mastered those crutches and his balance, just don't let him try to do too much too soon.'

'Merry Christmas to you and your family,' she said. 'And thank you for the lifts, the advice and your kindness.'

'Merry Christmas to you too,' he said. 'Jimmy's a lucky man having a lovely wife like you. Remind him of it now and again, and don't treat him with kid gloves, he's a grown man, not a sick child.'

As Belle went back indoors she saw Garth coming out of the bar with a glass of whisky in his hand.

'If that's for Jimmy, take it back,' she said quietly. 'It won't help him one bit.'

'One glass just to steady him can't hurt,' he said with that stubborn look he had so often.

'If he starts relying on whisky to get through the day it will be terrible for all of us, not just him,' she said fiercely. 'It's bad enough for him managing those crutches sober, drunk he'll be falling over and hurting himself. He can have a couple of drinks in the evening when he's upstairs, but not otherwise.'

'You, my girl, are becoming a shrew,' he said, then turned and went back into the bar.

They had supper in the kitchen at six as usual, before Garth opened up for the evening. It was Mog's special steak and kidney pie, which had always been Jimmy's favourite, but he pushed it around the plate and only ate a few mouthfuls. Belle willed Mog not to remark on it. But he did do justice to the rice pudding and preserved plums.

'You made rice pudding the first time you cooked for us in Seven Dials. I hoped then that you'd stay,' he said.

Mog blushed. 'Fancy you remembering that,' she said, clearly delighted. 'But then it was a pleasure to feed you and Garth. My goodness, you could put food away!'

After Belle had helped wash up she told Jimmy they would go upstairs to the living room. 'The fire is lit there and it's more comfy and quieter,' she said. She didn't trust Garth not to try to lure him into the bar if he was down here.

A flicker passed over Jimmy's face and she wasn't sure if it was panic or irritation. But he hauled himself out of his chair anyway.

In the hall he sat down on the stairs, and holding on to the banister went up one step at a time on his behind, the way she'd seen him do at Haddon Hall. She followed him up with his crutches.

As he went into the living room and saw the Christmas tree and decorations and the fire, he showed some emotion for the first time since getting home. 'It looks so homey and lovely,' he said, turning to her and smiling. 'Like the first Christmas after we got married.'

Belle drew the curtains as he sat down in the chair by the fire. 'We could play cards. Or read. I got some books from the library I thought you might like.'

'Or we could just sit here and look at the fire,' he said. 'You never used to be so jittery. Is it because of me?'

'I think it's just because we've been apart for so long,' she said truthfully. 'It must be the same for you. We can't turn the clock back to where we were before you went to France.'

She sat down on the hearthrug next to his chair. 'We hardly ever got to do this before,' she said. 'You were always working in the bar, and I'd be up here drawing hats.'

He reached out and touched her shoulder. 'We always had so much to say to each other then, though. You'd think after all this time away we'd have even more.'

'I expect in a few days we'll be like that again,' she smiled up at him. 'I felt very strange coming back here, and it must be even stranger for you.'

'Everything was easy at Haddon Hall,' he said thoughtfully. 'No one expected anything of me, the other men had been through the same as me, we didn't have to talk.'

'No one expects anything of you here either,' she pointed out. 'Especially me. But you must say what you want; mind-reading isn't one of my talents.'

He smiled at that. 'Would you think me miserable and ungrateful if I said most of the time all I want is complete silence?'

She shook her head. 'That's understandable. I often feel that too when Mog is wittering on. David, he was the stretcher bearer I worked with, once told me he couldn't bear to go home because he knew his mother would keep questioning him. I knew exactly what he meant.'

'Maybe we'll be all right then,' he said.

Jimmy looked very troubled when he wanted to go to bed and found the boxroom was still just that, full of boxes. 'You didn't have time to clear it?' he asked Belle.

'I didn't try,' she said. He'd mentioned this room at her last visit, but mindful of what Dr Cook had said, she'd ignored it. 'You are sleeping where you belong, with me in our room.'

He looked panicked then. 'But I'll disturb you if I have a bad dream. I can sleep on the couch.'

'No, Jimmy,' she said firmly. 'You belong with me. And if you have a bad dream you can tell me about it. I've put your pyjamas on the bed. I'm just going downstairs to get you some hot milk. By the time I get back I expect to find you in bed. No more arguments.'

It was just on closing time. Garth was still in the bar and thankfully Mog appeared to be in there with him, otherwise Belle knew she'd be firing questions at her. As she heated up the milk in the kitchen she struggled not to cry. Jimmy hadn't shown any signs of wanting to kiss her all evening. Apart from the odd pat on the shoulder, he hadn't touched her either.

She didn't know how to say, 'You don't have to make love to me, just hold me.' But how could that be? There was a time when she could say anything to Jimmy. Mostly they hadn't even had to speak to make themselves understood.

How could she break through that wall he'd built around himself? What was he thinking?

As she went back upstairs with the milk, she half expected him to be back in the living room on the couch. She was too tired for confrontation tonight, so if he was, he could stay there.

To her surprise he was in bed, hunched up over to the right, with the covers up to his ears as if he thought he could make himself invisible. She put the milk down beside him and said she wouldn't be long, then went into the bathroom.

He had drunk the milk and was back in the same position when she returned in her nightdress. She got into bed beside him, turned out the light and said goodnight.

Belle waited. He had never, ever failed to kiss her goodnight since they got married. But she could feel how rigid he was without even touching him.

Finally, unable to stay silent any longer, she spoke. 'If I had been wounded instead of you, I'd still want you to hold me,' she blurted out. 'I can't remember one night in this bed that you didn't fall asleep with your arm around me.'

He didn't answer.

'Don't pretend you're asleep,' she snapped at him. 'Ignoring me won't make this problem go away.'

'Don't whores know everything about men?'

His reply, though almost whispered, seemed to reverberate around the dark room. She couldn't really believe he could say such a cruel thing.

She was too stunned to come back at him quickly and just lay there in the darkness.

'I can't believe you'd say something so cruel,' she said eventually, her voice shaking. 'I know what I was, but you used to be the kindest, most selfless man I ever met. As your heart appears to have been blown away along with your leg and arm, I might as well go back to France and leave you here to rot alone in self-pity.'

She got out of bed then and stumbled off to the living room. She felt as if he'd struck her.

It was impossible to sleep. She was cold as there were no covers and she couldn't go and get any without alerting Mog that something was wrong. She was angry and deeply hurt because she had never imagined that Jimmy would throw her past at her, especially to avoid any physical contact with her.

She hated that she was trapped now. He could be as nasty as he liked, but she couldn't walk out on him. It wouldn't be right to expect Mog to pick up the pieces.

Maybe he was just lashing out at her for making him sleep with her. But in almost all his letters in the past years he'd said how he dreamed of being cuddled up with her in bed. He must remember that, and however afraid he was that he'd lost the ability to make love, surely he would still want her close to him?

She heard him get up in the night and the clonk of his crutches as he went to the bathroom. She held her breath, so

349

sure he would come and find her and apologize, but he went straight back to the bedroom and shut the door behind him.

Long before it was light, when there wasn't a sound out on the street, Belle got up, put her clothes on in the bathroom, brushed her hair, pinned it up again neatly, and then went downstairs. It was Christmas Eve, the busiest day of the year for the pub, and Garth and Mog would be down soon to get ready for it. She dreaded seeing them, as whatever lie she told them, Mog would see through it.

So she put on an apron and laid the table for breakfast, her intention being to brave it out and pretend she had just got up early to help them. She laid a tray for Jimmy too, because if she gave him breakfast in bed, by the time he came downstairs later, Mog and Garth would be too busy to notice anything was amiss.

She was frying bacon and eggs when Mog came down. 'Ooh ducks! What a lovely surprise, but you should've stayed in bed and let me do that,' she said, her small face wreathed in a smile. 'How's Jimmy?'

'He was still asleep when I came down,' Belle said. 'I'll take his up to him.'

She took Jimmy's tray up as Garth and Mog sat down to eat their breakfast. He was lying the way he had been the night before, hunched up on his side as if he hadn't moved all night.

'Your breakfast, Jimmy,' she said curtly. 'It might be a good idea if you stayed up here for now. I don't want Mog to realize something's wrong and get upset.'

He turned over on to his back and she saw his eyes were red and swollen. 'I'm sorry, Belle. That was unforgivable of me.'

Half of her wanted to accept his apology and say she

knew he hadn't really meant it. Yet the other half was still too hurt to forgive that readily. 'Nothing's unforgivable given time, and some evidence you didn't mean it,' she said cautiously. 'But right now I feel wounded, so sit up and eat this so I can go and get on with the chores.'

'Please stay and talk to me,' he begged her.

'I can't. There's too much to do downstairs. I understand that you feel only half a man, and that you've got to come to terms with what's happened to you. But shutting me out and being spiteful about my past is not the way to deal with it. I'll talk to you later.'

She told Mog and Garth Jimmy was tired and was going to stay in bed. As they had so much to do, neither of them questioned it. Belle went into the bar with Mog to clean it, and Garth went down to work in the cellar.

Later on Belle went outside to polish the brass on the bar door. It was bitterly cold and the fog so thick she couldn't see across the street. She felt desolate, scared and overwhelmed by the prospect that this would be her life from now on, with domestic chores being the only way to work off her frustrations.

Around mid-morning she took tea and cake up to Jimmy. He was sitting up in bed reading a book, and as she put the tea down beside him he tried to catch hold of her hand, but she shook him off and left the room.

Mog took him up some sandwiches and soup at lunchtime. She reported that he looked 'peaky', and had said that he'd stay upstairs so as not to get under anyone's feet.

'He's a brave lad,' she said fondly. 'It'll be nice tomorrow when we can all be together with no bar to worry about. There's that many people in there now! Four deep at the bar when I took some clean glasses in and it'll be even busier tonight. I wanted to go to the midnight service but God will have to excuse me this year, I don't think I'll have the strength to walk up there after we close.'

Belle was glad there were plenty of glasses to wash and sandwiches to make. After the bar closed for the afternoon, she swept it out and washed the floor again, then cleaned the outside lavatory the customers used, to avoid sitting with Jimmy. Her anger had gone now; she just felt bruised and very tired.

It was well past eleven when Garth finally pushed the last of the drinkers out of the door and locked up. He had been drinking steadily all evening and was swaying on his feet. Mog pushed him off up the stairs, and then she and Belle collected glasses and wiped off the tables and bar.

'The rest can wait till Boxing Day,' Mog said, surveying the floor swimming with spilt beer and cigarette ends dropped on it. 'I'll just put the takings away, and then off to bed.'

It was Belle who went around checking the doors and window were locked and turned the lights out. She was dead on her feet and knew she couldn't face another night on the couch, but she didn't want to have to face Jimmy either. She knew he wouldn't have found it pleasant during the evening in the bedroom with all the shouting and laughter in the bar below. She'd last seen him at half past six when she'd taken him up a cold supper of ham, cheese and pickles. But then, he knew what it was like at Christmas in a public house, so he wouldn't have expected any of them to go in and see him.

He was reading in bed when she came into the room in her nightdress.

'Garth sounded drunk,' he said. 'He was muttering to himself out on the landing. You've all had a busy night, and you look very tired.'

'Yes, I am,' she said. 'I could sleep for a week.'

'I'm really glad you've come in with me,' he said. 'I am so sorry, Belle. I was horrible to you, and I wish I could take it back.'

'It's all in the past,' she said, and reached out to stroke his face. 'It'll be Christmas Day in a few minutes. Mog used to tell me when I was little that there's magic in the air at Christmas, so perhaps we'll wake up tomorrow and everything will be right with the world.'

She got into bed and he turned out the light. As she was dropping off to sleep she felt him kiss the back of her neck, and he whispered that he loved her.

Chapter Twenty-Three

On Christmas morning Belle got up at seven while Jimmy, Mog and Garth were still sound asleep, and lit the fire in the living room.

She had woken to find Jimmy curled into her back and it felt so good she decided to put aside her hurt, and make sure everyone had a really nice day.

After she'd got the fire going she went downstairs, cleared up from the night before and put the turkey in the stove to cook. Later, when she heard Mog moving about upstairs, she took up a tray of tea and suggested they all went into the living room.

Mog had made a real effort with her appearance. She was wearing a rose tea dress with darker pink embroidery on the bodice that Belle had never seen before, and it made her rather sallow complexion brighter. She looked delighted that for once someone else was organizing things and happily sat down in the living room.

'I thought I'd make us all bacon sandwiches to eat up here, then we can open our presents and have a nice lazy time,' Belle said, putting the tea tray down by Mog for her to pour.

Garth came in then. He was clearly suffering a little from the excesses of the night before, but he'd put on a sparkling white shirt with a winged collar and a dark green jacket.

'Is that tea? And did someone mention bacon sandwiches?' Jimmy said at the door. 'My word, you all look very posh. I must look like the poor relation.'

'You don't at all,' Belle said. He was wearing the brown

cardigan Mog had knitted for him, and she could appreciate that made it a great deal easier for him to get on one-handed than if he'd been wearing a jacket. 'And yes, you did hear bacon sandwiches mentioned, I'm just going down to do them. You make Mog stay here and put her feet up.'

Jimmy sat down in an armchair, his crutches beside him. Belle bent down to kiss his cheek before leaving the room. 'You look more rested today,' she said.

He put his hand on her cheek and looked into her eyes. 'I slept better with you beside me,' he whispered.

It turned out to be a lovely day. Outside it was as bitterly cold and the fog still just as thick, but that just made it seem cosier by the fire. Mog's presents to them were all things she'd made herself. She must have planned it all a year ago as there was a handsome dark green cardigan for Garth, a soft flannel shirt for Jimmy and a red lacy wool shawl for Belle.

'I couldn't buy anything for any of you,' Jimmy said sadly.

'You gave us the best Christmas present of all just by being home here with us,' Belle said, putting her new shawl around her shoulders.

Garth looked surprised as Jimmy and Belle opened the presents from him. Everyone laughed, knowing full well Mog had bought the pyjamas for Jimmy and stockings for Belle. But Garth had bought Mog's present all by himself and got the shop to wrap it. It was a silver fox fur to wear over her coat, something she'd always wanted. She screamed with delight when she opened it, then leapt at Garth to hug him.

'I didn't think you were listening when I kept on about it,' she said. 'I've never had anything so lovely before. I'd better start going to church again so I can show it off.'

As Garth had let Belle in on the secret, she'd hidden away

in her bedroom to make a hat to go with it. It was a cloche style which suited Mog, a silver grey satin base with slightly darker grey trimming and two toning satin rosettes to one side. She'd bought Garth a green and white silk cravat, and Jimmy a chess set. She knew he'd played chess a lot while at Haddon Hall, and she hoped he would teach her so they could play together.

Mog made them all laugh by putting on the hat and fox fur and swaggering around the living room like a duchess. Belle realized it was the first time she'd really laughed since she'd come home from France, and it was good to see Jimmy looking relaxed and happy to be back with them all.

Annie had sent Belle a box of very grand chocolates. But lovely as they were, Belle would have been more pleased with a letter showing some concern for Jimmy and asking how they all were. There wasn't even a brief note in the package.

'I really wonder about her sometimes,' Mog said indignantly. 'I wrote to her too, you know, when we heard about Jimmy. She didn't bother to reply. Yet I bet if she was in a tight corner she'd be over here at the speed of lightning.'

'Well, she won't get any joy from me if she does,' Belle said. 'I'm not even going to thank her for the chocolates. Thank heavens for you, Mog! One of you is worth a hundred of her.'

Later Belle and Mog went downstairs to see to the dinner, leaving Garth and Jimmy playing chess.

'Jimmy's much better today. Or maybe it's just because you are being nicer to him,' Mog said pointedly as they prepared the vegetables.

'I kept away from him yesterday, because he said something horrible to me,' Belle blurted out. 'I didn't deserve it, and I'm not going to put up with any more of it. But it's over now, I said my piece and it's forgotten.'

356

'I hope you can go back to how you used to be,' Mog said wistfully. 'But I suppose that's crying for the moon; this war has changed us all.'

'Maybe one day we'll find it's changed us for the better,' Belle said, and went over to Mog and hugged her.

Mog broke away after a few moments and caught hold of Belle's face between her two hands. 'I know you better than anyone,' she said, looking right into Belle's eyes. 'So I know something happened to you in France. Not just Miranda being killed, or the sights you saw. Something else. Whatever it was, you can tell me.'

Mog had always been able to sense if there was anything troubling her, and Belle remembered from the past she'd always felt better by unburdening herself, but she was an adult now, and some things were better kept secret.

'I just grew up,' she said and smiled at the older woman fondly. 'When Jimmy and I got married I had everything I'd ever hoped for. I believed all the bad times were over and we'd live happily ever after. I know you thought the same too when we moved here and you married Garth. But it didn't turn out that way. Maybe we need bad times to make us fully appreciate the good ones.'

'Today seems a good one,' Mog said.

'Yes, it does, so let's just be glad of that.' Belle said. 'I'm going to lay the table and we're going to stuff ourselves to bursting. We'll forget about the war and what the future might bring and just be happy together.'

'It was a lovely day,' Jimmy said as they got into bed that night. 'You and Mog worked so hard to make it good, the best dinner ever; if the boys back in France knew what we'd had they'd be drooling.'

He had mentioned various friends during the course of

the day, and it was clear to Belle that he was missing the comradeship of the army and realized that even if he could get back to work behind the bar he was never going to find that depth of friendship in civilian life. It was the same for her too, but Jimmy's disability was going to make it hard for him to make new friends.

'You must write to some of them,' she said. 'I'm sure they'll want to know how you are getting on, and maybe you can even get together again once it's all over.'

'I suppose I should,' he said thoughtfully. 'It would be good to hear first hand what's going on over there too, the newspapers don't tell it like it really is. Do you write to that friend of yours back in the hospital?'

'I've written to Vera several times,' Belle said. 'There's more wounded Australians, New Zealanders and Canadians being brought in now. She worries about her two brothers, half expecting them on the next ambulance train. I miss her.'

'I miss the blokes I was with,' Jimmy admitted. 'We were always arguing, taking the rise out of one another, I used to think that some of them were idiots. But now when I look back what I see is the brothers I always wished I had. Pals like I never had in civilian life.'

'You never had a chance to make friends before, you were always too busy working,' Belle said. 'I never had a real friend either, not till I found Miranda. We've got one another, Jimmy, we were good friends too, but it isn't quite the same as friends of your own sex, is it?'

'No, sweetheart, it's not. But I'd rather have you as my only friend than a whole battalion of male pals.'

'That's good to know,' she said, and cuddled closer to him.

'Night night,' he said, turning his back to her.

Belle lay there for some time feeling sad and disappointed.

It had been such a lovely day and surely it wasn't too much to expect a cuddle at the end of it?

On New Year's Eve, at Garth's insistence, Jimmy reluctantly joined him in the bar. He came out less than an hour later looking shaky and sat down with Mog and Belle in the kitchen. 'I couldn't stay there,' he said. 'Half of them wanted to know all the gory details of my injuries, the other half knew someone worse off and went on about it. I don't want to talk about wounds. Or who is dead. There was some poor sod in the corner coughing his lungs up too, he'd been gassed. I can't be doing with that.'

Belle thought she ought to be glad he didn't like it in the bar. One of her biggest fears had been that he'd want to be in there every night, and she'd have to help him up the stairs at closing time and listen to drunken ramblings. But she couldn't be glad. Although everything had been fine on Christmas Day, he had retreated back into himself since then, not speaking, not taking any interest in anything or anyone.

She had tried to bring him out of himself, talking about people and things he used to like, getting Mog to cook his favourite meals and asking about his friends in the army. But the wall he'd built around himself seemed to be getting higher each day.

The fog had lifted on Boxing Day, and then it snowed. Belle had gone for a walk up on the heath and saw scores of children dragging sledges, having snowball fights and making snowmen. She'd come home invigorated and suggested they bought Jimmy a wheelchair so he could go out. But he'd been contemptuous, asking how she thought she would be able to push him up the hill.

It was true that whichever way they walked from the Railway there was a hill, but she was strong, she could push him, or at least attempt it. Was he really intending to stay indoors permanently?

In another couple of hours it would be 1918. A time for being optimistic and hoping the year ahead would be a better one. Why couldn't he see it that way?

'I'm going to bed,' Jimmy said.

'Surely not this early?' Mog exclaimed. 'Stay up and see the New Year in.'

'What's to see?' he shrugged. 'Hundreds of glasses to be washed, the outside lav awash with piss and vomit, and drunks talking rubbish. I'd rather be in bed.'

Belle's heart sank. While she did understand that he must be feeling useless because he couldn't work, his negativity about absolutely everything was affecting them all.

'Go on then if you're going to be a wet blanket,' she said.

Mog turned on her as he left the room. 'Can't you find it in your heart to be kinder? You never used to be cruel.'

'Am I cruel to want him to talk to us? To accept what's happened and to think about what he can still do rather than all the things he can't?' she asked. 'For a start, he could take over doing the pub's accounts, Garth struggles with that.'

'Have you suggested it?'

'Yes, of course I have, but he nearly bit my head off. Said how could anyone follow Garth's system?'

'Garth hasn't got a system,' Mog said. 'That's the reason he struggles. I never knew anyone so disorganized.'

'Jimmy could make one, he's bright, he's good at sums. Besides, he used to do it before he joined up.'

'You are always so impatient,' Mog said. 'He's only been home a week. Can't you just let him alone for a bit? Let him find his own way?'

Belle wanted to tell Mog that she might be right, and it was Jimmy's coldness to her that was making her seem cruel and impatient, but she couldn't bring herself to admit something so personal.

For the next two weeks she made no suggestions at all to Jimmy about things he could do. She ignored his long silences and waspish remarks, and let him go to bed early without passing comment, even though she knew it was a ploy to avoid any lovemaking, or indeed conversation.

The weather was not on her side either. First snow, which quickly turned to dirty slush and more fog, and even when that lifted for a while the sky was like lead. It was so cold that just a short walk made her feel as though the skin was being stripped off her face, and although she found jobs to do at home, the days seemed endless.

It had been very quiet in the pub since New Year's Eve, so Mog and Garth also had a lot of spare time. She sensed they were both finding Jimmy's moods quite a strain too, as they were arguing about petty things. Mog kept complaining she had a headache, and Belle could feel pressure building up inside them all, which if it blew up could only result in more distress and unhappiness for everyone.

For all their sakes, Belle felt she had to get some advice about Jimmy, so one Tuesday afternoon she walked up to the Herbert Hospital in the hope that one of the sisters she knew might be able to recommend someone who could help him.

She went to her old ward, only to find the nurses, most of whom were unknown to her, settling in a batch of new arrivals. Belle had all but forgotten the frenzied activity at such times, and as she hovered at the door looking for a familiar face, she was shocked to see that most of the new patients were burned, their faces, shoulders and arms like raw meat, and there was a smell so bad it made her gag.

'Have you come to see one of the patients?' a nurse asked as she came in carrying a pile of clean bed linen.

Belle explained she used to work there and had been hoping to see Sister May.

'She'll be on another ward,' the nurse said. 'This one is just for burns now. Maybe one of the porters can tell you which one to go to.'

'Why are there so many burn cases?' Belle asked.

'Liquid fire,' the nurse said. 'This lot got it at Cambrai, poor devils. Of all the weapons they use in warfare, I think this is the worst. Those who survive it are scarred for life.'

Belle thanked the nurse and turned away. She realized that all the wards would be just as busy and that no one would have time or inclination to talk about a man who was no longer in a critical condition. She thought perhaps it would be better to go and see Dr Towle and get his advice.

As she started to walk home with the images of those badly burned men on her mind, the anger she'd been trying so hard to suppress for the last couple of weeks began to bubble up inside her. She wished Jimmy could see those men, perhaps then he'd appreciate that losing an arm and a leg could never be as bad as such terrible burns.

Yet as she walked she realized her anger wasn't just because of Jimmy, there was a whole raft of things causing it and she was projecting it all on to him because he was closest and she was with him daily.

How could anyone not be angry about a war that was killing so many tens of thousands of young men, and maiming still more? There were the widows with children left without fathers, some of whom were left in desperate situations, unable to pay the rent and struggling to buy food. It was becoming ever more common to see wounded men begging in the streets, and only a day or two earlier she'd read that in some poorer areas of the big cities malnutrition in children was as bad as it had been in Victorian times.

Then there were her own personal grievances. Not just the difficulties with Jimmy, but the lack of interest or sympathy from her mother, and the unfairness of Mog being ostracized in the village because of what Blessard had written in his gutter rag. Mixed with that was her grief at Miranda's unnecessary death, and the heartache and guilt she felt at Etienne coming back into her life.

She knew it was her impotence which was fuelling her anger. She could do nothing about any of these things. She couldn't stop the war, help those in need, or make Jimmy whole again. All she could do was endure, hoping against hope that time alone would bring solutions to all the problems.

Yet it seemed to her that she had spent too much time in her life enduring things. Just this once she would like to strike back, refuse to be like a leaf being blown hither and thither in the wind. To make a stand.

A memory of Miranda came into her mind. She was sitting up in her bed in the hut one night, writing a letter home. She was wearing a pink nightdress and her blonde hair was tumbling over her shoulders. But all at once she flung the letter down. 'I'm sick of trying to make her like me,' she blurted out and began to cry.

Belle had got out of her bed and gone over to her friend, putting her arms round her. 'Your mother?' she asked.

'Who else?' Miranda sobbed. 'She couldn't care less what I do here, she's just glad I'm out of sight, and that means out of mind too. I write every week, I try and make it interesting and impress on her that I'm good at my job, a regular little Florence Nightingale in an ambulance. All I get is a few lines back every few weeks, nothing about me, saying that

Amy is going to marry a viscount, how well my brothers are doing, and describing the society balls and parties she goes to. The only thing that would ever make her pleased with me is if I was to die out here, then she'd be able to boast to her stuck-up acquaintances that I gave my life for King and Country.'

The following day Miranda had apologized for the outburst, but she didn't say it wasn't true. And after she was killed and Belle was packing up her friend's things, she'd read the few letters from her mother that were in her locker. It was as if they had been written by someone who barely knew Miranda, even chillier than she'd said.

Remembering this added more fuel to Belle's anger. The odious Mrs Forbes-Alton hadn't even replied to her letter giving her more details of Miranda's death and saying how devastated everyone at the hospital had been by it. Instead she had spitefully blamed Belle and slandered her in the press, destroying Mog's happiness and good name, to the point where she felt she couldn't even go to church for fear of being snubbed.

Like a bolt of lightning from the leaden sky, Belle saw that this was one thing she didn't have to endure. She should have gone round to the Paragon as soon as she got back from France and had it out with Mrs Forbes-Alton. That was what Miranda would have expected her to do.

As an idea began to form in her mind, Belle could almost hear Miranda urging her to do it. Mog wouldn't approve, Jimmy would be appalled, but she didn't care what they thought. She was tired of allowing people to victimize her, and sometimes you had to fight fire with fire. She couldn't put the world to rights, but she could give that vile woman her come-uppance.

*

That evening Belle was able to ignore Jimmy's sullen silence because her mind was whirling with the finer details of her plan. It lifted her spirits in the same way sketching used to do.

And she intended to put the plan into action the very next day.

Miranda had once said that her mother held a bridge afternoon at her home every Wednesday. She had joked that she always knew when it was two o'clock as the front door bell rang on the dot, and her mother's cronies left the house just as punctually at four. Miranda had added that supper on a Wednesday was always a trial, as she was forced to listen to a rehash of the afternoon's gossip, and she wished she'd been able to do as her father always did, which was to absent himself.

At just on four Belle watched from further down the Paragon as the bridge players left the Forbes-Altons' house. It was already dark, but light from the hall at number twelve was bright enough to see Mrs Forbes-Alton silhouetted in the doorway, and Belle could hear her braying voice saying her goodbyes.

Two of the women got into a motor car waiting for them while the others scuttled quickly to neighbouring houses. The front door closed, and Belle strode purposefully up to it and rang the bell.

She had made a real effort to look stylishly eye-catching. It was important that she conveyed the message that she was tough and ruthless. A covetable scarlet pill-box hat set off her dark curls, and she wore a coat that Jimmy had bought her soon after they were married, navy-blue, fitted to her waist, and double-breasted in the fashionable Cossack style with fur trim at the hem, neck and cuffs.

As Belle had hoped, Mrs Forbes-Alton opened the door

herself, imagining it was one of her friends returning because she'd left something behind. As she saw Belle standing there, her smile vanished.

Belle put one neatly booted foot in the door to prevent her closing it. 'Yes, it's me. I think it's time we had a talk,' she said.

'I have nothing to talk to you about,' the older woman boomed. 'Get away from my house.'

She was taller than Belle remembered and very stout. Her grey hair was elaborately arranged in sausage-like curls on the top of her head, which only served to draw attention to her many chins. She was wearing a purple tea dress with a ruffle of lace across her big chest, and the colour made her look bilious.

'I don't need you to talk, just to listen,' Belle said with a hint of menace. 'If you won't listen I'll go straight to your chum Mr Blessard and speak to him. You won't like that.'

'How dare you come round here threatening me?' she said, her small pale blue eyes wide with shock at Belle's audacity.

'I haven't threatened you at all,' Belle said airily. 'I only said it would be better for you if you listened to me. There's no threat in that. Now, are you going to invite me in, or must I shout on your doorstep?'

Belle had expected to be nervous; her biggest fear was that she wouldn't be brave enough or articulate enough to deliver her ultimatum properly. But now she was here, standing in front of this woman who had given Miranda so much unhappiness, Belle could see she was just a bully, and like most bullies, all she feared was someone stronger than herself.

The older woman's face showed what she was thinking. She didn't want a scene on the doorstep that someone might overhear, and hoped that Belle would be intimidated once she was in the Forbes-Altons' grand house.

'I am not in the habit of talking to anyone but tradesmen on my doorstep,' she said and opened the door wider, turned and strode off across the hall. Belle smiled to herself. The woman thought this would make her falter, but Belle closed the front door behind her and followed Mrs Forbes-Alton into the drawing room. Two card tables and chairs were set up there, the cards still lying on them. Belle guessed the maid had already left for the day or she would have been clearing this away.

She walked around the two tables towards the fire and without being asked sat down in a winged armchair closest to it. 'A lovely room,' she said, looking round with interest. It was in fact very Victorian in style, with too much heavy furniture, sombre pictures and countless ugly ornaments. 'Of course Miranda described it in detail to me, so I feel I've been here before.'

'You are a very impertinent young woman. Kindly remember your place,' Mrs Forbes-Alton barked indignantly. She stood behind a chair glowering at Belle.

'My place?' Belle sniggered. 'What a delightfully old-fashioned notion. Not one I hold with at all.'

'What do you want?' Mrs Forbes-Alton asked, looking nervous now. Belle guessed that was because she was alone in the house.

'I want you to tell your friends and cronies in the village that you were fooled by Blessard into believing I was a woman of easy virtue. You are going to make amends for the hurt you have caused my dear aunt, Mrs Franklin, by making sure that in future she is invited along to all the social functions she always used to attend.'

'But you have been a lady of the night, that is fact,' Mrs Forbes-Alton snapped at Belle.

'The truth of the matter is that I was a victim of an evil man who was hanged for his crimes,' Belle said. 'I was just fifteen when I was abducted and taken away to France. But I haven't come here today to discuss your inability to separate fact and pure fiction about my past, or to take you to task for having no compassion for someone who has been treated so badly.' She paused to let that sink in.

'My aunt, Mrs Franklin, is one of the kindest, best women who ever lived,' she went on. 'And you have wronged her grievously with your malicious gossip and tittle-tattle. As you doubtless know, my husband was wounded in action, and because of this we cannot move away to somewhere where people are kinder. So you, my dear Mrs Forbes-Alton, are going to make things better for us all.'

'Why should I do anything for you, a mere trollop?' the older woman snorted with disdain.

'Because if you don't I shall shame your family name as you have done mine,' Belle said. 'Believe me, I know things about you all that would not just make people in Blackheath sit up and take notice, but would also reach the national press.'

'What rubbish! There is nothing whatsoever about our family that is shameful.'

'No?' Belle raised one eyebrow and smirked. 'A woman who gave out white feathers makes sure her sons have desk jobs for the war? How hypocritical is that? When her daughter is killed in France she basks in the reflected glory that she was doing her bit for the war, yet the truth is Miranda wanted to go to France to get away from you.'

'My sons are doing vital war work, and who would believe that Miranda wanted to get away from me?'

'People would believe it if I was to let the newspapers publish your letters to her,' Belle said. 'And I have them, I brought them home from France. It is hard to believe any mother could write such cold, unfeeling letters.'

'People of my standing do not wear their hearts on their sleeves like the working classes,' Mrs Forbes-Alton retorted. 'If they were published I'd get nothing but sympathy for my loss. It would be you who would be vilified.'

'I agree your class are not emotional about their children, possibly because you put them in the hands of nursemaids at birth,' Belle said. 'But of course there is also the matter of the abortion Miranda had in the summer of 1914. How does abortion go down among people of your standing?'

The woman blanched and caught hold of the back of the chair to steady herself. 'What can you mean? I cannot believe you'd claim such a vile thing.'

'Do sit down before you fall down,' Belle said sweetly. She was beginning to enjoy herself now and she could almost hear her old friend applauding her.

'She didn't do that, she couldn't have,' the woman blustered, but she sank down into the chair.

'Oh yes she did. That's how I got to know Miranda. I took care of her when she collapsed outside my shop after having it.'

'That is malicious rubbish!'

'Not at all. Think back. I'm sure you must recall the afternoon in August of 1914 when she telephoned and left a message with your maid to say she was staying the night with her friend in Belgravia? She telephoned from my shop. I walked back here with her the following morning once the baby had come away. She had a bruise on her forehead and she told you she'd fallen down in the street.'

Belle watched the other woman's face and she could see that she did remember that day.

'How can you make up such a thing when Miranda is dead?' Mrs Forbes-Alton asked, but the power had gone out of her voice.

'You know I am not making it up. I even have proof in a letter from her thanking me for my help,' Belle said. 'Even you must have wondered how and why we became such close friends.'

Again she saw something flit across the woman's face. No doubt she was remembering times when she'd berated her daughter for choosing the company of a 'common shop girl' instead of someone of her own class.

'She had an affair with a man she met in Greenwich Park. He was a scoundrel and a married man too. Poor Miranda thought he loved her, but as soon as she told him about the baby she was carrying, he disappeared. She risked her life having an abortion because she knew you would disown her.

'Of course I have no wish to drag my dearest friend's name through the mud,' Belle went on. 'But if she had lived to know what you did to my aunt and me, she would have been utterly disgusted by you and would have urged me to use every last thing I know about her to shame you.'

Belle paused again for a moment to let her words speak for themselves.

'I grew to love Miranda,' she said eventually. 'And she loved me too. In truth I was the only person who cared about her at all until she met Will Fergus, the American sergeant she met in France whom she intended to marry. I'll bet you didn't even reply to his letter after her death, did you?'

The woman opened her mouth and then closed it.

'I thought not,' Belle said. 'And he was a good man. Miranda was the happiest she'd ever been in her whole life when she met him. But you couldn't understand why he and I were so distressed at her death, because you never cared

370

about her. What sort of a woman are you that you couldn't love your own child?'

'I did care for her,' Mrs Forbes-Alton said weakly.

'No, you didn't. She was right in thinking you'd throw her out on to the street if you'd known about the baby. You destroyed my aunt's happiness too, and yes, before you ask, she knows everything about Miranda, yet she has never breathed a word of it to anyone, not even after what you've done to her. But I am not so kind. I want some rough justice.'

'How much do you want?'

Belle threw back her head and laughed. 'You think I want money from you? I wouldn't take as much as an old coat of yours if I was freezing. I've already told you part of what I want, and that is to see Mrs Franklin reinstated in all the village events. I want you to greet her warmly in church, in front of all those small-minded acolytes who suck up to you.'

Belle could see the woman was going to agree to that.

'You said "part" of what you want,' she said cautiously.

'Yes. I want to see Mrs Franklin happy again, but the other part is that you speak to Mr Blessard's superiors on that rag of a newspaper he works for. You tell them he twisted your words when you were griefstricken about your daughter, and that what he printed about me was lies. And you make sure they dismiss Blessard.'

'How can I do that?'

Belle was delighted to see how scared she looked.

'If you and your husband can get your sons safe desk jobs in Whitehall for the duration of the war, this little thing shouldn't prove a problem. You must stress that I could have sued the papers for slander, as all I was doing in Paris was learning millinery. And you can point out that my husband is a war hero, and that I've spent the war caring for men at the Herbert and driving ambulances. As long as they print an apology and the scurrilous story is quashed for good and my sweet, kind aunt can hold her head up in the village again, that will do.'

'I don't know that I can do this.'

Belle shrugged. 'Well, if you don't, you know what's going to happen. I'll start talking, very loudly. I'm betting you won't want your other daughter's chances of marriage being scuppered by this — I heard she's become engaged to a viscount.'

Pure terror flitted across the older woman's face. 'Please don't do that, Mrs Reilly,' she begged. 'I'm sorry that I hurt you and your aunt. I was very upset at Miranda dying and that man put words into my mouth, but I'll try and put it right.'

'You must do more than try. I'll give you just two weeks. Keep firmly in your mind that I have nothing left to lose. The war has made my husband a cripple, I've lost my best friend and my good name. You on the other hand have everything to lose. If this matter isn't put right within two weeks, then I shall start my own little campaign against you and your family.'

With that Belle got up, smoothing down her coat, and walked proudly to the door. 'No need to see me out,' she said. 'I can find my way out of anywhere and anything.'

Chapter Twenty-Four

Mog came running into the kitchen one afternoon in April, her small face flushed with excitement. 'They asked me if I would run the cake stall at the summer fête,' she blurted out. 'I can't believe it! Mrs Parsons said that I was the best cake maker in the village and I was an inspiration to the younger women.'

Belle was doing the ironing, and although Mog's triumph was hardly important when just a few days earlier they'd heard the sobering news that the Germans had broken through the Allied lines in France, it was a victory for Mog. Belle stood the flat iron on its end, and went over to hug Mog. 'Quite right too,' she said. 'If anyone deserves something good to happen, it's you.'

Jimmy was sitting by the stove reading a newspaper and looked up with a smirk. 'I've been telling people for years you are the best cake maker in London.'

Mog glowed even more at that. 'But how will I get the ingredients with it all on ration?' she asked anxiously.

'They'll expect you to make Garth pull some strings to get them,' Jimmy said.

Garth did keep in with black marketeers, and the odd pound of ham, butter or cheese came his way, but Belle felt the way Jimmy had phrased his remark implied that Mog had only been shown favour today because of her husband's ability to get hold of anything.

Jimmy had never been cynical before he went to war, but he was now. His old warmth and sense of humour did surface again now and then, but sadly most of the time he was very dour.

'The ladies on the fête committee wouldn't know about such things,' Mog said. 'But maybe they'll have something in their store cupboards to help me out.'

Belle was tempted to pull Jimmy up on what he'd said, but decided it was better to let it pass as Mog hadn't appeared to see it as a slight. In the past couple of months he had improved in some areas. He talked more and he had taken over doing the accounts. He also had fewer nightmares.

Yet even though Belle felt sad she couldn't bring the old Jimmy back, at least she had succeeded in getting Mog accepted back into the community, because Mrs Forbes-Alton had done exactly what she had insisted upon. An apology had appeared in the *Chronicle* which said that the reporter Mr Blessard had wilfully exploited Mrs Forbes-Alton's grief following the tragic death of her daughter and had made claims about her friend Mrs Belle Reilly that were unfounded.

It went on to report that Jimmy had been seriously wounded in action, and that the newspaper was very sorry to have added to the family's distress at such a difficult time. The final statement was that Mr Blessard had been dismissed.

The article was on the inside of the paper, so well tucked away that not everyone would have spotted it. But regardless of how many people saw it, Mrs Forbes-Alton must have been frightened enough by Belle to make certain that the story got round the village, and she immediately included Mog in several fund-raising teas she had organized. One such tea was in her own house and Mog had come back from it incandescent with delight that she was no longer being snubbed.

Belle felt she had triumphed over the woman, but she had never told Mog anything other than that she'd spoken to

Mrs Forbes-Alton about Miranda. Then a few weeks after the piece in the *Chronicle*, PC Broadhead called in at the Railway to say that Blessard had been arrested for throwing a brick through the newspaper office window while drunk. Blessard claimed he'd been unable to find another job and had lost his home as he couldn't pay his rent. The police had shown no sympathy, instead telling him he should enlist immediately which would solve his problems.

There was no doubt that the army needed more men, even weasels like Blessard. They had raised the age limit for conscription to fifty-one, and Garth, who had only recently passed that milestone, joked that he'd never been so glad to admit his true age. The Americans had finally arrived in large numbers in France and gone into battle, and although they were inexperienced they had given Britain a surge of real hope that victory was possible.

Belle had received a letter from Vera saying that Etaples had been bombed, though fortunately the shells missed the hospital. But she said other hospitals nearer the front had been hit, power lines had gone down and operations had to be done by oil lamps. There were so many wounded coming in that in one four-day period 273 operations were carried out, the doctors and nurses starting work at eight in the morning and carrying on till one the following morning. With so many American doctors and nurses moving to the new American hospitals, the staff that remained were all overworked, sometimes with just one nurse on duty alone at night in a big ward.

At the end of March Germany's Big Bertha gun shelled Paris from seventy miles away. Vera said it made everyone fear the gun could be turned on them next, as if it wasn't already bad enough with enemy planes flying overhead nightly.

None of this alarming news was being reported in the newspapers, but they made much of the Red Baron, Germany's famous ace pilot who had finally been shot down. Perhaps the press felt it was important to raise morale with some good news, as everyone was so weary and despondent.

The government had put up posters urging everyone to 'Set their Teeth and See it Through', and that was all anyone could do. People were afraid of the Zeppelins and bombers and struggled with prices that kept on rising, with food shortages, rationing and long queues just for a loaf of bread or half a pound of sugar. In every town and city there were many men out on the streets with missing limbs, blinded or with other serious injuries. Hospitals, nursing and convalescent homes were full to capacity, yet still more wounded were brought back daily and the death toll rose remorselessly.

Shell shock was something people hadn't heard of until the battle of the Somme, and then it was generally thought to be an excuse for cowardice. Back then, thanks to the glorification of the war by the press, few people fully appreciated the horrors men at the front had to endure. But that view had begun to change as wounded men revealed the true nature of war. Many women had observed a husband, brother or son home on leave who shouted out involuntarily at sudden loud noises, had nightmares or was withdrawn, and now the public were becoming far more sympathetic.

Yet sympathy alone couldn't help the worst affected. Many would never be able to hold down a job again, some became violent, others turned to drink or even suicide. Still more would languish in mental asylums and would never recover.

Likewise, at the start of the war most people thought that all deserters were cowards and should be shot. But the tide had turned there too, for even though courage was still applauded and cowardice despised, the vast majority of people thought it wrong to execute someone who ran in a moment of pure terror.

Belle could see the war had changed so many things. On 6 February women over thirty had been finally granted the vote. This was something Mog was thrilled about, but which Garth viewed with anxiety. Some of the social niceties that Belle and Mog had to learn when they first came to Blackheath were virtually extinct. Class distinctions were less marked now as people were drawn together in grief at the loss of loved ones. Society women mixed with working-class girls for the war effort; officers often became indebted to the men they commanded.

Chaperones were a thing of the past; young couples seized the moment, never knowing if it would be the last. Women had risen to the challenges of wartime and had not only taken over traditional male jobs, but were excelling at them. No one was surprised any more to see female conductors on the trams and omnibuses and there were many female ambulance drivers in London. Factories, farms, shops and offices all over England had as many women on their staff as men, and women could even go into a public house now without eyebrows being raised.

Garth had finally set aside his long-held prejudice on this, though it was more to do with economics than a true change of heart. If he didn't let a soldier on leave bring his wife or sweetheart in, they'd go elsewhere. Mog helped him serve most nights, and Belle too at the weekends, but only because their help came free.

Yet the change Belle had really hoped for had not materialized in Jimmy. He might talk a little more and help Garth by doing the accounts, but he was making no attempt to help himself. He was fitted for an artificial leg, but he wouldn't persevere and practise walking with it. Dr Towle had tried to persuade him to see a psychiatrist friend of his to get him out of his dejected state of mind, but he refused. As for lovemaking, Belle had tried every sensual trick she'd ever learned to get him interested in it again, but he had set his mind against it, and often called her a whore for trying to please him. Even if she just cuddled up to him, he stiffened, and she couldn't remember when he'd last kissed her. Now she rarely even tried any more, it was just too hurtful to be rejected.

There were many nights when she lay awake sadly remembering the man who could barely wait to get her into the bedroom. Sometimes they had made love the whole night, only falling asleep at daybreak, and back then he'd worshipped every inch of her.

She never undressed in front of him now. On past occasions when she had, he'd claimed she had no shame. She had raged at him, but all that did was create an atmosphere which permeated the whole house. He wouldn't talk about it, he refused to get help, and Belle had finally accepted that this was the way it was going to be for ever.

Keeping busy was her way of getting through each day. She altered clothes for neighbours, she made a few hats for a dress shop in Lewisham, and she'd taken over cleaning the house and bar so Mog had more freedom. But there were times when she despaired. Seeing couples walking hand in hand, mothers laughing as they chased toddlers up on the heath, and families having picnics in Greenwich Park were reminders of what might have been if Jimmy hadn't been wounded.

She told herself that thousands of other women accepted the cards they'd been dealt, and that she was lucky she and Jimmy had a home with Garth and Mog. But even though she could accept all the limitations that came with a disabled man, she resented Jimmy wallowing in self-pity. And she was afraid that one day she would crumple under the weight of responsibility for him.

'Will you help me organize the cake stall?'

Mog's question brought Belle back to the present.

'Of course I will,' she replied. Whatever else was wrong in her life it was good to see Mog bubbly and happy again.

'I thought maybe you could paint a nice banner for above the stall,' Mog said. 'With cakes and things, really jolly and eye-catching.'

Garth came into the kitchen with a letter in his hand. 'That bloke in the hardware shop just brought this in,' he said, handing it to Jimmy. 'It was addressed wrong. Looks like it's from France.'

'Yes, I could do a banner,' Belle said, but her attention was on Jimmy rather than Mog. Despite saying he was going to write to some of his army friends, he hadn't done so. She just hoped this letter wouldn't be bad news and make him even grumpier.

'Who's it from then, Jimmy?' Mog asked.

'Bin,' Jimmy said as he pulled out the letter from the envelope. 'Well, his real name was Jack Cash, but we called him "Bin" because he was always saying he'd "bin there". He's the only one of the mates I made when I was at Etaples training that's survived.'

Jimmy carried on reading, while Belle and Mog discussed the cake stall.

'Bloody hell!'

Jimmy's exclamation made both Belle and Mog look at him. 'What is it?' Belle asked.

'He's only gone and found out about the Frog that rescued me,' Jimmy said. 'Seems he's a real hero, been awarded the top award, Croix de Guerre, that's like our VC.'

'I always thought he was a hero for saving you,' Belle laughed. 'But I didn't know the French gave medals out for that!'

Jimmy smirked wryly. 'He didn't do me any favours, did he? He should've shot me and put me out of my misery.'

'Don't say that!' Mog looked horrified.

'He would've been put on a charge for leaving his men and returning to his lines. But according to Bin, he dropped me off and went right back into the fray. Singlehandedly he took out a Boche machine-gun emplacement, then shooting like a madman he found his men and took them on to that day's objective. Bin reckons his actions saved dozens of Frogs, and they took over fifty prisoners.'

'How wonderfully brave,' Belle said. 'Sounds like he really deserved a medal.'

'But the strangest thing is that Bin claims it was a man we'd met before,' Jimmy said. 'We were sent down to Verdun back in 1916, to pick up a couple of our men suspected of desertion who'd been picked up by the Frogs. We stopped at this *estaminet* to get directions for the HQ and this bloke helped us and bought us a drink. He spoke perfect English, never got his name, but we talked for some time. Bin reckons that's why he rescued me, he recognized me by my red hair.'

'Fancy that!' Mog exclaimed. 'So there is some advantage to having red hair.'

Belle thought this story was amazing, but more importantly to her it was good to see Jimmy animated about something for a change.

'Bin said that too.' Jimmy managed a little chuckle. 'He said, "And we all thought red hair was a curse, now we all want it." He says the story has become one of the legends of Ypres. He said he was intending to find this Sergeant Carrera to thank him personally. But he's gone west now too.'

Belle almost gasped aloud at the name but she checked herself just in time. 'He got killed too?' she asked.

'That's what he says. So I didn't imagine he'd called me by my name. He did know me.'

Jimmy had told Belle back in the hospital in France that he thought the man who rescued him had called him by his name. But because of the pain he had been in at the time, he didn't know if he'd imagined it.

Belle had to turn away from Jimmy so he wouldn't see the horror and guilt which she was sure must be etched on her face.

Surely it couldn't be Etienne? It was far more likely to be just another Frenchman with the same surname. Yet somehow she knew it was him. And now he was dead.

She took up the iron again, putting it back on the stove to heat up, and busied herself by folding a pillowcase neatly. But Mog was caught up in the story and wanted to know more.

'So you'd met this man before? What was he like?'

'I can't remember that much now. He was older than me, tough looking, he said he'd learned English in London years before the war. That day we mostly talked about the fighting and stuff. I liked him, well, we all did. But another little mystery has been solved now. You see, I was told he gave my name when he took me in. I thought that was because he'd just looked on my tag. But maybe it wasn't, because that day at Verdun, Bin and the other lads were calling me Little Red Reilly, and he asked me if I'd just got the nickname since coming to France and what my real name was.'

Belle's legs were turning to jelly and she felt queasy. When she tried to pick the flat iron up again she was shaking so much she almost dropped it.

'Isn't that a wonderful story?' Mog said. 'What's up, Belle? You've gone very pale.'

'I could do with some fresh air,' she said hastily. 'It's very stuffy in here.'

'I'll carry on with that ironing,' Mog said. 'Go on up and have a lie down. You never seem to sit down for five minutes these days.'

Belle did retreat to the bedroom, and fell on to her bed sobbing. In the forefront of her mind was a picture of Etienne kissing her goodbye that last time outside the hospital and telling her that it would all work out and one day they'd be together.

She had lost all hope of that when she heard Jimmy was wounded, and although a day hadn't passed since then that she didn't think about Etienne, she had prided herself on doing the right thing.

But it wasn't right that he was dead. Not killed out on that battlefield, buried in a mass grave. Her strong, brave Etienne who meant more to her than she could ever adequately explain, even to herself.

But why didn't he tell her he'd met Jimmy back in 1916?

Was it because if he'd admitted it that evening he came to the hospital, it might have stopped her from going off for the night with him? It almost certainly would have done as it would have made an image of Jimmy spring into her mind.

Yet for whatever reason he chose to keep quiet about that meeting, it was so honourable of him to rescue his rival. Was he tempted fleetingly to let him die? If he was, it made his actions even more admirable.

Her insides began to churn alarmingly. She couldn't remember if she'd ever told Jimmy that the surname of her rescuer in Paris was Carrera. But Noah definitely knew it and if he was to call here and Jimmy told him about this, he would recognize it immediately and wonder why she hadn't spoken up; after all, that was the natural reaction for anyone, unless they were hiding something.

She turned her face into the pillow as images of Etienne kept jumping into her mind. It had been hard enough to try to erase thoughts of him all these long months, and now she knew Jimmy, Mog and Garth would be talking about this for weeks to come. How should she react? Should she go downstairs now and say she'd just remembered that Etienne's surname was Carrera?

But she knew she couldn't do it. Not yet. Just saying his name out loud would surely bring tears to her eyes. She had to hold it inside her.

That evening Jimmy seemed much brighter after getting the letter from his old friend. He even suggested lighting the fire up in the living room, when normally he stayed in the kitchen until about eight then went to bed.

'We could have a game of chess or do a jigsaw together,' he suggested.

Belle thought it somewhat ironic that she'd tried to get him to do just that on so many nights without success, yet on the one night she really wanted to be alone, he had a change of heart. But she went upstairs and lit the fire anyway; it was after all a step forward.

'It was good to hear from Bin and all the news of everyone,' he said once they were both up there. The bar downstairs was quiet, and with the curtains drawn and the fire blazing the living room was a warm and comfortable retreat. 'I'm going to write back. Though I haven't got much to tell the lads.'

'They'll just be happy to hear you're well,' Belle said. 'You can tell them things you've read in the papers. Or remind them of funny things you shared.'

He sat back in his chair by the fire looking thoughtful. 'I hated it out there,' he said at length. 'In a quiet five minutes I used to close my eyes and imagine being here, just like this.'

'But now you are here you wish you were back there?' she asked.

He managed a smile. 'Not quite. I just wish I was whole again. Working behind the bar, going for walks with you, not feeling so hopeless. But I do miss my mates out there.'

In the past she would have moved over to him and given him a hug if he was sad. But she had found to her cost that any demonstration of affection made him prickly.

'Tell me about some of them,' she suggested.

'There was one we used to call "Gannet" because he would finish up any food you didn't eat. He was a laugh, always scavenging around; somehow he always managed to get drink, some eggs, a chicken or a rabbit. He worked a stall in a market with his dad in the East End before the war, I suppose he learned the art there. Only eighteen but a great lad.'

Belle smiled. It was good to hear him talking the way he used to before he was wounded.

'Then there was "Father"; we called him that not because he was old, but because you found yourself confessing things to him. I said once that he ought to become a priest, but he said he liked women too much.'

'What sort of things did you have to confess?'

Jimmy shrugged. 'Being scared before going over the top; that I often wonder about my father.'

'Do you?' Belle exclaimed in surprise. 'You've never, ever mentioned thinking about him to me.'

'I never used to, not till I got out there. I suppose it was to do with meeting so many different kinds of men who often talked about their fathers. I always believed that he was rotten to the core because he walked out on Ma, but maybe there's another side to that story.'

'Have you asked Garth about him?'

'No. He'd take Ma's side, and there isn't anyone else to ask.'

'I often wonder about my father too. But as Annie doesn't even keep in touch with me, she's hardly likely to want to talk about him. I wish Mog knew.'

Jimmy smiled at her. 'He'd be a good, kind man, and creative too. You don't get any of that from your mother.'

Belle's eyes prickled at the compliment, but she didn't think she deserved such praise. All at once she felt she had to partially unburden herself about his rescuer.

'The man who saved you, you said his name was Carrera. Well, that was Etienne's name,' she said.

'What! The man who took you to America?'

'I'd rather remember him as the man who helped Noah find me in Paris,' she said.

Jimmy was silent for a moment but he was looking at her intently.

'That day in Verdun, he asked if I was just called Red in the army, that was after he'd heard me called Little Red Reilly. Looking back, that's an odd thing to ask; no one usually cares what your real name is. He even asked what I worked at before the war. I told him I was Jimmy back home, and about the pub; I told him about you losing the baby and mentioned your name. So if it was the same man, why didn't he tell me who he was?'

'Maybe he didn't make the connection till later,' Belle suggested. 'But if he had, perhaps he thought it best not to bring up the past because you were with other men. I told him quite a lot about you while we were on the way to America, and of course two years later he knew from Noah that you'd searched everywhere for me.'

'So he saved me for you?'

'I doubt he looked on it like that. It's more likely he just remembered you from the day at Verdun and couldn't bear to leave you there helpless.'

Jimmy made a sort of agitated whistling noise. Belle didn't know what to say now; when she looked at him she could almost hear his brain ticking over, assimilating all the strands of the situation.

'He felt he owed me my life? Why? I'd done nothing for him. He risked being put on a charge for stopping for me. I doubt if his CO would consider rescuing a Tommy any kind of priority when there were dozens of French wounded all around there. So you have to be the reason for it. He loved you!'

Belle's stomach turned over. She wished now she hadn't said anything. Jimmy was a thinker; he'd dwell on this, turn it this way and that, and he'd want answers to anything he couldn't work out.

'You know very well that he always felt very bad about taking me to New Orleans,' she said. 'That is exactly why he came to Paris to help find me. I'd say that was proof he cared about me, but there was nothing else between us. I've never been so glad to see anyone as when he broke the door down where I was being held. But after, I couldn't wait to get back to England to see you and Mog.'

'Funny that you said so little about him on your return,' he said, his voice tinged with suspicion. 'I mean, a man saves your life yet you don't want to keep in touch with him?'

'Of course I would've liked to, but I thought it would be hurtful to you. Oh Jimmy, don't make this into something it's not. I'd been through several kinds of hell back then, I was home, safe again, I wanted to forget it all and start again.'

He reached for his crutch and heaved himself out of the chair. 'I think I'll go to bed now,' he said.

'That's right, stir up something then back off to brood,' she thought, but couldn't bring herself to say aloud. That was what he always did, and she felt she couldn't stand much more of it as it was like walking on eggshells.

'I wish I could have my old Jimmy back,' she said sadly. 'You can't imagine how much I miss him.'

He leaned on his crutch looking down at her, his mouth curled into a sneer. 'How can you expect me to be the same when half of my body is missing? You aren't the same Belle I married either. What excuse do you have for that?'

He turned then and hopped away across the room. Belle could only watch him go, her heart even heavier.

Chapter Twenty-Five

Belle hesitated at the open door of Dr Towle's consulting room. He was sitting at his desk writing up some notes and for a second she felt she couldn't go through with it.

But he looked up and smiled. 'Come in, Mrs Reilly, I don't bite,' he said.

The doctor had something of a reputation in the village as a ladies' man. As Belle knew him for his kindness when she had lost her baby and the sympathy he had shown Jimmy when he first arrived home, she thought this reputation was unwarranted. But he was undeniably easy on the eye. Tall, well built, with a ready smile, good teeth and a twinkle in his dark eyes. His dark hair was tinged with grey, the only clear indication he was over forty, and she thought it was very sad that stupid people misconstrued his understanding of women's problems.

She sat down at his desk very aware that once she'd voiced her problem with Jimmy she could never retract her words.

'You look tired and pale,' he said, his deep brown voice soothing and sympathetic. 'Are you unwell? Or is this visit about your husband?'

'Yes, it's about Mr Reilly,' she said, hanging her head. 'I'm at my wits' end, doctor. He's so sullen, so . . .' She stopped, overcome by tears she couldn't hold back. 'I'm sorry,' she managed to say as she fished in her pocket for a handkerchief.

It was near the end of July and the weather had been so hot for the last two weeks that it had been impossible to sleep well at night and it was hard to raise the energy to do even the simplest of tasks during the day. But she could have coped with the heat, food going off before it was even cooked, the dust that seemed to coat everything, if only Jimmy would rise out of his black moods.

Time and again he had asked her questions about Etienne, usually to blame the man for rescuing him, but sometimes with suspicion that there had been something between them in Paris. At least she wasn't guilty on that count, but he also fired questions about her time at the hospital, what the male drivers and stretcher bearers were like. He was like a dog with a bone, going to it again and again, to the point when she felt like screaming. There had been moments when she was sorely tempted to walk out of the door and never come back. It was only the thought of what that would do to Mog that stopped her.

The doctor leaned forward, putting his forearms on his desk. 'I have observed that this appears to be one of the many troubling side effects for wounded men once they come home. Even if they hated every moment of it over there, there was purpose to each day, and now they have none. You and many other wives learned to cope alone while your husbands were away. However much you missed them and wanted them back, it must be very hard to adjust to their return when they are no longer the strong, capable man you said goodbye to.'

Belle nodded and dabbed at her eyes.

'I've had many a devoted wife in here confiding how much attention her husband demands, how critical of her he is, and some say they no longer show them any appreciation. Is this what you are finding?'

Belle took a deep breath. If other women could confide in him, so could she. 'Yes. He's a different man now. Everyone

389

liked Jimmy before this, he cared about people, he was generous with his time and affection. Just a lovely man. But that's all gone now. He is so bitter, so difficult.'

'It will get better, Mrs Reilly,' he said.

'Will it?' she asked bleakly. 'He's barely been out the door since he got home. He won't persevere with his artificial leg. He doesn't talk to me. He looks at me sometimes as if he hates me. He's wearing me down to the point I want to run away from him.'

'And how is he with Mr and Mrs Franklin?'

'Not as nasty as he is to me, but there are times when they despair too. I won't run away of course, I couldn't possibly be that unfair to Mr and Mrs Franklin. But it is affecting us all, and I don't know which way to turn.'

'In what way is he nasty to you? Has he hit you?'

'Oh no, he wouldn't do that,' Belle said quickly, even though he had moved to do it on several occasions, and she'd jumped nimbly away. 'But he brings up things about my past, he's suspicious of me. There is no joy in him any more, not about anything.'

Dr Towle raised one dark eyebrow questioningly.

'That doesn't happen,' she said, guessing that was what he wanted to know about, but wouldn't have risked embarrassing her by asking. 'He rejects any kind of affection from me.'

'Could that be because he is afraid of you having a baby? I did tell him after you had the miscarriage that it wouldn't be advisable.'

'You did?' Belle exclaimed. 'He never told me.'

She was stunned by this news and she began to cry again. 'Do you mean I can never have a baby?'

'I am so sorry, Mrs Reilly, I assumed your husband told you this once you recovered. I didn't say you couldn't have another child, only that I felt there was a risk of miscarrying again.'

Belle sniffed back her tears. 'Well, it's not likely to happen anyway the way things are,' she said.

One of her greatest hopes for the future had been a baby. She'd thought that would be the one thing which would buck Jimmy up. She had thought too it would blot out all memory of Etienne, and a baby would bring joy into Mog and Garth's life too. Now that had been denied her as well.

'It could be that he's not just frightened for you, but also fears that he could not support a child,' the doctor said gently. 'Men are very sensitive about such things.'

'If he persevered with the leg he could run the bar,' Belle said. 'But he seems to enjoy wallowing in misery. I want to shout at him and point out that other wounded soldiers are forced to beg on the streets to put food on the table. But he doesn't appear to be aware how fortunate he is to have a roof over his head and people who love him.'

The doctor nodded in sympathy. 'It is only recently that doctors and psychiatrists have begun to recognize the effects this war is having on soldiers' mental health,' he said. 'There wasn't the constant bombardment of heavy guns in previous wars, nor such prolonged fighting. Most men died of injuries like Mr Reilly's. All of us in the medical profession are aware now that in this war it isn't only the physical injuries we need to treat, but the mental ones too. Sadly at present there is no medicine to help; all we can recommend is rest, peace and quiet, and hope that talking to our patients will eventually dispel the hideous images in their heads.'

'But what if they won't talk? Or try anything?' Belle asked, tears streaming down her face. 'Jimmy won't even think of allowing me or his uncle to take him out in the wheelchair we bought for him. A walk on the heath or in Greenwich Park might help him, but he refuses. It can't be doing him any good sitting in a dark kitchen day after day, never seeing a bird, flower or tree.'

'I agree totally,' the doctor said. 'He needs sunshine, nature and conversation with others to help bring him out of this. I will come and see him and try and make him see that.'

'He'll probably refuse to see you,' Belle said glumly. 'When I suggested that he talked to you, he said all he wanted from a doctor was for him to put him down.'

Dr Towle nodded. 'That has been said by many injured men, but I don't believe that is really what is in their hearts. I will drop by tomorrow morning while I'm out on my rounds. Don't tell him I'm coming or he might find an excuse not to see me. Did you say you were coming to see me today?'

'No, I didn't. It would just have started another row.'

'Then I won't mention that you called either. The only advice I can give you, Mrs Reilly, is to stand up to your husband. If he is sulking, let him and walk away. Don't try to appease him all the time, that doesn't work, and it will just make you more angry with him. And try and get some rest. You look exhausted.'

After Belle had gone, Dr Towle sat for a moment looking at the brief notes he'd made while talking to her. She had always intrigued him, ever since she and her aunt had lived a few doors down from his surgery when they first arrived in Blackheath. Her looks were enough to get her noticed, but it was more than just that; she had none of the simpering girlishness he was accustomed to, she looked people in the eye, and had a bold manner he found very attractive.

All the time she had her hat shop in Tranquil Vale she was a regular topic of conversation with both sexes. She was

392

admired for her talent, flair and looks, but there was something more that no one could really put their finger on. Some said she was worldly, and used words like 'confident', 'poised' and even 'racy' to describe her, but even his own wife, who was renowned for her incisive summing up of people, could only suggest she thought Belle had 'a past'.

Belle was much admired for her voluntary work at the Royal Herbert. Word got around that she was conscientious and capable, yet when she went off to France many people thought driving an ambulance was inappropriate work for a young married woman. The poisonous Mrs Forbes-Alton fanned the flames by claiming she was leading her daughter Miranda astray, and the gossip mounted. Later, shortly after Miranda's tragic death, there was that scurrilous article about Belle in the newspaper, which people passed around gleefully.

He remembered the trial and subsequent hanging of the man Kent. At the time he'd felt great sympathy for all his innocent victims, and was shocked to discover that Belle Reilly was one of them. Yet as he had pointed out to his wife, who sadly was almost as bad as Mrs Forbes-Alton in condemning Belle, it took great courage to survive and make sure the man was brought to trial.

So what could he say to her husband to make him buck up? Would it be fair to drop a hint he might lose his lovely wife unless he did so?

Belle missed the doctor calling on Jimmy as she had gone out in the afternoon to try to buy some meat and queued for over an hour, only to find by the time she got to the counter that the butcher had nothing left to sell. She managed to get some eggs and cheese though and was planning to make a savoury tart for their supper.

She was very hot and weary, and when she got back into the kitchen to find Jimmy still sitting there just as he had been when she'd left, it was on the tip of her tongue to say something sharp. But to her surprise he looked up and smiled at her.

'You look all in,' he said. 'Did you have to queue a long time?'

It was the first time he'd even acknowledged there was such a thing as a queue to get rations, much less shown any sympathy.

'Over an hour, to get nothing at the butcher's,' she sighed. 'I hope Garth manages to wangle a rabbit or something from someone tonight.'

She went to the sink and filled a glass with water, gulping it down in one. 'Where's Mog?' she asked.

'She went off to the sewing circle and Garth's taking a nap. Dr Towle called round earlier.'

'Really?' Belle said. 'So who let him in?'

'I did. I can open the door,' Jimmy replied, but there wasn't the usual sarcasm in his reply. 'He gave me a lecture on apathy.'

Belle sat down at the table, arranging her face with a suitably surprised expression.

'He said I must get outside more, and I should practise walking with the peg leg every day, gradually keeping it on for longer.'

'And what did you say to that?'

'That I would.'

Belle really was surprised now. 'That would please us all,' she said. She wanted to add that she'd said the same thing over and over to him for weeks now but he'd ignored her.

'I suppose I have been apathetic,' he admitted. 'The doc

pointed out that the muscles in my remaining leg and arm will grow weak if I don't use them. And being out in sunshine will make me feel better.'

'So what about a spot of practice now?' Belle suggested. 'You could do it in the bar while it's closed. There's not so many obstacles in there to get round.'

'Not now. I'll start tomorrow when Garth's around to help me.'

Belle thought that sounded like a delaying tactic.

'I will do it, Belle. I promise,' he said. 'You aren't strong enough to support me. And I'll be better with Garth.'

To Belle's surprise Jimmy didn't renege on his promise. Every morning, once Garth had finished the work in the cellar, Jimmy went into the bar with him and practised. The counter was just the right height to hold on to with his remaining arm, and when he reached the end unaided, Garth helped him to turn, then supported him on the way back.

Each day they did a little more, gradually increasing the time until he was walking for an hour. At first he got sore patches on the stump of his missing leg where it rubbed on the socket of the artificial one, but Belle or Garth massaged the stump each night with surgical spirit to harden it.

Belle was so delighted to see the effort Jimmy was making that she overlooked his tetchy moments, and in the afternoons she helped him out into the back yard to sit in the sunshine for a while. At long last he was brighter in himself, and one Sunday afternoon he even agreed that he would go out in the wheelchair as long as Garth felt up to pushing him.

Belle and Mog were thrilled that they could all go out together. They both dressed up and put on their prettiest hats, and Garth wore a striped blazer and a straw boater.

Even Jimmy entered into the spirit of the occasion, allowing Belle to help him into the green linen jacket he used to wear behind the bar.

It was hard work pushing the chair up the hill on to the heath, but once there the going was easy. As always on a Sunday afternoon, there were crowds of people out enjoying the sunshine. But there were few men between eighteen and fifty; those they saw were all in uniform and home on leave, walking with their wives or sweethearts. The groups of children having picnics or playing ball games were being watched over by mothers and grandparents.

Jimmy seemed more at ease when he saw other men with arms in slings or on crutches. There were even a couple of men in wheelchairs too, but he was visibly saddened by the number of women wearing black, or a mourning band on their arm.

He reached out for Belle's hand at one point, a silent gesture that said he was at last thinking of the plight of others rather than just his own disability.

When they got to the boating pond, Garth and Mog left Jimmy and Belle while they went off to get ice creams for them all.

Belle sat on a bench next to Jimmy, watching the children sail their boats. 'Do you remember that day we came over here from Seven Dials? You said your mother had brought you here when you were about seven?'

He looked round at Belle and smiled. 'Yes, I remember, that was one of the best days ever. I never thought that six years later I'd be sitting here in a wheelchair though.'

'At least you are sitting here,' she said reprovingly. 'You could be in one of those mass graves in France. And I'd be just another one of those hundreds of war widows with nothing left but my memories. We can't alter what's already happened, but we can still choose our future.'

He held her eyes with his for a few long seconds. 'Maybe if I can master the peg leg, we could still get the guest house by the seaside,' he said.

'That's the spirit,' she said, reaching out to caress his cheek. 'We've got through the worst of it now, it can only get better.'

Vera's disturbing letter about men dying of Spanish flu over in France arrived the day after Mog had read out a report in the paper that there were cases of it in London and in various other cities around the world.

Belle had been inclined to think that the newspapers were exaggerating this so-called 'epidemic' because they had run out of steam in reporting on the war. But she knew Vera wasn't an alarmist.

'*They are dying overnight,*' Vera wrote.

It's absolutely terrible. I took in six sitting cases one day, all with injuries that could be patched up in no time. Two days later three of them had high fevers, one died on the first night, the other two the next day. They are putting suspected cases into an isolation ward, but it comes on so fast, one minute they look fine, the next they are sweating buckets and losing all control of everything. The strangest thing is that it's it's taking the fit and young, old folk and children don't seem to get it.

Vera's letter had come in early August, and within a week Mog reported two deaths from Spanish flu in the village, both women in their mid-twenties. Garth noticed that the bar was becoming less busy, he thought because people felt it best to stay out of crowded places. In the queues at the shops everyone seemed to know someone who had this terrible flu, or had already died from it.

Soon it was obvious that the press weren't scaremongering or using the epidemic as a diversion from reporting on the war. The flu was here, cutting down people who had been healthy and strong. Belle saw two hearses pass the door of the Railway in just the time it took her to clean the brass on the doors one morning. Fear was in the air; she saw it in women's faces as they hurried to the shops, and Mog's sewing circle stopped meeting, whist drives were cancelled and people walked rather than catch the omnibus.

Then Garth became ill. Mog had never known him even to have a cold before, but he complained of a sore throat at midday, and by four in the afternoon he was shivering so violently he had to take to his bed.

Dr Towle came that evening and told Mog she was to wear a gauze mask over her mouth and nose while taking care of him. All he could prescribe was plenty of fluids, and to sponge Garth down if he grew feverish.

'Stay away,' he said firmly to Belle and Jimmy who were hovering by the bedroom door. 'Leave Mrs Franklin to nurse her husband. And keep the bar closed for the time being.'

Belle heard Mog come out of her bedroom during the night and slipped out of bed to catch up with her as she was going downstairs, her arms full of bedlinen.

'How is he?' Belle asked. 'Can I do anything?'

'He's really poorly,' Mog said, her lower lip quivering. 'He's lost control of . . .' She stopped short in embarrassment and Belle realized the sheets were soiled. 'He's delirious. I'll just take these down to put into soak.'

'I'll do that,' Belle said, taking the bundle. 'I'll make you some tea too. Would you like a sandwich or something?'

Mog shook her head. 'I couldn't eat, I'm too scared. I know he's a strong man, but this is really serious.'

'Things always look worse at night,' Belle said to reassure

her. 'You go back in with him and I'll see to these. I'll tap on the door with your tea in a minute.'

'Could you get me some more sheets and another towel?' Mog said. 'I've changed the bed, but it's bound to happen again. I could do with some more hot water too.'

The next morning when Mog came out of the bedroom again, her face was grey with exhaustion. 'He's even worse,' she said. 'I've sponged him all over, tried to make him drink, but I can't bring his temperature down. He doesn't even know me.'

Belle washed the soiled sheets and towels and hung them out to dry. She made some beef broth and tried to persuade Mog to let her sit with Garth so she could get some sleep.

'He's my husband and I have to look after him,' Mog said. 'I'm worried enough that you might catch it just from being in the same house. So don't come close to me. And don't you dare go in that room.'

Belle and Jimmy felt they had to obey her wishes. Jimmy sat in the yard outside while Belle busied herself with chores. Later she managed to get Mog to eat some scrambled egg and toast, but she scuttled back upstairs immediately afterwards, and as she opened the bedroom door, from downstairs Belle heard Garth call out something unintelligible.

'I'm going to go and get the doctor again,' she said to Jimmy. 'I'll be as quick as I can.'

A stout, middle-aged woman answered the door at the surgery. She was wearing a navy-blue dress and looked like a housekeeper. 'The doctor is out on his rounds,' she said curtly, when Belle asked that he called to see her husband. 'As you can imagine, he's rushed off his feet with this epidemic. He's been telling those he can't get round to see to cool the patients down and make them drink; there is nothing more he can do.'

'But I'm afraid Mr Franklin will die,' Belle implored her.

'I'll tell him you called,' the woman said. 'That is all I can do.'

The doctor didn't call. By midnight Belle knew he wasn't coming and she was getting more and more frightened. Mog was exhausted, she'd washed and changed Garth dozens of times, tried to make him drink, and she wouldn't allow Belle to take over so that she could get a couple of hours' sleep.

'I'm not having you falling ill too,' she said through the closed door. 'I can doze in the chair here, you and Jimmy go to bed.'

They did go to bed, but although Jimmy fell asleep, Belle couldn't as her ears were pricked for a call from Mog.

She must have finally dozed off as she woke with a start at a sound from the landing. It was light now, so she guessed it was around five in the morning. She jumped out of bed and rushed out of the room. Mog was standing by her bedroom door, tears pouring down her face.

'Has he . . .?' Belle asked.

Mog held her hand out as a signal to come no closer. 'No, but he's going to. His face has turned black. He's barely breathing now.'

Through the open door Belle could see Garth. He seemed to have shrunk, and his normally ruddy face was tinged with black, his red hair slicked down with sweat, and there was a vile smell wafting from him.

'Does he know you now?' Belle asked in a whisper.

'No, not now, he did a while ago, and I thought that meant he'd turned a corner,' Mog sobbed. 'He asked me what was for supper, and said I made the best meat pies in London.

I told him I'd make the biggest pie he'd ever eaten if he'd just get well. Then he drifted off again.'

'Oh, Mog.' Belle wished she could hold her and comfort her, but each time she moved nearer Mog held out her hand to stop her. 'Shall I run for the doctor again?'

Mog shook her head. 'Only God can save him now, and I don't think he's inclined to. The only man I ever loved and he's taking him from me.'

She turned then and went back into the bedroom, shutting the door and leaving Belle shaken to the core at her words.

Garth died just after seven that morning. Belle had been sitting on the stairs in case Mog called her, and she heard a prolonged wheezing sound which then stopped abruptly. Seconds after she heard Mog cry out. The sound of heartbreak.

Jimmy was in the bedroom and he called out for Belle.

'I think he just died,' Belle said, going over to him where he was sitting on the bed.

Jimmy's eyes filled with tears and Belle put her arms around him and rocked him to her breast. 'I'm so sorry,' she said.

As she held him while he sobbed against her, she wondered what else could be taken from them: Jimmy crippled and now Garth gone. She didn't care if they couldn't run the pub, she didn't care if the Germans won the war, or if no one in the village ever spoke to her again. But the prospect of Mog having to go on without Garth was just the saddest, cruellest thing of all.

Chapter Twenty-Six

'You don't look too good, son,' Mog said to Jimmy after they'd finally closed the pub doors on the last of the guests at Garth's wake. It was half past eight in the evening, and although Mog was touched that so many people had come to the funeral, she'd been afraid they would never leave.

'Always so thoughtful of others,' he said, reaching out for her hand from his seat in the wheelchair. 'You've lost your husband, taken care of everyone here this afternoon, and now you're worrying about me.'

'I guess I was born for worry.' She smiled weakly, and leaned down to kiss his head as he hugged her awkwardly from his chair. 'I really don't know how we're going to manage without Garth.'

'We'll find a way,' Belle said, looking round at them as she stacked the plates and glasses on to a tray. But as she looked at Jimmy, she saw Mog was right in saying he didn't look too good. She moved closer to him, turning the wheelchair so she could see his face more clearly. 'You're sweating, you've gone very pale. Are you feeling all right?'

'It's nothing, just the funeral making me realize how much I've always depended on Garth, and how much he meant to me,' he said. 'You two don't look your best either. You've been run off your feet all day, and I'm only sweating because it's hot in here.'

Belle and Mog exchanged glances. It wasn't hot in the bar, in fact it was decidedly chilly as they'd opened the windows to let out the cigarette smoke.

'I think you need to go to bed, Jimmy,' Belle said gently. 'You've had a very long and distressing day. I'll make you a hot toddy.'

'I'll go to bed as long as Mog does too,' he said. 'She's barely slept at all since Garth got sick.'

'I can't go to bed, there's too much to do,' Mog replied indignantly.

'I can do that,' Belle said firmly. 'Jimmy's right, you haven't slept properly. So go on up, both of you. I'll make you both hot toddies and bring them up in a minute.'

She wheeled Jimmy out of the bar to the staircase, then helped him to get out so he could shuffle up the stairs on his bottom. Mog took his crutches and carried them up behind him. As Belle watched them she noticed how slowly Jimmy was moving. He normally went up the stairs almost as fast as she could walk.

A pang of fear shot through her. They had taken all the precautions the doctor advised: Jimmy hadn't been anywhere near Garth, she and Mog had boiled all Garth's bed linen, any cups, glasses or anything else he might have touched had been washed in boiling water. But people had been talking about the epidemic all afternoon, and some knew families where only one person had got it, while in others they had all gone down with it. No one seemed to know how it spread, and no one knew how to cure it. In some parts of London dozens of people had died from it, in others they were very ill but recovered.

But the epidemic wasn't just here in England and Europe, it was all over the world according to the newspapers. The only thing everyone seemed to agree on was that young children and old people weren't dying from it. It mostly only killed those between eighteen and fifty-five.

Belle took the hot toddies up a little later. Mog was already in bed, looking very small and vulnerable with her hair unpinned.

'I thought I'd have Garth beside me until I was a very old lady,' she said, and her eyes filled with tears. 'I really can't imagine how I'm going to get on without him.'

'I don't know what to say,' Belle admitted. 'He was so strong, so full of life, never a day's illness till this. But you'll always have me, Mog. You aren't going to be on your own.'

'You are a comfort,' Mog said and tried to smile. 'But you go and see to Jimmy. He's really cut up about losing his uncle, as if he didn't have enough troubles already.'

Belle found Jimmy sitting on the side of the bed, his starched wing collar half undone and sticking up by his ear. The only thing he'd taken off was his jacket. She put the hot toddy down on the bedside table, turned on the light and drew the curtains.

'I don't feel right,' he said and held out his hand to her.

Belle took it and rubbed it between her two hands. His eyes looked heavy and he had beads of perspiration on his forehead. 'You are just tired,' she said, trying to make herself believe that. 'Let me help you get undressed and into bed.'

He never normally let her help him. Right from when he first got back from the convalescent home he had always gone to great lengths to dress and undress in private because he didn't want her to look at what was left of his arm and leg. He had relented in letting her put surgical spirit on his leg stump, but she had never once seen him naked. When he first came home he got Garth to help him in and out of the bath until he could manage it on his own.

But now he let her unbutton his shirt, take his braces down and unfasten his trousers. He lifted himself up enough for her to pull his trousers off, then his long underpants.

If he'd ever allowed her to help him like this from the

beginning, she would have remarked on how neat the stumps of his leg and arm were. They certainly weren't gruesome, not something she'd have been afraid to touch, and nor were the scars on his belly and buttocks. But this wasn't the time to say anything; she sensed he was barely aware that he was naked from the waist down, and that in it self was evidence that he was ill.

She got his pyjamas on and made him drink the hot toddy, then tucked him into bed. 'Go to sleep now,' she said, stroking his forehead as if he were a small child. 'I'll be downstairs clearing up, but if you need me just call out.'

Leaving the door open and the landing light on, she went downstairs.

Everywhere was too quiet. Normally at this time of the evening the bar would be busy and noisy. The rumbling sound of voices, bellows of laughter, stools scraping on the wooden floor and the clink of glasses would waft into all the rooms, upstairs and down. Until Garth became ill his presence was a large one; his booming voice, heavy step and just the size of him seemed to fill the whole place. Mog had always said she knew the moment she came in through the street door whether he was in or out.

Belle went into the bar to close the windows and stood looking around for a moment. When Garth was behind the bar, he dominated it. The mirrors behind the bar doubled the effect, the width of his shoulders, his thick red hair. Jimmy had often described how he'd seen his uncle lean over the bar and grab a troublemaker round the throat with just one hand. There weren't many men brave enough to take him on; they almost always backed away in fear.

Yet that fierce reputation was just a facade. Garth was gentle and tender with those he cared for, and Belle had heard some of the men at the wake today saying how he'd

405

been known to shove a ten-shilling note in the pocket of someone who'd lost their job, or who had a sick child or some other problem. He would often give away pies or sandwiches to someone he suspected was hungry.

Belle remembered when she was a child, people in Seven Dials considered him to be a brute, but he took Jimmy in when his mother died, and he hadn't hesitated to offer Mog and Belle's mother a home when theirs burned down.

It was Mog's love that mellowed him and brought out all his good points, and his love for her had made her become more assertive instead of the little mouse she used to be. She had always wanted a home of her own, she loved to cook, clean and take care of people, and she had a flair for home-making which showed everywhere in soft colours, warmth and comfort.

Her influence was even present here in the bar, although Garth had been fierce in keeping it as his domain. The polished brass, scrubbed floor, gleaming counter and shining glasses were her doing. There was always a roaring fire in winter, and the settle beside it was bright with cushions she'd made. Although there was nothing beneath the glass dome at the back of the bar now, any other day it would be filled with home-made pies.

It was too soon even to think of when they could re-open the bar, but Belle's instinct told her that although she and Mog could probably manage to run it adequately between them, without Garth's huge presence behind the bar keeping the customers under control, it would soon flounder.

She finished clearing up, swept the floor and put all the clean glasses back behind the bar, then closed and locked the windows and went back into the kitchen. A letter of condolence had come from Lisette, Noah's wife, that morning, and as Belle hadn't had time to read it properly then, she took it down from the dresser and read it again.

Lisette said that Noah was over in France so was unable to come to the funeral, but she was expecting him back very soon. She said she knew he would want to come over to see them all to offer his help, as he would understand that running a public house without Garth was going to be difficult for them.

It was a kind, very sincere letter. Noah had become very close friends with Jimmy at the time they were searching for her, and Belle had much affection for Lisette for the kindness she'd shown her at the time of her terrible ordeal in Paris.

They had come up in the world since then. Noah was a highly respected journalist and Lisette the perfect wife and mother to Jean-Philippe, the boy she'd had already when she married Noah, and now to Rose who was three. Lisette ran their beautiful home in St John's Wood as if she had been born to wealth and privilege. Yet money and position hadn't changed either of them; as soon as they heard Jimmy was wounded they'd written, and Belle knew that they would come here as soon as Noah was back in England, and that he would want to help in any way he could.

Belle hadn't written to Noah about Etienne's death. Used to death and destruction as he must be while reporting on the war, he would, she knew, be very sad to hear he'd lost his friend. But it was more to spare Jimmy's feelings; she knew that if Noah wrote back or called and wanted to talk about Etienne, it would just start Jimmy off again. Every now and then he questioned her about her time in Paris, and although she had done nothing to be ashamed of with Etienne at that time, while defending herself she might give away her true feelings for the man.

In the main Jimmy had become a great deal easier to live with since Dr Towle talked to him. He had continued to practise walking, and a few times he'd walked to shops nearby. He often laughed the way he used to.

But he still had days when he was very sullen and nasty to Belle. She had only to make an effort with her appearance before going out for him to question where she was going. He still wouldn't attempt any lovemaking, and when she tried to talk to him about it he just clammed up.

Garth's death had been a terrible shock to Jimmy. He'd broken down completely and been inconsolable. He said that he so much wished he'd told Garth how much he valued him, that he'd been better than a father. He also regretted not going into the bar with him all these past months as it would have meant so much to him.

All Belle could say was the truth: that Garth had been so proud of Jimmy and loved him like his own son. She knew Garth's death would create greater problems for Jimmy too. He couldn't take his place, and that was going to make him feel even more useless.

Hearing a loud thump from upstairs, Belle jumped to her feet and ran up the stairs. She found Jimmy on the floor beside the bed.

'What happened?' she asked, but as she bent over to help him up and found him soaked in sweat, she knew immediately that he must have wanted to go to the lavatory and hadn't remembered he only had one leg.

He was too confused even to help himself get up, so she ran to the bathroom to fetch an old chamber pot left in there. Then, hoisting him up on to the side of the bed, she directed him to urinate in it.

She made him drink some water when he'd finished, then tucked him back into bed. 'Don't try to get up again, just call me,' she said. 'I'll be right here.'

Belle spent the night in the easy chair with a blanket round her, but every hour or so whenever she heard Jimmy make a sound, she got up, sponged him down because he was burning up and tried to make him drink a little. Although she was frightened and felt very alone, she was glad Mog hadn't woken.

It was a relief to see the first signs of dawn in the sky and hear a bird chirruping somewhere close by. But as the early morning light began to come into the room she was horrified to see Jimmy's face looked grey and sunken.

'Will you drink some more water for me?' she whispered when she saw his eyelids flickering as if he was trying to open them.

'Let me go,' he croaked out.

'No, Jimmy, you must try and fight this,' she said, putting her arm beneath his shoulders and lifting him so he could drink.

He opened his eyes then, and as the light caught them they looked like molten gold, the way they had when she first met him at the age of fifteen in Seven Dials. 'I can't. I'm tired of fighting. You'll have a better life without me.'

'I won't, Jimmy, I need you,' she pleaded. 'We can have a good life, we belong together.'

'We've already had all the good there can be,' he said, and his voice was clearer now, his eyes fixed on hers as if daring her to interrupt. 'The man you loved died out there in Ypres, long before the shell crippled me. Even if I'd come back in one piece, I wouldn't have been the Jimmy you knew: the filth, the brutality, the stink of dead bodies, the mud and the roar of guns killed him off. I don't believe in anything any more, not King and Country, not God, I've got nothing left inside me.'

'You might think that now, because you are sick, and your uncle has just died,' Belle sobbed, horrified by the ring of truth in his words, yet desperate to make him believe otherwise. 'All that horror you went through is over now. Look at what I went through in Paris! I thought the same as you, that I could never forget it and be happy again. But I did, because you didn't give up on searching for me, and when I got back you made me feel whole again. I can do that for you too.'

'No, you can't. All living with me will do is pull you down,' he said, his voice growing weaker again. 'Let me go, Belle, remember me how I used to be.'

She put both her arms around him, held him tightly against her shoulder and wept. She could feel tremendous heat coming from him and that made her break away to lay him down again. His eyes had closed and his breathing was laboured. She unbuttoned his pyjama jacket and began sponging him down with cold water.

'I'm not going to let you go,' she said fiercely. 'I love you, so does Mog, we need you. We can make you forget the war, we'll move to the seaside, we'll get the best artificial limb maker in the country to help you. You are still the Jimmy I married, I know you are.'

'What can I do to help?' Mog's voice at the door interrupted Belle.

Belle turned her head. 'Don't come in, but will you go and get Dr Towle?'

Mog said she would, and Belle heard her going down the stairs and the sound of the side door opening and closing behind her.

A few minutes later Jimmy retched, and before Belle could get a bowl or even help him sit up, he vomited. It came spouting out of his mouth, bilious yellowish-green and foul smelling, all over the pillows and himself. Belle removed the pillows and was just about to take off his pyjama jacket, when she noticed another smell and she realized he'd defecated too.

She knew this had happened to Garth several times, but

until now Belle had not considered how Mog, such a small woman, had managed to strip him, wash him and remake the bed with clean linen by herself. Belle had dealt with such things before in the Royal Herbert, but not alone.

Gritting her teeth, she pulled back the covers and stripped off his pyjamas, using them to clean up the worst of it. She quickly got some fresh linen from the cupboard on the landing, and some hot water from the bathroom, and washed him on the folded-over sheet. He was moaning softly, becoming delirious, and once she'd got him clean she put a new sheet on one side of the bed, then rolled him over on to it and managed to pull the rest from under him and tuck it in all round.

She had finally got the covers over him again, not attempting to put clean pyjamas on him, when Mog got back.

'The doctor said he'd be here as quickly as possible,' she said from the doorway. 'He's got to see another patient first. I'll take the dirty stuff down and make you a cup of tea.'

It was nearly nine that morning before the doctor arrived, and during that time Belle had had to change the bed twice more. It had begun to rain, and with the windows shut she knew the room must smell like a farmyard.

Dr Towle was dishevelled, unshaven and his eyes were red-rimmed. Clearly he too had been up most of the night. But he managed to smile at Belle and offer his commiserations before examining Jimmy.

'Mrs Franklin said he was taken ill after his uncle's funeral yesterday evening,' he said, then went on to ask how quickly the high fever and sickness had come on.

'Could he go to hospital?' Belle asked.

'I'm afraid there isn't a bed free anywhere,' the doctor said. 'And even if there was, subjecting him to the journey now would only make his condition worse. Sadly, Mrs Reilly, you are already doing everything that can be done to help him.'

'Is he going to die?' she whispered. Jimmy appeared to be unconscious but she couldn't be sure of that.

Dr Towle made a gesture with his hands that implied Jimmy was in God's hands now. 'About a third of the patients I've seen so far have recovered, but none of them had such high temperatures as your husband. With any other illness youth and strength are a great advantage, but it doesn't seem to be so in this particular one.'

'We can't lose him too!' Belle looked at the doctor in horror. 'Isn't there anything you can give him?'

'I wish there was,' he said glumly. 'Try and get him to drink warm water with a little brandy. Sponge him down, keep the room warm but well ventilated. That is all I can offer. I'll come back this evening to see how he is.'

All that day Belle struggled to get Jimmy to drink, and when the liquid just ran out of his mouth because he wouldn't or couldn't swallow, she resorted to using a glass dropper from a medicine bottle and squeezed a few drops of water mixed with a little brandy between his lips. He drifted in and out of consciousness, in and out of delirium when he said things that made no sense. But now and again he spoke a few words that she could understand.

'I looked at the picture of you so often that it cracked in the end,' was one thing. Belle knew he meant a picture that was taken of her on their wedding day. She'd found it was missing from the other photographs after he'd gone to France.

'The other men used to tell me no woman could ever love a man with red hair,' was another thing he said.

But mostly he spoke the names of friends he'd made in the army, and although she didn't know who they were she was glad he was thinking about good times.

Dr Towle came back in the evening as promised, praised Belle for using the dropper and seemed pleased to hear there had been no further vomiting. 'There is no real pattern to this disease,' he said. 'Some of my patients have appeared to be at death's door, but then they recover. Others don't seem so seriously ill and they just slip away. I find it baffling, and I so much wish there was more I could do.'

'It's a comfort that you called,' Belle said. 'While he's quiet like this I feel hopeful.'

'Can you cope another night with him? You look worn out, Mrs Reilly. I could find a nurse to help you.'

'I think he's better with just me taking care of him,' Belle said, remembering the dragon of a nurse he'd sent when she lost the baby.

'Well, try and get forty winks while he's quiet,' the doctor said. 'I must go now, I have dozens more patients to call on. But I'll be back in the morning, and hopefully by then there will be an improvement.'

Belle slipped downstairs later and ate some soup, bread and cheese that Mog had prepared, but as soon as she'd eaten it she was back with Jimmy. She managed to nod off in the chair for over an hour, but awoke to find him delirious again.

Again she sponged him down, dropped the water and brandy into his mouth, changed the sheets that were soaked with both sweat and urine, and tried to comfort him as he rambled incoherently. 'I couldn't find our lot,' he said at one point, grabbing her hand so hard it hurt. 'I couldn't see, I kept slipping in the mud, and I fell over dead men.'

Belle guessed he was remembering that last attack. He rattled out words that had no meaning for her: creeping barrage, Very lights, Aunt Sally and Forby. But it didn't matter that it made no sense to her, she had a feeling he thought he was talking to another soldier.

'A man was cut in half by shrapnel,' he said at one point. 'His bottom half kept running for a while.'

'Shhh,' she said, bathing his forehead. 'You are safe now, you'll never see such things again.'

About two in the morning he became lucid for a little while. He turned his face towards her and tried to smile. 'It is you, Belle! I thought I was dreaming. I told the lads I had to stay safe to get home to you. And I did.'

'Yes, you did, and now you have to drink some of this to make you better,' she said, offering him a glass of water. He even lifted his head on his own and drank a mouthful or two before slumping back on the pillow.

He closed his eyes then and Belle felt he'd turned the corner and was sleeping, so she went back to her chair. Around an hour later she got up again on hearing him making an odd rattling noise in his throat. She moved the lamp a little closer to him and saw his face had grown darker, just the way Garth's had.

'Oh, please no!' she exclaimed. She felt for his pulse and found it was weaker, and when she put her hand on his forehead it was very hot. Frantically she sponged him down again, talking to him and begging him to rally round. But there was no response. His eyes fluttered open now and again, but he didn't even try to speak.

'Jimmy, you must stop this,' she said in the firm voice she used to speak to the soldiers in the ambulance. 'You can get better, you must get better. Do it for me, don't leave me alone.'

Suddenly Mog was beside her. Small in stature she might be, but she seemed to fill the room with determination. 'Come on, Jimmy,' she said. 'Don't upset Belle like this. We both need you. We love you.'

His eyes opened. 'I love you both,' he said in a rasping whisper. 'Look after one another, I can't stay any longer.'

Belle looked at Mog in horror and could see from the expression on her face that she knew he was dying.

'I never told you before but I think of you as my son,' Mog said. 'I'm that proud of you!'

He tried to smile, but it was just the slightest movement of his lips. 'You were like a mother to me,' he whispered. 'Don't let Belle grieve for me. Stay close to her.'

'I'm here, Jimmy,' Belle said. 'And I'm telling you that you must fight this.'

His eyes turned to Belle and his hand fluttered as if he was wanting to lift it to touch her face. 'My Belle, my beautiful Belle,' he said. 'I'm sorry for everything, but it's for the best.'

Belle picked up his hand and kissed his fingers. 'You've got nothing to be sorry for, and it's not for the best,' she said brokenly as tears rolled down her cheeks.

She felt his hand go limp in hers and her fingers felt for his pulse. She could feel nothing.

'Oh, Mog!' she cried out.

It was Mog who took Jimmy's hand and laid it down. She closed his eyes and kissed his cheek. 'Goodbye, son,' she whispered. 'Garth and your mother are waiting for you.'

'No, Jimmy,' Belle sobbed. She slid down on to her knees on the floor, her head resting on his chest. 'There was so much more I wanted to say to you.'

The two women stayed there for some time, both crying, then Mog got up and lifted Belle up, rocking her against her shoulder the way she used to do when Belle was a small girl.

'Everything is worse in the night,' Mog said softly. 'But he was right, it was for the best. He hated being so helpless. He knew it would never get better for him. You come and get into bed with me now. We can't do anything until it's light.'

Chapter Twenty-Seven

Belle heard a knock on the side door of the pub as she and Mog were sitting in the kitchen, but she ignored it. It was a week since Jimmy's funeral and people had been knocking ever since. Occasionally it was someone calling to offer help and sympathy, but mostly just to ask when the bar would be open again. There was a notice pinned to the door that it was closed due to bereavement, but that had not deterred them.

Both Belle and Mog were finding it hard to get through each day. Time hung on their hands with no one for them to take care of. They felt empty and tearful and had no real idea of which way to turn. The constant knocking made it worse, as it was a reminder there were decisions to be made.

The knocking grew louder. 'It could be Dr Towle,' Mog said.

Belle got up wearily. Mog might be right, at the funeral the doctor had said he'd pop by in a week to see how they were.

'All right, I'm coming,' she muttered as she walked to the door.

But it wasn't the doctor, it was Noah. He took off his hat as he saw her and smiled hesitantly.

'Oh, my goodness,' she exclaimed. 'Noah! What a surprise!'

It was at least three years since she had last seen him, but although his impeccably tailored pale grey tailed coat, waistcoat, pin-striped trousers and hand-made shoes told of his success, his rosy, still boyish face held an expression of such sympathy and understanding that Belle was taken right back to the time in Paris when he'd done so much to help her. Just seeing him made her instantly feel better.

'I hope I haven't called at a bad time? I was in France and didn't get your letter till I got back yesterday,' he said. 'I can't tell you how sorry I am that I wasn't here to support you and Mog when you needed it most. Both Lisette and I wept for you both when we read your letter, and we were so sad that we'd missed the opportunity to pay our last respects to both Garth and Jimmy.'

His sincerity was very touching and it pulled her together. 'I wouldn't have wanted you to come and risk infection,' she said. 'But I am so pleased to see you now. We haven't been opening the door to anyone, but I'm very glad I did this time. Come on in.'

As the door closed behind him he put his arms around Belle and hugged her tightly. 'I know a gentleman isn't supposed to take such liberties,' he said gruffly. 'But you know that I've always thought of you as family.'

Belle hugged him back and kissed his smooth cheek, which smelled of sandalwood shaving soap. 'If I could've picked a brother, I'd have picked you,' she said, emotional tears springing into her eyes. 'Shall we go in the kitchen? Mog's just made some bread.'

Mog appeared then in the kitchen door, her apron and her cheeks still dusted with flour. 'Oh, Noah,' she cried and ran over to embrace him, 'how good it is to see you! We were only saying this morning that you'd know what we should do.'

'Dear Mog,' he said as he held her. 'I am so sorry you lost Garth. I thought I'd still be seeing him when he was a very old man. It was such a cruel blow for both you and Belle to lose your husbands. How did you get through two funerals?'

Because of people's fear of infection and their own grief, both Belle and Mog had agreed that Jimmy's funeral should

417

be a very quiet one. They had served tea and cake afterwards to the few people who had insisted on coming, but the number of people who came to the church and those who left letters of condolence and flowers at the pub showed how highly Jimmy had been thought of.

'We coped quite well until the day after Jimmy's,' Mog said, wiping her eyes on her apron. 'But it's been awful since.'

Noah looked at Belle and she nodded to confirm this. There had been nothing to fill the void the men had left. The place was too quiet, too tidy. Even the closed bar seemed like a reproach. But even if they had felt up to opening it again, there were proprieties of mourning to think about. It wouldn't be seemly for two such recently widowed women to be working in a public place.

Mog had pointed out that even if they wanted to open again, neither of them had the strength to bring up barrels from the cellar, or had any real knowledge about the different kinds of beer or how they should be treated because Garth had always handled that side of the business.

It was only today that Mog had rallied herself enough to make some bread. Up till now they had been picking at food left from the tea after Jimmy's funeral, as neither of them had any appetite.

Noah's presence in the kitchen was like a light being switched on. Mog made tea, laid her fresh bread, still hot from the oven, on the table, got out the butter and cheese, and as she busied herself she told Noah how it had been.

He had always been a good listener. As Mog talked and poured the tea, he nodded, taking it all in.

'Tell me how it was after Jimmy came back from France,' he asked Belle after a little while. 'It must have been very difficult for both of you.'

Belle made her account as brief as possible. She and Mog had talked and talked about it all week, and they were now at the point when they didn't wish to go over it again.

'You tell us about Lisette, and Rose and Jean-Philippe,' she said after telling him the absolute minimum. 'We could do with hearing something cheerful.'

'We rented a cottage in Devon to get them away from London,' he said. 'I thought the children needed some sea air, green fields and less sadness around them. I couldn't stay with them for the whole time unfortunately, I had to go over to France. But Jean-Philippe learned to swim while I was away and it was good to see roses in their cheeks and Lisette looking more relaxed when I got back. She wanted to come today but I thought it was better to come alone.'

'I wouldn't have wanted her to come here so soon after,' Belle said. 'A mother needs to stay healthy for her children.'

'Lisette thumbs her nose at the risk of infection,' he smiled wryly. 'She wanted me to stress that isn't the reason and to ask you both if you'd like to come back with me today and let her look after you for a while.'

'That is so kind,' Mog said, her lower lip quivering. 'You married a good one, Noah.'

'As we all did,' he sighed. 'Without Garth and Jimmy's influence in the past, I wouldn't be where I am now, nor would I have Lisette. I don't really need to tell you how much we care for you.'

'You always did have a way with words,' Belle said fondly. Noah had never suffered from the usual male reticence to say what was in his heart. But he was a man who backed up his words with action too, and she knew any advice he gave them today would be sound.

'You say you don't know which way to turn,' Noah said,

looking from Belle to Mog. 'On the way here I was thinking that might be the case, and I do have suggestions that might help.'

'It's the pub really,' Mog said wearily. 'We don't know how long we should be seen to be in mourning, not just wearing black, but before it would be acceptable to open the bar again. We are both perfectly capable of serving at the bar, and we know a little about ordering beer and spirits. But there is so much more we don't know, Noah, and the pub needs a strong man at the helm.'

'Yes, of course it does,' Noah said. 'Most of your anxieties could be solved by taking on a manager. Neither of you would need to be seen in the bar then. But let me tell you, the etiquette of mourning is virtually dead itself. Almost everyone in the country is mourning someone. Widows have to go out and work to keep their children, and people can't afford to spend what little money they have on black clothes. I understand you both think it right and proper to be wearing black for a while, and not appearing in public places. But quite honestly, only very old people with a limited outlook would expect you to stick to that now.'

That had been Belle's view too, but Mog had been affronted when she raised it, and insisted they both wore black dresses. Noah could say such things to her, however; Mog saw him as the fount of all knowledge.

'A manager?' Mog said. 'I hadn't thought of that. Wouldn't that be too expensive?'

'You won't have any money coming in if you keep the pub shut,' he said. 'I could help you with advertising for someone and interviewing the applicants.'

'Yes, but it would be so easy for a manager to fiddle us,' Belle said. 'You know how it is, Noah, men in this trade are not always the most honest. Garth himself knew every trick in the book.'

Noah nodded agreement. 'I think the real question is whether you even want to stay here.'

Belle and Mog looked at each other. 'I don't particularly,' Belle said. 'But then, it all belongs to Mog now. She has to decide how she feels.'

Mog looked troubled. 'I don't really want to be here any more either, not after so much sadness. But I'd feel I was letting Garth down by leaving. He loved this place.'

'He loved you more,' Noah pointed out. 'I know he wouldn't turn a hair at you selling it. Remember his views on women in bars!'

Both Belle and Mog managed a weak smile. 'He'd never have allowed anyone in a skirt to come through the doors if he'd had his way,' Belle said.

'Well, he did mellow on that,' Mog chipped in. 'I was serving with him for most of the war. Only because he couldn't really afford to pay a barman, and he did eventually let soldiers bring their wives and sweethearts in there too.'

'So we agree then that he wouldn't expect you to try and keep running it?' Noah said. 'I think we also know he'd turn in his grave if it failed. So why not sell it, Mog? You could buy another little business that you both liked and would be good at. Maybe Belle could make hats again? A tea shop? A small hotel?'

'I'd love a tea shop,' Mog said. 'One of those pretty places with a garden where we could serve tea outside during the summer.'

Belle smiled. Mog had mentioned that in the past, and she certainly had all the talents to make it a success. It was also good to hear her talking with some animation again. 'Wouldn't you miss the friends you've made here?' she asked.

'What friends?' Mog said with a touch of bitterness. 'The women who snubbed me when they read all that about you?

421

They only came round later because I was useful to their different causes.'

'That was a shameful episode,' Noah agreed. 'And it is another very good reason for upping sticks and moving away. Unless of course you both feel you need to be close to where Jimmy and Garth are buried.'

'Garth said such things were sentimental nonsense,' Mog said sadly. 'And if Jimmy had been buried in France, Belle wouldn't have been able to visit his grave.'

'Then there's nothing stopping you. I think you need to be born into the licensing trade to be really good at it, not to mention being as hard-headed as Garth was. I'd say you two would be much happier with a more feminine business.'

'I certainly wouldn't want to have to clean out that lavatory at the back every day for the rest of my life,' Mog grimaced. For a second she looked and sounded much more like the old Mog.

Noah grinned. 'Well, would you like me to contact agents to sell it? You could do that yourselves of course, but they might browbeat women into settling for a lower price.'

Belle looked questioningly at Mog. She hesitated for just a moment. 'Yes, Noah, I'd like you to do that. The sooner it's sold the better.'

Belle got up from her chair and hugged Mog. 'That is very brave and very sensible,' she said. 'We can get a little flat to live in while we decide where we want to go and what we want to do.'

'Sooner than later is good,' Noah said. 'The longer the pub is closed the less attractive it becomes to a potential buyer. Blackheath is a good area, with a reliable train service. I'd stake my reputation on it becoming a very popular place to live once the war is over.'

'Will that be soon?' Belle asked. Noah would know the

real truth about it, and she didn't think he would give her one of those idealized versions printed in the newspapers.

'I'd say before Christmas,' he said. 'It's run its course now, too many millions dead, and the Germans are as demoralized as us. They are calling the third battle of Ypres, the one where Jimmy was wounded, Passchendaele now, after some benighted blown-apart village they have yet to gain. I'd like to hear the whole sorry episode known as the Atrocity of Passchendaele. If I had my way I'd see General Haig horsewhipped through the streets for sending the cream of Britain and the Commonwealth's young men to be blown apart or drowned in the mud. It has been, and still is, a pointless, wicked sacrifice.'

'You were there?' Belle asked. The sheer passion of his words seemed to confirm it.

'Yes, I stood on the Menin Road, amongst burned-out tanks, dead men, horses and mules and observed awesome, terrifying shelling. Where the shells hit the mud they exploded like geysers a hundred feet up in the air, bringing with them body parts of the dead. I saw thousands of men like ants bent double under weight of their packs, trying to run through that bog under heavy fire, yet bravely holding their rifles out of the water even when they were cut down. Sometimes it took four stretcher bearers to carry a man just a hundred feet, the mud was so thick. There were wounded that lay up to their necks in water and amongst the dead for four days before being rescued. And all the while the generals drank tea from bone china cups in safety behind the lines and planned to send still more men to their deaths.'

Belle covered her face in horror.

'I wrote a piece telling the truth but the paper wouldn't print it.' He pursed his lips in disgust. 'But after the war ends I shall write that truth in a book. It will be a testament to the horror, barbarity and senselessness of it all. And perhaps too it will make the widows, mothers, fathers, brothers and sisters of the tens of thousands of men like Jimmy understand how brave their men were.'

A little later Mog excused herself, saying she had some jobs to do upstairs. Belle felt it was her tactful way of allowing her time to talk to Noah alone.

'How are you really feeling now?' he asked once Mog was out of earshot. 'Lisette told me that you confided in her about how difficult Jimmy was after he came home.'

'To be truthful, I'm confused about how I feel,' she admitted. 'I feel terribly sad of course. It just doesn't seem right that Jimmy had to go through all that misery of being wounded, and just when he was beginning to deal with it, he got that terrible flu.

'But I won't lie to you Noah, he was very difficult to live with, especially when he first came home. So many awful moods, he said nasty things, and he wouldn't let me get close to him. Mostly the future looked very bleak. So sometimes I feel relief that it's over. But just to think that makes me feel so guilty.'

'I can imagine how confused you must feel,' Noah said soothingly. 'On the day you married Jimmy I really believed that from then on your life was going to be so happy. You'd had more than your fair share of misery, and with Jimmy, Mog and Garth beside you, I thought I needn't ever worry about you again. But this damned war! Nobody has been untouched by it.

'I don't think there's many that went through the battles Jimmy did, who aren't changed by what they saw. And to come back with a missing arm and leg too! I was terrified out there, Belle. And I didn't have to do anything but take shelter and observe. The smell, the filth, the noise – it was a scene from hell with the added spice of sheer terror as you didn't know if and when you were going to be blown up.'

He paused, looking at her. 'But you did all anyone could possibly do for him. You loved him and you cared for him. Now it's time you thought about yourself.'

She couldn't reply, she was too choked up by his sympathy.

'You are thin and pale, Belle. You've got to be kind to yourself now,' he went on. 'I did suggest you came home with me, but seeing you both, I think it might be more beneficial if you went away to the seaside for a rest. Recoup your energies. Think about your future.'

Belle began to cry again and Noah moved his chair closer to her and drew her into his arms.

'You've been through more than anyone I ever met,' he said in understanding. 'Etienne once said you had been manipulated by other people right from a child. And he was right. But now is the time to break out of that, to decide what you want. You are still a young woman with your whole life ahead of you.'

The mention of Etienne brought a flood of new tears. It was him she wanted, but that had been denied her too.

'Do you remember I wrote and said it was a French soldier who rescued Jimmy? Well, it was Etienne,' she blurted out.

'Etienne!' Noah exclaimed. 'How could it be? I don't understand.'

'Jimmy had a letter a while back now from a friend in the same regiment. He named his rescuer as Sergeant Carrera. He was awarded the Croix de Guerre because he singlehandedly took out a big gun and got himself a hero's death.'

'He's dead?' Noah gasped. 'Oh, no. Not him too?'

'I'm afraid so. It was because of the medal that they got all the details.'

Noah frowned. 'Can you be sure it was Etienne? Not just another man with the same surname?'

'Jimmy's friend said it was a man they'd met before, near Verdun in 1916. Jimmy described him to me, and things that had been said, and I just knew it was him. Besides, it all sounded so typical of Etienne, disobeying orders to take Jimmy back behind the French lines to safety. Jimmy always said the man had called him by his name too.'

She wasn't surprised to see Noah's eyes fill with tears, she knew how much he'd liked and admired Etienne. And she felt a surge of relief that she could talk about the man to someone who cared as much as she did.

'Didn't Jimmy tell you he'd met him in Verdun?'

'No, but then he never knew the French sergeant's name. It was clear though that Etienne knew his; Jimmy said he asked him questions about where he lived in London and suchlike.'

'Etienne always did play his cards close to his chest. I had a couple of letters from him earlier on in the war,' Noah said. 'I was astounded he survived Verdun, not many of the French came through that. We talk all the time of British casualties, but the French lost even more. Twenty-five per cent of their army have been killed. But I thought he was indestructible. Stupid really, no man can be that.'

'I thought it too, Noah,' she said and put her hand on his arm. 'Look, I never admitted this to Jimmy or Mog, but I saw him in France. He came to the hospital.'

She told Noah briefly how it came about. 'He told me he was going to put you down as his next of kin. Of course, it might have slipped his mind, but don't soldiers get reminded to do that before a big battle?'

'Yes, they do. Even if they've got nothing more than a watch or a spare pair of socks, the CO gets them to write it down. If Etienne did do this I should have been informed of his death.'

Belle hadn't thought of that. 'Well, I don't suppose the French are as organized as us. With so many casualties it must be hard. And maybe his CO hadn't passed the information on to someone who could write in English.'

Noah nodded. 'Yes, that could delay things. He said in his last letter – that was back in April, I think – that he hoped when the war was over I'd bring Lisette and the children down to Marseille. He wanted us to see his farm. I could never imagine him with chickens and pigs. But then he was always full of surprises. Why would he put me down as his next of kin though? Surely he wouldn't want to leave the farm to me? He knows I know nothing about farming.'

Belle realized that as soon as Noah was notified about Etienne he would be even more puzzled by why he had left the farm to her.

'I think he planned to leave it to me,' she said.

Noah stared at her for a moment then frowned. 'Why would he do that, Belle? Wouldn't Jimmy have found it strange? Not to mention suspicious?'

'Yes, I suppose he might have.' Belle could feel her colour rising because of the way Noah was looking at her. 'But Etienne said you were the one person he knew he could trust to deal with it, and he said you would be able to explain to Jimmy that it wasn't strange or troubling as he was my friend and rescuer in Paris.'

'Etienne would think that way, but I doubt Jimmy would have agreed,' Noah said thoughtfully. 'I'm not sure that I would either. After all, I remember how you felt about him back when we were leaving Paris. I always suspected it was returned too. How did you feel towards him when you saw him again?'

Belle had forgotten how intuitive Noah could be, and years of journalism had honed his skills.

'You fell for him all over again?'

It wasn't a question but a statement, and Belle couldn't deny it. 'Yes,' she said in a small voice. 'So help me, I did.'

The silence was broken only by the ticking of the clock in the hall.

'You considered leaving Jimmy?'

'No! Well, maybe for a little while I wondered if I could do it. It was a moment of madness, my friend had been killed, I was so sad. And I suppose I was swept along with Etienne saying that one way or another we'd be together eventually. But he went back to the front, and then Jimmy was wounded and I came back to England with him.'

'You must've been in turmoil,' he said in a hushed tone that was so sympathetic she felt she must admit how bad it had been for her.

'Yes, I can't even begin to describe it,' she sighed. 'I wrote to Etienne the same night I heard that Jimmy was wounded. I said he must not contact me again. He only wrote back to say he understood and wished both Jimmy and me well.

'Of course I know now he stuck to that because he was dead. But back then I was riddled with guilt. I even felt Jimmy being wounded was a kind of punishment for me. I tried really hard never to think about Etienne, but it was very hard when Jimmy was being so cold and difficult.'

Noah just sat there deep in thought for a little while. He lit a cigarette, and Belle looked at him nervously, wondering what was going through his mind.

'The most astounding thing about this is that he rescued Jimmy!' Noah burst out suddenly. 'His way to have you would have been clear if he'd ignored him. But then, he did have his own kind of honour; I know if I was ever in a tight spot, I'd want him beside me. And you haven't told Mog any of this?'

'No, how could I? I was tempted to go and confide in Lisette when I first came home. I was feeling so wretched, ashamed of what I'd done, and I felt she was the one person who might understand. But I couldn't. I thought it better to blank him from my mind and concentrate on rebuilding my life with Jimmy.'

'So how did you keep your feelings for him in when you heard he'd been killed? That must have been so hard, especially when Jimmy was being so difficult.'

'Yes,' she admitted. 'The hardest thing, and Jimmy kept talking about it. But it's all over now, both of them have gone. And I must pick up my life and start again.'

They could hear Mog coming back down the stairs, and Noah changed the subject and went back to his earlier suggestion that they went away for a little holiday.

'That would be nice.' Mog's face lit up. 'We could go to Brighton. I've always wanted to go there.'

Noah stayed for about another hour, and before he left he asked Mog if she wanted to go ahead with him finding a buyer for the pub. Mog must have given the subject some serious thought while she was upstairs because she said she would.

'You do have Garth's will?' he asked.

Mog said she did and asked if he wanted to see it. 'He left everything to me, except for some money for Jimmy and Belle.'

'You must take it to his solicitor then,' Noah explained. 'It has to go through Probate before you have the right to sell the property. But the solicitor will explain all that to you. Now, do you need any money to tide you over?'

'No, we're all right,' Mog said. 'Garth always had some cash tucked away. He wasn't very trusting about banks.'

'Well, if you need some more, just ask,' Noah said.

As he was about to leave he asked Belle if she'd seen her mother recently.

'No, she didn't even bother to reply when I wrote and said Jimmy was wounded. There was a box of chocolates at Christmas, but not even a note with it. Then in February I got the briefest of letters asking why I hadn't been to see her. I wrote back saying that I didn't have time to go across London to visit with a crippled husband to care for. I haven't heard another word since. We haven't told her about Garth's and Jimmy's deaths.'

'My advice would be not to inform her,' he said with a little smile. 'Relatives have a habit of coming out of the woodwork when people die. And as I recall, Annie isn't the kind to come visiting unless she wants something.'

'Our relatives are thrust upon us. Thank goodness we can choose our friends,' Belle laughed. 'And you've been the best of friends, Noah.'

He kissed them both goodbye, reminding them that he and Lisette were on the telephone if they wanted to talk about anything, and that they were welcome to visit whenever they liked.

'I'll look for an agent close to here and come back when they want to value the property,' he said as he left. 'Until then, you go away and have a real rest.'

Three weeks after Noah had called on them, Belle and Mog returned to the Railway after ten days in Brighton. The agent Noah had asked to find a buyer for the property had come up with someone who was extremely keen to buy it. Now they just needed Garth's solicitor to tell Mog she was legally entitled to go ahead with the sale.

'It's lovely to do nothing for a while, but I don't think I'm ready to be a lady of leisure just yet,' Mog said as she put the kettle on. She looked around the kitchen and frowned. 'My word, it's gloomy in here! I never really noticed before, but I suppose after our lovely room on the seafront being so full of light, anywhere would seem dark.'

Belle smiled. Mog had really perked up while they'd been away; she talked about Garth and Jimmy a great deal, but in a positive way, as if she was coming to terms with their deaths. She talked about the future just as much though, wanting to go into tea shops, being critical of their baking, and discussing improvements she'd make if it was her business. They had studied advertisements for properties too, and light-heartedly argued about where they'd like to live. Mog favoured somewhere in the country, but Belle felt a small market town would be better for both of them.

Yet all the way home on the train Mog had been talking about giving the pub and their living quarters a spring-clean, and Belle thought she'd had a change of heart and wanted to stay. She'd enjoyed walking on the promenade in Brighton, she thought the pier was wonderful and loved going to the theatre and the music hall. But it was quite clear that she missed her domestic chores. In the last few days Belle had noticed her checking the hotel's banisters for dust. She'd tutted over the brass knocker on the front door which hadn't been polished and she'd begun to criticize the evening meal. But her remark about the kitchen being gloomy suggested she'd be even happier doing domestic chores somewhere new.

'Then we'll make certain that wherever we move to is light and bright,' Belle said.

Mog looked at her, her head cocked on one side like a little bird. 'You can't wait to leave here, can you?'

Belle thought the time had come for complete honesty. 'No, I can't,' she admitted. 'All I can feel here is sadness, I'm numb to anything else. I don't think that until we lock the door here for the last time I'll ever come out of it.'

'Jimmy gave you a hard time, I know that,' Mog sighed. 'I tried to talk to him about it several times, but he wouldn't listen. You are right, it's best that we move on and try just to remember the good times we had here, not the sad ones.'

Belle put her arms round Mog and hugged her. Words were unnecessary. As always, Mog was resilient, loving and understanding. And they both knew that wherever they went or whatever they did, they could be happy again as long as they were together.

'Will you go through that pile of post?' Mog asked a little later, indicating the heap of letters she'd picked up as she came in and put on the table. 'I'll make the tea and a list of groceries we need.'

Belle sorted through it. There were more letters of condolence for both her and Mog from people who hadn't got to hear of the men's deaths until recently. A few bills, and a great many advertisements for everything from chairs and tables for a bar, to glasses and new beers. Among them was a letter from Vera from France.

Belle had written to her friend while she was in Brighton and told her about Garth and Jimmy dying. But it seemed their letters had crossed in the post, because Vera was planning to go home to New Zealand.

'I've had enough,' Belle read.

'I'm exhausted, I've got boils on my neck. I look like an old lady, and I really can't bear the misery all around me any longer. Men are dying like flies of this Spanish flu. The hospital has been shelled several times, driving at night with no lights is a nightmare. I've done my bit, now I want to see my mother and father, to sit and look at clear blue sea, and have no responsibilities. That sounds so selfish. And I suppose it is. Anyway, by the time you get this I'll be on my way to England. I'll only have three or four days there before I get the ship home from Southampton. My plan is to go straight to London, I'm really hoping I can stay with you, but if you can't manage it, I'll find a cheap hotel somewhere near. Don't even think of going to any trouble. Just to see you will be the very best tonic anyone could give me. I hope seeing me will cheer you too.

Your loving friend Vera

Belle whooped with delight. Vera's letter was dated a week earlier, so she might very well arrive tomorrow.

'Good news?' Mog asked.

'Yes. Vera's coming on her way back to New Zealand. I can't wait to see her.'

Mog smiled affectionately. 'I'm glad. An old friend to make you laugh and to remember that you're still young, that's just what you need right now.'

Chapter Twenty-Eight

Vera pulled a silly face as Belle opened the door to her. 'I hope you got my warning letter?' she said. 'If you didn't, you've got two seconds to shut the door.'

Belle laughed. 'I did get it and I was thrilled to hear you were coming,' she said, reaching out to take her friend's suitcase. 'But I suspect you didn't get the one from me that must have crossed yours in the post.'

'Was that the one where you said don't ever turn up at my door?' Vera said as she stepped into the hall.

'Yes, that was the one,' Belle replied, but aware that she must tell Vera about Jimmy and Garth before she introduced her to Mog, she put the suitcase down, opened the front door again and drew her back outside.

'Fair enough. It was nice to see you if only for a second,' Vera said, but her wide smile faded when she saw Belle's anxious expression. 'I've come at a bad time?'

'No, it's a good time, but I need to tell you what's happened before we go back in. It was in the letter you didn't get. Both Garth and Jimmy died of the flu, less than a week apart.'

Vera's jaw dropped.

'It was four weeks ago. We're both over the worst of the shock now, well, at least we've come to terms with it.'

'I can go,' Vera said in alarm. 'I am so sorry. I don't want to intrude at such a time.'

'You don't need to do that. Mog was as glad to hear you were coming as I was.' Belle caught hold of Vera's arm to stress that she meant it. 'We could do with a little light relief from one another.'

Vera just looked at her for a moment. 'I can hardly believe it. I am so very sorry, Belle,' she said. 'Oh, my goodness! Could I have arrived at a worse possible time?'

Belle smiled. 'Your timing is fine. I just wish I'd written straight away so you'd had advance warning. I don't want you to feel awkward. Now, come on in and meet Mog.'

Vera was hesitant as Mog came forward to greet her. 'I'm so sorry for your loss, Mrs Franklin,' she said. 'Belle's just told me.'

'And Belle told me what a good friend you were to her in France,' Mog replied, and opening her arms she moved forward to embrace Vera. 'You are very welcome here, my dear, and do call me Mog.'

Belle felt easier then. Mog liked to have someone to fuss over, and she knew Vera would appreciate a bit of mothering too.

Over in France Belle had often observed that Vera could enchant people. It was partly her cheeky, freckled face, her wide grin and irreverent sense of humour, and partly her keen interest in anything and everything. When she told a story she painted a picture with words, and she was a good listener too, one of those rare people who made whoever she was listening to feel they were the most fascinating person in the world.

After they'd had their dinner Belle lit the fire in the living room upstairs. September had been warm, and now in October it was still mild during the day, but cold in the evening.

It was good to sit round the fire and talk, reminding Belle of Sundays before Jimmy went off to the war. Back then, Sundays had been special because the pub was closed. They would have a huge roast dinner and then go up to the living room to relax and chat. Garth and Mog invariably fell asleep, but later they would play cards and Garth would regale them with some of the gossip he'd heard over the bar during the week.

Mog used to hang on Garth's every word, laughing at all his jokes, but now it was Vera's spell she was falling under. Belle felt like hugging her friend for taking Mog out of herself, telling her funny stories about the hospital, or about her family back in New Zealand. Mog loved the fact that they had a bakery, and she and Vera swopped stories about baking cakes or making pastry with almost identical passion. Later Mog talked about Garth's death, something she perhaps hadn't felt able to do with Belle, and as Vera had seen so many men with the Spanish flu she was able to convince Mog that she'd done all anyone could do for Garth.

Around eight in the evening Mog went off to bed, but before she went she suggested that the next day they took Vera up to see Trafalgar Square, Buckingham Palace and the Changing of the Guard. 'We could go in that new place we read about in the newspaper. Lyons Corner House,' she said. Then she looked at Belle and smiled. 'And let's not wear black. I'm sure Garth and Jimmy wouldn't want us looking like two old crows.'

'You've really helped her,' Belle said once Mog had gone and the door was closed. 'We've only just come back from the seaside and she became a lot brighter while we were there, but today she's been the way she was before I went to France. Thank you for that.'

'I think she's a treasure,' Vera said. 'She and my mother would get on like a house on fire. They are remarkably similar in many ways. But tell me about you, Belle. The whole thing. I know all about Garth but nothing about you and Jimmy.'

Belle had told Vera a few things in her letters, but she'd made light of the difficulties she'd had with Jimmy. However, as she started to open up, Vera picked her up on various points until she was finally able to spill it all out: the anger, hurt, loneliness and disappointment she felt, plus her guilt because of Etienne. Vera was shocked to hear he was dead too.

'How dreadful for you to hear it that way!' she exclaimed. 'No one to confide in, keeping your feelings hidden. I wonder you didn't go mad.'

'I deserved it all,' Belle said sadly. 'When I think of all the nights I lay awake thinking about Etienne and wanting him so badly, how could I be hurt that Jimmy never wanted to make love to me?'

'Didn't he ever?'

Belle shook her head. 'Not once. I really thought if I could bring that back we'd be all right. But he wouldn't. He got angry with me for trying to make him. In the end I just gave up. Yet I did love him, Vera; what I felt for him was quite separate from my feelings for Etienne. He said he was sorry when he was dying, and I know he meant for rejecting me.'

'How odd it was that Etienne rescued him!' Vera said thoughtfully. 'He knew who Jimmy was yet he saved him. I'd say that was because he knew he'd never be able to face you again if he didn't.'

'Maybe. The irony of it was that Jimmy wished he hadn't been saved. I often ask myself how I would've felt if he'd died then and I'd been free to be with Etienne. Perhaps it's just as well it didn't work out that way.'

Vera reached out and wiped a tear from Belle's cheek. 'I'm not going to let you wallow in guilt any more. You did the right thing by Jimmy. No one could've done more. So what now? The war is going to end very soon. You can start a new chapter in your life and you've got to make sure that whatever you do, it's for you, not for anyone else.'

'An old friend said more or less the same thing,' Belle said. 'Mog's selling this place as we can't and don't want to run it. Mog wants a tea shop.'

'Here in Blackheath?' Vera asked.

'No, we want to move right away, but we don't know where yet.'

'Why don't you come to New Zealand?'

Belle laughed. 'Don't be silly. We couldn't do that.'

'Why not? A real new start, a beautiful place, lots of space and opportunity. We speak English, in fact most of us are of British stock. You'd love it. I'd get both of you married off in no time.'

'When you haven't even got yourself married off?' Belle raised one eyebrow.

'I wanted different things then, namely adventure. But after what I've seen in France I'd happily settle for everything my mother has – a kind man, children, peace of mind and good friends around me.'

'New Zealand does sound wonderful,' Belle admitted. 'When I came back here I often used to daydream about things you told me, going out on a boat to fish, the sunshine, the turquoise sea. The sea was grey in Brighton, and very cold.'

'My parents would be glad to put you both up till you got settled,' Vera said. 'Mog could have a tea shop in Russell, you could make hats again, or you could take in paying guests. My mother is always saying we need a haberdashery shop. If women want dress material, cotton or buttons they have to order it from Auckland and wait for it to come on the steamer.'

'Mog wouldn't want to go to the other side of the world.'

'I bet she would, she's got an adventurous soul.'

Belle giggled. 'The most adventurous Mog gets is trying a new recipe.'

'I think she'd surprise you. From what I've seen today, I'd say she'd be game for almost anything, just as long as you were with her. What have you got in England to keep you here?'

Belle thought for a moment, but nothing sprang to mind. She had a mother, but she wouldn't lose any sleep about not seeing her again. The only true friends she had were Noah and Lisette, but they had their family and a life of their own. The thought of being somewhere where her past would never come up again was very seductive.

'You want to come, don't you?' Vera crowed.

'Maybe,' Belle said cautiously.

They moved on then to talk about the hospital in France. Belle wanted to hear about all the people she had made friends with there.

'Captain Taylor died of the flu,' Vera said. 'David has a sweetheart, a nurse called Charlotte West.'

'Is that the one in Ward M, with a birthmark on her cheek?'

'Yes, that's her. Nothing to look at, but really jolly. David is totally smitten with her. Sally was mean about it, said they'd be perfect for each other as they are both misfits.'

'If ever there was a misfit, she's one,' Belle giggled. 'I'm glad for him, he's a good man and he'll be improved after a bit of passion.'

'I hope I get some before long,' Vera said impishly. 'I want to be wild and reckless like you and Miranda were.'

'Maybe you'll get the chance on the voyage home,' Belle laughed.

They took the train into Charing Cross the next day. It was a cold but bright day. Both Belle and Mog had abandoned mourning clothes but chosen outfits that were quietly digni-fied. Belle wore a pale grey peplum-waisted costume she hadn't worn since before she went to France, and a grey hat with pink velvet roses on it. Mog chose a deep lilac wool jacket over a paler mauve dress, her beloved fox fur, and a hat trimmed with purple feathers.

Belle had given Vera an emerald-green brocade coat of hers which she felt was too frivolous for a widow but perfect for her red-haired friend. She teamed it with a hat that had been unsold when she closed the shop, a frothy paler green confection of tulle and velvet.

Vera was thrilled by her appearance. All her clothes, and she had very few, were drab and utilitarian, and she said she was sick of the sight of them. She had told Belle when they were in France that women in Russell were not a bit fashion-conscious, mostly because it was so cut off from bigger towns and cities. But being in France, and with influence from Belle and Miranda, her interest in clothes had been awakened. She said she planned to buy a new dress and some more elegant shoes so she could catch the eye of an officer on the long voyage home.

It had been a very long time since Belle and Mog had been into London's West End and though the buildings hadn't changed, it seemed everything around them had. The Strand and the area around Trafalgar Square were teeming with automobiles rather than the hundreds of horse-drawn cabs, carriages and carts they remembered. Four years of war had made everything seem tired; it was reflected in people's faces and the shop windows. There were so many men in uniform, either home on leave or going back to France, and on every corner there seemed to be a man on crutches or blinded, sell-ing anything from matches to shoe laces and newspapers.

Outside Charing Cross Station there was a queue of ambulances collecting wounded men from a hospital train.

Belle and Vera paused to watch a couple of women lifting stretchers into them, a poignant reminder of France. They had already seen a tea stall on the station run by a couple of well-dressed ladies which had made Belle think of Miranda and brought a lump to her throat.

'We must get away from here,' Mog said firmly, perhaps aware of what Belle was thinking. 'We want Vera to go home with good memories of London.'

Vera was beside herself with excitement as they went down the Mall and she saw Buckingham Palace ahead of her. 'I can't believe I'm really seeing it at last,' she said. 'We had a picture of it at school and I used to imagine what it was like inside.'

Belle couldn't help but remember the day Jimmy had brought her here to see it. She was just fifteen then, only eight years ago, but it seemed more like twenty because so much had happened in the intervening years. The memory of that lovely day with him in the snow had sustained her after she was abducted.

As she and Mog pointed out St James's Park, Clarence House and other points of interest, accompanied by a potted history, Belle had the sensation Jimmy was close by, urging her to put aside the past and plan a brand-new future.

She put her hand in Mog's, and smiled at her. 'Shall we go to Seven Dials later and say a final goodbye?' she asked.

Mog squeezed her hand and nodded agreement.

It was while they were in the new and very imposing Lyons Corner House that Belle raised the question of New Zealand. All three of them were tired now, they'd walked what seemed miles, and seen so much. Yet it had been the last port of call, Seven Dials, to see the Ram's Head, Garth's old public house just along the street from Annie's brothel where Belle had been born, that had affected them all most deeply.

Vera knew much of the story, the burnt-out brothel and how Garth took Mog and Annie in to live with him and Jimmy. But to see the dirty, narrow streets, the poverty and the deprivation in Seven Dials after the splendour and majesty of palaces, royal parks and Westminster Abbey was quite a shock for her.

For Belle and Mog a thousand and one memories came flooding back, both good and bad, as they stood across the street from the Ram's Head and remarked on how shabby and small it looked. It was also a jolt to realize how far they had gone and how much they had changed since those days.

They saw prostitutes lurking in doorways, and evidence that there were just as many brothels, if not more, than in their time. The ragged children who called out to them for pennies were just the same too, as were the mangy dogs, the ancient old crones sucking on pipes and the drunks reeling down the street.

They didn't linger, just paused briefly in front of the Ram's Head. Mog shed a few tears, and told Vera about the first time Garth had kissed her and said he loved her. As they went down through Covent Garden Belle thought of the seventeen-year-old Jimmy holding her hand as they ran and slid down the icy streets, and how good it had been to find a real friend.

He had been the very best of friends. Without his dogged persistence in searching for her she would probably have died in Paris. He and his uncle had loved and cared for Mog too.

At least she could say truthfully that they were friends to the last and he would always have a special place in her heart. But now she must stop agonizing over what might have been and the wrong she'd done, and start a new life.

All three of them were very excited to go into Lyons Corner House on the Strand. Owned by Liptons, the tea people, who had made their mark by opening these large places with several floors, it was so modern and elegant. The ground floor sold chocolate, cakes, biscuits and flowers, but each of the restaurants on the upper floors had a different theme, with musicians playing.

They went into the one on the first floor which was more of a tea shop and also served special ice creams. The waitress served them with tea, and brought a two-tier china cake stand arranged with dainty sandwiches, scones and a selection of cakes.

'Vera suggested we could go and live in New Zealand,' Belle said bluntly. 'What would you say to that, Mog?'

Mog was just pouring out the tea, and was so surprised at the question that she overfilled the first cup.

'I don't know,' she said. 'Are you being serious?'

'Never more so,' Belle replied. She took the overfilled cup, drank some of the tea and tipped what was in the saucer back into the cup. The Corner House was very busy, and it had a lovely romantic atmosphere as a man in a tailed coat was playing a piano, and there were scores of men in uniform with their wives and sweethearts. 'You liked the sound of everything Vera told you yesterday. You could have your tea shop there, or a haberdashery shop, whatever we found was most needed when we got there. Vera said we could stay with her parents until we got settled.'

'You could probably get assisted passages too,' Vera said. 'What have you got to lose, Mog? You could always come back if you didn't like it.'

'If all New Zealanders are as nice as you I wouldn't want to,' Mog said. 'But what about my furniture? I've got some things I wouldn't want to part with.'

Belle knew by that question that Mog liked the idea. She grinned at Vera, who then began to tell Mog much more.

They were in Lyons for over two hours, talking over everything from the weather in New Zealand to what clothes to wear, whether they had the same money as in England, everything and anything. It was only when the waitress pointedly asked them if they might like to have dinner in one of the other restaurants that they realized how the time had flown.

'We'll have to talk to Noah about this,' Mog said as she paid the bill. 'He'll know more about how we should go about it.'

'Then you want to go?' Belle said, taking Mog's arm as they left.

'Well, it sounds a lot more exciting than Tunbridge Wells,' she said. 'I've always wanted to go on a long sea voyage.'

'I don't suppose you'd get a passage until the war ends,' Vera said. 'There's still the danger of being shelled or torpedoed. I'm going back on a troop ship and I'll be helping with the wounded going home. But everyone is saying there is going to be an Armistice any day now.'

While Belle and Mog were in Brighton they'd heard much the same thing. But as people had been saying for the last four years that the war would all be over by Christmas, they didn't want to get their hopes up until there was an official announcement.

'We couldn't go yet anyway, not until all our affairs are straightened out,' Mog mused. 'But what a wonderful thing to look forward to!'

That evening after Mog had gone off to bed, Vera and Belle discussed it further.

'I can hardly believe Mog was so excited about it,' Belle said.

'I think going back to Seven Dials did it,' Vera said thoughtfully. 'I noticed she looked horrified some of the time, like she thought she might end up there again.'

'Maybe,' Belle said. 'When this place is sold it will be the first time in her life she's ever had more than a few shillings of her own. She's also aware that she's got the responsibility to make it work for her. I expect she thinks it will go further in New Zealand. Will it?'

'I'd say a great deal further,' Vera said. 'My father seems to think there will be something of a boom in New Zealand when the war's over. Not straight away obviously, but in the next two or three years. Russell is tiny, Belle, it's had a shocking past, but that history makes it appealing to visitors. And of course there's the sailing, fishing and the lovely scenery. Pop's farsighted. He started the bakery with next to nothing and built it up; if he thinks visitors will come for holidays, then I'd be inclined to put my shirt on it. But even if you find Russell is too sleepy for you both, you can always go to Auckland, Wellington or Christchurch.'

Belle smiled at her friend. She had worked a small miracle on her and Mog, brought them out of themselves and given them new hope.

'We're going to miss you so much after you've gone,' she sighed. 'You've cheered us both up, you've given us so much to think about. I can't thank you enough.'

'It won't be goodbye, only au revoir,' Vera grinned. 'Anyway, we've still got tomorrow.'

Across London in St John's Wood, Noah was in his study typing up an article for a magazine when Lisette came in. She had put on a little weight after giving birth to Rose, but she was still a very pretty woman with her lustrous dark hair, creamy skin and delicate features. Noah had always considered her to be the personification of French elegance, and today he thought she looked good enough to eat in her cream and brown striped dress.

'Come to distract me?' he asked.

'Would you welcome distraction?' she said in her delight-fully accented English.

'Always, from you,' he said, holding out his arms for her to come and sit on his lap.

She ruffled his wavy hair with her fingers. 'Theese needs cutting,' she said. 'It is like a bush.'

Noah laughed. 'Is that all you came to say?'

'No, I was thinking about Etienne,' she said. 'What proof is there that 'e is dead?'

'Jimmy got a letter from a comrade about him getting the Croix de Guerre.'

'Yes, I understand that, but the Engleesh always seem to think that honour only goes to Frenchmen when they die in battle. That isn't so.'

'Isn't it? But surely the man who sent the letter must know if Etienne survived?'

' 'Ow would he? You of all people must understand that stories get twisted and added to as they get retold,' she said. 'If Etienne had received such an honour on 'is death, I believe the French army would 'ave written to you immedi-ately. That medal is a very special one, it means great honour.'

'We've got no way of knowing if Etienne got around to informing anyone that I was to be contacted. The French army were late in getting to the lines at Ypres. The assault had already been delayed because of that. You, my sweet little wife, have no idea of the confusion at such times. Even the best-laid plans go awry.'

'I think you should try and get confirmation one way or another,' she said. 'If 'e is dead, then 'is affairs will need to be put in order. But if 'e is alive, 'e won't contact Belle because 'e thinks she is taking care of Jimmy. 'E will have no way of knowing Jimmy is dead now.'

'Did I ever tell you that you are a very caring, clever woman, as well as a very beautiful one?' Noah said.

'Not often enough,' she laughed, kissing his nose. 'Belle and Mog are making plans for their future, and from what you 'ave told me, Belle 'as grieved long over Etienne. If 'e is dead, then 'is farm in Marseille should go to her, and if 'e is alive, then maybe she should go to 'im.'

'What if he is alive and badly wounded like Jimmy was? Wouldn't that be even worse for her?'

'Should we be the people to decide that?' She raised one black eyebrow questioningly. 'And you, Noah, you are 'is friend. Don't you want to know if 'e needs 'elp?'

'Well, yes. Until you brought this up I didn't question whether he was really dead. Tomorrow I will make some inquiries. But we must not give Belle false hope. This is just between us until we know for certain, either way.'

Lisette held his face between her hands and kissed him on the lips. 'Je vais garder l'espoir d'un regroupement romantique, mon chéri.'

Chapter Twenty-Nine

The bells were ringing out all over to London to celebrate that the war was over. People were out on the streets shouting, laughing and hugging one another in shared joy.

Although Mog and Belle felt happiness and huge relief it was all over at last, and had gone out on the street earlier to add their voices to the gathering joyful throng, like so many others who had lost husbands, sons and brothers, they hadn't got the heart for any wild celebrations.

They had spent their day sorting and packing, and once that was done they sat by the fire together and talked about the good times before the war. Tomorrow, 12 November, they would be leaving the Railway for good.

A gentleman by the name of Charles Wyatt wanted to buy it, and as he was anxious to start trading as soon as possible, Mog was renting it to him as a temporary measure until Probate was settled. When everything was finalized her solicitor would act on her behalf to exchange contracts with Wyatt, and then pass on the proceeds of the sale to Mog.

Thanks to Noah and his knowledge of business, it had worked out well, as Mog would be getting rent from Wyatt until the sale. He was delighted that he could move in, and Mog and Belle could move away knowing the building was in safe hands. Wyatt had already purchased all the stock in the bar and cellar, and most of Mog's furniture.

They had decided that New Zealand was where they wanted to go. After Vera left they discussed it endlessly. Oddly enough, it was Mog who wanted to go the most; she claimed she'd never had an adventure in her life and never been on any ship, apart from the river boat on the Thames.

Belle had brought up many counter-arguments – that Mog might be seasick the whole way, that she might find it dull living in a small, isolated place with no theatres, big shops, trams and markets. This wasn't because she herself didn't want to go, but she wanted to be absolutely certain Mog knew what she was letting herself in for.

But Mog just laughed. 'I've only been to two or three theatres in my whole life, in fact I've spent most of my life indoors, cooking and cleaning. I want to see new places, try food I've never tasted before. I really love the idea of starting all over again.'

Noah was very shocked when they told him what they intended to do. He said it seemed so drastic, and couldn't they wait a couple more years? But when he saw they were serious about it he admitted he was being selfish, because he knew he was going to miss them. He did agreed that New Zealand would be a much pleasanter country to live in, with no bitter winters, and that it would be good for them to leave the past behind. But he made Mog promise that when her financial affairs were sorted out, she would put some money aside just in case they ever wanted to come home.

All Mog's favourite things, items she and Garth had bought or were given as wedding presents, including a velvet button-back chair, her sewing machine, an ornate mahogany dressing table, chest of drawers and their bed, were being taken into storage until they could be shipped to New Zealand. Belle had kept only the very smallest of keepsakes, and her millinery blocks and steamer.

For now they were moving into a beautiful apartment in St John's Wood. It belonged to a friend of Noah's, who had gone to America and was anxious to have someone reliable

449

there to look after it. If everything went to plan they'd be leaving for New Zealand in February.

'I'd forgotten how cold it can be in this place,' Mog grumbled, pulling a shawl around her shoulders and huddling closer to the fire in the living room. 'But we'll be beautifully warm from tomorrow. Imagine us living in a place with heat in every room. I never saw the like before.'

Belle smiled. The apartment block they were moving into had a boiler in the basement which sent up hot water to heat radiators in all the apartments. Mog thought this was miraculous; she couldn't really believe she wouldn't be called on to stoke the boiler.

'A kitchen full of light and a huge bath with constant hot water too,' Belle reminded her. 'We won't know ourselves. And we can see more of Lisette and the children.'

'Are you sure you don't want to go and see what's going on out there?' Mog thumbed towards the window. The noise had grown steadily louder all day as people up the street had joined together for a party. There had been banging on the pub door too, despite the notice pinned to it explaining why it was closed. It seemed very odd to hear such commotion; Blackheath was usually such a quiet, genteel place.

Belle winced. 'No, I don't. It's cold and I'd sooner be in here with you and remember all the good times.'

Mog smiled. 'We had a lot,' she said. 'My wedding, then you opening the shop. Do you remember when this whole room was full of hats, feathers and artificial flowers? Then there was your wedding. And Garth got so drunk I had to leave him down on the bar floor all night.'

Belle laughed. They had tried to get him upstairs but failed because he was a dead weight.

She remembered the lovemaking with Jimmy that night too. He was so nervous she'd had to undress him. He'd scuttled under the bedclothes to hide his nakedness, yet he'd watched her undressing with eyes full of wonder.

'Your body is so beautiful,' he said in such an awed tone it made her eyes fill with tears. 'How did I get so lucky to have such a treasure?'

'Because,' she said filling two glasses with the champagne she'd rescued from the bar downstairs, and holding one of them to his lips to drink, 'someone up there knew what a good man you are and what a bad girl I can be, and decided you had to rescue me.'

As he drank the champagne, his hand reached out to caress her breasts. She had been afraid he would grab at her and remind her of moments in her past she wanted to forget. But his touch was sensitive and erotic, and she was instantly aroused. When she slid into bed beside him and her skin met his, he moaned with pleasure and enfolded her in his arms.

'I've been imagining this moment for months,' he said before he kissed her.

That first time was fast and furious, yet there was such tenderness in his touch, love in every fevered kiss. And although it was over too soon for her, she sensed that she'd only had the hors d'oeuvre and the banquet was yet to come.

How right she was. The next time he was only intent on pleasing her, the pace was slow and sensual, and he put his hand over her mouth because she was making so much noise.

They had a fit of helpless giggles about it later, and pulled the eiderdown over their heads so Garth and Mog wouldn't hear. She doubted she would ever experience such joy again in her lifetime. Or feel such sorrow that the war changed them both for ever.

Mog still had many moments when she cried over losing Garth. But the excitement of starting a new life in

New Zealand and all the packing and other jobs to be done had helped to distract her. She had bravely said that when she closed the door of the Railway for the last time, she wasn't going to cry any more, just smile at the lovely memories Garth had left her with.

They were still hearing of neighbours dying from the flu, and it was frightening to read in the newspapers that it had spread all over the world. But for today the end of the war was the only subject on everyone's lips, rationing, bombing and other hardships all put aside because soon all the men who had survived would be coming home.

On 12 January 1919 Noah arrived home late. Lisette was sitting by the fire in the sitting room doing some mending.

'You are very late,' she said. 'But I kept your dinner warm. Did you 'ave any luck?'

'None,' he said dejectedly. 'Another wild goose chase. I hate to say this to you, Lisette, but your lot don't seem able to keep tabs on anyone. Not even one of their heroes.'

They had got firm confirmation a week before Christmas that Etienne had received his medal while still alive. Included was the citation which said exactly what he had got it for, and that had been the same day that he rescued Jimmy. Noah had intended to tell Belle in time so that she could talk to Mog, explain what Etienne meant to her, and then they could all celebrate together on Christmas Day.

But then just two days later he received an official letter from Etienne's commanding officer informing him, as next of kin, that Sergeant Carrera was missing, presumed dead. This had happened in late October, but there was no explanation as to why Noah hadn't been informed earlier.

To have his hopes built up and then crushed so shortly afterwards was terrible. If it hadn't been for Lisette pointing out that Etienne was only 'presumed' dead, Noah would have given up then and there.

Lisette hadn't seen the battlefields. Like most people who hadn't witnessed the carnage, she imagined the dead were all lined up in neat rows, evidence of their identity noted, then buried with prayers.

Noah knew it wasn't like that at all. Hundreds of men were blown to so many pieces their body parts were scattered to the four winds. Others had sunk so deep into the mud they buried themselves. Many of the dead were found to have no identification on them. And as a senior officer had told Noah out there, 'They are dead. We can't help them, and we have to concentrate on saving the wounded who might survive.'

But Lisette kept on insisting that Etienne could be badly injured in a hospital, or he could have been taken prisoner. She urged Noah to say nothing to Belle yet, but in the New Year he must try to find out more.

Both Noah and Lisette were anxious to know the truth before Belle and Mog booked their passage. But the days went by and all Noah's renewed efforts came to nothing. He made telephone calls and wrote dozens of letters, but the letters weren't answered and on the telephone he was always directed to someone else.

Then Belle booked the passage to New Zealand, and now, as the day of their departure drew ever closer, she and Mog could talk of nothing but buying a trunk, and which clothes they should take and which they should leave behind. Mog had bought enough dress material, sewing cotton and buttons to take with them to make dresses for half the female population of Russell.

Today Noah had had an interview with someone from the Red Cross who dealt with prisoners of war. All he could say was that it was far more likely Etienne was dead than alive, but that he would look into it.

'France is in chaos, Noah,' Lisette said soothingly. 'There are so many men unaccounted for, you know this. Some soldiers 'ave gone home, others still 'ave duties. But your letters, they will be passed on, and soon they will come into the hands of someone who knows what 'appened.'

'But Belle will be leaving England in a month. They have a passage booked. What if I find he is alive and she's already gone?'

He didn't believe Etienne was alive, not now. A man might choose to disappear if he had something to hide, but Etienne was a war hero, and if he had survived that last assault, someone would know.

Lisette went over to Noah and put her arms around him. 'It won't matter if she's gone. If 'e is alive and 'alf the man I believe 'im to be, 'e'll go and claim 'er,' she said. 'Now, come with me and I will get your dinner.'

'Don't cry, ducks,' Mog said to Belle as the HMS *Stalwart* weighed anchor and began to move slowly away from the dock at Southampton. 'We can always come back if we don't like it. But you and I are made of strong stuff. We'll make a good life for ourselves out there, you'll see.'

Belle wiped her eyes and smiled at Mog. 'I'm not sad at going. I'll miss Noah, Lisette and the children, but there isn't anyone else. This just reminds me of going off to France with Miranda.'

That wasn't strictly true. She had thought about Miranda earlier, remembering how excited they'd been as the ship left Dover. But what had really made her cry was thinking about the trip from New York to New Orleans with Etienne. She'd had her first glass of champagne with him on her sixteenth birthday, and she thought she was in love with him and tried to seduce him. There was a kind of irony in that all these years later she was on another ship, this time going right to the other side of the world, yet even though he was dead he was still dominating her thoughts.

'Let's go and unpack and make our cabin feel like home,' Mog suggested. 'It's cold enough to freeze a witch's tit out here.'

Belle laughed then. She hadn't heard Mog use that expression since they left Seven Dials and she became set on being ladylike.

'Only another two days and we'll be there,' Belle sighed. 'I can't wait to walk down a street, to look in a shop, to see grass and trees. And won't it be good not to have to listen to any more people complaining?'

It was April now, and they had been through every kind of weather. The first storm of the voyage in the Bay of Biscay had been a baptism of fire for Mog when there had been waves as big as church steeples crashing over the ship. But although she turned green, she hadn't become really ill.

There had been winds so strong it was impossible to walk without hanging on to the ship's rail. They'd had hailstones as big as marbles which rattled on the decks like gunfire, rain and thick fog, and sometimes the sun was so intense that in just a few minutes it burned any exposed skin.

As they drew closer to the equator the sultry heat made it impossible to sleep at night, and there were tropical storms too. But it was cooler now, still stuffy in the cabin, but pleasant to walk on the deck when the wind dropped.

Boredom had been the biggest trial. The days seemed endless with nothing to do. They had both brought embroidery and knitting with them, and they read books, played cards and waited for meals, but it was being cooped up, and the lack of exercise, that prevented them enjoying what should have been like a relaxing holiday.

There were of course many other passengers to talk to: a group of officers, all wounded, but not so badly they needed to be on a hospital ship, around forty immigrants like themselves, and some New Zealanders who had sailed for England before the war and had to remain there because of the danger to shipping. But although most of these people were pleasant enough to while away an hour or two with, none of them were terribly interesting, and some were downright dull. Because Belle and Mog were stuck together in such a confined space, they often snapped at each other. They both had to make a concerted effort to give each other some privacy and time alone.

But now the voyage was nearly over, past irritations had vanished. Mog was being positively girlish, flirting with the ship's crew and beaming at everyone.

They disembarked in Auckland to warm sunshine. To them it felt like a spring day back in England, and it was strange to think it was autumn here. The small guest house they found about half a mile from the docks was a pretty clapboard house with a view of the sea from their room.

They had five days there before boarding the *Clansman* to sail to the Bay of Islands, and their delight at last to be able to walk around on dry land was almost intoxicating. Everyone they met wanted to talk about England to them. Even those who had been born in New Zealand all seemed to have English or Scottish parents or grandparents. People were friendly and helpful, advising them on places to visit, local customs, items they might need to buy in Auckland that they wouldn't be able to get in Russell. They were regaled with stories about the Maoris and their culture, something they found fascinating and knew nothing about before. Then there were the tales of the hardships early settlers had endured when they came out on immigrant ships in the last century. They were also shown a great deal of sympathy for losing their husbands.

In many ways New Zealand wasn't so different from England. It didn't have the very old buildings, it wasn't so crowded, and they hadn't seen anywhere they'd call a real slum, even if the locals considered them to be so. The climate was similar to back home, people had the same kind of priorities and beliefs. Yet the Spanish flu had killed people here too on the other side of the world. Their landlady told them around 6,700 people had died, but that she'd been lucky that everyone she knew who got it had survived. She described how the trams stopped running for fear of spreading infection, and that carts, trains and trucks were pressed into service as hearses.

The effects of the war were very similar to those back in England too. Thousands of New Zealanders had enlisted for the same reasons as British men, and as high a proportion had died. And just like at home they saw men with missing limbs, and blinded and disfigured, out on the streets of Auckland. They were told that most of them were casualties of Gallipoli and that there were over 4,500 of them. A further 2,700 had been killed. But that wasn't all; as many again who had been wounded in France had not been brought back yet. Despite almost everyone here having lost a family member, however, the New Zealanders seemed very stoic about it, and took great pride in the courage of their men. Both Mog and Belle were touched, too, by their sympathy for everyone in Britain, because they'd had to cope with not only huge numbers of deaths and casualties, but also bombing, food shortages and rationing.

'I feel as if I've come to the place I was supposed to live,' Mog said one night as they were preparing for bed. 'Don't you just love it that they don't seem to have pokers up their arses?'

Belle roared with laughter at that. Mog meant the seeming lack of class distinctions. Belle wasn't entirely sure that this was a general attitude; they were after all staying among ordinary people. But she was hopeful it would be the same in Russell, because she remembered Vera had always been rather puzzled and amused by the snobbish attitude of the other women drivers in France.

'You'd better not bandy the word "arse" around until we know people well,' she warned Mog.

As the *Clansman* headed into the Bay of Islands, both Mog and Belle gasped at the beauty of it. They might have had it described by Vera and seen pictures of it in Auckland, but the reality of it was far more astounding. The sea really was turquoise and so clear they could look down and see fish clearly. The trees on all the little islands were a vivid green and grew right down to the water's edge.

They had seen dolphins as they sailed here; they had come and played around the bows of the ship, lifting their shiny heads out of the water and opening their mouths as if smiling in welcome, and that had moved both Belle and Mog almost to tears. They had seen a huge whale in the distance too, and all this had been so exciting, sights they'd never expected to see. Yet to see this magnificent bay spread before them, which outshone all the wonders of HMS *Stalwart*'s ports of call, was truly humbling.

'If we can't be happy here then we won't be happy anywhere,' Mog said, wiping an emotional tear from her eye.

As the ship approached the jetty at Russell they could see

a great many people gathered there waiting. They had already been told that the north had no proper roads, and that a ship was the only way to get there. The *Clansman* was the town's weekly lifeline. It brought not only passengers but mail, food supplies and other goods. The first European settlers had come here, and it was once intended to be the capital city of New Zealand, because of its splendid and safe natural harbour, but in the end Auckland was chosen because of Russell's isolation.

'There's Vera!' Belle exclaimed, pointing her out to Mog. 'I wonder how she knew we'd be coming today?'

'Well, it looks like the whole town turns out whenever the ship comes in,' Mog said. 'But look at those pretty little houses! What a picture it is!'

It certainly was a picture, a clutch of pretty little white or cream clapboard houses which looked like dolls' houses. Up behind the town the wooded hills rose up as if protecting it, and in front of the houses was a narrow strip of sandy beach. Dozens of small boats bobbed up and down at their moorings, and gulls were wheeling overhead, hoping to snatch an easy meal from one of the fishermen.

Vera was jumping up and down with excitement even before the ship was moored and a gangway fixed to the jetty. She was wearing a green print dress, her red curly hair loose on her shoulders and gleaming in the sun. An older, stout, short woman was with her, who they thought perhaps was her mother.

Finally people began to file off the ship and they joined the queue. They had already been told their trunk and other luggage would be placed on the jetty after everyone had disembarked.

'Belle, Mog!' Vera yelled as she elbowed her way through people on the jetty. 'Welcome to Russell!'

*

459

It was around four in the afternoon when they arrived in Russell and the remainder of the day passed as if they'd walked into a party where they knew no one but found they were the guests of honour. Vera and her mother, Mrs Reid, who immediately said she was to be called Peggy, took them home to the family bakery, where Mr Reid – Don, as he wanted to be called – was kneading a mountain of dough for the next morning's bread. He broke off from this to plant a kiss on both Belle and Mog's cheeks, apologized for his flour-covered hands and said they were to think of his home as theirs.

Peggy was the kind of woman who could do ten things at once and talk at the same time. While laying the kitchen table for tea, she shouted through the back door at a man to go and collect their belongings on a cart. She took a fantastic-looking tart with a latticed top out of the pantry, served up five large portions and added a dollop of custard to each. She asked about the trip from Auckland while making a pot of tea, and almost by sleight of hand the cups and saucers appeared on the table.

'Right, sit down now,' she said. 'I won't stand on ceremony with you as from what Vera's told me about you I already think of you as family. This is just something to tide you over as there's people coming to supper soon who are dying to meet you.'

Vera rolled her eyes, which Belle felt was a silent message that she knew her mother was a bit exhausting on first meeting, but she would ease up soon.

Don came in then, having washed the flour off his hands and taken off his apron, and his smile was as warm as his bakery. 'Vera told us what a good time you gave her in London,' he said. 'She's as pleased as punch you've come over here to live, but you're going to find it very slow after London.'

'We like slow,' Mog said and took a spoonful of the tart. 'Oh my goodness, this is lovely,' she exclaimed.

'We were happy to leave London,' Belle said. 'There's nothing left there for us. It's beautiful here, and we intend to make a go of it.'

'Tomorrow I'll show you all round,' Peggy said. 'That won't exhaust you, it only takes half an hour. And that would be the long tour,' she laughed, and her big bosom shook with it.

Belle laughed too. She had a feeling laughter was something that was in plentiful supply in this house.

They had barely drunk their tea and eaten the delicious tart when people started to arrive: first the couple that ran the post office, Frieda and Mike Lamb, who told them they had both been born in England but had come to New Zealand as small children with their parents. They were around their mid-forties and had met at school in Christchurch.

'It's good to have new people coming here to live,' Frieda said as she plonked a plate of cooked sausages down on the table. 'Our folks in Christchurch thought we were crazy coming here. They said it was all right for a holiday, but we'd be bored and fed up in no time. But we've been here ten years now and we haven't got time to be bored.'

Women came in thick and fast after that, all bringing a dish of food. Vera said that was customary when there was a party or gathering. She also explained that their menfolk would be along after the 'six o'clock slurp'. When Mog and Belle looked puzzled at this she explained that the pubs closed at six in the evening all over New Zealand, a law which was supposed to make men stay at home with their wives and families in the evenings. But as she laughingly explained, all it did was make the men drink as much as they could in the last hour, then go home to fall asleep.

Yet drunk though many of the men were, they still came, and Belle wondered how she would ever remember which man was which woman's husband, or anyone's name as there were so many of them. They all wanted to know what she and Mog intended to do here, and each one of them had a different idea about what sort of business was needed. Belle's dress was admired by all the women, though to her it was drab, just grey cotton with a thin white stripe, a sensible, everyday dress which was ideal for travelling in, and made by Mog. But compared with the clothes worn by the women here it did look stylish because it fitted properly. Their dresses were shapeless, and she suspected they were either bought readymade or run up by someone with only rudimentary knowledge of dressmaking. She guessed that most of these women had no concept of fashion, and it crossed her mind that perhaps this could be an opening for her and Mog.

The party spilled out into the back yard, but it wasn't until it grew dark and Peggy and Don began lighting oil lamps that Belle and Mog became aware there was no electricity in Russell. They didn't remark on it, partly because they felt they ought to have known such a remote spot wouldn't have it, but mostly because it really didn't matter to them. They'd both grown up with oil lamps, and even back home they hadn't progressed to buying an electric iron or a fire as so many people had. More worrying was finding there were only outside privies, one echo of the past they didn't relish much.

Later candles were lit and placed in jam jars in the back yard, a gramophone was wound up, an Irish jig played and an old man entertained everyone with Irish dancing.

'So how is Russell so far?' Vera asked when she finally managed to get a moment alone with Belle out in the back yard. 'Too much, too soon, I expect. I did suggest we held off on the party until you'd been here a day or two. But as you might have noticed, Ma does everything fast.'

'We are touched by such a warm welcome,' Belle said. 'I like that it's so informal too. Everyone is so nice.'

'You might change your mind about that and decide they are just plain nosy soon,' Vera said. 'Don't tell anyone apart from me anything you don't want spread around Russell. My mother is one of the worst for that, so be warned.'

'You haven't told her about my past?'

'Of course not,' Vera cut her short. 'Anything you told me in France stays with me alone. I told her Mog was the housekeeper in your mother's guest house and she brought you up. I said too that you learned millinery in Paris. Trust me, Belle. I valued your confidences, I will never tell anyone about them.'

Belle thanked her and assured her she did trust her, then asked if there was any further news of her brothers.

'Last time we heard they were waiting to go on a troop ship. As we've heard nothing more we think they must be on it now. We are so thankful they made it. Spud was wounded at Ypres but nothing serious, a bit of shrapnel in his arm. Tony said he's got nothing worse than flea bites. So you'll meet them soon, but for now you've got their room, which Ma has spent the last few weeks getting all smartened up for you.'

It was after midnight when they finally got to bed. Their room was large, with twin beds, each covered in a brightly coloured patchwork quilt. Like in the rest of the family house, the furniture was old and battered, but it had a very comfortable feel about it. The walls had recently been painted a pale green, there was an embroidered cloth over the small table by the window, and on it was a vase of white, daisy-like flowers.

Their trunk and other belongings had been put in the room and as Mog unpacked their nightdresses she looked across at Belle undressing and smiled.

'We did the right thing, it already feels like home. But let's find a place of our own really quickly, shall we?'

Belle knew exactly what she meant. Mog wanted her own things around her, to cook her own meals and have her own door which she could shut to be alone when she felt like it. Peggy and Don were the nicest of people but it was plain to see that they would become wearing.

'You are such a nest builder,' Belle said fondly. 'Don't worry, tomorrow we'll make it clear that's our first priority.'

The next day Peggy proudly showed them around. First to Christ Church, the oldest church in New Zealand, and the police station which was once the customs house but looked far too pretty a building to be used for either purpose. They saw the canning factory by the beach, and watched for a while as fishing boats came in with their catch. The Duke of Marlborough public house right on the shoreline was an impressive size for such a small town, and they dropped in to see Mr and Mrs Clow at their boarding house next to it. The piece of waste ground that lay between York Street where the Reids had their bakery and Church Street was still known as the swamp even though there were a couple of houses built on it and cows grazing. Peggy told them that in the old days when Russell had been known as the hell hole of the Pacific because of the wildness of the whalers who came and drank here, there had only been a few grog shops and shacks by the shore, then behind them nothing but mangrove swamp all the way back to the forested hills that surrounded the town.

There really wasn't a great deal to see apart from the post

office which sold a variety of goods, the Reids' bakery, a general store, a butcher's, a small hotel and various workshops. Peggy had waved her arm in the general direction of a few shacks at the back of the town and said, 'Natives live there.' Belle had seen quite a few brown-skinned people as they were walking around, some of whom had greeted Peggy, but she hadn't introduced them. Belle was dying to know what the situation was between the Maoris and the settlers but she thought it best not to ask Peggy, thinking Vera would give her a more balanced view.

They were going back to the bakery when Mog noticed a small house on Robertson Street that looked abandoned and neglected and she asked Peggy about it.

'Jack Phillips, a shoemaker, lived there,' she said. 'He died two years ago.'

'So is it for sale or to rent?' Mog asked.

'Henderson the solicitor would know,' Peggy said.

As Peggy had to get back to the bakery and relieve Vera who had been working with her father since early that morning, Belle said they would go and see Mr Henderson straight away if she would direct them where to find him.

'No time like the present,' Mog said cheerily as Peggy pointed out his house.

'She wasn't very enthusiastic,' Belle said as Peggy left them to go home. 'I wonder why?'

'You can ask Vera later,' Mog said. 'But my guess is that she's the kind that loves lots of people around her and is just a bit disappointed that we are already talking about a home of our own the second day here.'

Within twenty minutes Mog and Belle had the key to the empty house and were letting themselves in. Like all the buildings here it was wooden, the outside very plain and desperately in need of some replacement clapboards and painting. The steps up to the front door were rotting away and as they opened the door a musty smell made them both wrinkle their noses. A small square hall had four doors going off it and a narrow staircase. The room to the left had been the shoemaker's workroom and was still littered with scraps of leather, cobbler's lasts and a long work bench. But it had two windows, as did all the downstairs rooms, one at the front and one to the side, which would make it very light once the windows had been cleaned. The room to the right of the hall was a parlour crammed with very old, worn-out furniture. At the back to the left was a bedroom, again so full of old furniture they could barely get into the room. To the right was an antiquated and filthy kitchen. But there was a door leading from it to a garden. It looked as if it had been well cared for until Mr Phillips' death, as there were flowering shrubs, rose bushes and what looked like a vegetable garden, all overgrown with long grass and weeds.

Upstairs there was just one big room, the windows set into the roof at either end. Apart from an old iron bed with a stained mattress there was nothing else up there, and they assumed the owner had lived downstairs for many years.

'I can live with the outside privy,' Mog said, though she wrinkled her nose. 'But I can't be doing with getting water from a pump outside. All the furniture needs burning too. But it is light and bright. And the floorboards seem sound.' She jumped up and down to illustrate this.

'I suppose we could build a bathroom on to the back or the side and a plumber would be able to pipe water into the kitchen too,' Belle said thoughtfully. 'We could get a veranda built along the front of the house. Put up one of those white picket fences. It could be lovely. And we could use the workroom: you do dressmaking, I'll make hats and we could sell haberdashery too.'

They were looking at each other speculatively when they heard Vera call out.

'Come on up,' Belle yelled.

Vera came running up the stairs. 'I used to come here quite a lot when I was a kid, Mr Phillips made us all shoes,' she said breathlessly. 'His wife was nice, she used to make a fuss of us because they didn't have any kids of their own. She died before the war. It's a real mess now though.'

'But it's got possibilities,' Mog said, her small face alight with enthusiasm. 'Mr Henderson said he'd just got notification from the nephew who inherited it that he would get whatever he could for it as he needs money now. I have to make an offer.'

'Well, nobody else will want it. Everyone is down in the dumps over the war and the flu, and no one's got any money.'

It was the first time in Mog's life she'd had money, a great deal more than she ever dreamed of. But just the same, she didn't intend to be reckless with it.

'How hard will it be to get someone to fix it up?' she asked. 'We'd need a bathroom and a range in the kitchen to give us hot water. Then all the outside and the roof needs to be made weatherproof.'

'There will be men queuing at the door to do the work,' Vera said. 'But what you need to think about is whether you are sure you want to stay here in Russell. You haven't been here long enough yet to really know that.'

'I knew I wanted to stay here the minute I stepped off the boat,' Mog said. 'It feels right for me. But I don't know about Belle. You young people need to be somewhere with a bit more going on.'

Vera looked questioningly at Belle. 'Do you feel that?'

'We haven't been here long enough for me to even think about it. But I like the peace and quiet. Anyway, it's Mog who has the money to buy a house, not me,' she shrugged. 'It's her decision.'

'Yes, it's up to me whether I buy this house or not,' Mog said. 'But what I'm trying to say is that it doesn't mean you have to be tied here too, Belle. It will be your home, but you must plan what you want to do with your life. I'd hate it if I thought you stayed with me because you felt you had to.'

Belle frowned at her. 'But we planned to build up a business together.'

'I know, and I'd like that, of course I would. But there are no young men here, Belle. I don't want you ending up an old maid. I'd like to see you marry again.'

'You'll wait till hell freezes over then,' Belle laughed. 'I'm never going to love another man.'

'I think that too, now,' Mog said. 'But that's just because we've only been widowed a few months. I'm getting on, though; you on the other hand are young and beautiful. Jimmy wouldn't have wanted you to spend the rest of your life alone.'

'Mog's not quite right about there being no young men here,' Vera said. 'My brothers will be back soon, and there's another couple of lads due home too. But I can't imagine you going for any of them, Belle. Look at me, I'm a good example of what happens to the flowers of Russell! I'm seen as an old maid already!'

'Then maybe you two should clear off to Auckland,' Mog said.

Vera laughed. 'I am so tempted to do that. Ma drives me mad. It was bad enough before I went to France, but much worse since I came home. I don't want to work in the bakery for evermore.'

She began singing a song, 'How Ya Gonna Keep Them Down on the Farm, after They've Seen Paree?'

Belle spluttered with laughter. 'Did you just make that up?'

'No, not me. Some of the Americans at the hospital used to sing it. They'd heard it in a music hall in New York before they left for France. I heard it played on a gramophone too, apparently it's really popular in America. But that's another thing you'll find here, we're very cut off from the rest of the world. Music, fashion, art, new books, we don't get to hear about any of it.'

'I don't mind that,' Mog said.

Vera sighed and looked shamefaced. 'I feel bad that I didn't warn you about any of that, but you see, I didn't notice it myself until I got back, and by then you were on your way.'

Mog put an arm round each of the girls and drew them to her. 'Well, we're here now, and I like it. But if it's too dull for you two after seeing Paree, then you must find a place you like better.'

'I'm not running off without giving it a good crack of the whip,' Belle said firmly. 'I like it here too, and before we start considering alternatives, let's look objectively at what we could do here.'

They spent about an hour looking round the house and Mog made a list of things which needed doing to it. 'I'm going to mull it over for a few days,' she said as she locked up before leaving. 'I'll need to find out what it's worth and how much all the repairs will cost before I decide.'

April slipped into May with them barely noticing how quickly the time was passing. Mog enjoyed helping Don in the bakery, and she'd shared some of her cake recipes with him and was delighted to find the finished products not only sold quickly but people came back for more. With Vera's help, she had got prices for all the work that needed to be done on the old Phillips place, and once she had it all settled in her head, offered Mr Henderson a hundred pounds for the property. She expected him to be affronted at such a low price, but he accepted it cheerfully and threw in all the legal costs for the purchase too.

Belle took up painting in water-colours, and though it was often a little chilly sitting for long periods down at the beach, she liked painting the sea and the boats so much that she hardly noticed it. Often when she was painting down on the shore she realized that there had never been a time in her life when she'd felt so relaxed and peaceful. Even during the period before Garth and Mog got married, when she and Mog had lived in a room in Blackheath while Garth arranged to buy the Railway, there had always been tension. Back then it was because they were both striving to become ladies, so they would be accepted in the village. Then Belle got her shop and had the anxiety of that. She had been very happy, marrying Jimmy, making hats, seeing her business grow, but there had never been long, lazy periods of doing nothing like there was here.

The war had taken a great deal out of everyone, whatever their occupation or personal circumstances, with fear of losing loved ones, grief when they did, rationing, bombing and all the other hardships, including the horror of the flu that came at the end. But all that was over now; Belle had read in a newspaper that it was said to be 'the war to end all wars'. She hoped so. She also felt that she and Mog had finally found a place where they could be themselves, where they didn't have to pretend to be ladies, or be afraid to voice their opinions. Here they could put aside the sorrow and the hurts of the past for ever.

*

Spud, Tony and two other young Russell men finally arrived home at the end of May, and the whole town joined in the celebrations.

Vera's younger brothers were very like her in nature, both outgoing, warm and friendly, with a great sense of humour. They were both much taller than Vera, with brown hair, but had the same duck egg-blue eyes. Everyone remarked that they had left Russell as mere boys and come back as men.

Peggy was horrified to find that what Spud had called mere scratches on his right arm and leg were in fact very ugly scars, but Spud laughed them off and pointed out that he'd been lucky he hadn't got gangrene as he'd fallen into deep mud and lain there for hours before he was taken to a medical post.

Mog and Belle had intended to wait to move into their house until the new stove they'd ordered from Auckland had arrived and been installed, but the boys' return changed their minds. It had become very crowded in Peggy and Don's house, and it seemed wrong to expect Spud and Tony to have to sleep on the living-room floor, however much they claimed they didn't mind.

But as the damaged clapboarding on their house had already been replaced and the roof mended, it was at least weatherproof. Clearing the house had been a hard, dirty job; they burned the rubbish and put the furniture and other objects they didn't want outside for anyone to help themselves. To their delight most of it vanished within a day. But they kept the sturdy Kauriwood kitchen table as once scrubbed of years of grime it looked good, along with the iron bedstead, which Belle and Vera rubbed down and painted white. They kept a couple of kitchen chairs too, a chest of drawers and the work bench. Mog sent a telegram to

Noah asking him to arrange for her stored furniture to be shipped out as soon as possible.

The inside walls of the house were matchboard covered in scrim. They had been told plastering wasn't practical in wooden houses, and anyway, scrim supported wallpaper much better. Downstairs there were holes in the match-boarding, but as the big upstairs room had remained intact, they got a man in to hang the only wallpaper available in the general store. It was rather dull, pale blue with a swirly design in cream, but once up it looked surprisingly pretty. With lino-leum down which they'd ordered from a store in Auckland along with a new mattress, which would come on the *Clansman*, they planned to live in that room while the rest of the work went on in the house.

Spud and Tony intended to get work on the fishing boats or at the cannery, but for the time being they were only too pleased to get paid work helping the carpenter on Mog's house, building the veranda, making cupboards and shelves in the kitchen and renewing the damaged matchboard and scrim.

'Well, here we are in our own house at last,' Mog said on the night of 2 June as they prepared to get into the iron bed they had to share.

In the light of the oil lamp the room looked very attract-ive, with dainty cream blinds made by Mog in the windows at either end, a couple of rag rugs given to them as presents by women in the town on the linoleum floor, and the bed made up with linen, blankets and an eiderdown they'd brought from England in their trunk.

'I love Peggy, but it will be wonderful not to be woken by her shouting to Don in the morning,' Belle said as she slipped on her nightdress. 'And the stove will be arriving this week too. No more going there for dinner.'

'Shame on you,' Mog reproved her. 'Peggy and Don are kind, lovely people. Sometimes you can be very ungracious.'

Belle grinned. She knew Mog felt exactly the same as she did, in fact she'd had a far harder time because she missed being able to cook meals, and she'd been the one who listened to Peggy wittering on about nothing, day in, day out. 'Well, I'm going to make her a lovely Sunday hat, to make up for my ungraciousness,' she said.

'Changing the subject,' Mog did the pursed-lip thing she always did when she was disapproving, 'shall we take the *Clansman* to Auckland soon to pick out some furniture? Peggy said it's not wise to choose a couch or armchairs from a catalogue as they might turn out to be as hard as rock.'

'Hmm.' Belle thought for a moment. 'I think we should stay until the house is nearly finished and see what else we need. There'll be curtain material, and I need some hat-making stuff too. We'll be there for a week, so it's best to get everything we're likely to need all at once.'

They got into bed and Belle turned out the oil lamp. 'It's good not to hear Don snoring,' she said into the darkness. 'He snored so loudly that the whole house reverberated with it.'

Mog put a hand on Belle's arm. 'You, my dear, are becoming crabby. You need a sweetheart.'

Belle giggled. 'Are you going to order me one from a catalogue?'

'Write down your requirements and I'll check if they have a suitable one in stock,' Mog responded, with laughter in her voice. 'So go to sleep now and dream about him.'

Belle lay awake for a long time after Mog had fallen asleep, mentally compiling a list as suggested. She thought she would write it down in the morning to make Mog laugh.

Tall, slim build, fair hair, blue eyes, but as she reeled physical characteristics off to herself she realized she was describing Etienne. Just thinking about that one night they'd spent together made her feel such an intense longing that tears came into her eyes. She knew she wasn't the kind of woman to live a chaste life, she wanted to be held, to be kissed, and enjoy the bliss of lovemaking. Mog was right; she was growing crabby, and this was the reason.

Vera had told her that in the summer lots of men came here to fish, but the chances were they'd be married. Spud was sweet on Belle, she had seen the way he looked at her, but he was too innocent for her, even if she could get over the idea of a man called something as daft as 'Spud'. She'd overheard his brother Tony talking to him about a French whore he'd been with. He was clearly captivated by the experience, yet the derogatory way he'd spoken about the girl had made Belle wince.

She had no difficulty in maintaining the correct demeanour for a widow in a social setting, but if she should ever find a man she could love, she knew she wouldn't be able to hide her past from him. Jimmy had been a rarity in that he'd accepted it, but even he had fallen back on scorning her after he was wounded.

Belle thought the possibility of meeting a man who was as worldly and non-judgmental as Etienne, and who like him was also kind, fun and a wonderful lover, was as unlikely as waking up tomorrow morning and finding an elephant standing outside the house. So perhaps she ought to accept that she'd already had her fair share of passion, and resign herself to becoming an old maid?

Chapter Thirty

The work progressed on the house far quicker once Belle and Mog were living there and keeping the men at it. The stove arrived and was duly installed by a specialist who lived across the bay in Paihia. He not only put in a tank to store heated water from it, but ran a pipe from the outside water supply to a new sink in the kitchen, and another one for waste water to the cesspit outside. He said he would gladly come back again when they'd extended the house and fit a bathroom.

The veranda was built from Kauri wood, with the rails and balustrade painted white. Cupboards and a dresser had been built in the kitchen and the chimney had been swept so they could light a fire when it was cold. But they were still waiting for the wallpapers they'd ordered from Auckland for the downstairs rooms, and Mog's furniture from England.

It was the promised arrival of the wallpaper that made Belle walk down to the jetty when the *Clansman* was due in. Most people met the ship every week, not necessarily because they were expecting ordered goods, or to meet someone who was coming in on it, but just because the ship was a link with the outside world.

It was raining heavily that afternoon, however, and even Peggy, who rarely missed a week, hadn't turned out. Belle was wearing a long black waterproof coat she'd bought from the general store, a sou'wester hat and a pair of gumboots because the unmade up roads had turned to a quagmire.

She liked the bay in any weather, and as she stood on the jetty and looked out over the choppy water which was as leaden as the sky above, she thought it had a dramatic beauty which was just as lovely in its own way as it was in sunshine. The rain was acting like a semi-diaphanous curtain, giving only a very hazy view beyond a few hundred yards, and she could hear the engines of the *Clansman* approaching but she couldn't see it yet.

It was likely that other people who had goods on the ship were listening for that sound. They were probably biding their time until the ship moored before they came down to collect their parcels. They might not even bother because of the rain; after all, the goods would be stored in the shipping office and could be picked up later when it stopped raining, or even tomorrow. Mog had said to leave theirs, adding that the wallpaper would be heavy and it certainly wasn't needed right away.

But for some reason Belle had felt compelled to come down.

The *Clansman*'s engines were growing louder. Belle peered towards the sound and thought she could just make out a dark shape behind the curtain of rain. Then suddenly there it was, the funnel belching out smoke, and she could even see the crew members on the decks preparing for mooring.

She smiled to herself, remembering how when she and Mog had come on the ship they had stood at the rail for most of the journey from Auckland. They had watched the sea curling back, white-tipped as the bows sliced through the blue-green water. They had laughed at themselves for being mesmerized by it, when they had completed a long sea voyage only days before, yet they couldn't help themselves. They wanted to see every inch of the coastline of this new land they'd come to.

476

The engines cut out and the ship glided towards the jetty under the skilful hands of Captain Farquahar. One of the crew leaped ashore, as graceful and sure-footed as a deer, to help the onshore men bring her gently in the last few feet and secure her.

Even then the passengers made no move to brave the rain. They huddled back under the meagre shelter of the forecastle, save for one man in a long raincoat and a trilby hat. He stood alone at the rail, a small suitcase in his hand.

He was looking right at Belle, and she wished she could see him better as she thought he must be someone she knew from the town. But the rain was driving into her face, and his was just a blur.

The gangway was lowered and secured, and suddenly people darted forward to leave the ship. It occurred to Belle then that it would be quite some time, maybe more than an hour, before her box of wallpaper would be unloaded. She could feel her clothes growing damp beneath her coat, maybe from water trickling down from the sou'wester or creeping in on the shoulder seams, and she felt cold and clammy. But something stopped her from turning away to go home.

Mr and Mrs Brewster, whom she had met on her first night in Russell, came rushing up the jetty from the ship, Mr Brewster trying to hold an umbrella over both their heads.

'Meeting someone, Mrs Reilly?' he called out.

'No, just collecting a parcel,' she said. Then, remembering Peggy had told her they'd gone off to Auckland two weeks ago for the imminent birth of their first grandchild, she asked, 'What did she have, a boy or a girl?'

'A fine healthy boy,' Mrs Brewster called out. 'Mother and baby doing fine, but we're glad to be back.'

They hurried on by, and other people rushed past her too. A few she knew by sight and smiled at, but there were others she'd never seen before. Further down the jetty the crew and other men from the shipping office were already unloading some crates of chickens from another gangway, and what had been a silent and deserted place was now like an ants' nest of activity.

The man in the trilby hat was coming up the jetty now, and his straight-backed bearing and graceful lope were so like Etienne's she felt a sudden tightness in her chest.

She pushed her sou'wester back off her face a little and wiped the rainwater away. He stopped, looking at her, then lifted his hat and smiled.

It was an everyday polite greeting, but only one man she'd ever seen had a smile like that.

'Etienne?' she mouthed.

'Belle,' he said, and coming towards her faster now, he swept off his hat, and she saw that fair hair she knew so well, the sharp cheekbones and the blue eyes.

She thought her mind was playing tricks on her. He was dead! How could it be him? But he was as real as she was, coming towards her.

In that second she understood why in romantic novels women fainted from shock, even though in the past she'd laughed at such an idea. Her heart was racing so fast she thought it could burst. It really was him.

'I imagined you meeting me in sunshine, dressed in your best finery,' he said with that French accent that had remained imprinted in her head. 'Not in a waterproof coat in the pouring rain with a face so pale you look like you might faint.'

'I do feel faint, from shock,' she said in a shaky voice. 'I was told you were killed in France.'

'Then Noah didn't tell you he traced me?'

She could only shake her head.

'You weren't waiting here for me?'

'No, I just came to collect a parcel.'

There were people going past them on both sides. The rain continued to pour down, and Belle lifted her hand and reached out to touch Etienne's cheek. It was cold, a slight stubble coming through, but by touching him she knew for certain she wasn't dreaming.

He took her hand and kissed the tips of her fingers. 'I told you once before that I would go through fire, flood and any peril to be with you,' he said, his voice trembling. 'Please tell me now if you have someone else, or don't feel the same about me, and I will get back on that ship and go.'

Nothing in her life had ever been as moving as his words. There was so much she wanted to ask, yet at the same time the only thing which was really important was that he was alive, and he'd come right across the world to find her.

She drew his hand to her lips and kissed it. 'There is no one else. You took my heart back in France and you still have it. But we can't stand here in the rain. Come home with me. We'll talk as we go.'

'Noah tracked me down in February, he told me you had just left England,' he said as they began the path along the path by the shore. 'I thought he would've written to you about it, but as he hasn't, I'd better explain. I wasn't killed at the time Jimmy was wounded; it seems that his friend who informed him of that imagined that the French only decorate their dead. I was very much alive then. Noah was told this – I believe he said it was just before Christmas – but then he got a letter a couple of days later saying I was reported missing, presumed dead.'

'Why didn't he tell me this?' Belle shook her head in puzzlement. 'Mog and I were with him at Christmas.'

'Yes, he told me that. It seems both he and Lisette felt there was no point in telling you about it if I did turn out to be dead. So they decided to have it verified, one way or another, before they said anything. Lisette thought I could've been taken as a prisoner of war.'

'Were you?'

'No. I was just wounded at Passchendaele. Mistakes can be made if a man isn't taken to a dressing station by his regiment's own stretcher bearers. It seems I was picked up by Canadians, stripped of my uniform because of the mud on me, and my personal belongings went astray and my regiment weren't informed because it was thought I was a French Canadian.'

'But that's awful! Couldn't you tell them who you were?'

'It was madness there,' Etienne shrugged. 'So many badly wounded, too few doctors and nurses, but I didn't realize then what they thought. All I cared about was that I was warm and dry again, and in a bed. It would have come to light very quickly, if I hadn't got the influenza. As it was, I was put in a quarantine ward in the hospital, and by all accounts I was delirious for days.'

'But you came through it,' she said breathlessly. 'That is so wonderful!'

He laughed. 'Yes, I thought so! It left me very weak, and I went home to Marseille to recuperate. I did ask the doctor at the hospital to inform my regiment, but it looks as if more mistakes were made with that. The war ended, France was in turmoil, hundreds of men missing, and I was staying with friends, not at my farm, all of which were reasons Noah couldn't find out if I was dead or alive.'

'But he never told me he was going to check to see if you were really dead. What made him even think you might not be?'

'You'd told him that I'd said I would put him down as next of kin. He knew the army of any country is usually very good at notifying that person when someone is dead or missing. That made him suspicious. But he didn't voice these suspicions as he didn't want to give you false hope.'

'I don't understand why he didn't send a telegram or write when he found you were alive. We've had a letter from him since we got here.'

Etienne turned to her and stroked her cheek. 'I expected him to tell you. Maybe Lisette thought it was more romantic this way. Perhaps he thought it might cause problems with Mog. He said she was very fond of Jimmy.'

'She was, and it's going to be difficult to explain why you've come.'

'You could tell her that the parcel you were expecting wasn't there, so you collected me instead.'

Belle laughed. 'The parcel was wallpaper. She'll say you aren't much good to stick up on the walls!'

Etienne grinned. 'Then I must do my best to charm her.' He paused for a moment, looking concerned. 'I really didn't think much beyond finding you, Belle. But now I am here, and I find you haven't been able to prepare Mog, we must be very careful of her feelings.'

In the shock at his arrival Belle hadn't actually considered that. All at once she was fearful of Mog's reaction to her bringing someone home who was a stranger to her. They had no guest bedroom either.

'I think it would be better if I stayed in a hotel,' he said. 'Is there one here?'

'The Duke of Marlborough is just here.' Belle pointed to the public house a few yards ahead. 'If they have a room free, that might be the best plan. You go in and ask – I can't come in there with you, they don't allow women in bars here. But I'll wait for you just past it.'

Etienne went into the pub and Belle walked on a little way,

then waited. Her heart was thumping and she felt faintly sick with the shock, yet her heart was singing.

He was alive, her love had come right across the world to find her. She wanted to shout out her joy.

But she couldn't give him a hero's welcome as she would like. Mog was no fool. Whatever they said, she would know that no man would ever come this far to see a woman unless he loved her. She would question and question until Belle admitted the whole truth, and even though Etienne had saved Jimmy's life, she was likely to take against Etienne out of family loyalty.

Etienne came out of the pub just a few minutes later to say he had a room there. 'If it would be better for you to tell Mog about me tonight alone, I could stay here now and see you tomorrow,' he said.

Belle thought about that for a few seconds. 'No, that would look even more suspicious,' she said eventually. 'No one in this town would leave an old friend alone on their first evening here. And that is what you are, Etienne, an old and dear friend.'

He sighed and looked troubled. 'I think she will see from our faces that we are more than that.'

'Perhaps, but she has a lot to be grateful to you for, saving me in Paris and rescuing Jimmy. Just promise me that however much she probes, you won't admit we spent the night together in France. We'll admit you came to the hospital once, but only that.'

As Belle went up to bed later that evening with Mog, Etienne having just left to go to his hotel, she believed the meeting had gone perfectly.

Mog had been astounded to see the man she'd heard so much about in the past and thought was dead, brought to her house. For a few moments she could only stare at him, but she recovered quite quickly to fire questions at him. Why hadn't he written first? Wasn't it a bit odd to come all this way on a whim? Was he intending to stay in New Zealand? And why was he presumed dead anyway?

Etienne handled her questions with gentle charm. First he explained about being wounded, then the flu, and gave the reasons why Noah had been unconvinced he was dead.

'Noah and I had stayed in touch since Belle returned to you from Paris,' he said, giving her the full background. 'Through him I learned you had all moved to Blackheath and that Belle had married Jimmy. It was an extraordinary thing that I ran into Jimmy in France. He said things that made me realize who he was, and had we been alone together I might have told him who I was too, but such a conversation was impossible when he was with other men.'

'Extraordinary too that you happened to be there when he was blown up,' Mog said tartly.

'Not that odd. The French often fought side by side with the British,' he said, not rising to her sarcasm. 'I'm sure he told you so. I thought I saw Jimmy the previous night in the distance. Maybe thinking that meant I was subconsciously looking out for him. I can't comment on that, but I believe you have been told how it was that day, driving rain, mist so thick you could only see a few yards ahead. Both British and French got mixed up in the assault because we had to make our way round huge shell holes. I must have seen a hundred or more men killed or wounded that day, English and French. But when this man was hit close to me and his helmet fell off as he tumbled into the mud, I recognized him as Jimmy and helped him.'

'Why did you?' she asked. 'Jimmy said you weren't supposed to help the wounded.'

'Because of Belle of course,' he shrugged. 'Had there been any stretcher bearers close by I would've called them. But they couldn't come out under such heavy fire, and I couldn't leave him to drown in that water-filled shell hole.'

Mog warmed to him after that. She dished up the lamb stew she'd made for supper and it was she who told him how they'd coped with Jimmy's injuries and finally his and Garth's deaths from flu.

Just the way Mog was with him made Belle think she found nothing suspicious about an old friend turning up. Mog trusted Noah's judgment implicitly, and as it was he who had brought this about, that meant Etienne should be welcomed.

They talked about the house then, and the plans she and Belle had for dressmaking, millinery and selling haberdashery. The only question Mog did fire at him for a second time was to ask why he'd chosen to come to New Zealand.

'For much the same reason as you,' Etienne said with one of his Gallic shrugs. 'My farm had suffered while I'd been away, and there is so much sorrow and anger too in France. We lost even greater numbers than the British. I was already considering a new start somewhere. Then when Noah got in touch, and told me about everything that happened to you and that you'd emigrated here, New Zealand seemed a good place for me to start again. The climate in the North Island isn't so different to France; I could farm here, or fish, which is something else I like. So where else would I start but by going to a place where there is an old friend?'

Etienne left soon after that, and as Belle showed him out, he drew her away from the front door and kissed her. It was just the same as the first kiss back at the hospital, like a flame flaring up inside her. She knew then that the hardest part of this was going to be hiding how she felt about him. They wouldn't be able to conduct the leisurely, chaste courtship that

484

was expected of a recently widowed woman. She wanted him now, to be naked in his arms, to drown in ecstasy with him.

'Tomorrow we'll find a way to be alone,' he murmured into her neck as he kissed it. 'I love you, Belle, and together we'll find a way around all the obstacles.'

Belle went indoors then and leaned against the closed door to compose herself before facing Mog's inevitable questions.

There were no real obstacles. They were both free, although there were those prudish ideals about widowhood which others set such store by. Belle really didn't care if people chose to see her as a flighty strumpet who would be dancing on her husband's grave by carrying on with a Frenchman, but she was concerned that any improper behaviour would reflect back badly on Mog.

'He isn't as I imagined him,' Mog said when they went to bed.

'How did you imagine him then?'

'Low class,' Mog replied. 'Villainous looking!'

Belle chuckled. 'He does look tough. I was scared to death of him when we first met back in Brest.'

'I wouldn't like to see anyone get on the wrong side of him,' Mog said. 'But he's also got a soft, charming side.'

Belle was delighted that was Mog's opinion and she got into bed beside her.

The lamp was turned out and Mog fell silent. Yet Belle sensed she was deep in thought, not dropping off.

'Did you have a love affair with him back in Paris?'

The question seemed to fill the dark room.

Belle knew Mog meant after Etienne had rescued her from Pascal, not in France a year ago. 'No, of course I didn't,' she said truthfully.

'But you fell for him?'

It was tempting to deny it, especially in the dark when her face couldn't give her away. But Mog didn't deserve to be lied to.

'Yes,' she admitted. 'But he never told me he felt that way about me, and that was that.'

'I knew there was something when you came home. You didn't say much about him but I had a feeling. Why did you marry Jimmy?'

'Because I loved him, and because we were right for one another.'

'But you saw Etienne again. Was it while you were at the hospital?'

'Yes, he came to see me, it was after Miranda was killed. He knew her American sweetheart.'

'And you fell for him all over again?'

'No, it was just a friendly visit, nothing more.'

There was a long silence and Belle hoped Mog had run out of questions.

'You can't hope to fool me,' the voice that had admonished her so often as a child came through the dark. 'Just you remember I worked in a brothel for most of my life. I've seen hundreds of men at their worst, and now and again at their best. I learned to read what the expressions on their faces meant. Just the way a man walks tell me things most women would never know. And I know that Etienne loves you. I also know he's had his way with you. I saw it in his eyes.'

Belle lay there rigid with tension. Mog had never been a prostitute, she had only been the maid in Annie's brothel. It had never occurred to Belle before that this woman who had cared for her since a baby, as if she were her own child, had gained such depth of knowledge just by observing others.

486

'Now you'll tell me when it was. My guess is that it was just after Miranda was killed.'

Mog had often used the expression, 'Be sure your sins will find you out' in the past, and Belle knew this was the time of reckoning.

'Yes,' she whispered, 'it was. Just one night and then he went back to the front. I know I shouldn't have. Heaven knows I suffered enough guilt afterwards.'

'Then Jimmy was wounded and you came home?'

'Yes.'

Belle waited, expecting a tirade of 'How could you', followed by a list of Jimmy's virtues.

But it didn't come. Mog turned on her side towards Belle and put her arm around her. 'I knew something was wrong when you arrived back. I saw such sorrow in your eyes, which couldn't have been entirely because of Jimmy's injuries. Later, when he came home, I saw how defeated you looked when he acted so cold towards you. My guess is that you saw that as what you deserved?'

Belle began to cry. 'I wrote to Etienne before I left France and told him I could never see him again and that he mustn't try and contact me. I tried to make Jimmy happy, but I couldn't.'

'No one can make another person happy, they have to do that for themselves,' Mog said. 'I hated the way he was with you, I told him so, many times. But he was stuck in his own private hell, and I think he lost the ability to feel for anyone else.'

'But that doesn't excuse me being unfaithful. I did that when he was still well and fit.'

'Would you have left him if he hadn't been wounded?'

'I don't know. I thought of waiting until the war was over, then telling him I'd stopped loving him. But I still believed in "till death us do part" and I doubt if I could've brought myself to hurt him that badly. You see, I never stopped loving him, whatever I felt for Etienne.'

'And the day Jimmy got the letter telling him that Etienne saved him, and he had been killed. How did you feel then?'

'Like my heart had been ripped out,' Belle whispered.

Mog's arm went round her tighter. 'My poor love. I wish you'd told me all this.'

'You aren't angry with me? You don't feel it serves me right?'

'What right have I got to sit in judgment?' Mog said. 'I expect if you'd told me the truth when you first came back from France, I would've said all kinds of harsh things. I loved Jimmy, he'd become like a son to me. But I know deep down that Garth and I pushed you into marrying him. I so much wanted you to have a kind, decent man who adored you, and so I ignored the tiny voice that said you weren't entirely perfect for one another. I convinced myself I was just guiding you in the right direction.

'You were happy together before you lost the baby, so I really believed I had done the right thing.

'But tonight as I saw how you and Etienne looked at each other, the way your eyes both shone, I could feel the passion in you both. You and Jimmy might have had a good marriage, but it was never quite like that. I think Etienne is your destiny.'

'You have such a big heart,' Belle sighed. 'I was so afraid you'd be ashamed of me.'

'How could I be ashamed of someone who put aside her own needs to do the right thing for her husband? I heard some of the nasty things he said to you, Belle. But you stuck with him, and nursed him tenderly right to the end. That's what counts.'

'And now what do I do?'

Mog chuckled. 'I know what I'd do, get on the ferry with him tomorrow, go off to Paihia and find somewhere out of the way to stay until you've worn each other out with loving.'

'Mog!' Belle exclaimed.

'That's how it was with me and Garth, we hardly went out of the hotel room for our whole honeymoon. Of course you'll be putting the cart before the horse. But we don't want to alarm the good people of Russell before we can arrange a wedding and make it decent.'

'Where will you tell people I am, and how will you explain Etienne?'

'I'll think of something,' Mog said. 'Now dry those tears and go to sleep. You'll need to get up early to wash your hair, have a bath and make yourself beautiful for him.'

Chapter Thirty-One

Mog watched as Belle combed her newly washed hair, and smiled. Wearing nothing but a white lace camisole which reached to a few inches above her knees, with her dark curls cascading over her shoulders and a dreamy expression on her face, she looked so pretty.

'What are you going to wear today?' she asked. 'Not that dreary grey dress again I hope.'

'Lawd no! I thought maybe the mauve dress Lisette gave me,' Belle said. 'It's stylish without being too bold, and it doesn't have any old memories for me.'

'A good choice,' Mog said fondly. 'And you have that straw hat with the flowers on which will go well with it.'

'I didn't thank you for being so understanding last night,' Belle said, turning to the older woman to hug her. 'I don't know what I'd do without you. You always make me feel better about everything.'

Mog hugged her too, and bit back the tears that threatened. She had often said she hoped Belle would meet a special man again, but she hadn't anticipated it happening so soon. Her fear was that Etienne would want to whisk her away, as she couldn't imagine him wanting to settle in Russell.

He was a hard man to figure out. A loner, she felt, courageous and strong-willed, but with a dark past. She knew he was on his best behaviour last night, careful to say all the right things, and she had to admit his French accent was delightful. But she hadn't been able to see beyond his good manners and his looks.

Mog wouldn't call him handsome, his face was too bony and his eyes such an icy blue, but still he would make many a female heart flutter. She remembered Noah once saying that he was a man you would fear if he was against you. The faint scar on his cheek spoke of back-street knife fights and danger.

Yet those icy eyes had melted as he looked at Belle, and he had even saved Jimmy for her sake, so she knew they had nothing to fear from him.

'Will I do?' Belle said later as she came into the kitchen where Mog was washing out a few clothes.

Mog turned from the sink to see Belle looking a picture in her mauve dress and straw hat. Excitement had brought a pink tinge to her cheeks and made her eyes shine. 'You look beautiful, now off with you!'

Etienne was just coming down the steps of the Duke of Marlborough as Belle turned on to the path by the shore. He paused to look out at the sea; he hadn't seen her.

She pulled in the skirt of her dress tight and hid behind a tree to watch him. It was sunny and already the worst of the previous day's puddles had dried up. She wondered if he was thinking of hiring a boat to whisk her away somewhere because the sea was as calm as a millpond.

Yesterday's dark suit with matching waistcoat had been changed for a navy-blue blazer and light grey trousers and waistcoat, with a cravat instead of a tie. He looked far too well dressed for a place where most men only ever looked smart on a Sunday for church. She called out to him, then bobbed back behind the tree.

She giggled as she heard him running towards her. She waited till he was about to pass her hiding place, then jumped out with a 'Boo!'.

He laughed. 'You shouldn't do that to an old soldier,' he

said, catching hold of her hands, his smile almost as wide as the bay. 'With my lightning reactions I might have shot you.'

'Did you sleep all right?' she asked.

'Not much,' he said ruefully. 'I was haunted by dreams of you. How was it with Mog after I left?'

'She thought you were a bad lot and I was to meet you today and tell you to catch the *Clansman* back to Auckland.'

Still holding her hands, he leaned back against the tree. 'And are you going to obey her?' he asked, one eyebrow raised quizzically.

'You once told me you'd kill me if I tried to escape you,' she said, trying hard not to laugh.

'I don't think you put on that pretty dress to be killed in,' he said, letting go of one of her hands to touch her cheek lightly. 'So where shall we go? I'm told that a man called Old Tom can be persuaded to take us to Paihia.'

'Funny you should say that, I just happen to have a couple of overnight things with me,' she said impishly, showing him a small straw basket. 'Mog said she would tell anyone who asked that we'd gone to see some French relatives of yours over there.'

He beamed. 'So I have her approval?'

'That will depend on your future behaviour,' Belle said, fluttering her lashes at him. 'Maybe you need to go back into the Duke and get your razor and a clean shirt. Tell them you aren't sure how long you'll be gone for.'

'Gardez au chaud pour moi pendant cinq minutes,' he said, and turning, he ran off back to the hotel.

Belle walked slowly on, past the hotel towards the jetty. She wanted to dance and sing she was so happy, and she was very glad there was no one around who might stop and ask her where she was going.

Someone would have told someone else that a Frenchman had come in on the ship and that he was staying at the Duke. That's how it was in Russell. They would discuss why he might have come, who he might know, anything out of the ordinary was worth talking about. But if Belle had been spotted with him, the gossips would be hard at it by now.

Mog had been very sharp to remember that there was a small community of French people living in Paihia. No doubt she would airily tell Peggy that Etienne was an old friend of Jimmy's, that he'd come to pay his respects on his way to visit his relatives. Then she'd say he'd taken Belle with him today to give her a chance to see the community over there.

When Vera heard his name she was going to be agog. Belle wished she could go and see her and explain, but Mog had said she'd take her to one side and tell her the whole story.

Old Tom was not one for more than a few words. He was sitting on his boat mending a fishing net, and when Etienne asked if he could take them to Paihia he agreed without any questions.

Old Tom was only in his fifties, but he was called that to distinguish him from another Tom who was younger. He bundled up his fishing net, wiped off a seat and held out his hand to help Belle in.

Out in the bay it was chilly and very windy. Belle took off her hat and wrapped herself in her shawl. Etienne's fingers stole in beneath it and found hers and just his touch made her tingle. She was full of niggling anxieties: where would they stay, how would they get back, and even if it was wise to be rushing into this when she couldn't be certain what his intentions were.

But there was too much wind and noise from the engine to talk, so she just sat back, her fingers entwined in his, and looked at the scenery, as always thinking that the Bay of Islands must be one of the most beautiful places on earth.

Paihia wasn't as pretty and quaint as Russell. It sprawled along the shore, perhaps because there was enough space to build houses further apart. Yet the knowledge that no one knew them here was an attraction in itself.

Etienne went into the post office to inquire if they knew of a cottage he could rent for a few days. He told Belle to stay outside because he said when he told lies he didn't want an audience.

He came out smiling with a scrap of paper in his hand. 'It looks as if we're in luck. This Mrs Arkwright takes care of two or three places which are used for holidays. I can go and see her now, she's just around the corner from here.'

Again he didn't want Belle to go with him and suggested she looked in the shops while he was gone.

He was gone well over an hour and Belle became quite worried. Then suddenly he came haring along the road by the shore.

'What took so long?' she asked. 'I was getting anxious.'

'Mrs Arkwright took me to see the cottage, and once there she fussed about making up the bed, putting out towels, I couldn't hurry her up. But I've got the key and we can go there now. All we need to do is buy some provisions.'

'What's the place like?' Belle asked as they went back towards the grocery shop.

'You'll see when we get there,' he said.

'Did it cost a lot?'

He put his finger to his nose to signify it was none of her business.

After buying a bag of groceries, Etienne led her to the end of the road along the shore where a wooded hill rose. They took a narrow path up through the trees.

'Voilà!' he said as they came to a clearing. He indicated a tiny white-painted wooden house built with its back into the hill, a few steps leading up to a veranda which overlooked the sea.

'What a beautiful spot!' Belle exclaimed. It was entirely private as it was surrounded by trees. When they walked up on to the veranda to open the front door, Belle couldn't even see the roof of another house.

Etienne put the bag of groceries down to unlock the door, but before she even thought of moving, he scooped her up in his arms and carried her in. Then he put her down and kissed her.

All reason, modesty and even concern that the door was still open left her. Last night's kiss had awoken feelings that she'd almost forgotten she'd ever experienced, and now she was hungry for him. As he kissed her she was feeling under his jacket, frustrated that she couldn't reach under his trousers to touch his skin because a waistcoat and braces were in the way. She pressed against him shamelessly as his tongue darted into her mouth and inflamed her still more.

He threw off her hat and shawl, his fingers fumbling with the buttons at the back of her dress. He pushed it down low enough over her shoulders to release her breasts and bent to take her nipple between her lips.

She groaned with delight, and tried to remove his jacket, but she was so overcome with the waves of red-hot pleasure washing over her that she couldn't manage it. He pulled up the skirt of her dress and found his way beneath her petticoat, pushing her drawers aside, and as his fingers found their way inside her already hot and wet sex, she held his head tight against her breast and cried out that she wanted him now.

She hadn't even seen the bed or noted anything about the interior of the place they were in, and when he pressed her

495

up against a wall, stopping caressing her only long enough to unbutton his trousers, she wouldn't have cared if they were in a pig sty.

His hands were on her buttocks and he lifted her up and on to his erect penis, and held her there by the wall, pushing his way into her as he kissed her. It was frenzied for both of them, rough and crude sex, the kind Belle had seen in back alleys in New Orleans and at the time felt sympathy for the girls subjected to it.

But she needed no sympathy, she wanted him every bit as badly, and her whole body seemed to be melting into him.

She came in what seemed like seconds, before he did, and she heard herself cry out his name.

He was close behind, his fingers digging into her buttocks, his breath like fire on her bare shoulder, and with a roar he came too, and his grip on her loosened so she slithered down till her feet were on the floor.

'It wasn't meant to be like that,' he murmured, his head sinking to her shoulder. 'I meant it to be slow and beautiful.'

Belle could feel perspiration running down her face and between her breasts. Her legs had gone to jelly and if she hadn't been leaning back against the wall she might have fallen.

'We can do slow and beautiful later,' she panted out. 'For now hot and fast was just right.'

He lifted his head and looked at her, kissing her lips, her nose and her forehead. 'Your cheeks are all rosy now, you've never looked more beautiful.'

'Can I sit down before I fall down?' she said, caressing his face with both her hands. He had never looked more beautiful to her either. She could feel the scar on his cheek, she loved his full lips, his proud nose and his fair eyebrows. But most of all she loved his eyes; they were like the sea, so cold sometimes, darker when he was angry, but right now, even though the room was gloomy because the curtains were still closed, there was enough light from the open door to see they were as blue as a summer sky, and soft with love.

They adjusted their clothing and Belle went to put the groceries away. Etienne drew back the curtains, and it was only then that Belle took in that the cottage was a perfect hideaway. It was simply furnished, with just a sink, a table and chairs, a small stove with a rug before it, a couple of easy chairs and the china and cooking pots on shelves. But it was spotlessly clean and bright, and the other room was the bedroom, with just the bed and a chest of drawers.

'The water is rain from a tank,' Etienne said, turning on the tap to demonstrate. 'The privy is outside. I saw a tin bath hanging on the side of it too. And there's a shed with logs for the stove.'

'I've got everything I need right here,' she said, putting her arms around him.

Etienne lit the stove while Belle went outside on to the veranda to look at the view of the sea over the treetops. She could see Russell in the distance, but it could have been a million miles away. She had never in her life been this happy. There was no guilt now, no remorse, or even anxiety about the future. As Mog had said, being with Etienne was her destiny, and perhaps she had needed to go through all those bad things in the past year to know how right this was now.

Later, after a cup of tea and a sandwich, they went to bed. This time their clothes came off first – Etienne even hung up her dress so it wouldn't get creased – and the lovemaking was slow and beautiful.

Belle ran her hand gently over his scars; the one on his shoulder that she'd seen in France was fading now, but the newer one on his right thigh was still very livid. 'I was lucky that it missed my knee and I didn't get gangrene,' he said. 'Knee wounds usually leave you with a bad limp.'

'Did it hurt?'

'Not when it happened. I staggered back towards the line for a bit, using my rifle like a walking stick. But I must have passed out through loss of blood. I can just about remember the stretcher bearer picking me up. It was only when they cut my uniform off at the dressing station that it began to hurt, and it was hell then.'

'Did you know that you'd got the flu?'

'Not really. Only that I felt really bad, very hot and shivery at the same time. I don't remember much more, except I thought you were there.'

'Me?' Belle giggled.

'Yes, but like you were when I was seasick on the ship going to America. When I started to get a bit better one of the nurses asked me who Belle was. It seemed I'd been calling your name.'

'I'm very glad to hear it was me you were thinking of,' she said, kissing his scars.

'They said that all the other men who had been on the ward when I was taken there died of it. I don't know why I survived; there didn't seem to be any reason for it.'

'Because you had to come and find me,' she said.

It rained later, but the rattling on the roof and the wind in the trees only made it feel cosier inside. The stove made it beautifully warm, Belle lit an oil lamp, and together they made an impromptu supper of bread and cheese and a tin of soup.

Etienne wore only his trousers, Belle just her camisole, and as he opened a bottle of wine he'd bought he made a toast.

'To our long and happy future together,' he said, clinking her glass with his. He took a sip of the wine and winced.

'I may have to start a vineyard myself if this is the best wine you can buy here.'

'Could you?' she asked.

'Maybe, with the right land. The climate is right for it.'

'What about your farm in France? What have you done with that?'

'Noah bought it,' he said. 'I hadn't got around to telling you, but he came down to Marseille to find me.'

'He did that? What a wonderful man he is,' Belle said. 'And not a word to me!'

Etienne smiled. 'Yes, a true friend. You see, by then he'd discovered that I'd been sent home just before the war ended. But when he got no reply to a letter he wrote to the farm he decided to come and search for me. He tracked me down to the friends I was staying with, and then we went out to the farm together.'

'And he said he'd buy it?'

'He fell in love with it right away, I tried to talk him out of it, but he said Lisette wanted their children to have holidays in France and for Rose to speak fluent French like Jean-Philippe does. He argued that if I was coming out to find you it would just become more overgrown. He said he could afford to build a better house on the land. But I'd always be welcome there with you or without you.'

'So what now?' Belle asked. 'What will you do here?'

'For now I will make love to you until you beg for mercy,' he grinned. 'Then we must get married to save your reputation.'

'Isn't it customary to propose first?' she laughed.

'Will you marry me, my beautiful Belle?' he asked, reaching out for her hand.

'As soon as it can be arranged,' she said. 'I love you, Etienne, there's nothing I want more.'

He got up from the table and came round and pulled her up into his arms. 'We have both come a long way from that day in Brest when I had to take you on the ship to America. Did you know I began to love you when you took care of me while I was seasick?'

'No, surely not!'

'Not in a physical way! You were too young and vulnerable, yet you had so much spirit. Leaving you in New Orleans made me so ashamed; you were always on my mind afterwards.'

'You had to take me there, I knew that, I used to think about you all the time too. But you had a happy marriage?'

'Yes, I did love Elena, but I think our marriage was much like yours. We grew up together, and I thought what we had was all that could be expected. But it was never the way it is with you.'

'Tell me truthfully, did you have feelings for me after you rescued me in Paris? I know we talked about this a little at the hospital, but I need to know more.'

He put his hands on both sides of her face and looked into her eyes. 'Yes, I knew I loved you, and I sensed you felt the same, but it was the wrong time to speak out. You had been hurt by men so badly, I thought you needed time to heal. But it was more than that. I had done so many bad things, I thought I was bad for you.'

'How can you think that? You saved my life!' Tears were welling up in her eyes because of his low opinion of himself. 'If you'd only told me how you felt! Just a hint might have made all the difference.'

'I did, but like a coward I said it in French at the station and hoped you understood enough. But what was I to do? You were going home to Jimmy, I knew from Noah how he felt about you. Even if I had been good at writing my true thoughts in a letter, I would have been afraid Jimmy might read it. So I wrote as a friend would and hoped you could read my true feelings between the lines.'

Belle sighed, remembering how her heart sang when she saw a letter from him in the post, only to be disappointed that it was stilted and cool.

'Then you wrote to say you were marrying Jimmy and I knew my chance was lost. I told myself you'd be happier with him,' he said sadly. 'Even that didn't stop me thinking about you. That was why I came to your shop, I needed to see for myself that you were happy. I never expected to ever hear from you or see you again, but then came the chance meeting with Jimmy in France.'

'That was very strange,' she said.

'I think now it was fate colliding. I saw he was a good man, strong and principled. I really liked him and the way he spoke about you.'

'What did he say?' Jimmy had told her his version and she wanted to know if it matched with Etienne's.

'He told me about you being attacked in your shop and that you'd lost your baby. He said too that he regretted enlisting when he should have been home with you. I was both jealous of him and yet glad that you were with such a decent, caring man.'

'But you still came to the hospital to see me?'

'Yes. I couldn't help myself when I heard of your friend's death. It was just to see you, I had no hope of anything more. But once I saw you and kissed you, it was like being caught in a whirlwind.'

'Yes, it was for me too,' she agreed. 'A kind of madness that drove out all reason or even sense of duty and morality.'

Etienne sat down and pulled her on to his lap and wiped away a tear on her cheek. 'Would you have left him for me if he hadn't been wounded?' he asked.

'I really don't know. Maybe eventually the guilt, and wanting you so much, would have driven me to it, though back then I felt I couldn't. But what made you save him, Etienne? Tell me the truth.'

He sighed deeply. 'I have to admit that for a second I was tempted to leave him. But although letting him die would have meant the way would have been clear to have you, deep down I knew I would never be able to live with it. Of course I didn't have time to really think why I was doing it at the time. But afterwards I was glad, because for once I had done the right thing.

'But it didn't end there, Belle. When you wrote and told me how bad he was, and that was the end for us, I really wished I had left him there. Not just because I could have had you, but because of what your life would be like taking care of him. I've seen so many wives and mothers dealing with their wounded men, the poverty and hardships, and all too often their men take out their frustrations on them. Did this happen to you?'

Out of loyalty to Jimmy she wanted to deny it, but realized Noah might have already told him. 'Sometimes. Let's just say he wasn't the man I married any more.'

They were both silent for a little while.

Etienne broke the silence. 'I think it is time we talked about us and our future,' he said, sliding his hand up her bare leg seductively.

'That isn't talking,' she reproved him. 'What are you going to do for a living here? The choice is rather limited.'

'It is only a limited choice to a man with no imagination,' he grinned. 'Fishing, farming, building, I can do most things, and I have a bit of money too. What I meant was about getting married and where we'll live. But let's get into bed and talk about that in comfort.'

*

Belle woke as dawn was breaking. Etienne was sound asleep, curled against her back, his arm around her. They had made love for hours, and remembering some of the erotic things he did to her made her blush. She had always thought she knew more about men and sex than other women, but she'd found that she was wrong. Love lifted it away from the mechanical tricks she'd learned in her past life and turned sex into something beautiful and fantastic. Serge, the accomplished lover who had been hired in New Orleans to initiate her in the arts of love, had awakened her sexually with his skill. Yet even though it was a satisfying and thrilling experience, without love it was empty. Jimmy had all the love to give her, he had been an enthusiastic lover before the war, but he was somewhat inhibited despite her encouragement to be otherwise.

Etienne had no such inhibitions. He was red-blooded and understood women, being rough at the right time and gentle when it was not. He had taken her on a magic carpet ride of thrills, lust and passion, yet it was the tender, sweet moments when he sought only to please her that touched something deep inside her and made her cry. Despite all her experience she'd never felt that way before.

She was sore from lovemaking now, just as she had been after the night with him in France, but it was a good feeling. Sliding from under his arm without waking him, she reached for her camisole lying on the floor and slipped it on, then stole out of the bedroom.

There were still glowing embers in the stove, so she put some more wood in it, then went out on to the veranda. The sun was rising on the horizon, casting beams of gold through still grey cloud. A lump came up in her throat at the beauty of the bay with its silvery-blue water streaked with the gold from the sun, and the dark green of the trees all around it.

The huge emptiness of the scene before her seemed to be

503

telling her that this was where she and Etienne belonged. She had felt as soon as she got to New Zealand that it was a country that welcomed those with strength, determination, courage and imagination. Now, with Etienne beside her, she felt that nothing was impossible, even bearing his child.

She turned to see him behind her, just a towel around his waist. His hair was tousled and a faint shadow of beard was coming through on his face. The scar on his shoulder and the one on his thigh would remain a permanent reminder of the horrors of war, just as the faint scar on his cheek would also remind her of his less honourable past.

Belle had her scars too, though invisible ones. Two flawed people who together could accomplish anything they set their minds to.

He came up to the rail of the veranda, putting his arm around her, looking at the view. The sun had risen higher and a long, low wisp of white cloud now lay right across the bay.

'I love early mornings,' he said. 'Even at Verdun there were some beauties; they gave us hope that the day ahead would be better than the one before. But looking at this glorious one with you, I know God is on our side.'

Belle smiled. His words seemed to echo what she'd been thinking. 'So what will we do today?'

'Walk, explore, think of how we'll make our fortune here. Look and see if there's land fit for grapevines. Buy some fish for dinner.'

'You told me we'd be together one day, and you were right. So perhaps with you all things are possible.'

'Having fish for dinner is an absolute certainty,' he said, pointing to a fishing boat out on the bay. 'But the vineyard and the fortune might take a little longer.'

Acknowledgements

First and foremost to Glen Fisher as without his knowledge of the First World War, the books he directed me to and his enthusiasm for my book I might never have got started.

I read a huge amount of books in my research, too many to mention individually, but of special note were *The First Day on the Somme* by Martin Middlebrook, *The First World War* by John Keegan and *Voices of the War* by Peter H. Liddle.

Lyn Macdonald's books *Somme, They called it Passchendaele,* and *The Roses of No Man's Land* helped me understand the bigger picture so much better. I can recommended any of these books to anyone who wants to know more about the First World War.

Lesley Pearse

About Lesley

Lesley Pearse is one of the UK's best-loved novelists, with fans across the globe and book sales of nearly four million copies to date.

A true storyteller and a master of gripping plots that keep the reader hooked from beginning to end, Lesley introduces readers to unforgettable characters about whom it is impossible not to care. There is no easily defined genre or formula to her books: some, like *Rosie* and *Secrets*, are family sagas, *Till We Meet Again, A Lesser Evil* and *Faith* are crime novels, and others such as *Never Look Back, Gypsy* and *Hope* are historical adventures.

Remember Me is based on an astounding true story about Mary Broad who was convicted of highway robbery and transported on the first fleet to Australia, where a penal colony was to be founded. The story of the appalling hardships that faced the prisoners there, and how courageously determined Mary was to gain a better life for her children is one you are unlikely to forget.

Passionately emotive *Trust Me* is also set in Australia, and deals with the true-life scandal of the thousands of British children who were sent there in the post-war period to be systematically neglected, and in many cases, abused.

Stolen is a thriller – the first of her books with a contemporary setting – and was a Number One bestseller in 2010.

Painstaking research is one of Lesley's hallmarks; first, Lesley reads widely on the subject matter, and then she goes to the place she has chosen as a setting. Once there, digging up local history, the story begins, whether it is about the convicts in Australia, the condition for soldiers in the Crimean war, the hardships facing gold miners in the Klondike or the sheer jaw-dropping courage of the pioneers who forged their way across America in covered wagons.

History is one of Lesley's passions, and mixed with her vivid imagination and her keen insight into how people

'Lesley introduces readers to unforgettable characters about whom it is impossible not to care'

might behave in dangerous, tragic and unusual situations, she is soon able to weave a plot with many dramatic twists and turns.

'It wasn't until I was working on my sixth or seventh book that I became aware that my heroines had all had to overcome and rise above emotional damage inflicted upon them as children,' Lesley points out. 'I have had to do this myself; my childhood certainly wasn't a bed of roses, but the more people I get to know, the more I find that most have some kind of trauma in their past. Perhaps this is why so many of us like to read about triumph over adversity.'

Lesley's colourful past has been a very useful point of reference in her writing. Whether she is writing about a grim post-war orphanage, about a child that doesn't quite fit in at school, about adoption, about a girl who leaves home too young and too ill-equipped to cope adequately, about poverty or about the pain of first love, she knows how it feels first hand. For as Lesley laughingly puts it, 'my life has had more ups and downs than a well bucket.'

'Painstaking research is one of Lesley's hallmarks'

But the sadness and difficulties in Lesley's life are in the past now. With three grown up daughters, and two much loved grandsons, the latest one, Harley, born in March 2010, Lesley feels her life is wonderful.

'I live in a pretty cottage in Somerset, with my two dogs, Maisie and Lotte, and my garden there is an all consuming passion,' she says. 'I feel I am truly blessed to wake up each morning with such lovely choices: writing or gardening. They fit so well together; if I'm stuck for an idea in the latest book, I go out and dead head the flowers, mow the lawn or weed. Often I'm writing until two or three in the morning as there is complete silence then and no distractions like the phone to disturb my concentration. I have to confess to wasting a lot of time on Twitter though. It's like having a whole bunch of invisible friends, many of whom are writers too; we comment on things, tell each other what we are up to, and sometimes we get into conversations that are so funny I'm sitting there howling with laughter.'

Friends are very important to Lesley; some of them go right back to ones she met at school and as a teenager. They are her life blood and she likes nothing better than a girl's day out with shopping and lunch with a group of them.

'I love it too when I'm invited to give a talk; sometimes these are in libraries, where I get to meet my readers; sometimes as a guest speaker at lunches or dinner for a charity function. A writer needs to have direct contact with people – without it they would be working in a vacuum. The feedback you get is so valuable, which book they liked best, or least, and why. It's also a great opportunity to get out of my wellies and old gardening clothes, dress up in something glamorous and visit a part of the country I haven't been to before.'

Lesley's storytelling abilities are even more evident when she is speaking to a group of people, for she can trawl through her past and tell hilarious anecdotes that have her audiences in fits of laughter. One suspects she might have made a good actress if she hadn't drifted from job to job as a young girl. As it was, she was a nanny, a Bunny girl, a dressmaker, and spent many years in promotion work, along with more mundane temping office work. 'The companies I was sent to as a temp were usually glad to see the back of me,' she laughs. 'I was a distraction because I talked to everyone and I was an appalling typist. Funny that I now type fast and accurately. But back then I was always tempted to put my own words into letters I was asked to write, just to pep up the dullness of them.'

Lesley is also the president of the Bath and West Wiltshire branch of the NSPCC – a charity very close to her heart because of physical and mental abuse meted out to her as a child.

'In my ideal world all children would be wanted, valued, loved and cared for,' Lesley says. 'I know from research that child abuse is an evil as old as time, and the only way to stamp it out is through education. I wish every school would put parenting on the curriculum and drum into teenagers the importance of taking care to ensure that they are in stable loving relationships before embarking on having a baby.'

'Lesley's colourful past has been a very useful reference point in her writing'

About
The Promise

Congratulations, Lesley, *The Promise* is your twentieth novel – how do you feel about reaching this momentous stage in your career as an author?

Astounded! That's an awful lot of words. Sometimes I get a bit scared that I won't get an idea for the next book, but so far the ideas have turned up. I couldn't keep going without my loyal readers; they are always dying for the next book to come out and I don't ever want to disappoint them.

What inspired you to write a sequel to *Belle*?

I loved Belle so much I really couldn't forget her and move on to another character. This was a first for me, usually I feel sad to part with my heroines, but I know I've told their story and it's over. But Belle was different, she was so full of energy and fire, I couldn't let her go. I felt too that my readers would want to know whether she got her hat shop, what role she'd play in the First World War, and whether she succeeded in staying out of trouble! And there are the men in her life. Would she settle down with Jimmy, would she meet Etienne again? And, of course, how would they fare in the war?

Your descriptions of life on the battlefields of France are incredibly realistic and moving. Did you find you had to do a lot of research into World War One before you wrote this novel?

Long before I even thought about setting a book in World War One, I had read a great deal about it, because history and wars are two of my passions. World War One was such a terrible and cruel war, it changed almost every aspect of life for everyone. I wanted to write a fictional story illustrating the courage, hardship and the sheer horror that ordinary people went through – not just the brave young men who went to fight under such appalling conditions, but about their women back home. In order to get my facts right I had to read at least forty more books while writing *The Promise*. I also went to the war graves in Flanders and spent long hours in the Imperial War Museum.

Belle is a strong, courageous woman who is determined to maintain her independence – first as a milliner and then as an ambulance driver in France. What was it like being a married, yet working, woman at that time? How did society view working women?

Society tended to look down on working women in general before World War One. Not just factory girls, domestic staff and the like, but people in trade too. Women of the middle and upper classes rarely worked and were confined to their homes and families, but the war changed that for many. However, Belle wouldn't have felt bound by the normal constraints of that period, not even when she married, because of her past and the way she was brought up. An occupation such as being a milliner would have been considered acceptable because it was a feminine job, yet being in 'trade' would have also set her apart. However, once so many society women rushed to become war-time volunteers when war broke out, most people – whatever their class – would have admired women who helped the war effort. After the war a great many more women embarked on careers. They were very much needed when so many of the young men didn't make it home again.

Why did you decide that Belle and Mog should emigrate to New Zealand? What drew you to New Zealand in particular?

I felt that after the horrors of war Belle and Mog would want to start afresh somewhere else. They really had nothing to stay in England for. I chose New Zealand because I love it. I think if I were younger I'd like to go and live there myself. I also felt Mog and Belle had the right kind of pioneering spirit to make a go of it there.

The BOOKS

Georgia

Raped by her foster-father, fifteen-year-old
Georgia runs away from home to the seedy
back streets of Soho ...

Tara

Anne changes her name to Tara to forget her
shocking past – but can she really become
someone else?

Charity

Charity Stratton's bleak life is changed for ever
when her parents die in a fire. Alone and pregnant,
she runs away to London ...

Ellie

Eastender Ellie and spoilt Bonny set off to make
a living on the stage. Can their friendship survive
sacrifice and ambition?

Camellia

Orphaned Camellia discovers that the past she has
always been so sure of has been built on lies. Can
she bear to uncover the truth about herself?

Rosie

Rosie is a girl without a mother, with a past full of trouble. But could the man who ruined her family also save Rosie?

Charlie

Charlie helplessly watches her mother being senselessly attacked. What secrets have her parents kept from her?

Never Look Back

An act of charity sends flower girl Matilda on a trip to the New World and a new life …

Trust Me

Dulcie Taylor and her sister are sent to an orphanage and then to Australia. Is their love strong enough to keep them together?

Father Unknown

Daisy Buchan is left a scrapbook with details about her real mother. But should she go and find her?

Till We Meet Again

Susan and Beth were childhood friends. Now Susan is accused of murder, and Beth finds she must defend her.

Remember Me

Mary Broad is transported to Australia as a convict and encounters both cruelty and passion. Can she make a life for herself so far from home?

Secrets

Adele Talbot escapes a children's home to find her grandmother – but soon her unhappy mother is on her trail …

A Lesser Evil

Bristol, the 1960s, and young Fif Brown defies her parents to marry a man they think is beneath her.

Hope

Somerset, 1836, and baby Hope is cast out from a world of privilege as proof of her mother's adultery …

Faith

Scotland, 1995, and Laura Brannigan is in prison for a murder she claims she didn't commit.

Gypsy

Liverpool, 1893, and after tragedy strikes the Bolton family, Beth and her brother Sam embark on a dangerous journey to find their fortune in America.

Stolen

A beautiful young woman is discovered half-drowned on a Sussex beach. Where has she come from? Why can't she remember who she is – or what happened?

Belle

London, 1910, and the beautiful and innocent Belle Reilly is cruelly snatched from her home and sold to a brothel in New Orleans where she begins her life as a courtesan. Can Belle ever find her way home?

The Lesley Pearse
Women of Courage Award

was launched in 2006 to celebrate the extraordinary achievements of ordinary women; women who have done something special for themselves or someone else; women of courage.

Previous Winners

Nicole

'Winning the inaugural woman of courage award was a unique experience which I shall always remember'

NICOLE GALLAGHER from Kent was nominated by her best friend because of her care and devotion to her children who both suffer from rare medical conditions.

Karen

'I still have to pinch myself to remind me that I did actually win the award'

KAREN BAKER from Harrow was nominated by her colleague. She provides full time support for her disabled daughter, Nicky, gives support to her colleagues in a busy role, looks after her father who has Alzheimer's disease and is the key support for her husband who has epilepsy. As if that wasn't enough, Karen has been living with cancer for years.

Kerry-Ann

'Winning has filled me with renewed enthusiasm to continue working hard towards my goals and to assist others in achieving theirs.'

KERRY-ANN HINDLEY from Glasgow was nominated by her partner because she has overcome personal tragedies, hardship and a terribly troubled youth to take her experiences and turn them into something positive – helping others.

Siobhan

'Winning the award was further reinforcement to me that child abuse will not be ignored in our society, and it has had the double effect of renewing my campaigning efforts.'

SIOBHAN PYBURN from Southampton was nominated by her ITV Fixers project worker for her courage in taking back control of her life and using her own experiences of abuse and incest to help others.

Sheila

SHEILA MEANING was nominated by her friend for her selfless dedication to the homeless over the last 21 years.

PLEASE TURN OVER TO FIND OUT HOW YOU CAN NOMINATE SOMEONE FOR THE AWARD

'I know there are real heroines out there who would put my fictional ones to shame, and I really want to hear about them'
Lesley Pearse

IS THERE AN AMAZING WOMAN OUT THERE WHO DESERVES RECOGNITION?

Whether it is someone who has had to cope with problems and come out the other side; someone who has spent her whole life looking out for other people; or someone who has shown strength and determination in doing something great for herself, show her how much she is appreciated by nominating her for an award.

The Lesley Pearse *Women of Courage Award*
gives recognition to all those ordinary women who show
extraordinary strength and dedication in their everyday lives.
It is an annual event that was launched by Lesley and Penguin in 2006.

The winner and her family will be invited to London for a
sumptuous awards lunch with Lesley, where she will be presented
with a specially crafted commemorative award, a framed
certificate and £200 of Penguin books.

Let us know about an amazing lady you know
and make a difference to her life by nominating
her for this prestigious award.

To nominate someone you know:
Complete the entry form, or send us the details required
on a separate piece of paper, and post it to:

The Lesley Pearse *Women of Courage Award,*
Penguin Michael Joseph, 80 Strand, London, WC2R 0
or visit:
www.womenofcourageaward.co.uk
where you can print out a nomination form, enter your
nominationdetails on to our online form and read all abou
the award and its previous nominees and winners.

OFFICIAL ENTRY FORM

NAME OF YOUR WOMAN OF COURAGE:

HER ADDRESS:

POSTCODE:

HER CONTACT NUMBER:

YOUR RELATIONSHIP TO HER:

YOUR NAME:

YOUR ADDRESS:

POSTCODE:

YOUR DAYTIME TELEPHONE NUMBER:

YOUR EMAIL :

On a separate sheet, tell us in no more than
250 Words why you think your nominee deserves to win
The Lesley Pearse *Women of Courage Award*

For terms and conditions please visit

www.womenofcourageaward.co.uk